# Skilled Hands

He was handsome. He was electric. He remembered names and told jokes and brought in pizzas. In no more than a matter of weeks, he had proven a rare talent, attracting some of the area's wealthiest women into his practice with one flash of his unforgettable smile. Dr. Dale Hunsacker was an up and coming commodity in one of the most cutthroat business venues in St. Louis—medicine. So what if he wasn't the best OB/GYN to hit the halls.

Dale was a great guy, a real dream. But could he also be every woman's worst nightmare?

# A MAN TO DIE FOR

## EILEEN DREYER

## HarperPaperbacks
*A Division of* HarperCollins*Publishers*

This is a work of fiction. The characters, incidents, and dialogues are products of the author's imagination and are not to be construed as real. Any resemblance to actual events or persons, living or dead, is entirely coincidental.

HarperPaperbacks   *A Division of* HarperCollins*Publishers*
10 East 53rd Street, New York, N.Y. 10022

Cover photograph by Herman Estevez

First printing: July 1991

Printed in the United States of America

HarperPaperbacks and colophon are trademarks of HarperCollins*Publishers*

10 9 8 7 6 5 4 3

# Acknowledgments

My special thanks to all the people who helped make this book possible. To Lt. John Podolak of the St. Louis police force, for his patience, insight, and experience. To the most fashionable homicide detectives in the Midwest for their hospitality, and Steve Ballinger for the ballistic information. If mistakes were made, they were mine. To all my friends at Tony's and John's who made it worth walking onto the work lanes all those years. There's nobody like you guys. To Katie Wilson Lucas, who is directly responsible. To Karyn Witmer-Gow, friend, mentor, and the best midwife a book could have. To Steve Axelrod who believed in me and Karen Solem and Carolyn Marino for taking a chance.

And most of all, always to Rick. This one's really for you.

It was difficult for the Angel of Death to kill everybody in the whole world, so he appointed doctors to assist him.

—Nachman of Bratzlav
Jewish mystic, 1771–1811

# Prologue

*CONTROL YOUR IMPULSES,* her mother had always said. Stifle your urges, the church echoed. She should have listened. The next time she had an urge like this one, she was going to lock herself in a closet until it went away.

"Honey, why are we here?"

"I have to make a stop before I take you home, Mom."

A stop. She had to report a crime. Several crimes. That wasn't exactly a run to the local Safeway for deodorant.

Gripping her purse in one hand and her mother in the other, Casey McDonough approached the St. Louis City Police Headquarters like a penitent approaching the gates of purgatory. It seemed amazing, really. Casey had been born no more than fifteen miles away, but she'd never visited this place before. She'd never even known precisely where it was.

A stark block of granite that took up the corner of Clark and Tucker, the headquarters did nothing to inspire comfort. Brass grillwork protected massive front doors and encased traditional globe lamps that flanked it. Unmarked police cars and crime scene vans hugged the curb. Police in uniform or windbreakers and walkie-talkies hovered near the front door, chatting among themselves. Civilians edged by, sensing their intrusion, much the way they would enter her hospital.

Casey didn't want to be here. If she could have, she would have approached her friends on the county police force instead. She would have pulled one of them aside when they'd come into her emergency room and proposed her theory in a way that could be considered an inside joke instead of an accusation.

"Say, Bert, what would you think if I said there's something just a little more sinister than fee-splitting going on around here? What if I told you that some of the bad luck around this place is actually connected? And not just because I know all the people involved, either."

Bert would laugh and deflect her fears with common sense, and the issue would have gone no further.

Only none of the crimes Casey suspected had actually happened in the county. Bert wouldn't know anything about them. He couldn't do her any good. If she wanted any relief from the suspicions that had been building like a bad case of indigestion over the last few weeks, she was going to have to find it with the city cops. Cops she didn't know. Cops who didn't know her.

Casey pulled on the heavy glass-and-brass door and winced at its screech of protest. It sounded as if it resented her intrusion. The way everybody else ignored the noise, the door must have been objecting for years.

Inside, the foyer was a high square of marble, cool and hushed. Casey held the heavy door open for her mother to follow inside. Sketching a quick sign of the cross, the little woman instinctively reached for a holy water font.

"It's not a church," Casey reminded her.

It was hell. She was in hell for what she suspected. But Casey just couldn't keep it to herself any longer. It was time to let somebody else help shoulder the weight of this rock she was carrying around her neck.

"What do you mean it's not a church?" her mother asked, swinging around on the gray marble floor, her voice echoing in the cavernous lobby. "Who's going to take care of St. Joseph?"

Heads turned. The female officer at the control desk at the far side of the room came to a kind of careful alert, like a guard dog catching an unfamiliar scent. Two middle-aged black men slouching against the wall of the diarrhea brown and green waiting area interrupted their conversation to assess the new entertainment.

"It's a police station," Casey whispered, a hand on her mother's arm so she couldn't get far. "It'll only take a minute."

She shouldn't be thinking of her civic duty. She should be thinking of her personal duty. She had a mother to take care of. A mother nobody else really wanted to be saddled with. What was going to happen to Helen when Casey was without a job, without a career, without any kind of future? Because if she took another step, that was exactly what was going to happen. This simply wasn't the kind of action the medical hierarchy overlooked.

"Can I help you?"

This was stupid. She had no business being here.

She had no choice. Evelyn had been her friend. Casey stepped up to the desk.

"Couldn't I just go to confession?" Helen asked in a little whimper. "I only pruned her roses."

The officer frowned. A petite, precise black woman with very little humor in her expression, she considered Casey's mother like a bad joke. Casey couldn't blame her. But then, Casey didn't know that the sergeant was going to like Casey's story any better.

How did she say it? How did she pull all the suspicions

whirling around into some kind of recognizable order? How did she relay them so that she would be taken seriously, so that she'd be able to hand off the responsibility and avoid recriminations for making accusations about respected people committing crimes?

Crimes. A euphemism. A generality that didn't carry the impact of the truth. She'd been avoiding the issue by calling it a crime, instead of what it was. She'd been dancing with inevitability, because the minute she gave voice to the suspicions that had been hovering like unwelcome ghosts, there wouldn't be any retreat. There wouldn't be any chance of calling her fears a mistake.

"Ma'am?" the officer nudged without appreciable patience.

"Murder," Casey blurted out ungracefully.

The officer scowled, hands on hips. "Take your roses seriously, huh?"

"Have you ever thought of the convent?" Helen asked, reaching across the dark wood desk.

The officer flinched.

Casey pulled Helen back just in time. "Say a rosary, Mom." When Helen nodded agreeably and began to dig into her purse, Casey returned to the officer. "It's about the murder the other night, Crystal Johnson. I may have some information about it."

That elicited a long, considering look. "You wanna tell me?"

Casey didn't know whether she wanted to laugh or cry. Didn't this woman understand how tough this was? Didn't she know that all Casey had were intangibles, feelings, instincts, for God's sake? Didn't she understand that Casey couldn't betray herself out here in the open, where an echo could carry her suspicions to the wrong set of ears?

"It's a long story," she hedged miserably. And somebody's going to see me here, somebody from the hospital like me who never comes into the city except to shop and eat, but who maybe got their car stolen or impounded for a ticket, and they'll go right back to work and report just what I was doing at the city police headquarters.

The officer took one more look at Helen, then Casey. "You're not confessing, are you?" She sounded almost hopeful.

"Not without a priest," Helen piped up.

Casey ignored her. "I suspect somebody else," was all she could manage.

A nod, a quick look around the lobby, at nothing at all. "Well, in that case, I'll do you one better. I'll get you a Bishop."

Casey considered herself rightfully frustrated and depressed. She should have known better. She wasn't really frustrated or depressed until fifteen minutes later when she stepped into the Bishop's office for the first time. One look at him made the rest of the situation pale in comparison.

Even so, she straightened as much as she could, shoved her mother into a seat, and challenged the officer. "There's somebody you and I need to talk about."

# Chapter 1

*HIS ARRIVAL WAS* foretold like the second coming of Christ. Administration, that great hospital prophet of profit and loss, whispered his name with reverence and hope. Men in three-piece suits said novenas, drunk with his potential, aquiver with his proposed patient load. Silver-haired corporate giants wept with joy. A great wind of change was sweeping over Mother Mary Hospital, and its name would be Hunsacker.

The labor and delivery staff took up the song the minute he first crossed Mother Mary terrazzo, the nurses entertaining the cafeteria crowd with psalms to his looks and charisma, teasing the unanointed with his proximity, congratulating themselves on their incredible luck to be so privileged with his presence.

The floors followed, and then surgery, until the reputation of Dr. Dale Hunsacker threatened mythological proportions.

He was handsome. He was electric. He remembered names and told jokes and brought in pizzas. The administration loved him because he had managed to siphon the wealthier pregnancies their way when he decided to name Mother Mary his primary hospital, and the labor and delivery nurses loved him because he inspired administration to cough up some badly needed money for their unit. So what if he wasn't the best OB/GYN to hit the halls. Neither were any of the other OBs on staff, and not one of them was nearly as pleasant.

Dr. Dale Hunsacker, doctor of Obstetrics and Gynecology, late of the finer neighborhoods of Boston and New York, had decided to escape the pressures of the East Coast for the settled, homey atmosphere of St. Louis. In no more than a matter of weeks in his new home, he had proven a rare talent, attracting some of the area's more wealthy women into his practice on weight of word of mouth and an unforgettable smile. Dr. Dale Hunsacker was an up-and-coming commodity in one of the most cutthroat business venues in St. Louis—medicine. And much to the chagrin of the more traditional moneyed hospitals in the area, Mother Mary had him.

Dale was a great guy. Dale was a dream. Dale was a hell of a team player. By the time Casey met him, she knew she was either going to end up hating him or having his children.

Given a choice, she would have picked almost any other night to finally meet the newest staff legend. Friday night was bad enough in the emergency room, but a full moon was worse. And to top it off, the weather was warming up. All those bananamen out there who had been waiting out the cold weather to go back into action were revving into high gear.

Five hours into her shift, Casey was tired, hungry, and crabby. The idea that all this was just a preview of the months to come depressed her immensely.

"It's like a zoo in here tonight," she complained to Janice Feldman when they met at the medprep where the medications were kept.

Tall, elegant, and irritatingly spotless at eight o'clock at night, Janice grinned and waved a manicured finger at Casey's freckled nose. "Watch it, hon. One of the surgery nurses got fired for bandying about that particular euphemism. Administration thinks it's derogatory."

Casey lifted a dry eyebrow. "It is," she assured her friend. "That's why I said it." Drawing up fifty of Vistaril, Casey capped the needle and turned to consider the long hall. "Sounds like it's feeding time, too."

Babies wailed, drunks howled, one particularly colorful psychotic screamed a series of numbers out loud to keep them all from disappearing, and the radio babbled nonstop. Phones rang, monitors beeped, and sirens moaned on their way in.

"Hold ye there, virgin!"

Casey stiffened and spun around. "Oh, shit, Ralph. I told you to watch him!"

A close relative of Gentle Ben was bearing down on her, hair and beard flying, eyes glittering, arms outstretched to her. The leather restraints he'd been wearing flapped in his wake. He was buck naked and ugly as sin.

"Save me, virgin!" he howled, scattering security guards like bowling pins. "Die for me!"

Casey planted herself foursquare in his path. "I have affidavits," she yelled at him, hands on hips, fighting a grin. St. Paul came in every other month when he forgot to take his Prolixin and tried to sacrifice a redheaded virgin to ensure the safety of his virility. Unfortunately, Casey was the only redhead around. "Witnesses. Participants. I—am—not—a virgin!"

"I'll swear to it!" Dr. Belstein yelled from room three where he was sewing up a toddler's chin.

"Me, too," Michael Wilson added, hand in the air

from where he was adjusting a pair of crutches at the other end of the hall. "She was great!"

"Nae!"

"Did St. Paul live in medieval Scotland?" Janice asked as security gave it another try. Two of them grabbed restraints. Two more tried flying tackles.

"What I want to know," Casey answered, watching the foray passively, "is whether he's only been this ugly since he fell off that donkey."

St. Paul finally came down when Casey just stuck a foot out and tripped him. The ensuing crash of people tumbled two chairs and sent a stock cart rolling into the telemetry desk. Janice delicately lifted a spotless white shoe just in time to have St. Paul slide neatly beneath. Spittle dotted the floor, but not her uniform.

"You'll need to fill out an incident report," Ralph informed them from where he lay amid the tangle of arms and legs.

Casey waved him off. "I'll just copy off the last four."

She was turning back to close up the cabinet when a wild howl split the air. Both she and Janice turned in the direction of room eight, which had been empty only moments earlier.

"What's that?" Janice demanded as the voice rose again, somebody's impersonation of a screech monkey.

"Your gomer du jour," Barb announced as she stepped out the door. "Mr. Wilson Macomber. Ninety-two and holding."

Janice groaned. "Again? I just sent him home."

Barb's smile was smug as she handed over the paperwork from the nursing home that had transferred Mr. Macomber in. "He misses you. I need rooms, kids. Clear something out."

"So I can get *Mrs.* Macomber?" Casey demanded. "No, thanks."

Barb just looked down at the floor where security was still trying to convince St. Paul he wanted to go back to his room—or Thessalonia, as it had been dubbed for the night. "Don't forget to fill out the incident report."

Casey and Janice turned back to their task, handily ignoring the scuffle that still continued behind them and the newest member of the Friday Night Choir.

"We really want to do this, right?" Casey asked.

Janice knew Casey well enough to laugh. "More than sex."

At that, Casey sighed and cleaned up her equipment before racing off. "I wouldn't know," she admitted. "I haven't had sex in so long, it would be hard to compare."

"Trust me, then," Janice suggested.

Casey turned, hearing the sudden tension in the other nurse's voice, but Janice was way ahead of her. "Heard from Dr. Wonderful yet?"

"Hunsacker?" Casey shook her head. "He's still missing in action. Which just proves that he's not stupid. God knows, I wouldn't want to face that bitch when she's in full cry."

Janice huffed self-righteously. "The price of courting the rich."

"Casey!" one of the other nurses yelled from the far end of the hall. "Mrs. VanCleve wants you!"

Casey's mood took an immediate nosedive. "He'd better get his butt in here fast," she threatened blackly.

"He will," Janice promised with a commiserating pat to the shoulder. "And from what I've heard, it'll be well worth the wait."

Casey stopped just long enough to shoot her friend a particularly derisive look. "Honey, he's gonna have to fart flowers to impress me after this." And then she headed off to face the glacial Mrs. VanCleve.

Casey's feet ached. Her calves ached. Come to think

of it, her hips ached. She'd walked on to a full house and hadn't stopped moving since, sending three patients to surgery, two to intensive care, and waiting to get one to Fantasy Island before somebody really did make him disappear. She'd held babies, comforted confused old people, pacified drunks, and dodged St. Paul. And to top it off, she'd gotten stuck with Mrs. VanCleve.

She knew Barbara had dumped the woman on her out of spite. Barbara didn't like Casey, and tended to use her shifts as triage nurse to drive home the point. Whenever Barbara triaged, Casey's patient load was Herculean. It also encompassed the far end of a badly laid out hall, so that Casey would suffer the maximum amount of inconvenience.

The Emergency Department, like everything else at Mother Mary, had been designed by architects whose specialty must have been racetracks. Constructed in a long L shape, its twenty-five rooms demanded a lot of running and a constant strain to keep an eye on all the patients.

Well, Casey thought again as she slipped into Mr. Willington's room to give him his pain medicine, at least she got her exercise. Be thankful for small things, her mother always said. Well, this was about as small as it got.

Pulling the cap off the syringe with her teeth, Casey aimed for the right upper quadrant of Mr. Willington's emaciated backside and slid the needle home.

"I'm going to turn off the lights now," she told him quietly, because anything hurt him at times like this. His skin was like leather by now, but he refused to flinch. Casey retrieved her empty syringe and dumped it in the waste, the cap still caught in her teeth like a toothpick. "And we'll see how it does. Would you like me to get your wife?"

"No," he moaned, turning as best he could. "Let her get away from me for a while."

Casey settled him with patient hands, smiling because that was all she could offer him now when the pain medicine wouldn't even really work anymore, smoothing his hair back from a clammy forehead, trying to ease his discomfort as much as she could before consigning him back to the floors that he so seldom left anymore. "Well, you get some sleep," she crooned, already wearing the edge off her molars against the plastic needle cap she'd begun to chew like old gum to work away the stress. "I don't want any wild music or dancing in here."

He managed a small grin at her wan joke. "Not unless I'm feeling particularly frisky."

She flipped off the lights and eased back out the door, hating the futility of aching for him, wishing he'd die quickly so she could stop torturing him.

"Yes, Mrs. VanCleve." Leaning into the room next door, Casey kept her voice level and concerned, even though she had long since decided that the only thing Mrs. VanCleve needed was a high colonic and a fast boot out the door.

For Mrs. VanCleve's part, she was comfortably ensconced on the cart like a Victorian hostess, hair perfectly coiffed and hands weighted down with enough diamonds to support a third world economy. Her nails were blood-red and her lipstick matched. Her eyes were harder than the stones in her rings and brimming with disdain.

"Do you know who I am?" she demanded yet again, her voice scathing.

Casey overcame the urge to say, Yes, of course. I've been in this room every thirty seconds since you walked in the door. I should damn well know who you are by now.

"We've tried everything to reach Dr. Hunsacker," she

explained yet again. "He isn't on his beeper, and he's left the other hospital. Like I said, Mrs. VanCleve, since you didn't let Dr. Hunsacker know you were coming in, he couldn't be here to meet you. You can wait for him, or if you'd like, one of our doctors can still see you."

She'd given that speech so many times in the last forty-five minutes she was thinking of printing it on a laminated card, like Miranda rights. Mrs. VanCleve was no more impressed than she had been the other ten or twelve times.

"I will not see some . . . intern! You get out and find Dr. Hunsacker now! I have a dinner to attend, and I will not be late."

Casey was still counting for patience when Michael screeched to a halt alongside her.

"Casey, Billie Evans is coming in in full arrest."

Immediately Casey lost interest in the society queen with the bladder infection. Without even closing the door, she turned on her tech. Instead of the crutches he'd been working on, he held out a set of scrubs. "What do you mean?"

Scrubs meant one thing. Trauma. Public relations still demanded white uniforms in this part of town, but if the nurses had the time when trauma was expected, they were allowed to change into the more practical scrubs.

"She was hit by a car. 264 just called it in. Five-minute ETA."

Casey grabbed the greens. "Have the secretaries place another call for Hunsacker. And ask them if they'd give me the log times on those calls so I can chart it. Might as well make some use out of all this paperwork. Then get respiratory, lab, and X ray up here. Notify OR."

He ran. Casey moved to follow him.

"Don't you just walk out on me," Mrs. VanCleve demanded.

Casey leveled a set of equally cool blue eyes on her patient. "I have no choice. Someone is dying. Surely you can understand that that has to come first."

"I don't—"

Casey didn't wait for the rest. She was already on her way in to set up for Billie.

She was shaken. Billie was the head nurse down in recovery. Not a popular person, by any means. A past master at the art of territorialism, Billie ran her unit rather like someone with the surname of Bonaparte, alienating everybody within range of her powerful voice and imposing figure. But Billie was one of them. You took care of your own, because nobody else sure as hell did.

The room was set up within three minutes. Respiratory s☐☐d by, lab had been called, one of the other nurses ☐☐d run for blood, and a call was out to the trauma doctors. Fluids hung from poles, their lines snaking down toward the waiting gurney. The plastic morgue wrap had already been stretched beneath the paper sheet, just in case. The code drugs were laid out in neat rows on the shelf, and all the myriad forms waited to be filled out on one of the stands. Now, there was just the waiting.

"Casey?"

Flipping a sterile towel over the instrument tray she'd just opened, Casey turned to answer, and found herself face-to-face with Dr. Hunsacker.

She'd never met the man, but there couldn't be any mistaking just who he was. Leaning in the doorway, his hand on the wall, dressed in rugby shirt and chinos, he looked tousled and handsome. Something out of an old romance, Dr. Kildare, come to heal and comfort.

"Dr. Hunsacker?" she answered, a little surprised at his appearance. A little disconcerted by her own fascination. His looks weren't all that great. Certainly nothing to catalog along with natural wonders. He was tall and blond, with a nicely squared chin, blue eyes, and a jogger's build. Big deal.

And then he smiled.

"Barb told me to look for the cute little redhead with the scowl on her face," he said brightly. "I assume that's because you've had the dubious pleasure of meeting Mrs. VanCleve. Can you tell me what's going on?" He punctuated the question by leaning more easily against the door, assuming a posture of patience and interest. He wasn't going anywhere. He was making it a point to let Casey know that her work here was more important than his.

"She was a little pissed that you didn't meet her," Casey offered.

"I'm sorry it took so long to get here," he apologized, and then flashed those perfect white teeth in a show of sheepish humor. "I forgot to take the beeper into Haagen-Dazs."

It was the smile. Casey could almost hear the delivery nurses sigh four floors away. Hunsacker was nice-looking until he smiled, and then he was unforgettable. It hit you right between the eyes and left you a little dizzy. It made you smile back, no matter what else you wanted to do.

Casey suddenly understood just how he was hooking all those rich patients. He just invited them into his office and smiled at them. She was sure the blatant flattery didn't hurt any, either. The day Barb called her cute would be the first ski championships from hell.

"I sent off a urine specimen when she first came in," she reported, ignoring not only the cozy charm but the fact that Haagen-Dazs seemed to have included bourbon in its list of flavors. She could smell it on his breath. Oh, well, at least it proved he was human. There'd been some question. "Mrs. VanCleve has urinary tract infection symptoms. Burning on urination, frequency, suprapubic cramping. She hasn't let any of our docs see her.''

Hunsacker rolled his eyes a little. ''I know,'' he admitted, leaning a little closer, allowing a conspiratorial grin. ''She can be a real pain sometimes. Well, I'll go in and smooth her feathers. Where's her chart?''

Moving toward the door, Casey pointed past the scurrying staff to the clipboard on room twenty's door. Hunsacker didn't move to give her more room. He seemed to like that close-contact approach to the staff. He was wearing cologne, too. Smoky cologne that smelled really good.

''Code blue, trauma room one. Code blue, trauma room one.''

Instinctively Casey looked up toward the dismembered speaker voice. ''Ambulance is here,'' she said, the adrenaline jolting through her. ''I'm going to be tied up for a while.''

Hunsacker waved off the disclaimer, his eyes avid at the sight of the assembled trauma staff. ''You'll probably be having more fun than I will.''

Personally, Casey agreed with him, but she didn't know him well enough to say it. Besides, the approach of pounding feet and a laden ambulance cart already had all her attention. She turned away from Dr. Hunsacker and forgot him.

For years Mother Mary had been a solidly third-rate hospital run by the only fiscally naive order of nuns in St. Louis. Staffed with ex-interns unable to find a home in any accredited residencies, its emergency room had garnered more disdain than chiropractic centers and laetrile clinics. Surrounding hospital staffs had dubbed the place M and M, not so much for the candy as Morbidity and Mortality, the twins of medical failure. The desperate and the uninformed went to Mary Mother's emergency room. The same was true of the staff. All that had changed when the financial crunch had hit the medical community.

Bowing to the inevitable, the good sisters had handed over the reins of power to a lay board untroubled by matters of compassion and spirituality. The combination of ruthless administration and safe parking had seen the hospital shoot past the two near contenders and survive when several others had failed. Now Mother Mary boasted an open heart unit, three MRI scanners, the largest pediatric psych center in the county, and a newly remodeled and expanded ER to up the trauma rating and attract those all-important rescue helicopters.

The luck was all on Billie's side when she came in. The emergency room was at full operating capacity, everyone present spoke a variation of the same language, the trauma surgeons on call weren't busy at a benefit of any kind, and the blood bank was stocked. There were enough nurses on to handle a trauma and a surgical team standing by in case she made it that far. Which Casey realized was just a message that it was Billie's time to die. Because she did.

"Dead feet," Abe Belstein pronounced as he walked in the room right behind the priest.

Casey had seen them the minute Billie had been rolled in. One of the classic signs of futility, the waxy, almost yellow cast to the feet of a trauma victim, kind of the sign that the body had already given up on servicing them, it was only going to be a matter of time before everything else quit, too.

Everything else was already long gone. The team tried to reinflate Billie's collapsed lung with chest tubes, forced her to breathe through the endotracheal tube in her throat, squeezed blood into her chest with MAST trousers, x-rayed everything with a bruise, and shot her with enough chemicals to get a truck in gear. They pumped in bloods and fluids and pumped out the same blood and never once got more than a marginal heart pattern.

Billie's eyes were open and flat, already opaque and anonymous. Her skull was shattered and her chest in pieces. Whatever car had hit her had sealed her fate on the spot. The frantic lifesaving measures they took in that room were for principle, not for effect. Nobody liked Billie, but they fought for her.

"What's the status on the car?" Casey asked the paramedics thirty minutes later as she copied off times from her scribbled notes before calling the medical examiner. The room was empty but for Casey, the paramedics, and Billie. Thick with the smell of blood, strewn with piles of used equipment and packaging, and spattered with any number of bodily fluids, the scene looked like the aftermath of an explosion.

Casey was as blood-spattered as the room and twice as disheveled. Her feet hurt even worse. She was chewing hard on another needle cap and she had an empty, ashes feeling in the pit of her stomach as she stepped over puddles of blood to get to her chart.

"No car, no witnesses. She was just found on the side of Rott Road," the paramedic answered as he cleaned off his equipment. "Evidently she tried to get across the street."

Casey nodded absently. "Evidently she didn't make it."

He didn't even pause from his work. They'd shared too many of these scenes. "Bert's here already. Ernie stayed back at the scene."

Bert and Ernie, the two county detectives who always seemed to be called out on Casey's shift. A Mutt-and-Jeff team that had survived every *Sesame Street* slur they'd encountered. Ernie even had the hand puppet in the car. Casey liked them.

"Well, the evidence is as plain as the tracks on her face."

Alongside her the door inched open to the hallway. Casey looked up, not wanting any visitor wandering in this particular wrong door. It wasn't a visitor. It was Dr. Hunsacker.

He never even looked at Casey. His eyes were on the body on the table. "Somebody said that was Billie Evans."

Casey took a quick look over her shoulder. She'd seen it often enough. Whatever it was that set a person apart disappeared in death, so that features took on an unnerving sameness. A person who didn't know would have to look twice to prove Billie's identity.

"Yeah," she acknowledged. "Hit and run."

Not moving from where he stood just in the doorway, Dr. Hunsacker shook his head slowly. "That's too bad, too bad. Although, I'm not sure I wouldn't want to die the same way."

Casey stared at him. "Hit and run?"

It took Hunsacker a moment to pull his gaze from Billie's still form. When he did, he proffered another sheepish smile. "Surprised," he said. "I'm not the kind to eke out every minute of life just to be breathing, ya know? I think I'd be the kind to opt out fast."

Casey wasn't sure what to say. She didn't know Hunsacker well enough yet to know how to answer. He didn't seem in the mood for black humor, and that was all she had left.

"Do you ever get used to it?" he asked, looking back at where Billie lay.

Casey took another look. Nothing had changed. It was a scene like a hundred she'd faced that year. "Yeah," she admitted with a little surprise, and felt even worse. It made her realize just how burned out she was getting, to have nothing more to say for someone she'd known.

"Six, nine, thirty-two, ninety-five, eighty-eight! Eighty-eight! Eighty-eight!"

Nothing broke a mood quite like a jumpy psychotic. Thankful for the interruption, Casey quickly gathered her notes together. "Oh, hell," she groused. "I was hoping the Lithium fairy had already scooped him up."

Hunsacker straightened to let Casey pass. "Mrs. Van-Cleve's still here, too."

That almost stopped Casey right beneath his outstretched arm. She didn't want to say something like "Oh, shit," to a doctor she hardly knew. With cops or paramedics it was different. They understood it. They expected it. Doctors who catered to rich patients might not see it the same way.

"I'm sorry," he apologized with that smile. "I would have had her out of here before you got out, but there wasn't anybody to help."

Casey blinked up at him, walking out into the hall to deposit her work before calling the officials. "Help?" she asked. She was as surprised that he couldn't get any of a half-dozen women who were even now ogling him from different distances, as that he needed help at all. A little hand-holding, a quick prescription for antibiotics and Pyridium, and Mrs. VanCleve should have been out the door. In fact, Casey had spent the whole code counting on it.

Letting the door close behind him, Hunsacker nodded, the hint of melancholy that had crept into his expression in that room disappearing. Once again he was the bright boy. "I need to do a pelvic."

"Casey, medical examiner's on line one," Barb announced from the edge of the hall. "State San's on line two. They don't want Mr. Ricks, and you still haven't filled out the AMA form for that little kid whose parents dragged him out of here."

The noise level was, if anything, higher. Barb stood there implacably, hands on slim hips, a small, feral, supremely unhappy woman who was three years out of training and already soured, her ire all Casey's tonight.

Casey looked longingly at the chair and knew she was never going to feel it against her backside. Mr. Ricks was now doing primary numbers, and the lights showed that she had three new patients she hadn't seen yet. And she still had to finish with Billie.

"Pelvic?" she echoed instead, eyes up to Hunsacker, unable to quite keep the exhausted challenge out of her voice. "What for?"

Some conditions needed pelvics. Some didn't. Mrs. VanCleve didn't. And Casey didn't want to do one, especially with that woman. Not even if Dr. Hunsacker were Mel Gibson and took off his shirt to do it.

"I do pelvics on all my patients," Dr. Hunsacker answered easily, as if that would be all Casey needed to know.

Casey heard the steel beneath all that velvet. "Did I miss something?" she asked anyway. "I thought there weren't any gynecological symptoms. The UTI symptoms were fairly specific, and the urinalysis was diagnostic."

"And I want to do a pelvic," he said.

"Casey, come on!" Barbara shrilled from the far end of the hall. "Take your calls. The ME's called back twice!"

Casey struggled to control the sudden burst of irrational anger. It was just all the work, all the headaches, Billie lying in there like a slab of beef without dignity. It was just that Hunsacker didn't need to do a pelvic any more than Casey needed to ask Mrs. VanCleve's opinion on nursing procedures, but he'd end up doing it anyway. With Casey.

"Let me talk to the medical examiner first," she said, knowing that he was wrong. Knowing that it didn't make any difference. "Then I'll be in."

He didn't even answer. He just nodded and headed toward Mrs. VanCleve's room, stopping on the way to get close to a couple of the other women in the hall. Casey took several slow breaths. Then she picked up line one and greeted the medical examiner.

Casey had never heard anyone whine and coo at the same time. Somehow, that was exactly what Mrs. Van-Cleve was doing when Casey walked back into her room. Hunsacker was holding the woman's hand, assuring her that the pelvic was perfectly necessary, and the woman was batting her eyes at him like Scarlet O'Hara while complaining that she was just too sore for a pelvic. They were so *uncomfortable*—even, unfortunately, when Dr. Hunsacker did them.

Casey busied herself setting up for the exam. Her mind was, in truth, still with all her other chores more than this one, and most particularly with Billie, who, it seemed, would die unmourned. No relatives, no close friends to notify. The hospital had been her life. A frequent target of Billie's ire, Casey suddenly wanted to go in and apologize to her for having to die alone.

Too late now, she wanted to talk to her, to ask how she'd come to be like she was. She wanted to ward that wasted, bitter ghost away from her, because that lonely, unmourned body looked too suddenly like her own, and she wasn't sure she could bear it.

"Okay, now, Vivian," Dr. Hunsacker crooned, speculum in hand. "This will only take a few minutes."

Casey wasn't really paying attention. She stood behind Hunsacker and to his right, directing the light and thinking of the pile of paperwork that still waited for her before she could redirect Mr. Ricks. Then Mrs. VanCleve yelped.

"Come on now, Vivian," Hunsacker was saying, his tone reminiscent of a father chastising a recalcitrant child. "Be a big girl. That doesn't hurt."

Casey's attention was caught. Not just by his words, or the curt tone of voice, but his actions. Maybe it was her imagination. Maybe she just wanted to find fault with him, but he sure did seem to have a rough hand at the old check and see. The next time Mrs. VanCleve protested, Casey almost did, too.

Asshole OBs. Sometimes they had the sensitivity of gorillas. Casey wanted to see somebody do a rectal on him with that much finesse and see him be a big boy.

"Now, stop it and hold still, Vivian." For a minute there, he even looked angry. Casey could only see the corner of his jaw from where she stood, but it clenched tight. A tendon popped up along his neck, and his fingers seemed to dig a little too deep as they palpated.

Vivian held still. Hunsacker finished and flipped the sheet back down over her knees. "Good girl," he praised her and climbed back to his feet to head for the sink.

When Casey saw his expression, she thought she must have been mistaken. He looked as genial as a big brother, smiling and friendly and at ease.

"Am I all right?" Mrs. VanCleve asked in a curiously small voice.

"Just fine," he assured her, rinsing his hands for the second time. "Nothing more than a bladder infection."

Casey didn't say a word. She did watch, though, as Hunsacker methodically dried his hands and returned to take hold of one of Mrs. VanCleve's as he gave his instructions.

"I want to see you in the office on Monday just to check," he said, his voice soft. "You'll be there, won't you?"

Mrs. VanCleve was back to simpering. "Of course I will," she promised, her eyes glowing.

Hunsacker nodded and patted and talked about the party Mrs. VanCleve was to attend, the people she knew. Casey finally lost interest and walked on back out. He followed her within a few minutes, drying his hands yet again.

Dropping the paper towels in the waste can, he met her at the desk where her paperwork still lay in a disordered heap. "Thanks for the help, hon," he acknowledged with that same silky tone of voice.

Casey didn't bother to sit to write on Mrs. VanCleve's chart. She just bent over the desk. Hunsacker came right up alongside her and leaned in close, as if the two shared a secret. His Dock-Sides bumped against the back of Casey's nursing shoes and he settled a hand on Casey's shoulder.

Casey wasn't sure why she reacted the way she did. Maybe the close contact, maybe the force with which he'd conducted that pelvic. Maybe just the sense that Hunsacker never questioned Casey's attraction to him. For whatever reason, the hair stood straight up on the nape of her neck at his touch. Shying away, she walked to the other side of the desk.

"Do you have her script so I can dismiss her?" she asked, surprised at the chill in her voice, a little confused about her sudden antipathy.

For a moment there was an uncomfortable little island of silence in that crowded, noisy hallway. When Casey looked up at the doctor, it was to discover a curious flatness in his expression. A distance, as if he'd just disappeared, even standing right before her. He held a notebook in his right hand, but didn't even seem to notice it.

"Dr. Hunsacker?"

It was like hitting a switch. One minute his eyes were as animated as Billie's, the next he was smiling as if Casey were his best friend. "Sure. You know the routine, I'm sure." Picking up one of the script pads, he quickly scribbled. "What do you like on your pizzas?"

Still trying to catch up, Casey blinked. "Huh?"

Hunsacker ripped the prescription off the pad and handed it over, smiling and relaxed. "Mushrooms? Anchovies? I owe you a pizza for putting up with Mrs. Van-Cleve for me."

"Mushrooms," she answered instinctively, wondering at the odd, niggling little feeling in her chest.

"Casey, do you have any empty rooms?" Barbara asked in that tone of voice that relayed to everyone that Casey was goldbricking.

"I'm dismissing twenty right now," Casey assured her, the frustration bubbling close again.

"Thanks, hon," Hunsacker said, his attention on his notebook. He seemed to be carefully scratching out notations and adding more. A list maker. "Next time I'm here I'll ask for you especially. You've been a doll."

Shutting the little book, he returned his attention to Casey. Flipped on the voltage and laid a hand on her arm whether she wanted it there or not. And Casey, knowing that at least four women in the room envied her, didn't like it.

It wasn't until the end of the shift, when the bunch of them were scattered over the nurses' lounge like shaken rag dolls, that Janice even had the chance to bring up the subject of the wonder doctor.

"So, Casey," she said, head back against the chair, eyes closed. "Have you asked Hunsacker to bear your children yet?"

From where she sat sprawled on the threadbare old couch in the corner, Casey couldn't even manage a shrug. She was measuring her visual acuity by trying to read the notices on the bulletin board across the room, or as they'd dubbed it, the BOHICA board, for Bend Over, Here It Comes Again. Three new forms were displayed that needed to be filled out for every surgery patient. A sign said no change-of-shift parties were allowed in the lounge. The refrigerator was for patient food, and the microwave for the doctors.

"He sure did seem to like you," one of the other nurses admitted, pulling off her shoes to massage her toes. "Damn it."

"I'm not sure I like him," Casey answered quietly, trying to analyze the discomfort she felt about Hunsacker's friendliness.

For a moment she didn't notice the stunned silence around her. She was still thinking of that pelvic, those clenched fingers. That smile. All that familiarity.

Another notice said that Libby Kelly had been replaced as head nurse on telemetry. Word was that she'd bucked one of the doctors up there and lost.

"Are you crazy?" Barb demanded. "How many other doctors would have taken Mrs. VanCleve off your hands?"

"How many doctors would have smelled that nice doing it?" Janice countered, taking a last, long drag from her end-of-shift cigarette and grinding it out in an ashtray on the table they'd stolen from the fourth-floor waiting room. "Why in heaven's name don't you like him?"

When Casey looked over to answer, it was to discover the degrees of outrage that met her words. There wasn't a sympathetic face in the room.

"I don't know," she had to admit anyway. "I just don't know."

Nobody agreed with her. Nobody really understood. And Casey couldn't think how to make them. She just had a hunch and a set of nervous neck hairs, and nobody in their right mind would count those as irrefutable evidence of anything. All the same, Casey couldn't shake the suspicion that Dr. Dale Hunsacker wasn't the person everybody thought he was.

# Chapter 2

CASEY DIDN'T DWELL on Dr. Hunsacker. In fact, once she got past the mushroom pizza he sent the next day, she barely thought of him in the weeks that followed. He showed up in the emergency room on occasion, but never found reason to work with Casey. The closest Casey got to him was as amused spectator to his elaborate game-playing and the general adulation that met him wherever he went.

The whispering about him persisted, with the rumor machine inevitably gearing up. Hunsacker was handsome and he was single, and that was more than enough to stir the hospital grapevine interest, not to mention imagination.

All except Casey's. She had enough on her plate without having to deal with anything new.

"It was so nice of you to fit us into your busy schedule."

Flat on her back beneath the first warm sun of the year, Casey lazily lifted a hand. "I try not to forget the little people."

It was a Tuesday. Casey was off, and as far away from the hospital as possible. Well, as far away as she could

afford at the end of her paycheck, which was her back-
yard five miles away.

When she'd heard the weather forecast she'd vowed
to waste her only day off this week offering obeisance
to the spring sun. When she'd found out that two friends
were also available on short notice, she'd decided to
share her task with them.

The sunshine was warm. Spring had returned to Webster Groves with its old Victorian homes and lush, tree-
laden lawns. Fruit trees spilled petals and perfume, and
bulbs exploded into bright chains of color along walks
and drives. The first lawnmowers of the season droned
like heavy flies. A fresh breeze rustled through the huge
old oak trees that ringed the yard, and in the distance
a siren that didn't need to be answered moaned. The
three women were stretched out around the pool, cool
drinks in hand, romance books open, music drifting from
the stereo. A day made in paradise.

Of course, since the pool was a four-foot wader, the
drinks tea, and the music rock and roll from a jam box
with only one working speaker, it took a little imagination to come up with the good life. But then, if Casey
hadn't had a vivid imagination, she wouldn't have been
such a sharp trauma nurse. It was a gift she'd inherited
from her mother.

"I'm tellin' ya, Casey," Poppi Henderson insisted,
"it's the chance of a lifetime. I really think this is the
one."

Casey didn't move. "Of course it is, Poppi." It was always the chance of a lifetime with Poppi. Casey had
known her since fifth grade, and Poppi had never
changed. There was always something grand and wonderful about the world, marvels just beyond our reach,
mysteries to untangle for the betterment of mankind and
Poppi Henderson.

Of course, it might have made a difference that Poppi had wasted much of her misspent youth on marijuana and acid. It was bound to affect somebody's views of the world. Especially since Poppi hadn't completely moved on into maturity.

"You weren't tripping when you came up with this idea, were you?" Evelyn Peters asked from the third lawn chair.

Poppi didn't even bother to express denial. "Some of my best ideas come then," she said. "And I'm tellin' you, this one's a natural."

Casey just smiled. To anyone who didn't know her, Poppi looked just like all the other Baby Boomers who strolled the sedate, shaded lanes of Webster. A pageboy blonde with big blue eyes and a taste in Laura Ashley, she looked like she'd just stepped out of a Junior League meeting. And to make matters even more fun, the Muffies and Buffies in the decidedly upscale Republican neighborhood took her diminutive as one of their own. It didn't seem to dawn on them that Poppi had metamorphosed from Pauline sometime around 1970 when names like that meant something completely different.

Poppi never bothered to correct misconceptions. She was perfectly happy with her facade. Nobody looking at her would guess that she was still heavily into experimentation.

"When do you get any work done?" Evelyn asked.

"That's all relative," Poppi assured her with a languid wave of her arm from where she was sprawled in the pool.

Taking a sip from her tea, Casey had to laugh. "Relative's the word, Poppi. I'd probably have the time to work up board-game ideas if I worked for *my* father, too."

"Not just any board game," Poppi insisted. "Nirvana.

The game of reincarnation. I'm tellin' you, it's the game of the nineties."

God, Casey needed this after the last week. There was nothing like Poppi to scatter reality like a storm cloud. After eight straight days on, Casey felt battered, abused, and overwhelmed. She was getting too old to take it anymore. She was too tired, too strung out from trying to keep up, too experienced to expect relief. As predictable as spring thaw, her seasonal depression had hit.

Most people dreaded the cold, the darkening days of winter where the primitive mind still expected death. Casey dreaded the sun. Like most emergency-room staffers, she looked to the summer and only saw the crush of numbers, the unrelieved burden of exhaustion and dread.

Mother Mary was particularly susceptible, having situated itself at the merger of highways 270 and 44 in the county, favorite routes for summer escape, and having decided with its refurbishment to court the injured and sick everywhere with billboards and public-sponsored events. It had worked, and it now had the second busiest ER in the metropolitan area.

The patient load was already beginning to geometrically increase. Children fell from bikes, homeowners committed suicide with a variety of lawn implements, motorcyclists steered for grease spots. Swimming pools were open for drownings and rivers for boating accidents. Heat shortened tempers and increased recklessness.

And as much as she dreaded it, Casey couldn't think of anything else she'd rather do. Well, except for one. And thirty-two was just a little late to become a lead singer for a rock band.

"You'd invest in me, wouldn't you, Mrs. McDonough?"

"Of course I would, Poppi. God bless you."

Casey hadn't even heard her mom come out into the yard. Squinting against the glare of the sun, she caught sight of her mother as she headed down the path toward the garden with her bucket and scrub brush, almost oblivious of the company only feet away.

A small, birdlike woman, Helen McDonough walked with a stoop, dressed only in dull brown, and always wore a matching scarf over her hair. Casey had seen her in nothing else since her father had died twenty-four years earlier. She closed her eyes again, much too familiar with the sight.

"What's your mom doing?" Evelyn whispered.

Casey didn't bother to open her eyes. "What day is it?"

She heard the small pause before Evelyn managed an answer. "Tuesday."

Casey nodded. "Then it's Mary's day for a bath."

"Mary . . ."

"Around the back," Poppi offered. "The madonna in the garden."

"Oh."

They heard the first, tentative notes of "On This Day, O Beautiful Mother" as Casey's mother began her chore. Casey just concentrated on the gentle harmony of America and the fresh sweetness of apple blossoms from the neighbor's yard.

"Is that why you came back here?" Evelyn asked. "Because she's getting . . . uh . . ."

Casey had to laugh. "She's not getting anything, Ev. She's been like that as long as I can remember. She chose my dad over the convent and never forgave herself for it."

There was another stiff silence, then another small "Oh."

Poppi, as usual, jumped to Mrs. McDonough's defense. Poppi related to Mrs. McDonough, especially when she was stoned. "Oh, she's okay," she protested. "You just don't have any patience with her anymore, Case."

Casey got one eye open and leveled it on her closest friend. "And you don't have to live with the Chapel of Eternal Vigilance in your attic," she countered.

Evelyn was even more confused. A friend from Casey's days at St. Isidore's, another hospital in the area where Casey had worked right out of training, Evelyn had never before crossed the McDonough threshold. They'd always met in neutral territory, and much less often since Casey had defected for newer pastures at Mother Mary some four years earlier.

"The chapel—"

"Third floor," Poppi answered. "Lots of candles and holy cards. Didn't you smell the incense when you walked in the house?"

Evelyn lifted an eyebrow. "I thought that was *you.*"

Poppi offered a particularly insulted scowl, which, coming from a woman reclining in six inches of water and surrounded by Donald Duck and Goofy, lost some of its impact. "I have much more taste than that. What do you think I am, a channeler?"

Evelyn was obviously at a loss for an answer. Casey couldn't blame her. One had to become acclimated to Poppi, kind of like cold water or weightlessness. Evelyn had met her enough times over the years to know the basics. That didn't necessarily mean she was used to them.

To add to that, Evelyn was one of the most blatantly normal people Casey knew. An earth mother by temperament, she was a great hand-holder and commiserator. She'd also been one of the lousiest ER nurses Casey had known. ER nurses were aggressive and decisive. Evelyn was not. She was much happier lavishing support on young mothers in St. Izzy's high-tech postpartum unit.

"You could just move," Poppi nudged. "Like you've been threatening to for the three years you've been back."

Casey waved off the objection. "If I moved, who'd whitewash the statues?"

It wasn't something to discuss on a warm, bright spring day. Casey had only this day off, and she didn't want to spend it on recriminations and frustration. If she wanted to do that, she could just go back to work and get paid for it.

Pulling herself up, she swung her feet over the side of her chair and settled them into the cool tickle of the new grass. "How about if we change the subject?" she suggested abruptly, trying to ignore the tremulous voice that still drifted from the other side of the garage.

Instead she noted that her thighs were pinking up a little. "Scoot over, Poppi. I want to do a few laps."

Poppi obliged, and Casey sank into the tepid water, iced tea in hand. "Ah," she cooed. "This is living."

"Hey," Poppi said. "You want to change the subject, I have one. I need a new GYN. Mine died or something. You guys have the scoop on that kind of stuff, don't you?"

"I'm better at trauma surgeons," Casey admitted, settling her head back against the inflated side and sipping her tea. "But Evelyn's your girl for gynies."

Poppi peered over her big, round sunglasses to where Evelyn was rearranging herself to start a new chapter on her book. "Does that Hunsacker guy practice at Izzy's?" she asked. "I've been hearing a lot about him lately."

"You don't want him," Casey said instinctively.

Evelyn stopped midmove. Poppi swung her attention

to Casey, her blond hair bobbing a little with the sudden turn.

"Is there something you want to share with the class?"

Casey felt the intensity of Evelyn's silent interest. She couldn't understand why she'd spoken so quickly and with such finality. After all, she'd only worked with the man once. And she did seem to be the only one in her acquaintance who didn't like him.

"I don't know," she demurred, her attention on where she was rolling her glass against her leg. "I, uh, just don't think you two would get along."

At that Poppi straightened a little. "Which means he's either a Reagan Republican or he's gay."

"He's not gay," Evelyn piped up, and then blushed.

Now Casey was looking over. "You've heard the rumors, too?"

Disconcerted, Evelyn shrugged and looked down. "Have you met him?"

Casey nodded. "Yeah."

Now Poppi's attention was swiveling back and forth, her eyes avid with curiosity. "Oh, this sounds like it's going to be good. I take it you've already counted him out as a potential date, Case?"

"I don't date doctors," she retorted. "You know that."

"You don't date anybody," Poppi shot back. "But you married a doctor once, why not again?"

"He wasn't a doctor," Evelyn spoke up with some disdain, having known the lovely ex-Mr. Casey McDonough. "He was a psychiatrist."

Something else that didn't bear bringing up on a nice day. "Have you worked with Hunsacker?" Casey asked instead.

Evelyn nodded, her gaze sharp. "Do you think he's for real?"

Casey thought of her single close encounter with the

good doctor. She thought of the rumors, the still-growing reputation, the praise from all strata of medical society. "He makes me nervous," she admitted. "Ya know?"

Finally Evelyn allowed a smile, albeit a small one. "Well, thank God. I thought I was the only one. He's so pretty sometimes I forget how much he frustrates me. And he's just a wee bit obsessive-compulsive. We're running out of Phisohex from all his scrubs."

"It's more than that," Casey agreed, seeing those eyes again, remembering the doubts and unease. "He gives me the creeps. Like he's laughing at me the whole time he's calling me honey and telling me what a swell person I am."

It was all Evelyn needed. Swinging into sitting position, she leaned forward. "I've heard he's been doing the fifty-dollar special."

Casey gaped. She'd been harboring unkind suspicions about Hunsacker, but nothing that big.

"The what?" Poppi demanded impatiently, head still swinging.

"The fifty-dollar special," Casey repeated. "The pelvic with that . . . extra touch."

Now even Poppi was gaping. "You're kidding. You mean he's coppin' a feel beneath the sheets?"

For a nurse, Evelyn relied heavily on euphemism. She scowled at Poppi's terminology. "We call it the three-finger pelvic. It's just a rumor, mind you. But I do know he's been seeing at least three of the nurses out at Izzy's on a regular basis."

"The guy must be a marathon runner," Poppi crowed with salacious delight. "Well, you know, come to think of it, I wouldn't be averse to doing a little . . . undercover investigation for the benefit of society."

Casey actually laughed. "And when Jason found out

and threw your cute little ass out, you could come live with Mom and me and the saints.''

"Poppi's coming here?" a voice piped up from behind Casey. Casey cringed, wondering just how much her mother had heard, instinctively knowing that she'd tune out anything unpleasant. After all, that's what St. Francis would have done. Or any of the myriad St. Catherines or all those martyrs. "That's lovely, Poppi dear. You can join us for mass in the mornings."

"I'm not Catholic, Mrs. McDonough," Poppi reminded her, the ritual as old as Poppi's first visit.

"Of course you are, dear," Mrs. McDonough crooned with a pat to Poppi's head as she passed with her bucket on her way back into the house.

Poppi watched Mrs. McDonough climb the stairs to the porch and then turned to Casey. "How old am I?" she demanded with a broad grin.

Casey took a long sip of tea. "Twelve."

Poppi nodded fatalistically. "I thought so."

The fifty-dollar pelvic. Casey wondered whether it was really true. Evelyn hadn't been able to come up with any more than vague rumor, and rumors tended to swirl around Dr. Dale Hunsacker like smoke around a magician. The whole talent to dealing with a hospital grapevine was learning how to separate chaff from wheat. The problem was, after working with Hunsacker just once, Casey couldn't say she didn't believe this one.

She was being unfair, and she knew it. Casey had always maintained a certain reserve around male obstetricians. After spending those years at Izzy's where the OBs were as thick as roadies on a Stones tour, she'd developed some pretty firm opinions about them.

Obstetricians, she had long since learned, either loved women, or they hated them. There was no in-between.

And the thing that was really scary was that some of the doctors with the most loyal patients were the worst of the women haters.

She'd never quite figured out why. Those guys usually had a good knack with the patter. They were great at holding hands and telling the women to leave everything to them, but when push came to delivery, they were usually nowhere to be found. They were rough and manipulative and heavily into control.

There was no better friend, no kinder, more sincerely empathetic man than the obstetrician who loved woman. There was no bigger asshole than his opposite. Casey just couldn't figure yet into which category Hunsacker fit.

She would have been intrigued to get a chance to observe him. Unfortunately, the next time he showed up at the emergency room, so did an entire bus of senior citizens who hadn't quite gotten to their bingo game and a sizable percentage of the county's preschoolers.

It was Casey's night to triage, and she'd been dealt a full house. Not only that, but Abe Belstein was on his second twelve-hour shift in a row, and on a tear about the other doctor he got to work with.

"Somebody better light a fire under her ass!" he screamed at Casey, hands on hips and chin thrust forward. At five-two, Casey was the only nurse shorter than Abe, so he brought his problems to her. Like she could solve them.

Abe was short, squat, and had a face like rising bread dough. Fuzzy red hair ringed his mostly bald head, and he had the temper of a six-year-old. But Abe was good, Abe carried his load and respected the nurses, so everybody overlooked the tantrums.

"Abe, you're the doctor," Casey reminded him, trying to placate him and update the triage log at the same time. "They pay you the big bucks to deal with the other doctors. They don't even pay me enough to listen to you yell."

"*Do* something about her!"

Dropping her pen, Casey finally sighed. "There's a county cop in the work lane. How 'bout if I just have him shoot her and be done with it?"

Abe decided not to hear the sarcasm. "Just do it soon," he demanded and whirled to leave, shoving his yarmulke back into place.

He didn't make it more than two feet. One of the twisted limbs he'd treated that evening was attached to the inelegant young lady who suddenly presented herself before him. Clad in shrink-wrapped tank top, jeans, and heels, she was a vision of dyed black hair and feathered earrings. She was also about six inches taller than Abe.

"Oh, hey, Doc. There you are," she accused, pulling to a halt scant inches from his nose. "Good. That nurse in there wouldn't give me nothin' for pain. And I hurt more now, ya know? In other places."

Abe began looking around for escape. And for good reason. In point of fact, there was more than just the red hair that made Abe distinctive. Living proof of the law of compensation, Abe's short height and homely looks were offset by a truly awesome genital endowment. It provoked hushes of reverence in the locker room, rampant speculation among staff, and some really unique reactions from women everywhere. Especially, though, women in the emergency room.

"I don't think . . ."

He never had a chance.

"Just look, will ya?" the patient asked. Before Abe could move, or at least back up, she yanked up her shirt to prove that not only was she without a bra, but that Harley Davidson owned her considerable heart. Abe, unfortunately, was eye to eye with Harley's eagle.

Casey choked. Abe yelped. Several mothers hovering near the front desk grabbed their children and ran.

"Casey!"

Casey just smiled and walked on by. "Well, I can see you're busy, Dr. Belstein. I'll go talk to Dr. Miller for you."

Her mood much improved, Casey headed off in the other direction to scout for empty rooms. Her waiting room was filling with walking wounded with nowhere to go. And Dr. Miller was, true to Abe's complaint, spending much more time with her medical manuals than her patients.

"Hey, Dr. Miller, Abe just told me that you guys are getting a bonus for every extra patient you see tonight," she lied shamelessly on the way past.

She didn't need to stop for a reaction. The resounding slam of a textbook said it all. Now Casey just had to get the nurses in gear. And they all knew better than to fall for the old bonus gag.

Well, she might not have the fastest working team in town tonight, but at least they were a kick to work with. Even though Barb was still spreading joy and light around the work lane, she had to do it around Millie, who couldn't answer a phone without doing it on point. Then there was Steve, who was practicing for his psychology degree on his patients, and Marva, nursing's answer to Jack Webb. She was great in trauma, throwing herself in front of a victim like a soldier facing a cavalry charge. Of course, anything else bored her. Tonight, unfortunately, she was bored.

Casey usually would have at least been able to count on Janice for some real output. For some reason, it seemed that tonight was going to be the exception. Disappearing from the work lane with puzzling frequency, Janice had not quite been able to keep up with the patient load on her end. She'd seemed brittle and distant all evening, which just wasn't like her. Knowing full well that dinner would be eaten on the run, Casey made a silent vow to be available for her at end of shift.

"Janice, is room fifteen going to be open anytime soon?" she asked, peeking in the half-open blinds to see a pretty young woman trying to get comfortable on the edge of the cart. Emerson, abdominal pain. She'd been here the requisite three hours waiting for tests, waiting for the doctor, waiting for spring.

"Dr. Hunsacker's coming in to see her," Janice answered without looking up from where she was charting.

Casey lifted an eyebrow. "Really. When?"

When Janice looked up to answer, Casey knew she hadn't been wrong. There was a new set of creases between Janice's elegant eyebrows, a funny white edge to her mouth. She even had a spot of Betadine on her uniform. Casey couldn't imagine what could be bothering her enough to excuse that.

"Any minute, I think. Twelve's gonna be leaving, though. Will that help?"

Casey found her attention returning to the smooth good looks of the woman on the other side of the window. She had the kind of beauty that could definitely be bought, all grooming and tailoring, sleek hair, and a tasteful amount of gold. A prime Hunsacker candidate.

"Casey McDonough, line one. Casey McDonough, line one."

Settling onto the edge of the table where Janice was working, Casey picked up the phone.

"Casey McDonough."

Silence.

"Hello?"

"Oh, honey, is that you?"

Casey struggled to hold on to her humor. It was like

an invasion, that quavering, uncertain voice intruding into work. Like a sudden slip, a faltering step in a fast run. Casey didn't want to have to deal with her mother here. She had enough crazies to handle without having to worry about her very own. She didn't want to have to say the words her mother needed, didn't want to acknowledge her mother's dependence on her. Or her dependence on a mother who preferred incense over flesh and blood.

"Yes, Mom. It's me. What's wrong?"

"Wrong? Oh, nothing, dear." Helen laughed, a high, tinkly sound, like a small girl. "I was just saying my evening prayers, and remembered that I needed to get to mass at St. Mary's in the morning. They have the traveling Infant of Prague, you know. And, well . . ."

Hunsacker. Casey caught sight of him at the far end of the hall. He was bent over Millie, moving his hands to mimic her latest pirouette. Smiling. Flattering.

"What time do you need to go, Mom?"

"Would you mind, sweetheart? I know it's unfair to ask you when you work such difficult hours and all. And I don't want to be a bother."

Casey concentrated on Hunsacker to prevent saying something unkind to her mother. "Just tell me what time, Mom."

"Nine. Nine o'clock mass. We could pray for Benny, don't you think?"

He had his hand on Millie's arm, stroking it as he smiled. An almost unconscious gesture of intimacy that seemed to make Millie purr. After Evelyn's report, Casey was intrigued anew.

". . . feel terrible about it, but you know you haven't been to mass this week, Catherine, and well, even though I don't like to insist, it would be so good for you . . . Catherine? Honey?"

The worry in her mother's voice snapped her back. One curiosity at a time. "That'll be fine, Mom. I'll see you in the morning."

Hunsacker laughed, a comfortable rumble, and Millie answered, delighted and coy.

"Be careful on your way home, sweetheart," Helen McDonough warned. "Not everyone is kind."

Casey's eyes were on Hunsacker when her mother spoke. It seemed the words were directed at him, at this smiling man who made women dip in attendance. Casey enjoyed a delicate shiver of fascination. Her mother was a little scary sometimes.

"Well, I haven't seen you in a while, have I?" Hunsacker asked with a broad smile as he approached.

Casey carefully hung up the phone. The smile she offered was leftover surprise, more than just a little curiosity. There was something just a little different about him tonight. An intangible, like wind currents, invisible yet present. Casey couldn't quite put her finger on it.

"Thanks for the pizza," she acknowledged, resisting the urge to squint her eyes, as if that could better focus the man before her.

What was different?

Same clothing, upper-class casual, striped Oxford shirt, pleated khaki slacks, those ubiquitous Dock-Sides. Same attitude, close body contact and teeth. Same throb of charisma.

"My pleasure," he assured her, reaching out to her much as he had Millie. It was as if words weren't enough with him. He fed on physical contact.

Casey was a physical person. She touched. She hugged and patted with the best of them. But there was something about his touch that crossed invisible boundaries.

Of course, they could have just been her boundaries. She hadn't trusted a toucher since her late unlamented marriage to the world's most professional patter and hugger. She might just be projecting all of Ed's worst faults on Hunsacker.

Or he could just be doing those three-fingered pelvics.

"Good to see you, too, babe," he greeted Janice with a lingering pat to her arm. "You have my lady here?"

"She's all ready to see you," Janice answered, snagging Casey's attention.

Janice had been distant before. Suddenly she was agitated. Almost jumping to her feet, she handed over the clipboard as if it were the holy grail. Casey had thought Millie glowed. Janice was positively flustered. For Janice, anyway. She took at least two swipes at her perfectly styled hair, and was trying to cover up that unsightly orange spot with her hand. It made her look as if she were pledging allegiance.

Hunsacker didn't even seem to notice. He skimmed the chart, nodded once, and then pulled out a gold Cross pen to make his own notations on the form. This entailed checking his watch, copying the time on the chart and the fact that he'd arrived. Then he pulled out that little notebook and made another memo to himself.

"Ready?" he asked Janice with that sudden, bright smile as he pocketed his personal notes. Without waiting for her answer, he took her by the hand and led her into the room. Casey just sat where she was and stared.

"There you are! Damn it, what the hell did you run off for?"

Casey didn't even look away from where Janice was closing the blinds for the pelvic. "Abe, do Jews believe in vampires?"

That brought him to a halt. "Romanian Jews, I guess. I want you to know I just escaped the clutches of that—that . . ."

"Slut puppy," she offered absently.

"Yeah. Right." His gaze followed hers, as if the closed blinds would offer explanation. "Did you see that damn tattoo?"

"Quite a beauty. I'm sure she was just showing you hers so you'd show her yours. I think he's a vampire, Abe."

"I tell ya, it's a fuckin' curse to be blessed—who's a vampire?"

"Hunsacker," she allowed, jumping off the desk. "It's the only reason I can come up with for Janice acting like a cocker spaniel puppy around him. She doesn't for you, ya know, and you have the Dick of Death. I bet he has thousands and thousands of red-eyed rats out in the parking lot."

Abe waved her off. "He has money and a great set of hands. And he's tryin' to make points. Once he has enough uteruses in his waiting room, he won't waste any more time on the help. Besides, he's taller than Janice, and she's archaic enough to think that makes a difference."

Casey heard it then, that funny little yelp. Just like Mrs. VanCleve. It made her flinch.

Suddenly it wasn't quite as funny. "I'm going to invest in garlic," she decided.

"You don't have to," Abe retorted dryly. "Your charming personality will save you."

Casey got home late that night, almost one. A bunch of teens out in Fenton had picked change of shift to play demolition derby. Casey hadn't had any plans to get in the way of staying, so she'd accumulated a little overtime, a lapful of vomit, and the undying gratitude of a set of parents whose hands she'd held. By the time she pulled into her drive, she didn't have any mercy or compassion left.

"Damn it."

The lights were on. Casey wanted to pull right back out and go someplace else. Anyplace else. Maybe Poppi and Jason would still be up. Maybe she could go into the city where the bars stayed open late. Maybe she could just run away from home. She didn't want to have to face her mother tonight.

She didn't want to face her mother any night. Casey remembered pulling up to this driveway three years ago, seeking asylum from a disastrously misadvised marriage. Seeking peace. Conveniently forgetting why she'd run in the first place.

It was a prison here, a stifling, airless limbo that smelled of despair and evasion. This sprawling Victorian confection of porches and windows, which young married couples slowed in the street to envy, was nothing but a shrine to decay.

It hadn't changed since she'd been a girl, since the very day her father had died at the dinner table. The very next day her mother had bought her first bandanna, made her first novena for forgiveness. The great Irish disease that had only lain dormant in the vague, maternal little woman had flared, malevolent and deadly, upon her husband's death and taken her soul with him.

Guilt, the Catholic motivator, the national suppressor, the parental rod. The cancer that sent her brother Benjamin first to the seminary and then to the road, figuring first to face it and then, finally, to outdistance it.

Casey knew better. There was no more running. No appeasement or atonement. There was only worship. And since her mother took care of that, she figured there was nothing left for her to do, either with guilt or the God who had thought of it.

But with her mother under the roof, there would be no ignoring it. Casey knew she should run. She knew she should get as far away from the madness as she could, just leave her mother to her prayers and her fasts.

Gathering her nursing bag and purse, Casey opened the car door and stepped out onto the driveway. The night was cool, the breeze fluttering the big elm tree that shaded the front porch. She could smell the hyacinth on the night air, cloying and heavy, like an old lady's perfume. She could hear the Jacksons' poodle yipping a few yards down. She saw a silhouette in the third-floor window and knew that Sister Helen was praying for her tonight.

Sighing with the weight of it, she walked on up to the house.

# Chapter 3

*IT WAS HIS* eyes.

Casey didn't realize it until a couple nights later when she was sitting in the lounge eating her dinner. There had been Hunsacker sightings earlier in the evening, and Millie and Barb had been fighting for time at the bathroom mirror. Casey watched and wondered why she seemed to be the only one in the entire building who didn't want Dr. Hunsacker's manicured fingers on her arm.

It might have been as simple as the fact that Casey didn't trust beautiful people. There was something about a man who just assumed that everyone would find him attractive that put her off. She had to work like a dog for every one of her advances. She had to try twice as hard to be noticed, and took none of her gains for granted. People like Hunsacker considered their looks not so much a gift as a right, and assumed that their fortune would naturally correspond. And, unfortunately, the world around them usually complied.

Growing up with the onus of coppery red hair and freckles, Casey knew that she was intimidated by physical beauty. She had never really had it, and never really would. In time the red had become fashionable and the freckles dimmed, but the gawky, shy girl in Casey had never died. She had gained a certain presence over the years, but she'd never know that effortless poise, that natural ease when dealing with her body or anybody else's.

Casey envied Hunsacker the swirl of attention, remembering all too painfully what it felt like to be invisible in a crowd. She resented him because a man with less talent than she thrived when she still struggled.

She hoped, though, that she had a less selfish reason for not liking him.

Hunsacker strolled into the lounge just after dinnertime. Casey was slouched in one of the swivel chairs, her feet up on an end table, reading a book and munching on moo goo gai pan, relishing the rare isolation.

Which meant that it was inevitable that he'd join her. He was in scrubs, somehow making those look as upscale as his chinos. Tonight, instead of fascinating her, it irritated her.

"Hey, babe," he greeted her smoothly. "Good to see you."

She'd had just about enough of that, too. Setting down the book, Casey eyed him as levelly as she could. "Casey," she said evenly.

He pretended not to understand. Affecting a wonderful expression of confusion, he settled into the next chair. "Pardon?"

Casey smiled. "My name. If you can't remember it, then 'hey you' is just fine."

On clicked the old electricity. He whipped out that smile faster than a sleight-of-hand trick and displayed it with just a modicum of hurt. "That's just the way I am," he protested, reaching out.

Casey backed away and returned his smile with a more cost-effective variety. "I'd also prefer not to be stroked unless we're formally engaged. Call me frigid, I'm just funny that way.''

He tried one more time. And that was when Casey saw the disparity. The intangible she hadn't been able to put her finger on the other night.

It was his eyes. No matter what the rest of his face did, no matter how much energy or empathy or delight he radiated, his eyes just didn't match it.

They glittered, like flat stones, a completely separate entity from the rest of him. It was as if while his body acted, his eyes watched. Unaccountably, Casey remembered her mother's words from a few nights earlier. ''Not everybody is kind.''

''Oh, Casey.'' He sighed, settling back into his chair and automatically recreasing his pants as he crossed his legs. ''You obviously don't know me well yet. When you do, you'll get used to me.''

Casey shrugged with a deprecating smile, intrigued by her instinctive reaction. She quelled the urge to move to a chair farther away. He was just too facile, too readily intimate. He was crowding her space, as Poppi would say. ''I just don't like being called babe,'' she explained. ''You understand.''

He said the only thing he could without being considered a jerk. ''Of course.''

''You have a patient down here?'' Casey asked, returning to her carton of food.

Hunsacker had pulled out his little notebook and begun making notations in it. ''A patient upstairs,'' he admitted with a smile. ''She's not progressing as fast as I'd want, but she insists on trying to do it her way, walking around the birthing room with her husband and kids. I'm also waiting to hear from postpartum at St. Isidore's on a lady I have there.'' Snapping his pen closed, he looked up. ''Didn't I hear you worked at St. Isidore's?''

Casey nodded. "About four years ago."

He nodded back and smiled. "Great people over there," he said, and his expression took on a curious cat-in-the-cream look. "Great people."

Must have been thinking of those three nurses he was chasing around Izzy's parking lot. He certainly seemed to derive a rather creepy satisfaction from the picture. Casey heartily wished that some of his acolytes here could see that look. Then she wished that they were self-assured enough to recognize it.

"So," he said with a brisk move to put his notebook away, "anything interesting going on here?"

Casey shrugged, wondering why she still felt so uncomfortable. Hunsacker had deliberately retreated, his attention now on a magazine he'd picked up.

"I've been in here for fifteen minutes," she said. "Before that I was holding a two-year-old for one of the plastic surgeons. Nothing to call out the news minicam for."

"Quiet, huh?"

Casey's head instinctively snapped up. "Don't ever say that," she warned, looking out the window by her head just to make sure.

Hunsacker's smile was disbelieving. "Oh, come on, you don't believe that, do you?"

"More than Einstein's theory of relativity."

No lights, no sirens. It wouldn't be long, though. Not the way that man courted disaster. Like Casey's supervisor said, it was worse than calling a game a no-hitter in the top of the ninth. The minute Hunsacker had said the word "quiet," a busload of hemophiliacs had undoubtedly slammed into a truckload of lawyers.

"Have a little respect for superstition," she begged. "Don't ever use that word down here again. Not if you want to live till morning. We've only had two codes so far tonight."

It was one thing the Irish were absolutely right about. People did die in threes. Which meant that they were still short one for the shift. In fact, they were still short another overdose, too, because death wasn't the only pastime that occurred in predictable numerical patterns.

"Did either of the codes make it?" Hunsacker asked, interested now, the magazine unattended in his lap, his attention once again hers.

"Nah," Casey answered, returning to her food before the disaster had a chance to interrupt her. "If you come in the door in cardiac arrest, chances are you'll go out the same way."

"Kind of fatalistic, aren't you?"

She shrugged. "Twelve years' worth."

His eyes widened with astonishment. "That's how long you've been doing this?"

She nodded, not wanting to face him and that charisma, preferring the safety of her water chestnuts. He was being pleasant, unaffected, and impressed. Casey shouldn't have still felt like somebody was walking on her grave. But she did. No matter what he said, he still gave her the creeps.

"That's incredible," he offered with what sounded like admiration. "I can't imagine surviving trauma medicine for that long. Sometimes obstetrics is more than I want to handle."

To Casey's left, the door opened. "I'll bet you lunch that that guy has an appendix," she heard.

Casey looked up with relief to see Janice and Barb walk in. When she saw who was sharing space with Casey, Janice stalled. Right on her heels, Barb bumped into her and cursed. Then she looked up, too.

Magic.

Casey silently watched as Hunsacker came to his feet

to greet the newcomers. Barb smiled like a tiger with prey in sight, and Janice seemed to gain height and poise.

"Barb, hi," Hunsacker greeted her. "You're looking great. What did you do to your hair?"

Barb's hand lifted instinctively as she gave him the nasty eye. "You're looking pretty good yourself," she purred.

He was already reaching out to bridge the gap between himself and the two women. Casey forgot the food on her lap. Barb she could understand simpering. Barb hadn't gained the nickname the Barracuda because she liked salt water. Janice, on the other hand, still had some explaining to do. Janice was just too damn intelligent to fall for this stuff.

"Congratulations," Barb was still purring. "I hear they've decided to add four new delivery rooms upstairs because of you."

Hunsacker flashed that self-effacing grin of his, the perfect reaction for flattery and Oscar acceptances, and Casey saw the bones actually soften in Barb's knees. "Don't kid yourself," he demurred, stroking her arm as if it were the nose of a horse. "They were going to do that anyway. But I do like the new wallpaper a lot better."

"Anything's better than that early institutional they had before," she agreed, doing her best to fill his entire field of vision. "Besides, you don't catch rich flies with bargain honey. Make 'em think they're delivering in Bloomingdales."

"Triage to the front desk. Triage to the front desk."

Barb immediately puckered up. "Damn. Don't go," she warned Hunsacker and whirled for the door to answer her page.

Hunsacker intercepted Janice before she got a chance

to sit. "How are you feeling?" he asked quietly, his voice rippling with concern.

Janice ducked her head a little, gave off an ineffective little wave. "Oh, I'm fine," she said with the carefully flat tone of somebody protecting a hurt very close to the core, like holding an arm close to broken ribs.

Hunsacker made contact. "You're sure?"

"Yeah." She smiled. "Thanks."

Caught by the revelation in their scant words, Casey remembered the promise she'd made to herself. She never had asked Janice what had been wrong. And, somehow, Hunsacker had.

She felt ashamed. She and Janice weren't especially close, but she should have talked to her before the resident gigolo did, should have followed up on a fragment of conversation that suddenly made unhappy sense.

She shouldn't feel resentful that he might have helped Janice when she hadn't. But she did.

Hunsacker and Janice still stood. "I was worried about you," he admitted in that same soft voice, his head bowed a little to her, his eyes on hers. Casey couldn't see his expression, couldn't tell if it still betrayed that troubling flatness. She wanted to think that Janice would have seen if it had. But Janice was still protecting herself too carefully to be perceptive.

Janice laid her hand on Hunsacker's other arm and smiled for him. "I appreciate that, Dale. You were a big help."

"Dr. Hunsacker, outside call. Dr. Hunsacker."

"Jan?" Casey said once Hunsacker had swung from the room.

Bent over the refrigerator, Janice turned to answer. "Yeah, Casey."

Casey wasn't sure exactly how to begin. "What do you think of Hunsacker?"

Surprised, Janice straightened a little. "He's nice. At least he has been to me."

Casey wished for subtlety. Normally Janice would have been the first one to see through Hunsacker. "He's been helping you out with something?"

Janice turned back to the refrigerator, preventing Casey from seeing her expression. "He listened. He really seems to understand . . ."

"Are you and Aaron having problems?"

Rather than answer right away, Janice continued her perusal of the refrigerator's contents. Considering that it consisted of various half-empty bottles of condiments and a couple cans of soda, it shouldn't have needed that much concentration.

Janice took a good three or four minutes to straighten and close the door.

"How long were you married?" she asked, turning to face Casey.

Casey had come to Mother Mary on the heels of her separation. Nobody really knew her ex or their history. She'd been more than happy to leave it that way. The look on Janice's face portended change.

"Four years," she admitted. "Why?"

With that Janice sat down, hands wrapped around each other, gaze on her knees, brows taut and troubled. "He was a doctor?"

Casey couldn't help a quick grin. "There's some discussion about that. He was a psychiatrist."

Janice was too preoccupied to catch the joke. She seemed to be looking into something yards away, assessing it, questioning it. Finally, she lifted her head.

"Can I ask why you left?"

If it had been anybody but Janice, Casey wouldn't have answered. Her ex still practiced in St. Louis, and nothing would infuriate him more than hearing about his more interesting idiosyncracies over the hospital grapevine. But there was something important behind Janice's question, something desperate.

"It was a lot of things," Casey finally admitted with a half smile. "Ed had a lot of problems that I couldn't solve for him."

Janice watched her now, eyes intense, dark. Casey wished she knew what Janice wanted to hear.

"You finally gave up?"

"Oh, in a manner of speaking. To give you an idea of the scope of things, he, uh, well, among other things—that the medical community doesn't know—he's a cross dresser."

Well, at least she'd pulled Janice's attention away from her own problem. The brunette's wide brown eyes widened even more. Her face compressed into a silent exclamation of astonishment.

"So . . ." She gulped down the surprise like raw fish and started again. "You, uh, divorced him because you caught him in your underwear?"

"No," Casey answered equably. "I divorced him because I kept catching him in other women's underwear."

"Code blue, emergency room four. Code blue, emergency room four."

"Oh, shit," Casey snapped, on her feet and out the door behind Janice before the announcement was repeated. "I knew it, I just knew it!"

"What is it?" Janice asked Barb as they rounded the corner by triage at a run. The lights were still flashing from the ambulance, washing the walls in red. The people who had been milling around triage stood back looking a little stunned.

"Gunshot to the face. He arrested at the door."

"All right," Casey agreed with a nod, following Janet into the work lane. "At least it's going to be fun."

The work lane was in pandemonium with the unannounced arrival. Doctors and respiratory techs crashed through the door from the stairwell. Michael was swinging the red trauma cart out of its niche by telemetry. Marva thundered on his heels with the crash cart. And dead center in the hall, right in their way, a toddler stood frozen in openmouthed astonishment.

Casey saw him and knew that neither Marva nor Michael could stop in time. It looked like the quintessential western scene with an unwary child caught in the path of the runaway stagecoach. And Casey was the only cowboy close enough to intervene. Spinning on her heel, she scooped up the little boy on a dead run and reached the far side of the hall just as the carts thundered past.

"Whoa, pardner!" she crowed, swinging the child up into her arms. He turned astonished eyes on her and she grinned. "Didn't your mom ever tell you to look both ways before crossing the street?"

"Child," Marva called to Casey from the doorway where everyone was congregating. "You should play football. You got great hands."

"That's what I've been told." Casey grinned back. "Anybody missing a pedestrian?"

She checked three rooms before she found the little boy's mother relaxing on a chair with the *Enquirer*.

"I'm going to close the door to the work lane," she offered, setting the little boy down and giving him a little push toward his surprised mother when he looked as if he was going to follow her back out. "You don't want him out in the work lane about now."

"He's bored," she protested flatly.

"Better bored than trampled," Casey retorted much more lightly than she would have liked and pulled the door shut after her.

"I can't get a line in!" Marva was protesting from across the hall.

Casey trotted on into the room and accepted goggles and gloves from Michael where he was stationed at the big cart. "What about a gown?" she asked. "I don't even have scrubs."

He shrugged. "Central supply's out."

Casey took a look at what was left of the victim to calculate potential danger and caught sight of the long-abused veins. "And I don't want AIDS," she decided. "Call surgery or isolation and get some up here."

Snapping the gloves in place, she grabbed a tourniquet and Cathlon catheter and went after a vein. It was her gift, her specialty. Marva called her a diviner. No matter what kind of condition the patient was in, Casey could usually get a peripheral vein to start IVs, especially in critical situations. Somehow the adrenaline rush improved her aim.

"I'll do drugs," she offered, noting that one of the paramedics was on top doing CPR and Janice was assessing as she cut off clothes. Marva was still trying for a line on the other side, and Steve was relegated to keeping track of everything that went on via flow chart.

"I heard that about you." Marva grinned.

"Everybody has to be good at something," Casey retorted, fingers probing the flaccid arm.

"Please, Jesus," Marva crooned as she slid her needle into the patient's other arm, "let me get this one. Please, sweet Jesus, help us out here, give your Marva the touch . . . Goddamn it, you son of a bitch, don't roll on me!"

Casey considered Marva the perfect Baptist trauma nurse. Casey, on the other hand, was a hummer. She was no more than eight bars into "Stairway to Heaven," when she felt a telltale pop at the end of the Cathlon.

"Damn, am I good!" she crowed, whipping her hand into the air like a successful calf roper. From just behind her, Michael handed her the end of the IV line. Slipping out the needle, she hooked the line up to the catheter and reached for her tape.

"Well, shit," Marva whined. "Why do I waste my time? All that heartfelt prayin' and you still beat me."

"Clean livin', girl." She wasn't going to have any teeth left in another five years between gnawing on needle caps and tearing tape. She was doing it again, ruining her incisors in her haste to secure the line.

"All right, all right, all right," a voice behind her announced in stentorian tones with more than a touch of the Middle East in it. "What do we have here?"

Casey gave way to a silent groan. Damn. "Never Say Die" Ahmed, the surgical resident with the record for the longest unsuccessful code in Mother Mary history. Portly, swarthy, and usually ill-mannered, he was not a favorite in codes. The units had long since dubbed him Rip Van Trachea for his unique intubation technique. Luckily, the patient already had the endotracheal tube in place, and the respiratory tech was bagging him.

"Looks to me like we've got a man without half a face," Casey answered without looking up from her work. Michael handed her a bristoject of epinephrine and she began to inject it into her line.

"Or you could say he's a man with half a face still left," Marva offered from where she'd just found similar success with her IV line and was hooking up the blood tubing.

Casey snorted in derision. "Optimist."

"Who shot him?" Ahmed asked.

"From the powder burns on his right temple," the paramedic answered. "I'd say he did."

"Would you like to follow ACLS protocol?" Casey

asked, passing the spent plastic prepackaged syringe back to Michael.

"Oh." Ahmed stood like an island of silence in the midst of the chaos.

"He's in arrest," she clarified impatiently. "Let's see a strip." The paramedic paused and Janice ran a strip. "Fine v-fib. How 'bout we defibrillate?"

"All right, all right all right. Let's go, then." Ahmed was beginning to gear up. Once he finally got into the picture, he wouldn't stop short of a power outage.

That was when Casey made a discovery. She'd been on the wrong side of the patient to see it, especially with everybody else crowded around. Of the injury she'd only seen the shattered remains of nose and eye socket, the blood and a bit of gray matter. She hadn't noticed until she really looked what lay beneath that wound. Or around it.

Quickly she scanned the entire body to verify. What she'd taken as the effects of self-abuse had really been disease. The patient was in his sixties, and he was cachectic, ribs standing out like a starved horse. That and the purple markings that showed at the edge of his ear clinched it.

"Oh, God," she breathed. "Chris, is the wife here?"

Rocking back and forth over the patient like an oil-well arm, the paramedic shrugged. "Wasn't at home when it happened. The neighbors were going to bring her in."

"Clear, all clear," Marva called, paddles in position. Chris pulled back.

"Does he have terminal cancer?" Casey asked.

Marva halted, thumbs poised over the red buttons.

"Shock him," Ahmed shrilled, furious at the pause.

Marva hit the buttons and the patient convulsed.

"Nobody said anything," Chris objected, leaning back into his CPR.

Casey turned to Janice. "Get out there and find the family. See if this guy has terminal CA. Find out what they want to do."

"CA?" Ahmed echoed.

Casey pointed to the marking, the shaved hair that they wouldn't have noticed beyond that devastating wound, the marking pen from where the radiologist had directed the radiation therapy that was meant to shrink the patient's tumor.

"Maybe the gunshot was superfluous," she suggested.

Until they found out there would be no choice. They would have to continue with full stops out. The patient had committed the cardinal sin of gunshot suicide, pointing the gun at his temple, almost ensuring failure. When the gun went off, it would jerk and send the bullet skipping toward the front. A survivable injury, a James Brady, they called it. Although this man had probably performed a self-inflicted lobotomy.

On the other hand, if he'd signed a statement forbidding extraordinary measures, there was no reason to revive him just to prolong his misery. If only they weren't lucky before Janice got back with the word. If only they didn't get him back. If only they could convince Ahmed to quit.

"I don't care!" he shouted ten minutes later when the verdict—and the notarized statement forbidding extraordinary treatment—came in. "We do not quit! Get some more blood into him. Put a call in to the neurosurgeon on call. Open up dopamine and run it in."

He was greeted by a forest of stricken faces. Nobody wanted to torture Mr. Melvin Tarlton any more than he had been. Nobody wanted to torture his wife or run up her already enormous bills. His private doctor had estimated him to have another month at best. The radiological oncologist had said that Melvin must have saved up what lucidity he had left to spare his family. And Ahmed wanted to drag them right back under.

Even so, it took Casey another ten minutes to finally reach her end point. They had long since passed into practice and experimentation, and she wasn't in the mood for it. And still Ahmed wouldn't quit.

"Ahmed, grow up," Casey snapped at him after pleading, wheedling, and coercion hadn't worked. "This is the twentieth century, and Mrs. Tarlton has a legal document. Let's call this damn thing and get the fuck out of here."

Only Casey had enough years to talk to him like that. Everyone else slowed their actions, inching toward finality.

Black eyes glittered with venom. "How dare you?" he demanded. "I am the doctor. I will have your job."

"Trust me," she retorted. "You wouldn't want it. We've been running the code for forty minutes already and haven't gotten squat."

"What about the dopamine?" he demanded, turning on Marva.

"Running." She shrugged, casting a glance up at the bag with a red tag on it. "Wide open."

"We're covered," Casey wheedled, hating the necessity, hating the game. Hating Ahmed for wasting everybody's time. "We've got the positive Nebraska sign, Ahmed. That EKG's as flat as Marva's chest. Mrs. Tarlton's not going to sue us for giving up now."

"We will call it when I say it is to be called," he warned her.

It took everything in her to keep from hitting him. The rage welled in her like a red fire, almost blocking out the sight of the crowded, littered, fetid room. "Then I guess you'll have to do it without me."

She stalked out. She knew that once she was gone it

would be safe for him to give in. After one more dose of epi and a stab at the pacemaker, he did just that. Four minutes and twenty seconds. Casey vented her rage on a plastic urinal that bounced with a satisfying clatter against the bathroom wall, and then washed her hands twice. She kept herself out of sight until she heard the dying whine of a discontinued monitor and knew she was calm enough to face Ahmed again.

She walked back out into the hall to bump into Hunsacker.

He was watching the desultory movements in the trauma room with interest, and didn't notice Casey until she was almost at him.

"Back again?" she couldn't help but ask. She was all set to walk on when Hunsacker turned his gaze on her.

Casey shuddered to a halt. Just for a second, as sudden as a death seizure, the light disappeared from Hunsacker's eyes. Casey didn't see recognition. She didn't see charm or interest or avarice. What she saw was a flash of deadly cold hostility.

She couldn't move, couldn't react. The weight of his animosity pinned her, upended her. She couldn't comprehend such venom. She couldn't imagine what could possibly ignite it or fuel it. But it was there, a hard glint so vicious that it paralyzed her.

"You can be a real ballbuster," he said, and that fast the light came back on. Steve was walking their way with the paperwork. Janice closed up equipment and Marva preserved tubes and lines for the coroner's perusal later. Hunsacker turned to watch them. "Those camel jockeys can be real assholes, can't they?"

Casey didn't know how to answer him. Was that what had frozen his expression? Had he watched the fight with Ahmed and sided with her? Could he possibly have that much hatred stored away to strike out so suddenly, so capriciously? Could he be that controlled that he could lock it back away so neatly?

Casey had to admit that with all her chances to cultivate prejudices, the only one she'd succumbed to was against certain doctors of the third world persuasion. Unaccustomed to respecting women as equals because of societal traditions, those men usually were the most difficult to deal with. Theirs often seemed the most severe kind of medical chauvinism, which to Casey often seemed like male chauvinism at its worst. And Ahmed was among the high priests of that particular sect.

But where she might have let off steam with Janice or Marva or Steve, she couldn't admit that kind of self-weakness with Hunsacker. She didn't want him to think she shared his bigotry.

"Your lady still not doing anything upstairs?" she asked instead, shaken enough to stare after him. Still unsettled enough from the aftermath of the code to wonder if she'd just imagined it all.

Hunsacker turned an appraising eye on her. Casey had the distinct feeling that he was disappointed that she hadn't snapped up his bait. She couldn't dismiss the feeling that he was watching her for something. "Oh, no," he finally said with another of those sudden smiles. "I've been forced to schedule her for a section. Then I have to go see that lady in at Izzy's. I guess it's going to be a busy evening for me, too."

Casey just shook her head and walked past. "I told you you shouldn't have said that word."

The rest of the code team was filtering out. Casey carried her paperwork to join them.

"I'll tell you something," Steve was saying to no one in particular as he sat down to fill in the medical examiner's information. "The cops have the right idea. You want results, you gotta bite down on the barrel. Anything else is just second best."

"I heard you were offering an in-service on effective suicide techniques," Marva offered from where she finished gathering personal effects. "Speaking of which, McDonough, we'll discuss that crack about my chest later."

Casey didn't need to answer.

"It'd sure save us some time," Steve groused. "I mean, that was a forty-five he used. Shit, he should have taken off his head and his next-door neighbor's head with that thing."

"Bite it, huh?" Janice asked dryly.

Steve nodded. "In far enough to get a good grip on it with your teeth. Like a real cold hot dog."

"Uh huh." She nodded. "Don't let me forget to write that down someplace so I won't screw up and disappoint you when my time comes."

Hunsacker hadn't moved, arms crossed, head tilted in consideration, eyes watchful. Casey dropped her charts next to Steve and pulled up a chair, still wishing she could say something about what she'd just seen, and then wondering just what it was she had seen.

"Now if I'd done it," Steve kept on, "I wouldn't have wasted my time with a forty-five. A thirty-eight gets the job done without all that mess, and no chance of taking out the bus driver down the street. Weapon of choice, ya know?"

"Well," Casey allowed, bent to her work in an effort to avoid Hunsacker's gaze. "You should know."

Steve lifted a cherubic face her way. "Did I tell you I got that Luger? The Krieghoff?"

"Oh, Steve," Casey teased. "Now you can die a happy boy."

"You just don't appreciate fine weaponry." He scowled.

"Me?" she retorted, hand to chest. "How can you say that? Guns are getting really close to motorcycles as top contributors for job security around here."

"A Krieghoff Luger?"

Casey started. Hunsacker was right behind her. Steve turned to him, lighting up like a kid talking about trains.

"An early thirty-six," he boasted. "Dated with plastic grips. I got it for under four thousand."

Hunsacker matched his expression delight for delight. "You really mean it. Do you collect extensively?"

"Only enough to supply the IRA into the twenty-first century," Marva offered as she walked by with an armload of equipment.

Hunsacker and Steve all but shivered with discovery. "I'm more of a modern aficionado than antiques," Hunsacker admitted. "I'm fascinated by the modern police and military firepower."

For a few moments Casey wondered whether Hunsacker was feeding Steve a line, but his jargon was too accurate. He and Steve tossed around ballistics figures and prices like arms merchants.

"If he wore yours," Janice said suddenly in her other ear, "whose did you wear?"

Startled, Casey laughed. Neither Steve nor Hunsacker had heard. "I wore mine, too," she admitted. "I tell you, I was to silk panties what Imelda Marcos was to high heels."

Arms ladened with trays to be sterilized, Janice leaned against the wall and grinned, her expression still betraying astonishment. "Well, just think, though. Now they're all yours. You could just about entertain the entire medical staff and not be seen in the same outfit twice."

"Are you kidding?" Casey demanded. "When we split, I got the silver. *He* got the underwear. I'm back to cotton briefs and socks."

Janice just kept shaking her head. "And it didn't . . . you know, bother you to . . . *see* him?"

"Sure it did," Casey admitted. "He looked better in my nylons than I did."

Janice swiped at her, laughing, and Casey thought she saw relief.

"You busy after work?" Casey asked. "We'd have a chance to discuss this without benefit of audience."

Janice's expression flattened a little. She dipped her head, clutching the trays to her like high-school books. "Another night?" she asked in a small voice. "I, uh, have somewhere to go."

Casey wanted to say something. She wanted to ease the crease that had returned to Janice's forehead. Something about her friend's stiff posture held her back.

"Of course."

"Hey, who wanted isolation gowns?"

Not only Casey and Janice but also Hunsacker and Steve looked up at the strident call from the doorway out to the service hall. One of central supply's finest stood there, several bundles in her pudgy arms, looking for all the world as if she'd just been asked to share the last of the firewood for the winter.

Casey made it a point to look at her watch. "Not bad. It only took an hour this time. Good thing we didn't really need 'em."

One look at her uniform belied her gracious words. Blood and Betadine spattered it like a Jackson Pollock painting. There would be little chance of getting it clean. Worse, if Mr. Tarlton had had the chance to pick up any hospital-born infections, Casey wouldn't be able to kill off the organisms in her wash. She'd just take them home to her mother and bring them back for the next shift of patients. It was too late for frustration. She just felt tired.

"Well, I got 'em," the tech protested. "Had to go to isolation. You want 'em?"

"Sure," Steve agreed. "That way when isolation needs 'em, they'll have to come to us."

"Ya know," Casey mused, accepting the load an hour too late. "If I come down with a bad disease, I'm gonna go right up to administration and puke on every one of them."

Janice shook her head. "Not good enough. Wipe a pustule on Nixon's face."

Steve lifted a hand. "Then have Ahmed treat him. Think how long he'd suffer."

"You guys are really into revenge," Hunsacker offered.

"Nah," Casey disagreed. "We're into justice. Revenge would be making him work down here under these conditions and then having to take home my paycheck."

"I still think you should consider my sniper idea," Steve offered. "We could all chip in. I'm sure the floors wouldn't mind."

"You certainly have the equipment," Marva agreed.

"Too impersonal," Hunsacker said suddenly, his voice flat and hard. "Get right in and cut his heart out."

Casey stopped breathing. She thought maybe Steve and Janice did, too. For an unbearably long moment the three of them froze, silent and waiting. Wondering how they could have just heard what they did. Wondering how they should react to a tone of voice that betrayed more than Hunsacker had intended.

Then, again, like the flick of a light switch in a darkened room, Hunsacker came to life and flashed them all a rueful grin. "At least that's what I always said about my ex-wife. Until I found out she didn't have a heart."

Casey was still sitting there, an arm full of packaged gowns, her mouth open, when Hunsacker strolled off toward the elevators.

"Dr. Hunsacker, line three. Dr. Hunsacker."

Instinctively Casey picked up the phone. It took her a minute to clear her throat to answer. "Dr. Hunsacker just left. Can I help?"

"He was down there?"

The outrage in the woman's voice brought Casey right around. "But he isn't now. Who's this?"

"Labor and delivery." Now she could hear gritted teeth. "We've been waiting for him for an hour to do this damn section he was so all fired to do."

Casey couldn't think of anything but the truth. "He was down here watching a code."

"Well, if you see him, you tell him to get his butt up here. He scheduled this damn thing two hours ago, and he hasn't said shit to his lady, and I'm damn well not going to get permits signed until he does. Of course, this gal'll probably pop the kid on her own before he gets here anyway."

Casey's attention was caught all over again. "I thought she was a failure to progress."

There was a small silence, and then an "Mmmm."

Casey knew a lot about those Mmmms. She used them often enough when she didn't need a doctor's wrath dropped on her head for an honest answer.

"He also said he has a lady over at Izzy's," she offered.

"I heard it was a date with a hot nurse for a late movie."

"Oh."

Casey's curiosity was piqued, now. She wanted to know more. Hunsacker certainly wasn't the first obstetrician to schedule a cesarean for his own convenience, but something about the extent of his stories intrigued her. Most OBs would have just given the failure-to-progress line and left it at that. He'd knitted an afghan out of it.

Casey wondered for the first time whether there really was a patient at Izzy's waiting for him, or whether it had just been another part of a good story. She wanted to know, suddenly, what the rest of the truth was.

When Casey hung up, she dialed Izzy's.

"Hey, Casey," Evelyn greeted her. "I was going to call you. I got some great scuttlebutt."

"First things first. Do you have a patient of Hunsacker's up there?"

Another one of those silences. "Why?"

"I'm just curious about something. He was just down here and said he was headed your way."

A longer silence, a gathering of calm. "When pigs fly." Evelyn knew she could trust Casey. "I just got threatened with my job for calling him the third time on a lady who's spiking a temp."

"He's not coming out?"

"Not until he damn well feels like it. Which, he says, will undoubtedly be rounds in the morning. Until then, and I quote, I can just keep my knees together. He says he has back-to-back sections at M and M."

It was Casey's turn for an Mmmm.

"Yeah," Evelyn retorted. "That's what I thought. Well, I'll tell you, I'm getting real close to shoving a piece of my mind straight up that man's alimentary canal."

"What's the scuttlebutt?"

That switched the tone of the conversation very neatly. "Oh, yeah. You haven't talked to Wanda Trigel over here lately, have you?"

"Wild Woman Wanda from labor and delivery? No,

not since the last time I was up at Izzy's for a transfer, why?''

"She didn't show up for work yesterday. They called her husband, and it seems Wanda drove off and hasn't come back.''

"Yeah, but that's Wanda. You know how bullheaded she is. She and Buddy probably had a fight. Give her twenty-four hours like always and she'll show up.''

"She disappeared three days ago. Buddy's really scared.''

"What do the police say?''

"That's the bunch out in Jefferson County. They think she ran off with somebody she probably met down at the Ramblin' Rose. They told Buddy he'll probably hear from her when the divorce papers come through.''

Wild Woman hadn't been named that for nothing. Blessed with the foulest mouth this side of Eddie Murphy and a taste in cheap hair bleach, Wanda was a crack operating tech and a world-class hell-raiser. Casey couldn't say she really disagreed with the police. "Well, Wanda's never been known to take my counsel, but if she does, I'll let you know.''

"Yeah, well, while you're in a counseling mood, tell Hunsacker to stop being such a jerk. I've come really close tonight to using vocabulary only Wanda would be comfortable with.''

Casey grinned. "Too bad she ran off. You could sic *her* on him. It'd be a great show.''

That seemed to improve Evelyn's mood. "Too late. She laid into him last week about something he did in a cesarean over here. I heard it was the best white trash fight L and D had seen in years. She told him she was better with a knife than he was. Then she told him half the gangs in North St. Louis were better with knives than he was.''

"Can't fault the girl for the truth."

"Not the way I see it."

"Of course, with Wanda's legendary taste, it was probably Hunsacker she met at the Ramblin' Rose."

"No," Evelyn disagreed. "If Wanda had faced off with Hunsacker, he'd be the one missing."

Casey was laughing along with her friend when Barb put an end to the conversation by announcing the arrival of the third overdose of the shift. Since Casey was the lucky winner for this particular grand prize, she hung up and pulled out a patient gown to keep a new mess from joining the one already on her uniform, all the while savoring the idea of Wild Woman facing off against Hunsacker.

Casey could just envision what their confrontation must have been like. Hunsacker might have a mean streak in him, but when Wanda was riled, she was like a pit bull. And it sounded like Wanda had been riled. It would have served Hunsacker right. Casey, for one, would have paid money to see him knocked down a couple of pegs.

It was too bad Wanda had decided to take off. Casey would have bought Wanda dinner just to be regaled with her version of the story. Wanda did have a way with words, especially when it concerned somebody she didn't like.

Come to think of it, it probably hadn't hurt Hunsacker at all that Wanda had disappeared so conveniently. There wasn't any doubt that if she hadn't developed an itch, she would have made it a point to entertain the grapevine with a vivid blow-by-blow account of the story of Dr. Hunsacker and the scalpel. Something Casey was sure Hunsacker wouldn't have been too fond of.

Grabbing a nasogastric tube the size of a garden hose and a couple liters of saline, Casey decided that Hunsacker must have already heard about Wanda's elopement. That was probably why he seemed so very pleased when he made that crack about the great people over at the Palace. Wanda had forfeited the match by disappearing, so he counted it a win. Too bad. Round two would have been a killer.

Right about at that point, Casey opened the door to room three to discover just what waited for her. All she thought about after that was where she'd rather be than pumping stomachs.

# Chapter 4

*ST. LOUIS IS* a city of neighborhoods. Originally defined by its immigrant populations—the Irish to the north, the Germans to the south, and the Italians in the west center—it matured into an untidy patchwork designed by parish boundaries, democratic wards, and ethnic preference. Primarily Catholic and conservative, it boasted a southern feeling of family and a northern commitment to industry.

White flight sucked away much of the population within the archaic boundaries of the city, and carried its neighborhood feel with it. Cities and villages quickly partitioned off surrounding county land and drew to themselves unique identities. Instead of considering itself a burgeoning metropolitan area, the growing population that spilled into surrounding counties continued to see itself as citizens of a small town, its loyalties and self-image tied to the neighborhood.

The Central West End was artistic, the South Side blue-collar union. Yuppies migrated to Creve Coeur and Chesterfield, and old money stayed close to Ladue. The Germans still favored Dutchtown, the best Italian restaurants were on the Hill, and the Ancient Order of the Hibernians held their St. Patrick's Day Parade in Dogtown. Blacks were seen about as often in Carondelet as whites were up on Cote Brilliant. The city was separate from the county, and surrounding counties measured their distance from the arch even as they kept their own unique flavors.

Metropolitan St. Louis was a community of settlers who never saw a reason for moving on. It was a comfortable, intimate big city with a good-old-boy network to rival the greatest societies, and a chronic inferiority complex. It was a crazy quilt of separate entities bumping and sidling against each other like passing acquaintances in a row of too-small plane seats that promote politeness but discourage curiosity.

This attitude had everything to do with why no one thought to look any sooner for Wanda Trigel. First of all, she disappeared from Arnold. A burgeoning Jefferson County city tucked into the southern side of the Meramec and Mississippi river merger, Arnold had long been one of the northern stops for migratory traffic along Highway 55. Poor, white, hard-line right-wingers, the initial core of Arnold had given the city its perception in the bi-state area.

The locals divided Arnold into three distinct areas, like the lobes of a lung. Upper Arnold was as upscale as it got, with its newer subdivisions and Walmart shopping centers. Lower Arnold, or LA, comprised an area of good old boys and girls, trailer parks and taverns. Life was hard, heads harder. Arguments were settled with pool cues and broken bottles, and the drug of choice was Busch.

The third area was UCLA, where Wild Woman had lived with Buddy. UCLA, or the Upper Corner of Lower Arnold, was where the river rats lived, the meanest form of life in the entire area. The police wore jackboots and the denizens stayed in the flood plain because they didn't have the means or the inclination to escape. Anybody who didn't like country music was a pussy, white supremacy was considered a religion, and the average entertainment entailed the illegal, the immoral, and the fattening. Anything went, and usually did.

The Millard boys ran that neck of the woods with brawn, bully, and the first automatic weapons south of St. Louis. Which was the second reason nobody thought much about Wanda's disappearance. She was a Millard, and apples didn't fall far from the tree.

The Arnold police department knew that, and so did Wanda's friends. They'd partied with her and even followed her onto home turf on one or two unspeakably foolish occasions. If Wanda finally tired of respectability, nobody could really find themselves surprised.

But no one thought to raise an outcry. The Creve Coeur police, who patrolled the area where Wanda worked, and the Jefferson County sheriff, who had jurisdiction over the last place she'd been seen, didn't think to get involved. It was Arnold's problem, and Arnold's attitude was that it was just a family problem. Just another woman who'd run out. What with the daily struggle to keep the peace in the growing, volatile area just south of St. Louis County, the police and sheriff figured they had more important things to worry about.

As for the Millard boys, they agreed with the police.

For Casey's part, she was a typical St. Louisan. Born and raised in Webster Groves, a solidly middle-class neighborhood in the near southwest section of St. Louis County, she had moved only as far as Creve Coeur for her freedom, and then Frontenac to marry. And now, she was home where she was perfectly comfortable shopping and entertaining within a ten-mile radius, where she was caught up more with her neighbors' problems than the county's, or the city's beyond.

Wanda was consigned to another world, to Casey's past at Izzy's, to another county where she had no control and very little contact, to a lifestyle that Casey minimalized through indifference.

The word of Wanda's disappearance lingered because the idea of Wanda and Hunsacker dueling was so delicious, but it didn't capture Casey's imagination or concern. Preoccupied with work, with her nagging disillusionment, with the spring holy days, Casey lost track of Wanda within days of her disappearance.

The Who spilled from Casey's headset and rain seeped in around the edges of her hood. It was a drizzly day, gray and indifferent, sapping even that fresh spring green from the young trees. Casey couldn't imagine why she wanted to be out walking. She was sweating and rain-damp at the same time, arms pumping, legs scissoring in rote movement as she ate up the sidewalk along Elm.

Casey tried to concentrate on the words to "Squeezebox," tried to match her stride with the rhythm. Instead she kept seeing the vivid images that had followed her from sleep that morning.

The dream. Bile rose in her chest again, a red, hot gorge of terror and frustration at just the memory of it. She'd never had the dream before. She would have remembered it. It had been in the apartment, in Creve Coeur. She could still see the spotless whites of the walls, the slash of a blood-red afghan against the black leather couch. She'd been standing close to the front door, but not too close. Not close enough to touch or escape. All the furniture looked so comfortable, but she couldn't use it. She couldn't sit, or lie down, or close her eyes. The door looked so inviting, but no matter what she did, she couldn't get out. She had to stand there, alone, frightened, angry, without moving. She couldn't rest no matter how tired she grew. She was three years old, which was stupid. She'd been over twenty when she'd first seen that apartment.

Casey couldn't understand why she should suddenly have that dream, why she should see that room after so many years. Unless it was the fact that her mother was pressing ever closer, demanding more time, more attention, more penance. Unless it was the fact that the job was squeezing in from the other end, the frustration mounting with every petty interference she had to suffer.

She'd been called into the office the day before. Just as she'd suspected, a complaint had been lodged. Not by Ahmed, though, or even Abe for the fact that she'd been merciless in staying on his tail that night ten days earlier. Besides, Abe would have dragged her off himself and just challenged her to a duel of four-letter words if he'd seen the need.

The complaint came from the mother of the little boy she'd dragged from the hall.

"Casey," Tom Nevers had said, fingers steepled over his '64 Cardinals World Series baseball. "You're in the big leagues. You know that you can't flip the bird at the fans."

Baseball. As far as Tom was concerned, the world had been created by Abner Doubleday and defined by Yogi Berra. A small, asthmatic man who looked more like Woody Allen than Ryne Sandburg, Tom could spend all day trying to couch unintelligible medical terms into anachronistic baseball ones.

"It's hardly flipping the bird," Casey reminded him, rubbing her forehead to ward away the headache this was producing. "I pulled the kid out of the way of a line drive."

His face lit with the analogy. Casey wondered how long she could keep this up. She attended more Cardinals' games than Tom did, but even Dizzy Dean had called a nurse a nurse—not a catcher (the unsung hero of the game, who really called the shots and made the pitcher—the doctor—look good).

"Casey, I'm afraid the fans are always right. Besides, that was Dr. Jordan's niece. He wanted the incident on your stats. I think if you just send a nice little note to the mother, he'll forget the whole thing. Especially since Dr. Hunsacker ran interference for you."

Wrong game, she thought instinctively. At least get your sports analogies straight.

Then the name sank in.

"Hunsacker?" she asked.

Tom nodded, a look of near reverence on his face, hands flat on the desk like a minister giving direction. "Dr. Jordan said something about it in his presence. You know, locker-room banter. Dr. Hunsacker insisted that he'd seen the incident, and managed to call off the fine. I think you owe him a lot, Casey. He really went to bat for you."

Casey winced. She'd been steeling herself against that one.

"Make sure you thank him, too," Tom said, sounding much like her mother discussing the blessed virgin. "Personally. After all, Jordan is head of staff. He could be your one-way ticket to the minors."

But she didn't want to thank Hunsacker. She didn't want to be in debt to him. Somehow, Casey had the feeling that he'd defended her just to see the deference in her eyes, and it pissed her off.

Casey turned the corner from Elm onto Swon and picked up the pace, instinct driving her. When she looked up to discover herself at the distinctive pink Federalist house, she understood. Without realizing it, she'd headed straight for Poppi's.

It shouldn't have surprised her. She always seemed to home in on Poppi when she needed a little relief from all the atonement in her life. If Poppi had ever thought it necessary to atone for anything, Casey had never heard about it.

"Are you decent?" Casey called, opening the door without invitation. Reaching a hand beneath the dripping plastic of her hood, she shoved the earphones back onto her neck and stepped in.

Silence. The first floor of Poppi's house remained as her parents had kept it, spare and elegant in cherrywood and oriental rugs. An impressionist print over the fireplace and brass candlesticks on the lowboy in the dining room. Upstairs was the real Poppi, with the waterbed and fabric-draped ceiling and old Peter Max posters.

"Poppi? Jason?"

"Ooooh, Ca-sey!" a voice whooshed from nowhere, as if suspended in the atmosphere. "Tracers!"

Shedding her coat, Casey chuckled. So it was surrealism time at the old Henderson house. Poppi would be stretched out, timing her heartbeat to the waves on the waterbed, choreographing the dancing lights in her head.

Casey stopped long enough to purloin a soda from the fridge, shucked her rain gear, and headed for the stairs.

"Oh, what is your wisdom, my seer?" she asked.

"On final approach," Poppi assured her in a voice that sounded like somebody being hypnotized.

She was, indeed, stretched out on the bed, eyes fixed to the gray paisley ceiling, hands tracing patterns in the air, stereo pouring out Wagner. Anybody else would have at least had the decency to trip to Zeppelin, maybe Santana. Poppi had always insisted that the classics were the really psychedelic music, since most of the composers had been crazy anyway. Listening to the muted wailing from the stereo, Casey couldn't really argue.

Pulling over one of the beanbag chairs, Casey collapsed into it. "Are you into dream interpretation?"

Silence. Poppi's hands drifted down. "Heavy."

Casey focused her own eyes on the intricate Celtic knot of a new Irish artist Poppi favored. Never ending, never beginning, it seduced you with its flow until you found yourself completely lost within the internecine tangle of its design. Once in, never able to escape.

"What haunts?" Poppi asked.

Casey rubbed between her eyes. The rain had picked up, silvering the light in the airy room. "My apartment in Creve Coeur."

"That makes sense. There's an aura, you know"—the hands fluttered again, as if caught in a languid dance—"red, with shimmers of green . . . like your very own aurora borealis . . ."

Taking a long slug of soda, Casey just shook her head. "No wonder I could never understand *Magical Mystery Tour*. When do you expect touchdown?"

"Fading. In another twenty minutes I'll be . . . on the phone to the League of Women Voters." Meaning sanity was returning fast. Poppi always slid to a three-point landing from these things. She'd been studied in the seventies and warned in the eighties, a person without addictions, one impervious to the worst effects of experimentation.

"Apartment?" she asked suddenly, her head turning fractionally. "That *is* heavy. What's it been?"

"Seven years. You know that. I dreamed I was locked in and couldn't get out. I kept fighting, yelling, you know. Couldn't touch the furniture, couldn't get out the door."

"Mmmm."

Which meant, processing. Poppi knew Casey better than anyone. She'd been there through it all, sharing the dreams, buffering the defeats, brightening the monotony.

"Work?" she asked.

"No more ludicrous than usual. I was chastised for doing my job and praised for not rocking the boat."

Good team playing was how Tom had put it. He didn't like hotshot players, none of this one wing down stuff when rounding the bases. Everybody pulled together, which meant that Casey shouldn't stand up and scream about inadequate staffing. It only reflected poorly on the rest of the club. It was a philosophy amazingly similar to that of the administration's. The only good nurse was a quiet nurse.

"Home?" Poppi asked.

Casey snorted. "We're into novena season there. I wouldn't mind so much if she didn't remind me every time she puts on her bandanna that it's my soul she's praying for."

"Echoes from the past?"

"Not a one. Ed is perfectly happy pretending he never knew me."

"Ed didn't live with you in Creve Coeur."

"I was getting to that." An even more difficult memory than Ed's massive passive-aggression. A real foray into denial. "Nothing there, either."

"Social life?"

"You're looking at it."

"Ah."

So, was the dream that mysterious after all? She did feel trapped, caught between a job she'd been at too long, a family more comfortable in the Middle Ages, a history of relationships that had worked out just about as well as her family, and a future that for all purposes looked like more of the same.

"Could be worse, you know," Poppi philosophized.

"I wish you wouldn't say that," Casey begged, taking another good swallow of caffeine and focusing her own attention on the patterns of rain against the big window. "Every time somebody says it could be worse, it usually is. The way my life is running, Benny will come home a Moonie."

"You have the power to change what you want," Poppi intoned. "Only you."

"Easy for you to say," Casey retorted. "You don't need anything changed."

"You came home," her friend countered with deceptive laziness. "From what I can remember, that didn't entail shoveling dirt on your head and chanting the Dies Irae."

"I want religious metaphors, I'll go home, thanks. Remember my talking about Hunsacker?"

Pause, grin. "Yeah. The man with the hands."

"I have to go pay obeisance to him the next time I see him at work. He intervened on my behalf."

"Nice guy."

"I don't think so."

Poppi's head made it all the way over now, and her eyes were fairly clear. "Why?"

But all Casey could offer was a shake of her head. "I still don't know. It's just a gut feeling, little things that don't mesh. It's the way he wraps everybody around his finger—especially the people who should know better."

"Jealous?"

Casey grinned. "Sure. But I've already gotten past that. This is something that bristles the hair on my neck. It's like instead of food, he ingests groveling."

Poppi turned back to her ceiling. "Check his forehead for the sign."

Casey gave up on the window and just settled her head back against all those beans, her eyes closing. Funny, the whispers of that claustrophobia still nagged at her. The dream hadn't quite let loose.

What was she so afraid of?

"I met him, ya know."

That brought Casey's head back up with a snap. "What?"

Poppi smiled lazily at the ceiling. "We favor the same fund-raisers. He's quite the golden boy."

Casey sat all the way up, feet flat on the floor, arms hanging over the sag of the chair. "What did you think of him?"

"Did you know"—Poppi's hands lifted slowly, as if tracking something in the air, and finally catching it—"that butterflies have teeth? Big, vicious ones."

Casey paused, not sure just what Poppi was addressing. It was always a hazard when getting an opinion from her.

"You can't see them, of course, until they bite you."

Then she smiled again, that dreamy smile of self-satisfaction that told Casey she'd made some enormous philosophical statement. Sometimes Casey thought she should show up here with an interpreter.

Then Poppi turned her face toward Casey's, and the smile dimmed. "Don't get bitten," she warned, and her eyes were as clear as a cold night.

At least Casey left Poppi's knowing that somebody else in this world didn't think Dr. Dale Hunsacker walked on water.

"I love him," Ms. Elliott gushed. "He's just so good to me."

Casey stood a bit stiffly, clipboard in hand, wondering

at the chance of Hunsacker coming down to see this doyen of the volunteer set for her leg cramp.

"I know he's busy," the little woman continued, plump hands fluttering about her Adolpho attire, her dark hair damn near spray-painted in place, and her face swept clean of lines by Fernando Alvarez, the plastic surgeon to the stars. "I even hate to bother him about it, but he did say to call him and only him about anything. He did say that he knew what was best for me."

Casey knew just what to say. "Mmmm."

"You don't think he'd really mind that I called him, do you? I mean, his nurse said he'd be here, after all. And it does bother me. You'll tell him that, won't you? That it really bothers me?" Her sudden smile was coquettish in a rusty sort of way, as if she were getting back into practice. "I don't want him mad at me."

Casey smiled and pulled out her stethoscope for vital signs. "Why don't I get all the basics and then call him, okay?"

Ms. Elliott hopped right up on the cart. Casey wanted to scream. After living with her mother for all these years, she had a really low tolerance level for passive-aggressive people. And the more she saw Hunsacker's patients down here, the more that particular trait showed up. Simpering, whining, executing elaborate flanking maneuvers just to keep from displeasing him when they needed to see him.

Casey slipped the stethoscope into place and wrapped the cuff around Ms. Elliott's arm. What she really wanted to do was tell her to be an adult. But of course she hadn't been thus far, so after fifty years what were the chances?

Casey was trying to figure out how she could arrange her dinner to escape Hunsacker, when she walked right out the patient door and found him at her desk. She hadn't seen him since that night she'd talked to Evelyn about him, and yet the hair on her neck went right back on alert.

"I hear you have a live one for me," he greeted her, his smile expectant, his legs crossed, his notebook out.

"Virginia Elliott?" she countered, freezing on the spot. Now that she was faced with thanking him, she didn't want to do it. She didn't know how to do it and keep her pride, because she was irrationally afraid that no matter how she handled this, he'd walk away with a piece of her.

She stood before a door, and couldn't get out, and it swelled in her chest like hot acid.

"Oh, yes, Virginia," he answered with a knowing nod, his face curling into a slight smirk. "The cocker spaniel of the Junior League. I often wonder how she decides what underwear to put on without consulting somebody on it."

Casey wondered whether she was supposed to answer. Did he have anything nice to say about any of his patients? Was he intentionally cruel, or just thoughtlessly? And should she feel worse because her own thoughts had so closely paralleled his words?

"She has a persistent cramping in her right thigh," Casey said carefully, handing over the clipboard. "She said that you told her to contact you about anything, so here she is. Want a potassium or calcium level?"

Slipping his notebook back into his monogrammed shirt, he pushed away from the desk. "Let me talk to her first. Go ahead and get the pelvic stuff."

Casey knew her mouth dropped. Her obligation to thank Hunsacker was lost.

Hunsacker seemed to be anticipating her. Leaning a little close, he smiled with some superiority. "Sometimes Virginia gets pelvic cramps that radiate to her thighs. I'll do a pelvic."

Casey hated him, right there on the spot, for controlling Mrs. Elliott, for controlling her.

"Why are you thinking of doing it?" she asked, knowing damn well she was going to get into trouble again for the loose hold she kept on her opinions. "To get back at her for something, or to get back at me?"

The light went out in his eyes. "It seems to me that I told you once, I do pelvics on all my patients."

"No matter what's wrong with them?"

He seemed to grow somehow, to harden. "I'm a gynecologist," he answered as if he shouldn't have to answer at all. "I do pelvics."

And what else? she wanted to say. Casey held her tongue just in time. Still, she didn't move. "I don't see any reason for a pelvic," she countered as calmly as she could, fists balled at her sides, back as ramrod stiff as Hunsacker's.

And just that fast, the dark emptiness in his eyes flooded with animosity. A hate so virulent that it left Casey shaking. The handsome man who was so good at flattery and affection suddenly became unrecognizable.

Casey looked around for witnesses, for verification, but for once the hall was empty. Everybody was in with patients, leaving only Casey to see the livid emotion in Hunsacker's eyes.

"I don't think you understand," he warned, bent so that his face was within inches of Casey's, his voice low and cold. "You really shouldn't challenge me on this. You don't have any idea how difficult I can make things for you."

If he'd screamed and ranted, Casey couldn't have been more shaken. Just the control in that soft voice of his was enough to make good his promise. But then, Casey had never been known for discretion. Her own temper got the best of her. After all, this was a public place, not an alley. This was the twentieth century.

"I know how difficult other doctors have tried to make it for me when I disagreed with them," she countered just as coldly, shaking with the effort to maintain her composure. "And I'm still here."

His smile was chilling. Cold and flat and frightening. "You still don't understand," he promised in a breath that fanned her cheek like a fetid wind. "You really don't. You don't want me mad at you. Now, go get the pelvic equipment, or believe me when I say I'll take matters into my own hands."

Casey was left standing alone in the hall, trembling and flushed. Afraid. She'd walked the halls for twelve years, been shot at, beaten by a drunk, threatened by innumerable addicts, prisoners, and belligerent relatives, gone one on one with manic depressives in full cry. But she'd never really been gut-deep afraid. No matter what, she'd managed to maintain a certain control. She was the one, after all, with the restraints, with the sedatives and the security guards.

Something about Hunsacker's warning, though, scared her. Really scared her. Something illogical gripped her, a cold snake of dread born of Hunsacker's words. More, of his voice, his eyes. Casey had seen deadly earnest before. She'd faced killers who promised to do it again. She'd talked down delusional psychotics who vowed revenge. Something in Hunsacker's expression reminded her of them. It wasn't the usual threat she heard from an insulted doctor—her job, her future, her salary. He'd struck something primal.

For the first time in a week, Casey thought of Wild Woman Wanda. She wondered if this had been what Hunsacker had looked like during that famous white trash fight. Had he leaned in really close and threatened her so that only she was afraid? Had Wanda, who wasn't afraid of anything, felt fear? Had she walked into the fight with her blithe assurance, her voice as sharp as his scalpel, and walked away trembling and uncertain, unnerved by his sudden silence, by the frozen wasteland behind Hunsacker's threats and promises?

What did Casey do about *this* threat? Did she tell somebody? Did she try and communicate just what had happened?

Nobody had seen it; nobody would believe it. So a doctor had threatened to make things very difficult for her. If nurses made out reports every time that happened, they'd have more documentation than the Library of Congress.

And this was not just any doctor. Tom likened Hunsacker to Steve Carlton. The administration didn't think to look further than the dollar signs the OB represented, and the community at large was dazzled by the way he looked in a tux. As for the other nurses, who could be counted on when no one else could for support in a situation like this, they were blinded by that smile, those nice biceps.

Maybe Evelyn. Casey hadn't talked to her since the last time she'd seen Hunsacker, and Evelyn seemed to have no love lost for the man. Maybe she'd heard more about Wanda, or maybe she had some insight into Hunsacker Casey didn't. Suddenly Casey had to know.

It was Millie who found Casey at the desk. Spinning on one toe, charts in hand, the tiny blonde came to an uncertain stop, her smile of greeting dying.

"Casey, are you sick?" she asked, her uniform skirt swirling to a stop after her.

Casey started badly, foundering for a minute. Rubbing the dampness from her palms, she turned a wry eye on the young nurse. "Dr. Hunsacker and I seem to have had a disagreement."

Millie's eyes widened in astonishment. "Oh, no," she retorted, though the tone was more "that couldn't happen" than "how bad for you." Millie was a definite acolyte, new to nursing, struggling for acceptance, uncertain of her attraction as a woman or abilities as a nurse. Perfect medium to cultivate Hunsacker worship.

Casey thought to tell her. She came close to explaining just what Hunsacker had looked like when he'd spoken, how he'd leaned so close that only Casey could hear his venom. But seeing those guileless eyes, she knew she wouldn't. Nobody'd believe her anyway.

"Can I help?" Millie asked.

And Casey knew that because Millie was still too new to question Hunsacker's judgment, she could help. It didn't do Mrs. Elliott any good, but it got Casey off the hook.

She was being passive-aggressive, avoiding conflict, skirting away from confrontation. Just like Ed. Just like Helen. Just like her when she'd stood in that damned living room so many years ago, eyes focused on the red slash of an afghan, fighting for courage and knowing she wouldn't find any.


"So, then they went in to check why this sixteen-year-old chickie hadn't been peeing," Marva was yelling over the music and crowd noise, "and pulled out six birthday candles!"

Casey burst out laughing. Evidently she'd missed all the fun up at the front end of the hall tonight.

"The best part," Marva said, waving off the laughter with her beer, "is that the mother says, 'Well, I never seen her eat them candles.' "

Both of them laughed now, oblivious to the jostle of

bodies around their tiny table at the back of the bar. Casey saluted the story with her own beer. "Gee, Marva, for my birthday, I'd be just as happy if they'd put the candles in a cake."

"What I want to know," Marva retorted, "is who she got to blow 'em out."

Casey was feeling better. It had taken six hours of unrelenting hell—three traumas, two MIs, and an assortment of hot bellies, fractures, and chronic lungers—not to mention a jaunt with Marva to the Body Shop, Mother Mary's local hangout, to effect it, but she found the persistent urge to look over her shoulder was easing. The further she got from Hunsacker's threat, the more she questioned it, the more she doubted her own impression.

She didn't like him, she didn't trust him, and she'd had her reason why tonight. The guy couldn't deal with it when he couldn't manipulate the people around him. Casey seemed to especially piss him off. She didn't like his familiarity or his greasy smiles or his control games with his patients, and he knew it.

So he was being a jerk. Casey'd known one or two doctors before him who'd been jerks. She was sure she'd trip over a few more before she hung up her guns.

But just the same, she was glad Evelyn had promised to meet them at the Body Shop for drinks. Casey needed to talk to somebody on her side. She needed to hear that Wanda had walked back into work unscathed and unrepentant.

"And this kid's mother says that little April hasn't ever known a man, so why isn't she intact in the 'you-know-where' place?" Marva continued, eyes sharp and wry, her head shaking. "Why do those people name their children like that?" she demanded. "April. Shit, that's almost as bad as Crystal and Dawn."

"You should talk," Casey retorted, "Your middle name's Placenta."

Marva's grin was wide and unabashed, lighting her whole face. "My mama thought it was the nurse's name," she explained yet again. "She saw the nurse walk in, and the doctor yells, 'Oh, look! Placenta!' He seemed so excited she thought he must really like her."

"Uh huh. So what did Jawaralal say to April's mom?"

"He said in that wonderful lilting little accent of his, so that the girl's mama doesn't even know what he's talking about, 'Excuse me to contradict you, my dear Mrs. Smith, but it is my personal opinion that your daughter has serviced more men than Central Hardware.' "

"How did you interpret it for her?" Casey asked. Interpretation was one of their most important functions, from Pakistani to street black and back again, from hoosier to French. It was too bad they didn't need dialect translators in the U.N., Casey'd be a shoo-in for the job.

"You kiddin'?" Marva demanded, downing the rest of her beer in a gulp. " 'Mrs. Smith,' I says, 'little April here's been in an accident with her bicycle at some time, hasn't she?' "

Casey chuckled. "God save me from OBs everywhere."

Her beer glass was empty. So, in fact, was Marva's. Casey decided that this needed rectification. It took the body an hour per drink to work off alcohol, and she had no intention of driving home drunk. If she had another drink, she'd have to stay till closing.

"I heard you and Hunsacker went a couple of rounds tonight," Marva offered.

Casey smiled. That would take her nicely to closing. "Let's get another round."

They elbowed their way to the bar, their swinging purses deadlier—and heavier—than any blackjack.

Brando the bartender saw them coming and turned for the appropriate tap.

"What do you think of him?" Casey asked, setting her empty stein down on Brando's spotless, gleaming oak bar.

Marva laughed, a rich contralto music that was always a surprise coming out of that pencil-thin body and angular face. "I been wonderin' when you'd finally ask me that."

Doing her best to ignore the pushy SICU nurse behind her who thought elbows were part of line courtesy, Casey blinked up at Marva.

"Why?"

Marva laughed again and held out a hand for her beer. Brando dropped it right into place and did the same for Casey. Casey led the way back to their little table.

"Because," Marva enlightened her back, "you been askin' everybody was they impressed with the man or not? All 'ceptin' me."

Marva had achieved her Masters in Nursing on full scholarship at Northwestern. She could quote Jane Austen and Eudora Welty, and wrote choral music on her off hours. Raised by professional parents, she'd never set foot near the projects in the inner city. But she could call up the patois when she thought it might serve. Evidently, it served tonight.

Casey shot her a wry glance over her shoulder. "Well?"

"Shit," Marva spat, although it actually sounded more like "Shee-it," which made it all the more emphatic. "What I want with his skinny white ass? He so busy lookin' in his mirror, I wouldn't have a chance at it."

Casey brightened even more. "You don't like him?"

Marva's grin was conspiratorial and sly. "We black

chilluns knows how to play the game, Missy Casey. We jus' smile and shuffle and get along.''

Casey climbed the rungs of her stool and sat down. It seemed Marva just bent a little. "God, Marva," Casey complained, "you're beginning to sound like Poppi. Just say it, will you?"

"I like my job," Marva answered, expression settling into that curious passivity that meant she was serious. "Where else can I have this much fun and not get arrested? If the hospital doesn't get me to quit in the next year, I'll be tenured, and I'm the only one around to put my children through college. Hunsacker's not important. He's dangerous, sure, but so is most of the staff at M and M. He's a little spooky with that 'pass the Kool-Aid' voice of his. But who cares? We don't have to deal with him enough to jeopardize our jobs by antagonizing the man. Ignore him and he'll go away." Taking a hefty hit of her new beer, Marva waved it in a signal of finality. "Shit, you let people know you'd rather somebody else assist him, the hall will look like a piranha fight over red meat."

Casey thought about it. The driving rock 'n' roll rhythm was numbing her brain and deadening her mission. The beer was buffing the edge off her anger. And Marva's wonderful pragmatism was cooling the fire of her zeal.

"Why is it that we're the only ones not dancing attendance then?" she asked.

Deeply involved with her beer, Marva just shrugged. "Nobody else down there is as strong as we is, child. They all jus' lookin' for somebody to tell 'em how wonderful they are."

Considering where her thoughts had been straying lately, Casey had to smile. "Yeah," she said with a wry nod. "You're right. I'm so strong, I don't need nobody."

For a minute she just let Bruce Springsteen fill her in about life in the steel towns. It was hard, real hard, and there was no place else to go. A man had to do what he had to do.

"I don't know," she admitted morosely. "I wish he were just stupid or obnoxious like the rest of the staff. Then I could blow him off in peace. But he's . . ." She shook her head, wishing she could verbalize the queasiness that had bloomed within the whispery terror of Hunsacker's threat. Wishing she wouldn't ever have to worry about it again. "I just wish I knew what to do," she finally admitted. "He threatened me tonight. Really scared the shit out of me."

Marva's eyebrows lifted. "You?"

Casey nodded, not facing her friend, the disquiet swelling again. "If it had been anybody else I could say he was just being a jerk. With Hunsacker, I really had the feeling that he came within about an inch of really hurting me."

Marva just shook her head. "You gotta learn to control those opinions of yours."

Casey looked up instead. "He was like a cat, Marva, and I kept feeling like the baby rabbit. What the hell am I supposed to do the next time we have a difference of opinion? I can't let him hurt his patients just to prove he's the one in charge."

"You can't let him get your job, either."

"So, what do I do?"

"I told you. Let somebody else take care of his patients."

"Well, that doesn't stop him, does it?"

"You got nothin' on paper, girl. When you do, that might change things . . . or is that what we're waitin' for your friend for? Did I end up in a plot to overthrow OB?"

Casey stiffened, shot a look at her watch. Oh, Lord, she'd forgotten about Evelyn. It was already almost twelve, and she hadn't heard from her. Maybe she should call and find out if Evelyn had gotten away from work. Maybe she should just tell her to make it another night.

"I'll be right back," she mumbled and slid back off the stool.

The phone was back by the rest rooms, sandwiched in between the cigarette machine and the two pressboard doors that never seemed to stay at rest. Popping in her quarter, Casey did her best to squeeze out of the way so she could let the steady flow of traffic through. After all, she figured, it would just take a minute.

She didn't know how worked up Evelyn was.

"This is it!" the nurse promised fifteen minutes into explaining why she was sending a patient to surgery instead of drinking beer with Casey, her voice brittle and trembling. "I'm filing a complaint. I've documented myself to death on this one, and I'm not going to take the fall for it. He didn't listen to me simply because I won't play his game, and now his lady's crumping. Damn it, and nobody pays any attention!"

"How much longer are you going to be?" Casey asked, finger in her free ear as she sidestepped the swinging door and tried to ignore the grappling couple in the back corner.

Evelyn sighed. "I have no idea, Casey. Could we maybe do this some other time? By the time I get out of here, the only thing that's going to be open will be on the East Side."

"You're going there?" Casey didn't mean to sound so astounded, but Evelyn wasn't the type to frequent the wide-open clubs that stayed open all night across the river.

"I don't know. A couple of people have suggested it.

I really need to work some of this shift off, that's for sure."

"I can wait."

"No. I'll call you later."

"Well, go get 'im, girl. And if you really do go over, be careful."

"I will. Bye."

She and Marva broke it up soon afterward. They both had to be back at the pit the next day, and the adrenaline high from the last shift had finally faded. It was time to crash among friends.

Casey only had home to go to. Her mother was asleep, but her cat, a female tabby of impressive proportions that usually never left Helen's room, was, unfortunately, in heat. So, Casey found herself wading through preening, screeching toms on the way into the house and absently wishing that one of those toms had two legs. Or one leg. She wasn't proud. Just enough equipment to make her yowl again.

The impromptu concert between Pussy (how did she explain to her mother that *nobody* named their cats that anymore?) and her admirers kept Casey up for most of the night, and a run up to the Catholic Supply House took up her morning, so that it wasn't until she was half-way through her shift at work that afternoon that she heard the news. Evelyn had never made it to the bar on the East Side the night before. Sometime around one-thirty AM, she had been shot to death at a stoplight in East St. Louis.

# Chapter 5

*IT WAS POPPI* who told her. Casey was in trying to get the whalebone girdle off a three-hundred-pound woman who was complaining of chest pain when the call came in. One foot up on the stretcher for leverage, and both hands somewhere amid folds of pale, cheesy-smelling skin, Casey knew she wasn't going anywhere fast.

"Hey, somebody answer that for me, will you?"

"Be careful," the patient gasped. "That's my best girdle."

It's my best back, Casey wanted to counter. It was no wonder the woman had chest pain. Between the weight of those tatas, a girdle built for someone a hundred pounds lighter, and a bra straight out of the Inquisition, she probably couldn't exchange enough air to keep her hair growing.

"We should have it off in a minute," Casey panted back, giving another mighty yank.

"A Dr. Leary for you?" Michael the tech offered, leaning in the door.

Casey almost grinned. Poppi and her codes. The staff wasn't allowed personal phone calls, so it usually took a certain amount of subterfuge to make contact. "I'll call her back, Michael. Would you have EKG and lab come in when I have Mrs. Heilerman assessed?"

Casey's back was to the door. Even so, she knew how much trouble Michael was having keeping a straight face. She didn't blame him. If anybody else were stuck doing this, she'd laugh, too. Unfortunately, it was her fingernails up in territory not seen by sunlight since the last world war. She just knew she was going to come away with her own supply of mushrooms.

Well, it could be worse. She could be Marva, who was next door with a foul-mouthed fifteen-year-old who'd chugged a bottle of Southern Comfort, and was in the process of puking it back up as noisily as possible, probably all over Marva.

When the girdle gave, it sprang Casey back almost to the wall. Mrs. Heilerman took her first good breath of the decade, and Casey was left with something that looked like a cross between a standing rib roast and a tent for munchkins.

The worst over, she did a quick physical assessment on the now-smiling woman and ordered a basic cardiac workup so the doctor would have normal figures to support his suggestion that Mrs. Heilerman ditch the girdle.

"Is this the eminent Dr. Leary?" Casey asked a moment later, phone balanced on a shoulder as she dried her hands. She'd washed them twice trying to get rid of dead skin before dialing Poppi's number.

Normally Poppi would have giggled. The fact that she didn't should have warned Casey. But Casey was being entertained by Marva and young Mr. Personality squaring off in room five. There were motherfuckers flying everywhere and remnants of the young man's last meal decorating one wall.

"Hey, I heard about Evelyn," Poppi was saying. "I'm sorry, Case."

Casey's attention snapped back to her call. "Evelyn?" she asked, premonition flaring in her gut. "What about Evelyn?"

A little silence, the background filled with the lush strings of Debussy. Music to deliver bad news by. "You didn't know? Evidently she made a wrong turn last night and ended up at a stoplight in East St. Louis. Somebody shot her."

Casey didn't even realize she'd sat down. Suddenly she was holding on to the phone with both hands, as if she'd drop it, elbows propped on a pile of unfinished charts. "Come on, Poppi. That's not funny. I was just talking to her last night at midnight."

"It happened around one-thirty they say, Case. No witnesses. Evidently she was headed over to Sauget and got lost?"

Casey's head sank. One hand cupped her eyes so no one in the lane could see the sudden tears. At the last minute she pulled over a drug company scratch pad to save the charts from water damage. "Uh, yeah, I know. She . . . uh, told me." She focused on the innocuous printing, anything but what she was hearing. Take two in the PM for a BM in the AM, it said. Somebody had scribbled in, "Better than having Ahmed's finger up your ass."

Casey had told Evelyn to be careful. Instead, Evelyn had ended up in the worst war zone in the bi-state area. Resembling Dresden after the firebombings, East St. Louis was a city bereft of middle class, business, and life. A wasteland within sight of the Gateway Arch, it had a mayor with bodyguards and a police force so strapped that men who wanted radios in their cars brought their own. Anybody out on the streets after dark was fair game. And it only took one wrong turn off the highway to land in no-man's-land.

"They don't have any idea what happened?"

Poppi's laugh was dark. The situation, as far as anybody in the area was concerned, was self-evident. "The cops figure somebody's financing a crack habit with her twelve dollars and forty-two cents."

"Casey," Barb announced from the end of the hall. "Dr. Rosario's coming down to set the arm in room nine. And your labwork's back on six."

Casey nodded, waved a little without looking up. She had to regroup before facing everybody. She had to get away.

"Thanks, Poppi."

"Later?"

"Yeah."

Hanging up the phone, Casey grabbed a handful of tissue and tried to stem the damage. Evelyn. Honest, reliable, responsible Evelyn. They hadn't been best friends. They had been, like most coworkers in emergency rooms, tight in the face of overwhelming odds. Like battlefield friendships, golden at the moment, surrounded, embattled, completely codependent, only to find not that much really in common once the war was over. But whenever the need had been there, because of what they'd shared, because of the people they were, they had come through.

"Where's that list of worst smells? I got a new one."

Blowing her nose, Casey looked up to see Marva, bedraggled, pungent, and scowling after her run-in with the Southern Comfort.

"SC, Big Macs, and onion rings. It beats the Ripple and navy bean soup all to hell . . . Casey?" Marva never invaded another person's space. Rather than touch or hold, she just stood, waiting. "What's wrong?"

Casey's smile was thin. "The other nurse we were going to meet at the Body Shop . . . uh, she was killed last night. Can you . . . can you watch my people for a minute?"

Marva never wasted her time with redundancy. The eloquent brown of her eyes said everything that needed saying. "Get out," she commanded, and gave Casey a push.

The grounds of Mother Mary had once been a private high school. Even though the drone of highway traffic filtered through the trees, it was still a pretty campus, landscaped with dogwoods and redbuds for the spring and sugar maples for the fall. The walks between buildings were lined with flowers. The grass was lush and thick, and quaint stone benches had been placed to face the best view.

After twenty minutes spent trying to walk off the surprise, Casey finally found one of the benches and watched the sun set over the highway. The day was hot, the first real taste of St. Louis summer, too early in April, with the humidity almost as high as the temperature. It softened the air somehow, hazing the sun and diluting the deepening green of the trees. The sky to the west was a heavy crimson, with jet trails slashing north in fire, and the moon hovering into sight like a ghost.

For a long time, Casey just sat, silent and overwhelmed.

There was a rock in her chest. A hot heaviness that bore as much guilt as grief. She should have insisted Evelyn meet her. She should have intercepted her. If there was one thing Helen had taught her well, it was to take responsibility for every calamity, and Casey was ready to shoulder her burden.

But there was more. There was something stuck in

Casey's craw, something more than just Evelyn's death. More than the senseless, random violence of it.

Casey was, by nature, an orderly person. Her job was to bring chaos into recognizable pattern. To identify, to assess, to correct. To do it all within the space of no more than three minutes. When she couldn't do that, she fretted and bitched and paced. And she felt like pacing now.

There was something more to this, an instinct that argued against simple bad luck, and she couldn't quite define or justify it.

"Why, hello, Casey. What are you doing out here?"

Chill chased recognition. Refusing to slow her pace, Casey turned, her hands shoved in her lab-coat pockets, her posture stiff. Hunsacker was closing fast, dressed for success today in a lightweight wheat double-breasted suit, blue shirt, and old school tie. Must have had a departmental meeting or something.

Last night, he'd fought with Evelyn. If he hadn't, she would have left work on time and sat with Casey for an hour or two and then gone safely home. She wouldn't have left the hospital late and found herself lost and alone in the middle of nowhere.

She wouldn't be dead.

Casey's step slowed with sudden, irrational anger. It was all his fault. "Hello, Dr. Hunsacker. How's your patient over at Izzy's?"

He frowned handsomely. "My patient? Which one?"

"The one you took to surgery last night. I was talking to Evelyn."

Why didn't he at least look surprised? Casey saw him consider her statement, saw the shocked concern flood into his expression right on cue as he slid his hands into his pockets and bent his head. But beneath it, she was plagued by the feeling that not only had he not been surprised, he'd been counting on her question. Casey couldn't say why, but she thought she detected a smug satisfaction behind the facade he was projecting.

Evelyn had bucked him and now she was dead. Did Hunsacker consider it just punishment? A sign from God that the doctor was still boss? Was he just off-center enough to consider this a punctuation to the threat he'd delivered to Casey?

"I heard about Evelyn," he admitted with just the right amount of solicitude. "You knew her?"

Casey nodded, never taking her eyes from his. A fresh chill crawled up her back. He was going to try to skate clear of Evelyn's threats. He was going to smile in private at her death, as if it were a delicious punch line to her ineffectual challenge. Casey's sense of justice, her control on her world, shifted a little. She battled the rage of impotence at his confidence. She shuddered at the hubris that would provoke that attitude.

"We used to work together," was all Casey said. "We were supposed to meet last night, but she had to stay late to get that lady to OR."

He was watching her, calculating. Casey knew it. She could swear she saw the wheels spinning beneath those bright blue eyes, heard the whine of an accelerating engine. It stoked her anger even higher. She wanted him to at least comprehend his culpability. Instead, he seemed to be savoring it.

The asshole. She wanted him to hurt even a little.

Letting his own gaze slip casually away, Hunsacker shook his head. "I know," he admitted, his voice heavy. "That was a bad situation. I actually called her supervisor to complain this morning before I found out about her. Now, of course . . ."

That brought Casey to a dead stop. "Complain? About what?" Evelyn had been the one so desperate and angry that she'd sobbed on the phone.

Hunsacker met Casey's eyes without faltering, the regret and compassion in his gaze sitting oddly on him. "I almost lost Mrs. Baldwin because of her. If I hadn't had a hunch and just gone on out . . ."

"But she called you," Casey insisted, straightening. "She said that she called you four times."

He smiled now, a smile of friends who knew better. "She was always calling me, Casey. If you knew Evelyn you knew that. She couldn't make any kind of decision on her own. When she called last night, she didn't say how bad her bleeding really was. If she had, don't you think I would have been right out there? The patient's husband is a lawyer, Casey."

I don't know, Casey wanted to say, stunned to silence by his words.

Yes, she did know Evelyn. Yes, Evelyn was the kind of nurse who couldn't take initiative. It had been one of the reasons she'd foundered so badly in the emergency room. But Casey knew that Evelyn wouldn't have made that kind of mistake. She wouldn't have failed to tell Hunsacker just what was going on. And once convinced, she wouldn't have been dissuaded.

But if her notes had borne her out, Hunsacker never could have complained. The proof would have been Evelyn's.

Casey didn't know what to do. Suddenly she didn't know who to believe. Hunsacker was right. If he'd known, wouldn't he have been out there? After all, hungry lawyers circled that area of West County like restless buzzards, waiting for disaster. If medicine was big business, malpractice suits were its unhealthy and thriving offspring.

Hunsacker might not be the best doctor, but he wasn't stupid. He wouldn't have been idiot enough to fly in the face of that most revered of medical dictums: Cover Your

Ass. Displeasing a patient was one thing. Displeasing her lawyer husband was quite another. If Hunsacker had thought there'd be any chance of that happening, he would have been out at that hospital at light speed.

"It won't reflect on Evelyn," Hunsacker assured Casey, obviously mistaking the distress on her face. This time when he settled a hand on her arm, she didn't back away. "I talked to the people out at St. Isidore's. Since Mrs. Baldwin is doing fine today, we thought the less said the better. Don't you think so?"

Casey tried. She really tried to consider this calmly. Could she have been wrong? Could she be reading something into Hunsacker that merely reflected her own frustrations? And yet, she felt the old rage bubbling in her, that feeling of an animal caught in a trap, unable to get out. She felt cornered by just the touch of his hand, and couldn't explain it.

Evelyn was her friend. She wanted Evelyn to have been right. She wanted to at least savor the sharp edge of self-righteous indignation at the thought that Hunsacker's selfish need for control had indirectly cost Evelyn her life.

Looking hard at Hunsacker, she tried to objectively interpret his expression. Still, she thought she caught the hint of satisfaction in his eyes, the smug enjoyment of the victor. And she decided that she didn't want to give him even that much.

"I don't know," she finally admitted, facing him. "I don't know that we should let it go at all."

Poppi evidently wasn't going to give Casey the opportunity to turn down help. When Casey pulled into her driveway at midnight, the bright red MG waited for her. All the lights were still on in the house, too, which meant that Poppi wasn't the only one ready to offer condolences. Casey gave brief thought to turning around and trying for one of those Sauget clubs herself. In the end she killed the engine in her import and opened the door to the muggy night.

The cats were once again lined up in the front yard, serenading like a class of second-grade Suzuki students, but Poppi didn't seem to notice.

"I brought some pretty good shit," Poppi offered quietly from where she leaned against her car door, her long, flowered skirt shifting in the sultry wind. For a minute Casey could almost imagine it was 1975 again, and that Poppi had shown up to dissect dates and the latest concert down at the River Festival.

"No, thanks," Casey waved her off. "That dims the outrage, and I want mine nice and shiny tonight. Besides," she added with a nod to the lights, "the convent frowns on that kind of thing. Don't step on any of the cats. I don't think they're here to dance."

Without further greeting the two walked back along the driveway to the kitchen door. The front door was for guests, for Girl Scouts selling cookies and the Jehovah's Witnesses selling salvation. The only time Casey walked in or out the front door was to sit in the glider on the wide wooden porch. If she could get past her mother, tonight would be one of those nights.

"Oh, Catherine," her mother greeted her even before the back door was fully opened. The little woman had been sitting at the kitchen table sipping at coffee and picking at her fingernails. The bandanna was firmly in place, even with her robe and slippers on. "Come sit down. Come talk."

Trapped again, pulled between her mother's suffocating concern and Hunsacker's smooth remonstrances, Casey fought down the almost physical urge to yank herself away.

"I've been praying," Helen said with a quick little nod of her head, as if this would settle it all. "Praying for poor Evelyn's soul in purgatory. But the virgin promises me that Evelyn will be in heaven soon, don't you worry. With your father."

Evelyn doesn't want to be with my father, Casey thought, still not answering, walking to the refrigerator instead and pulling out two beers. She wants to be with her husband. Besides, there wasn't any guarantee that Casey's father was in heaven. Flipping a can to Poppi, Casey leaned back against the cool, sterile white of the wall.

"I know, Mom," she said, desperate to be away from those pleading eyes. "I'm sure your prayers helped."

Helen smiled, her posture still anxious, like a small dog seeking to please. Casey didn't know what else to say. Rage and frustration were not emotions you brought into Helen McDonough's house, but that was all she could manage right now.

She wanted so badly to tell Poppi about her confrontation with Hunsacker. She desperately wished for the words that could convey the sense of menace Hunsacker had projected, the stale taste of avariciousness he left behind. She wanted Poppi to be able to see the unseen.

"It was Hunsacker's fault," was all she could end up saying as she took a sip of beer. "Evelyn only went to Sauget because she had to stay late to stabilize one of Hunsacker's mistakes. It's his fault she's dead."

Poppi tilted her head just a little, her voice carefully passive. "She might have wanted to go there anyway."

"He got her so worked up she couldn't go home, and it was too late by the time she got out to go anyplace close. That son of a bitch killed her as sure as if he pulled the gun himself."

"It was a senseless crime," Poppi countered. "She was

at the wrong place at the wrong time. Do you really think blaming Hunsacker for Ev's bad sense of direction is going to help?''

Casey glared at her friend, wishing she could explain away the guilt and frustration and fear Evelyn's death left behind. Wishing Hunsacker didn't unnerve her so much that she felt it necessary to blame him for what amounted to no more than a random tragedy.

Casey was an emergency-room nurse. She knew all about random tragedies. She was the world's leading expert, after caring for tornado victims and fire victims and drive-by shooting victims. Shit happens, and she saw it every day.

But for some reason, this felt different. This act of random violence stuck in her craw when she'd long since learned to shrug all the others off. She wanted retribution for it, balance. And she had nobody but Hunsacker available to make payment.

"I saw him tonight, Poppi. And I'll tell you something. I had the most unnerving feeling that he was actually glad Ev was dead. Like she was paying some kind of cosmic price for bucking him. Like he still won in the end, and that was all that mattered.''

"Casey—''

"There has to be something I can do, damn it. Some way to prove that Ev was right.''

Casey didn't even hear her mother get to her feet. She didn't hear the sly whisper of slippers on the Formica floor or see her mother's quick scuttle. Suddenly there was another hand on her arm, the fingers urgent and impassioned. Looking up, Casey realized that she'd walked right into a sermon.

"When your father died,'' Helen said, her voice breathy and trembling, "what did I say?''

Casey knew her role by heart. It wouldn't do any good to try and avoid it. "Why."

Helen nodded. "I said why, why my dear husband, why Mick McDonough, the finest man who walked the earth. I demanded answers. But I couldn't find them, could I?"

"No, Mom. You couldn't." For a Catholic, her mother would have made a great revival tent preacher. Instead of fire and brimstone, Helen's favorite topic was death. How to ignore it, how to deny it, how to wash away the guilt of it in fantasy and ritual so it couldn't chase you in the night. Helen felt strongly about death.

Another nod, another point made. "And how did I finally find peace?"

Peace? Casey wanted to demand. You call this peace, creeping around this mausoleum like an uncomfortable ghost, spending the last twenty years beating your breast and muttering mea culpas?

"How?" Helen insisted, digging her fingers in for emphasis.

"You offered your pain to God," she answered, the rote more ingrained than the Baltimore Catechism. "You surrendered to Him and let Him make your decisions for you." You became the ultimate passive-aggressive.

Helen usually smiled at this point. Tonight that must have seemed frivolous. "And for the first time in my life, I was content. I surrendered myself to God and let Him take charge. It's the only way we can manage, Catherine. God had a plan for Evelyn. He had a reason for taking her home, just as He did your father. And only He knows what that was. Our asking is presumptuous. We must simply have faith. Faith and submission. Only then will we have peace in our hearts."

Evidently, that was what Helen had been waiting up

to say, because at the end of her speech, she simply nodded one final time and turned away for bed. She pushed
open the swinging door just in time to hear a particularly
plaintive cry from the direction of her room.

"Listen to my pussy sing," she said, smiling. "How
Our Lord must love her music."

Casey didn't acknowledge the choking noises behind
her as Helen walked on through into the dining room.

"I don't think it's God she's trying to raise," Poppi finally managed.


But Casey didn't leave Evelyn to God. Casey hadn't
left anything to God since she'd been eight. Three nights
later at Evelyn's wake, Casey made it a point to approach
some of the postpartum nurse's co-workers from Izzy's.

She had to know. Once and for all, she needed proof
that Evelyn hadn't been at fault that night, that Hunsacker had fabricated his story and shirked his own guilt.
She needed to lay Evelyn to rest in her own way.

"I hear it was an AK47," Betty Fernandez was saying
to Marianne Wade with a sad shake of the head. "Damn,
when is somebody going to do something about the
weapons out on the street?"

Casey sidled up and exchanged greetings. "Do they
have anything else?" she asked.

Betty and Marianne both shook their heads, one tall
and thin, the other almost as round as Evelyn.

"I was the one who invited her over to Sauget," Betty
admitted, tears glittering in her soft gray eyes. "I waited
and waited . . . I just figured she decided not to come.
I should have figured she'd get lost."

It had obviously been said before. Marianne settled a
plump hand on Betty's arm and Betty shook her head.

"She was a big girl," Casey said, understanding. "You
can't be responsible for her, Betty."

It wouldn't really help; the three of them nodded anyway.

"I was talking to her that night," Casey offered, praying she didn't betray her anxiety. "Before you guys left. She said she still had to send that patient of Hunsacker's to OR."

"Oh, that." Betty's expression was indecipherable. "God, to have a night like that be your last."

Casey came close to holding her breath. "Did you hear any of her phone calls to him?"

Betty glanced over at the casket, as if afraid she'd be overheard. "What do you mean?"

Casey dipped her own eyes, doing her best to still her suddenly nervous hands. "I saw Hunsacker the day after. He almost reported Evelyn for not telling him how bad Mrs. Baldwin was."

She was answered with stricken silence. Betty looked at Marianne who took her own look over at the casket where Evelyn's husband stood at lone attention.

"No," Betty admitted, frustrated. "I know she called him. She was so worried, and she couldn't get him to answer or listen to her . . . at least, that's what she said. I kept saying that wasn't like Dr. Hunsacker, but Evelyn seemed so upset."

"And you guys left after Mrs. Baldwin went to surgery?"

Betty shook her head. "We left after she got out. Ev wanted to make sure she was all right."

Casey's hands went still. Her heart stumbled. "After she was out? Did Ev talk to Hunsacker again?"

Both women consulted. It was Betty who shrugged a qualified yes.

"Not around us. I think she might have run into him down by the parking lot. I heard one of the other nurses say later that she heard the two of them really having it out. But I don't know what they said."

Casey could just imagine. It didn't take much to resurrect that whisper, that deadly glare that accompanied his best threats. She wondered whether he'd warned her against reporting him, whether he'd told her that he could make life miserable for her.

She wondered what Evelyn would have said back. Evelyn who cared more passionately for her patients than any other nurse Casey knew. Evelyn who would offer up her free time, her boundless compassion, her own money, if necessary.

If the argument had been anything like Casey's, Evelyn would have been shaking when she got into her car. She would have been upset and distracted. She wouldn't have been paying attention as she drove off the lot or onto the highway until she found herself in unfamiliar streets surrounded by boarded-up buildings.

And Hunsacker had shown up the next day smiling.

"Well," Marianne allowed in a soft voice, "at least Ron has some finality. He can bury her and get on with his life. Buddy's still waiting."

Casey's head snapped up. "Buddy?"

Marianne nodded, her expression folded into concern. "Not a word from Wanda. The police still say she's run off, but I don't know. I think something happened to her."

Casey couldn't quite get a breath. Wanda. God, oh, God, she'd forgotten.

As quickly as the suspicion rose, she shoved it away. It was too ridiculous, too outlandish. But if Wanda hadn't just disappeared, would she have paid a cosmic price for arguing with Hunsacker, too?

"I heard she was having trouble with Hunsacker, too,"

Casey ventured gently, wondering why she asked. Wondering what she wanted to hear.

"God, yes," Marianne said. "If it hadn't been for the fact that I don't think she'd just leave Buddy like that, I would have said she quit because of Hunsacker."

"Why?"

She sighed. "Because of the fight they had the last day she worked."

Casey could do no more than wait. She didn't want to find a pattern. She didn't want to hear what she already knew was coming.

"I wouldn't have known about it except that I wandered into the lounge at the wrong time. He was standing really close to her, his voice so low I could hardly hear it. But Wanda was as red as a beet, and told him he could . . . well, it was anatomically improbable. She was furious, but she never said anything else about it. She just left."

Casey knew. And she didn't have to imagine what Hunsacker had said. She'd imagined it already. She'd heard it.

It was absurd. It was nothing more than a terrible coincidence. Anything more would be intolerable.

Still, she had to know. No matter what she wanted to do, she was going to end up picking at this like a sore, needing to prove that Hunsacker wasn't the golden boy everybody thought he was. He was a control freak, a smooth, manipulative, amoral narcissist who couldn't abide not having his way. At best, he was gloating over the impotence of women who had challenged him, and he'd damn well do it again to Casey. At worst . . . Casey couldn't even think the worst. She wouldn't. She'd just find out a little more in order to clip his wings a little and get her own control back.

Because that, she realized, was her Achilles' heel. She

couldn't offer control to anyone else, not God, not Hunsacker, not anybody. It had been why she'd ended up with Ed, and why she'd consigned herself after that to living alone. It was why she had to work ER, because nurses had the most independence there, and why she chafed so badly beneath the weight of frivolous administration and arbitrary physicians.

It was why when she looked to her future, she felt such desperation. She didn't know how to offer herself to anybody anymore, and because of that, she was going to end up just like Billie Evans, with no one to claim her and no one to mourn her.

Casey never had the chance to lay Evelyn to rest. She wasn't even allowed to forget Wanda, because suddenly Hunsacker decided that the Mother Mary ER was his second home, and Casey his best friend.

She never heard another threat from him. He didn't so much as mention the fact that he'd shown up at Evelyn's graveside for no reason at all, hugging Ev's husband as the nurses had looked on aghast. But he talked to Casey. He talked about how quiet things were over at Izzy's without Wanda's loud mouth. How he missed Evelyn's voice on the phone six or seven times a night.

Nobody else heard him say these things; only Casey. Nobody else thought they caught the glitter of silent challenge in his eyes. Casey was beginning to feel paranoid, as if Hunsacker were a figment of her overburdened imagination. Every sentence carried subtext, every look or smile a secret challenge, and she didn't know why.

She was beginning to see him where he wasn't and shuddering at the sound of his approach. And she knew, if he wanted to unnerve her, he was doing a hell of a job.

"You're obsessive-compulsive, you know it?"

Casey didn't even bother to look up from the newspaper she was reading as she waited for the nurse on Four West to pick up the phone. Marva wasn't talking about the paper, though. She didn't know why Casey had developed such a fondness for crime statistics lately. She didn't know that Casey was looking for Wanda to show up under the homicide column. Casey couldn't explain her growing obsession. Not to Marva or anybody else. Not even, really, to herself. She simply gnawed at the coincidence that two women last seen arguing with a prominent doctor were both in tough spots.

She'd also been plagued by the nightmare over the last two weeks, the one where she was locked in the apartment, impotent to free herself. It was the only recurrent dream she'd ever had—except for the one where Mel Gibson showed up at her door in nothing but a fireman's turn-out gear, but that was another matter altogether. That dream didn't make her feel frustrated and ashamed and frightened at once.

"Don't you read your literature, Marva?" she retorted. "Obsessive-compulsives make the best nurses."

"Once they stop washing their hands and turning off the oven, sure."

There had been two female homicides the night before. One courtesy of a boyfriend with a knife, and the other an alleged prostitute from the city's South Side. Assailant unknown, found beaten to death in her apartment.

Still no Wanda. Another nurse had died the week before, shot in a burglary. But no bleached blond OB techs had been found in any of the myriad ditches around town.

"You want some interesting reading," Marva offered, flipping through the paper without Casey's permission. "Read this."

The Everyday section, soft news and society tidbits. And there, right at the top of Millicent Adams' column in tux and patented smile, was Hunsacker, his arm over the shoulder of the mayor of St. Louis.

"Our boy's getting pretty popular," Marva commented dryly.

"It's enough to make you wanna puke." Adams, St. Louis' final word on the fashionable and powerful, had affixed the label "Superstork" on Hunsacker. How cute.

"This is Barkin. What?" The nurse on Four West finally picked up.

Casey came to attention. "Hi," she answered, quickly closing Hunsacker away behind the homicides once more. "This is the ER calling back to let you know Mr. Washington is on his way up to 423."

"They got eyes," Marva groused, reaching across Casey to wipe off Mr. Washington's name from the flow board. That only left fifteen patients waiting for disposition.

"They're also two nurses short," Casey retorted, hanging up the phone after receiving a curt reply to her announcement. "And the nurse I just gave report to was Millie Barkin."

Marva shot Casey a pained look. "Butcher Barkin? Oh, Lordie, poor Mr. Washington."

Casey dropped the chart remnants in an outgoing pile and pocketed her pen. "I rest my case."

She was about to fold away her paper and head in to start the migraine headache in eight when Tom blindsided her.

"Casey, listen, I've finally gotten the schedule finished," he announced, dropping it right on top of the chart she'd just pulled out. "You put in a request, but those aren't allowed on summer schedules."

"Since when?"

"Since you asked," Marva muttered from where she copied off lab results.

There was only one reason Tom would have forced her into looking at the schedule in a busy work lane. It was the "you won't make a fuss in an expensive restaurant" theory of management.

"July Fourth?" Casey shrieked, jumping to her feet.

"The patients," Tom objected, looking around as if she'd just dropped her uniform to the floor. "What have I told you about team playing?"

"The team's gonna have to play without me on the Fourth," she retorted, clenching the schedule in her hands like a weapon. "I played New Year's Eve and Easter. It's my holiday off."

"Nothing I can do. We go through this every schedule, Casey. You know I can't rearrange a road trip just for you."

Casey gained her feet, glaring. "I'd appreciate it if you'd tell that to Barb. She had New Year's off."

"She was sick, Casey."

"Bullshit, Tom. She was at the hockey game."

His face reddened. "I'm warning you, Casey . . ."

"I'll pick it up," Marva offered in a deadpan voice. "Bein' off the Fourth is against my religion."

Casey's first reaction was to tell her she was nuts. The Fourth was the worst holiday of the year, St. Patrick's Day and New Year's with detonators. But Tom was way ahead of her.

"You can't pick up other people's holidays," he said.

"Since when?" Marva asked.

"Since you asked," Casey retorted blackly.

"I don't know, Tom. Seems to me these women get more uppity all the time."

Stunned, Casey whipped around to see that Hunsacker

had managed to appear on the scene just when he was least wanted.

"Uppity?" Marva echoed with just enough lift to her left eyebrow to make a sane man dive for cover. Hunsacker smiled right through it.

Tom came right to attention. "Hi, Dale, nice to see you. You have a patient down here?"

Hunsacker pulled a hand from one pocket and waved at Tom like a rock fan. "Just on my way through to medical records."

"I saw you in Millicent Adams' column this morning," Tom offered, his smile unctuous.

Casey picked up the chart on her new patient, anxious to get away, her stomach already roiling.

"It's a filthy job," Hunsacker demurred with a conspiratorial grin. "But somebody's got to do it. Is that what you're reading, Casey?" he asked, motioning to the still-opened paper, his tone silkily offensive. "About me? I'm flattered."

Casey couldn't help but look up. She couldn't quite answer, caught by the new light in his eyes. The sudden challenge.

"Nah," Marva retorted for her, her own attention on the silent duel. "I have. *She's* been reading about murders."

Hunsacker was smiling. His eyebrow lifted, that same eyebrow that seemed directed right at Casey. "Really? I heard that you know you're getting old when you read obituaries. What does it make you when you read homicides?"

Marva again. "Morbid."

He was telling her something. Something vital. Casey could sense it, like the throb of static electricity. That smile wasn't without purpose. The expression in those eyes was too bright, too knowing. Too smug by half. She couldn't believe nobody else saw it. She couldn't believe he was delivering it in front of an audience.

"Is there anything in there worth reading?" he asked.

For just a minute, Casey wanted to turn to Tom for support, where he stood stiff and uncomfortable at her side. She wanted to demand that he recognize the sly malevolence in Hunsacker's expression. But she couldn't pull her own gaze from Hunsacker's long enough to do it. Like a deadly snake, he mesmerized her into compliance.

"Oh, just your usual mayhem," she said with a little shrug, her shoulders screaming with strain. "Crip shoots South Side Posse, burglar shoots cabbie, boyfriend stabs girlfriend. John beats hooker."

His smile broadened so minimally in response to that last bit of news that Casey knew no one else noticed. "It almost makes obstetrics sound boring in comparison."

Casey's heart stumbled. Her chest felt suddenly hollow. What was he telling her? Why had the challenge in his eyes suddenly grown?

Casey couldn't seem to breathe with the weight of his stare. She couldn't move. She didn't see anymore whether Marva or Tom were even still there. All she could see was that smile, and it made her think of Satan with a soul in his pocket. Dracula wiping his fangs.

"Well, I'll get going," Hunsacker said, still to Casey, only to Casey. "I had a hard night last night. And I'm on call tonight. Let me know if you need me for anything." Again his expression brightened by millimeters, his eyes dancing. "Anything at all."

He was already through the far door before anybody moved.

"What was *that* all about?" Marva demanded, looking after him.

Tom was more direct. "Casey, were you being antagonistic? What have I told you about that, especially to him. And why do I have the feeling you still haven't thanked him yet, after all the times I've reminded you?"

"For what?" Marva demanded.

"Marva, when I want you to have the signals, I'll give them to you."

Casey almost laughed. Tom had no idea what had just transpired. Her chest still hurt with the aftermath of that odd little conversation. She was overcome by the urge to grab that paper and reread the information about that hooker. And her supervisor was still trying to get her to read the playbook.

"Casey, are you listening to me?"

Slowly, Casey looked over from where she was watching the door swing shut behind Hunsacker. "Of course I'm listening to you, Tom. And, no, I wasn't antagonizing Dr. Hunsacker. If I were, I think you would have known it."

"What about thanking him?"

"Oh," she lied with a blithe smile. "I'm sure I did."

He nodded. "I hope so. You know, your evaluation's coming up soon, and I'd hate to see that kind of thing on it."

That kind of thing was always on it. Casey had a dangerously low AKQ, and unfortunately it wasn't going to get better. In terms of priorities, her ass-kissing quotient was somewhere below buying a leopard-skin coat and joining the Vanna White fan club. With Hunsacker sniffing around so much more lately, she was sure she was going to lose even more points.

"What," Marva repeated the minute Tom followed Hunsacker out the door, "was that all about?"

Casey considered the nurse, the keen intelligence masked by that deceptively lazy attitude. She thought of the frustration that was bubbling really close to her own surface and just how successfully she might relieve it by confiding in another person.

Marva was suddenly way ahead of her, as if she, too, had read that nonverbal communication a minute ago, and the meaning had just sunk in.

"Murder," she breathed, eyes growing so large with the revelation that the whites ringed them like the corona of an eclipse. Looking like a con being told the breakout was set, she grabbed Casey's arm and pulled her close. "You can't be serious, girl."

"I don't know," Casey hedged. "What if I am?"

Both of Marva's hands shot up as if fending off gunfire. "Stay away from me, you hear? I don't wanna hear *none* o' that stuff."

"But what if—"

Marva emphatically shook her head, waving Casey's words back where they came from. "I told you already. I got problems enough. So do you. You go makin' crazy accusations like that, you'll end up with a fine job in a McDonald's someplace dishin' hamburgers. For the *rest* of your life."

Casey was the one who ended up doing the relieving. She reassured Marva that she wouldn't do anything stupid and left it at that. Of course Marva knew she was lying, but they had both long since learned the value of silence. Marva's only answer was "Mmmm."

There was something unnatural about going to a gynecologist. Something invasive and demeaning. Sitting in her own GYN's office, Casey realized that the feeling was the same as waiting for confession.

Father Donnelly had been the pastor of St. Christopher's when she'd been a girl. A tall, raw-boned man with austere manner and saturnine features, he had heard all school confessions. Casey remembered standing in the cold, dim church, a second-grader at the end of each pew, inhaling the detritus of incense and beeswax, diminished by the echoes of creaking kneelers and nuns' whispers. Mesmerized by that little red eye that glowed over the confessional, shuffling a pew closer each time the eye blinked, palms clammy, heart thundering, brain empty of everything but the certainty that the next time she saw Father Donnelly he would somehow convey what an unworthy person she was for what he heard in that stuffy, claustrophobic little room.

Casey could still resurrect that terror, the shame, the dread that marked every long, slow procession along the side aisle of that church. She likened that feeling to the flutter of disquiet the minute she heard elevator music, saw *American Mother* magazine, and smelled disinfectant.

It wasn't just anatomy and physiology. It was mystery and secrecy. Morals and mores. A man never had to submit himself in a completely vulnerable manner the way women were supposed to. A man was never taught that his sexual organs were a precious gift to be secreted away until offered to one special person—only to be expected to expose them for regular and casual inspection by a stranger.

There was no one a woman instinctively feared or necessarily trusted more than her gynecologist, simply because there was no one else in the same position to take advantage of her. It was why good gynecologists were so very empathetic. It was also why it was so easy for bad gynecologists to cause so much damage and not even be reported. It would be like publicly denouncing one's confessor, only to compound the humiliation of private betrayal with the shame of public exposure.

Casey tried to imagine what it would be like to place that kind of trust in Hunsacker. To wait, exposed and unsettled, for the first touch of his fingers, the cold invasion of the speculum. Even sitting in a chair fully dressed, Casey found herself squirming.

Casey's gut told her that Evelyn had been right. Hunsacker was hurting people. Maybe he wasn't killing them, but he was humiliating them, manipulating them. Women surrendered themselves to him, just like Helen did to God, putting all their trust in his hands, and he abused it. She just couldn't ignore that as easily as Marva could. Those funny little yelps of pain she kept hearing from his patients haunted her—almost as much as the disappearance of her friends.

"Casey? Your mom will be out in a minute."

Startled from her reverie, Casey grabbed her purse and got to her feet. All around her women in various stages of ripening leafed through old magazines or hunched over needlework. And all Casey waited for was her mother. She allowed the old yearning to resurface for only a moment before turning to greet Dr. Burton's nurse.

"How'd she do?"

The nurse, an old classmate of Casey's named Sue who supported her alcoholic husband and four children with the wages of childbirth, proffered a smile of genuine delight. "I didn't know there was a patron saint of pelvics."

Casey scowled. "Probably somebody who died on the rack. What's new and exciting in the wonderful world of labor?"

They walked together through the door that separated office from waiting room. Casey heard Burton's melodious baritone and the clicks of PCs from billing. There were Mary Cassatt posters decorating the wall and a digital scale with a funhouse mirror in front of it that made people look thin. White-haired for her mother and worthy recipient of the Filthiest Joke Award for her, Burton was an OB who adored women.

"Scandal and dirt," Sue answered once safely beyond earshot of the uninitiated. "That's what's going on."

Casey pulled out her checkbook to pay for Helen's visit. "Usual stuff," she retorted. "VanDyke still trying to sneak those tubal ligations past the nuns?"

Sue's shrug was eloquent. "And Fernandez is on wife number five."

Casey's eyebrow lifted. "Damn, as fast as he's going through 'em, I should sign up now. I'd be set for life."

Sue grimaced. "Even alimony for life isn't worth two months with him. Besides, he swears this time, he's sticking to mistresses."

"Just my luck."

"Speaking of mistresses," Sue offered, her smile growing avaricious. "Wanna hear what I just overheard from the B man himself?"

Sue was leaning close, too close even for the clerical staff to hear, so Casey knew it was good.

"I'm all ears."

"What do you think of that new guy Hunsacker?"

Casey did her best not to betray her sudden attention. Even so, she took a calculated risk. "I heard he's been doin' the three-finger special."

Sue's eyes widened. "No kidding. Did you also know that he had quite an interesting mistress?"

Casey snorted. "From what I heard, he's had more women in bed than Sealy Posturepedic."

But Sue shook her head and leaned closer. "No, not regulation stuff. I'm talking about a hooker. One who specialized in the, uh, rough stuff."

It was getting hard for Casey to breathe. "From down South Chippewa way?"

Sue nodded, bristling with salacious outrage. "I guess none of the West County girls would put up with the Mike Tyson school of charm."

"How'd Burton find out?"

Sue shrugged. "You know him. He knows everything that goes on. My suspicion is he heard it down at the city clinic he volunteers at. He's told me before some of the girls frequent the penicillin gallery there. Of course, maybe we'd better put out warning posters that Hunsacker might be on the lookout again. Evidently his main squeeze lost an argument with her pimp. He beat her to death."

Except that the story in the papers was different. The story in the papers was that no one knew who killed the hooker.

The hooker who knew Hunsacker. The hooker whose death had been the slippery ball of contest Casey and Hunsacker had batted back and forth in full view of an unsuspecting audience. Casey wondered whether Hunsacker and the hooker had had an argument before she'd died, just like Hunsacker had had with Evelyn before she'd died, just like he'd had with Wanda before she'd disappeared. She didn't have to wonder anymore about what it had been that she'd seen in his eyes when they'd discussed it. She'd seen it the day she'd discussed Evelyn with him.

It was impossible. It was ludicrous. And yet, an hour later, Casey found herself in the Bishop's office discussing murder.

# Chapter 6

CASEY COULDN'T REALLY see him as a Bishop. More a monk, a hermit, the kind who used to scrape out a life in isolation at the windswept edges of Ireland. Beehive huts and meditation for the glory of God. Her gaze on his bent head and her hand at Helen's back, Casey wondered if he was a good cop, or just a zealous one.

He wasn't handsome. Sleek was handsome; well fed and muscled and carefully attended. He was lean and hungry-looking, with a kind of controlled ferocity to his movements and a wealth of the world in the network of crow's feet that betrayed his age as a few years up on hers. Angles and shadows, a lot of forehead and deep-set eyes, his face was all bone structure and character. The fluorescent lights made his skin look almost pasty in contrast to his heavy brown hair.

Casey was surprised by his undetectivelike attire: dark plaid shirt, knit tie, and pleated pants. It didn't even look right on a cop, much less a man named Bishop. Well chosen, a little loose on his frame. Casey could see him instead in homespun wool and rope sandals, exhorting the faithful to salvation. She wasn't sure she could see him waiting through her story.

"You have some information on the Crystal Johnson murder?" he asked without looking up from whatever he was writing.

Casey eased Helen down into one of the two chairs that took up the only free space in the crowded little office where four desks were jammed into the area reserved for one and file cabinets fought for space with bookshelves and computer terminals. The Bishop, as the duty officer called him, sat behind a nameplate that read Sgt. Barbara Dawkins, so Casey assumed he wasn't even using his own desk.

"I think so," Casey answered the only way she could, his indifference unsettling.

Helen was already trying to get back to her feet. "I have no place in your confessional, dear," she admonished. "Although why you wouldn't want to just go to Father Donnelly . . ."

That got the officer's attention. With the economy born of long practice, Casey slid her mother back into her chair and held her there. The detective watched in dour silence.

"It's not confession, Mom," Casey said, wishing desperately that she'd taken the time to get Helen home before coming down here. But if she'd gone home, she would have lost her nerve and stayed there. "It's a police station. I told you."

"I can accommodate a confession," he offered equably, his gaze settling disconcertingly on her. "If you feel the need to make one."

Casey scowled. "You must know the lady downstairs. She made the same offer."

She thought she caught the ghost of a smile tug briefly at the corner of his mouth. "We like to give people every opportunity to unburden themselves."

Casey almost found herself smiling back, even as the

perspiration began to slide down her back. "And don't think we don't appreciate it. But not today, thanks."

His nod was tight and a lot less congenial than it seemed. "Let me know. Now, about Crystal," he said, leaning back a little, his attention all hers. "You knew her?"

Casey had seen eyes like his before. The better psychiatrists had them, and Bert when he was questioning people. Deceptively passive eyes, almost hooded in their lassitude, as if their owner were only half-attentive. Casey called them crocodile eyes, because there was a mind behind those eyes as quick and surgical as a crock's jaw. Snap, and you were caught, before you could even cry out in surprise. They didn't make her any more comfortable.

"My name is Catherine McDonough," she introduced herself, settling into the other seat without letting go of Helen. "Casey. I'm an ER nurse out at Mother Mary Hospital. Do I call you the Bishop, or just plain Barbara?"

The only way she knew she'd caught him by surprise was the infinitesimal elevation of his left eyebrow. He motioned to the desk by the wall where a mountain of files and books vied for space with an old brass reading lamp, a Marine Corps paperweight, and a nameplate that read Sgt. Jack Scanlon.

"Sgt. Scanlon," he allowed, tapping the edge of his ballpoint slowly against the paper he'd been filling in. "I come here for lunch. Now," he said evenly. "Crystal?"

Casey didn't remember letting go of Helen. She just seemed to end up needing both her hands to tell her story. "I think I know who killed her," she admitted in a frustratingly small voice. So much was riding on what she said. So much needed saying, and she didn't have a clue how to best present it. So, she took a breath and fixed her gaze on Sgt. Scanlon's steely gray one. "But it's not going to make much sense unless I tell this in sequence."

All he did was lift a hand in a signal of acquiescence and lean farther back, folding one leg over the other. Casey took another breath and wondered if she'd end up hyperventilating.

She never got the chance to do even that. Before Casey could open her mouth Helen jumped to her feet. "You couldn't be diocesan," she insisted suddenly.

Casey grabbed her just in time. "Mom, sit down."

Instead of turning back, Helen faced the sergeant. "You're not Orange, are you?" she demanded with a hard squint. "I know they have bishops and such." The only worse insult than faithlessness to an Irish Catholic. Irish Episcopalianism.

"I'm sorry," Casey apologized, tugging at her mother.

Sgt. Scanlon looked very much as if he'd just been hit in the face with a fish. He kept still, but Casey had the feeling it was with effort.

Helen gave up and folded back onto her chair, her heavy black purse clutched to her chest. "Even Orangeman are coming to the true church," she insisted earnestly, then fell silent.

Casey sighed. She must have done something very bad to deserve this. It would be a cold day in hell before she ever tried to do a civic duty again. Now her carefully constructed history had fallen apart, and she couldn't seem to pull it back together again.

"Here," she said, pulling her own purse into her lap. "I brought a picture of him. It might help you ask questions around the neighborhood. I've heard he's been seeing Crystal." Pulling the crumpled paper from her purse, she ironed out the Adams column with her palm and passed it across. "At least, I think he's been seeing Crystal."

Scanlon uncrossed his legs and leaned up to the desk to take a look at the picture. "Who," he demanded. "The mayor?"

"No," Casey insisted, desperately trying to remain calm, one hand still on Helen. "Dr. Dale Hunsacker."

There, she'd said it. She'd accused him, shared her burden of suspicion, handed the weight she'd been carrying around over to the police. Now they'd take care of it, and she could go back to mass and trauma.

She should have known better.

He looked at the picture for all of ten seconds.

"McMurphy sent you, didn't she?"

Casey couldn't think of anything intelligent to say. "Pardon?"

Sgt. Scanlon lifted his eyes and impaled her on them, the gray colder than gunmetal. "She's paying me back for making her take that suicide last week and ruining her best suit. I can't help it if the dry cleaners wouldn't touch the damn thing."

Casey had been terrified, humiliated, unnerved. The sergeant's words finally ignited her anger. She didn't like being here. She hadn't wanted to come. After all, wasn't she the one with everything to lose? And now that she'd actually done it, now that she'd taken that gargantuan step into the police station with her suspicions, she got this?

"I'd appreciate it if you'd at least hear me out before you jump to conclusions," she objected, stiffening in the hard, institutional chair. "Believe me, Sergeant, I have better things to do than this."

"Mass, for one," Helen said, popping off the seat again. Casey didn't even bother to apologize for pulling her right back down. The little woman landed with a plop.

"Now, you want to hear the story or not?"

Sgt. Scanlon did that little trick with his eyebrow again. "I guess so. I don't want you yanking on *me* like that."

Casey glowered. Even so, she knew better than to waste her chance.

She began with the concrete stuff. Hunsacker's arrival, Wanda's disappearance, Evelyn's death, the fights. Then she tried to logically lay out the intangibles that brought her to this stuffy little brown and green office: the looks, the odd revelations about Hunsacker's sense of revenge, his facility at lying. His conflicting attitudes toward his patients.

Casey wrapped her fingers together as she betrayed the suspicion that Hunsacker was doing more than his fair share in exam rooms. Her chest grew tight as she described her confrontations with him. Especially that last one, over the paper. She'd gone home that night and showered for thirty minutes, plagued by the feeling that he'd had his hands on her even though he'd been four feet away.

"I thought it was just me," she admitted to her thumbs. "That I just hated the guy enough to jump to conclusions. And then I found out this morning from the hospital grapevine that Dr. Hunsacker had been frequenting a hooker down on Chippewa who offered . . ." Instinctively she looked over for Helen, uncomfortable with the images she had to relate. Helen was picking through her purse like a secretary looking for a lost file. Casey turned back to see that the sergeant had taken up tapping his pen again. "Who offered services for men who liked to hurt women. And that this hooker had been killed."

She couldn't tell if she had his interest. She couldn't even tell if he'd heard any more of her story than Helen, who had retreated to her rosary. The cheap plastic beads clicked erratically in her hands, a syncopated counterpoint to the tapping of Scanlon's pen against the desk.

"And you think it was Crystal?"

Casey jerked her gaze from Helen. Sgt. Scanlon was at least back to being passive, his eyes veiled and uninformative. At least she didn't see that disdain in them anymore. Maybe she had a chance.

"I don't know. It just seemed like an odd coincidence after the conversation I had with him about murders."

"Where nothing was really said."

*Click, click, tap. Click, click, click, tap.* The damn beads sounded like skittering hail against the window. In other offices, voices muttered and growled, male voices all. Outside the windows, a fire truck howled along Tucker Boulevard and horns bleated a frustrated protest. And Sergeant Scanlon still tapped that damn pen.

"Maybe I'm presumptuous," Casey offered stiffly, her fingers aching from the hold she had on her purse. "But I don't think Dr. Hunsacker's going to boast about murder to an audience."

"But that's what you think he was doing."

*Click, click, click, tap.* "In a way that nobody could prove anything."

Silence.

"Holy Mary, mother of God, pray for us sinners now and at the hour of our death, amen."

Casey jumped. The sergeant's gaze flicked over to Helen.

"Mom," Casey admonished, fighting a deathly shiver. "To yourself."

Helen swung a guileless look Casey's way, and smiled. "Of course, dear. Are we about finished?"

"I don't know, Mom. Pretty soon."

The sergeant hadn't even had the courtesy to take out

a statement form. He was only using his pen to keep time. Casey felt the frustration well anew in her as she turned back to him.

"I haven't anybody I can talk to about this," she said. "Nobody thinks Wanda's hurt but me, and Evelyn was killed in East St. Louis, and, well . . ."

He didn't even bother to help negate the end of an uncomfortable statement. Instead he leaned back again, his eyes heavenward (revelation? instructions? maybe the manual for dealing with difficult visitors was printed on the ceiling), and rubbed his hand over his face.

That was when Casey realized how weary he looked. She should have spotted it sooner, should have connected that tight set to his face with its bad color. Of course she'd bring the most monumental problem of her problematic life to this man when he wasn't feeling like dealing with it.

"Sergeant, check my work record," she pleaded abruptly. "I'm considered a pain in the ass, but not a cookie crumbler."

She caught the direction of his look before he even cast it. Yeah, well, how *did* you explain a phenomenon like Helen?

"I'll check your work record," he promised the same way Casey promised Mr. Philman she'd check the waiting room for Martians. "Mother Mary, you said?"

"And before that St. Isidore's up in Creve Coeur."

Still no pen. Still the sense that she was being humored. At best. The sergeant was beginning to fidget, tapping on his forms as if to remind Casey that he had things to do.

Again the anger flared. "You don't believe me."

Casey could almost see him flinch. She could even read his mind. *I just about had her out the door.*

This time he actually made it to his feet. Casey'd been

right. He had a rangy body that seemed to fight the room for space.

"Ms. McDonough," he began in his best pacifying voice. It still betrayed his irritation at ending up with her. "I don't know what goes on in Arnold or East St. Louis or even on the bridges across the river. Those aren't my jurisdictions, and frankly I have enough to worry about right here. I just got dumped with a fresh homicide that involves a five-year-old and his mother. I have a backlog of seven murders my crew's working. And I do know what goes on in my jurisdiction. Crystal was a hooker with a long list of priors, a habit for crack, and a nasty pimp. It's a simple equation, and I don't feel like screwing it up with mystery doctors."

Casey followed him to her feet. "You're not even going to check into it? You're just going to write me off?"

"Casey, look at this . . ."

"Sit down, Mom." She didn't even look over. She didn't think she could afford to break eye contact with the sergeant.

"I said I'd check with your work," he insisted, one hand on his hip near where a snub-nosed gun rested in its discreet holster, the other dropping the pen to massage an area that approximated his epigastrium. "I'll even call you when we convict Crystal's pimp, so you'll feel better."

Casey shook her head. "And Wanda and Evelyn?"

"I told you," he retorted. "Not my jurisdiction."

"I can't believe it." She wasn't stunned. She was furious. Frustrated. Damn, if she'd wanted to feel like this, she would have stayed back at Mother Mary and made this confession to Tom.

For a second the sergeant watched her, assessing. Rubbing unconsciously at his stomach, his forehead taut.

"Look at that picture you brought me," he finally said, his eyes suddenly sharp as flint. "See whose arm is around your suspect? My boss. I don't need his arm around my neck, too, right now, because I suspect it would feel a lot different. So go home and forget about Dr. Jekyll there. He's not your man, and we're both just going to get into trouble if you keep pursuing this . . . and get her out of my books."

"I told you!" Helen crowed just as Casey caught her by the arm. The book in her mother's arms went flying and the rosary cascaded to the floor.

"We're going home now," Casey snapped as she picked up the lurid pink beads from the dark brown linoleum. Her voice quavered with the effort it took to control the tears. That was the problem with being emotional. Tears went with every emotion, and fury was no different. Except that men read them as a weakness, and she was going to be damned if she'd afford the good sergeant the satisfaction of reinforcing that particular stereotype.

"No," Helen objected, going after the book. "I wanted to show you this." The sergeant grabbed it before she did.

"Not now," Casey commanded. Collecting both purses, she shoved Helen's at her and spun for the door.

"One more thing," she offered, turning to see Sgt. Scanlon holding the book to him like an injured child. "I hope you're treating that ulcer with more than just Maalox."

His eyebrow lifted yet again.

Casey flashed a sour smile. "You don't keep an eye on 'em, ulcers can kill you." Then she pulled Helen out the door.

The same three officers held down the steps down-stairs, or maybe it was three different officers, interchangeable in their blue uniforms and superior attitudes. Casey barely noticed the wide-eyed surprise on their faces as she swept past them, Helen in tow. She didn't see that the sun had broken clear of the morning cloud cover, or that it sparkled on the glass high-rises north and east. In her rush to get as far away from that condescending son of a bitch on the fourth floor, she almost dragged Helen right in front of a paddy wagon.

"Why did we leave?" Helen whined, still trying to pull away as they crossed Clark to get back to their car. "It's not polite, Catherine. I didn't even get to say good-bye."

Casey slung her purse out of the way and dug into her pockets for keys, her other hand still on Helen. "We had to go, Mom."

"We did not. I still had a thing or two to say to that charlatan."

"You didn't have anything to say," Casey snapped, the fury still bubbling too close. "God, no wonder he didn't believe me with you rooting around in his things. I might as well have walked in with a joy buzzer and a big red nose."

She was going to have to do it alone. She was going to have to find out about Hunsacker herself, because no one else was going to believe her. Not with Hunsacker in possession of that award-winning smile and Casey left with nothing more than supposition and enough eccentricity surrounding her to qualify her for a circus license.

It was a symptom of how cornered she felt that Casey forgot to restrain her tongue. "Come on," she demanded, giving Helen another yank to keep them ahead of the traffic that was bearing down from the highway. "Let's get you back to prayers and me back to reality."

Still only three fourths of the way across the street, Helen pulled to a sudden halt. It happened so fast, Casey was almost pulled off her feet.

"Damn it," she cried, whirling on the little women. "What do you think you're doing? I said come on!"

"Getting your attention."

Casey finally faced her mother. The two of them were ten feet from the curb, and traffic was bearing down on them fast. Horns sounded. Air brakes whined. But all Casey could see was Helen.

Helen was mad.

"How dare you?" she demanded, more fire in her eyes than Casey had seen in years. "Who do you think I am, a child? A dog to be dragged along on a leash?"

Casey barely heard the grind of gears as a truck closed in. She didn't see the policemen on the steps turn her way, poised for intervention.

She only saw her mother. Leave it to Helen to wait until they were in the middle of a busy city street to surprise her.

"You think you can just tote me around to your rounds without explaining? Without asking my permission or warning me? That was a police station we were in, Catherine. A police station. But you didn't tell me why we were going. You just expect me to sit quietly by like a child and wait till you're finished and then trudge home without asking questions?"

Casey flushed with sudden shame. Helen was absolutely right. It had been getting so difficult lately to think of her mother as anything more than a weight. A chore. "I'm sorry," she admitted, her voice hushed. "I didn't mean to hurt you. I'm just . . ."

"Frustrated," Helen finished, finally walking on toward the car and relieving the officers of their need to leave their cozy niche. "I know. I'm sorry he wouldn't listen to you. Because you're right."

Casey stared. "What do you mean I'm right?"

Helen just took a considering look at the flat gray sky

and smiled. "I wonder if I could have seen the sun dance at Fatima."

Book closed, cognizance vanished. She'd done it again. Left Casey standing out in the street in stunned silence, wondering just how much Helen heard and understood. Wondering what the hell she'd been talking about, whether she'd really comprehended the situation or just had a message from one of her saints. Or the sun. Whichever danced better.

But Casey didn't have time to worry about it. A semi was headed straight for her, and Helen waited by the car door to be let in.

More importantly, Hunsacker had to be stopped. And Casey was the only one around to do it. The sergeant had been a test, and she'd failed it. If he didn't believe her, nobody would. And it was obvious that he didn't believe her. Not only that, he didn't care. Casey was going to go into this fight all alone.

Dodging the last lane of traffic, Casey unlocked her car and let Helen in for the ride back home.

"And if he isn't a priest," Helen challenged without warning, "why did they call him the Bishop?" Then she retreated to her beads.

The sun washed the street, and a breeze lifted the litter in a dance. The day promised to be a real beauty. Casey cursed all the way home.

The fourth floor was quiet. The guys in juvy had headed off to lunch, and Brackman and Davis were off in search of a warrant. Down the hall Scanlon could hear the drone of a radio from the lieutenant's office, and farther along the stutter of computer keys from burglary, but for all intents and purposes, he was alone.

He had the field team's reports on the Washington murders to go over. He had to try to track down the chain of ownership on a gun used in a homicide six months earlier that had just turned up in a drug raid. He had to clean off all that crap on his desk as punishment for refusing to close three unpopular cases. Instead he sat at Dawson's desk with a newspaper clipping in his hand.

The steady tap-tap of his pen accompanied his observation. His gut was nagging him. Not the fire that had taken up residence just behind his rib cage in the last few months, his police gut. The one that got him so many arrests. The one that got him into so much trouble.

Crystal Johnson's file was back on his desk waiting for the autopsy report to come in, but he didn't turn for it. He stared at the grainy likenesses of the two men in tuxes. He thought of the absurdity of Casey McDonough's allegations. He tried his damnedest to do the smart thing and toss the clipping in the trash.

The fire burned higher in his chest. All he wanted to do was lay his head down on the desk and catch twenty or thirty years of sleep. Better yet, get in his car and not stop driving until he could sleep on a beach. Instead he pushed back his chair and climbed to his feet again. He began rubbing, as if it would ease the pain, wishing on an empty lamp for relief. It was time for lunch.

Scanlon had been brown-bagging it for a few weeks now, preferring his own company to the crowd down at Crown Candy since he couldn't eat the chili there anyway. His lunch waited in the pocket of his jacket where it hung on the coatrack.

He didn't even bother checking the hallway. One hand still full of clipping, he reached into his pocket and pulled out a can of Busch. He needed a cigarette, too, but he'd managed to give those up after the divorce.

Scanlon popped the can one-handed. Then, his attention still on those two smiling faces, he finished half the

contents of the can in one long pull. He didn't even notice the immediate flare underneath the can as he rubbed
absently at his midsection. He was too involved with con-
cepts like futility and common sense and survival. The
futility of bucking the system, the common sense of not
trying, the survival of those who don't. And, conversely,
the constant trouble for those, like Scanlon, who could
never seem to learn those fine lessons. Because he was
about to put his feet right in it again.

"Shit," he complained in a mournful voice, his forehead tight again, his eyes on his mayor. "Shit."

He did check the hall this time. It was still empty, the
eighty-year-old linoleum neatly telegraphing visitors.
Setting the can on his desk, he bent to his drawer and
opened it. Still watching for witnesses, he rifled around
beneath his phone books and procedure manuals and
dragged out a bottle of Maalox.

Scanlon didn't bother with measurements anymore.
He simply lifted the bottle and slugged until he felt the
cool fall of chalk soothe the frayed edges of his stomach.
Then capping the bottle again, he slipped it back into its
hiding place.

He took a moment to weigh his options, taking his
lunch back in one hand and the mayor in the other. He
thought of the alimony check, the hope for a quiet career
left to his own devices in homicide, and the chances he'd
end up pulling dawn patrol up in Little Beirut instead.
He thought of how tired he was already.

Tipping his head back, he finished lunch. Scanlon
scowled at it, scowled at the crumpled paper in his grasp.
Scowled at his unfortunate sense of right and wrong.

"Damn it to hell," he snarled, throwing the empty can
into the trashbasket with a resounding clang. "Wouldn't
it be just my luck if she were right?"

# Chapter 7

*SO, HOW EXACTLY* did one go about proving that a person was a murderer? Casey was sure if she were a cop she'd have some kind of game plan. They probably had a checklist, just like the one the hospital used for pre-op patients to assure that everything had been done in the right order. Consent form signed, check; pre-op medication given, check; false teeth out and catheter in, check. Evidence collected from scene, check; witnesses interviewed, check; body to morgue, check; no comment given to press, check.

Casey wasn't even good at the organizational patterns needed for nursing. It was why she was so perfect for the ER. Since she had no routine, surprises didn't bother her. Her sense of order was an instinctive thing, her approach to disease and trauma almost like rearranging a badly laid-out puzzle, rather than solving an algebra problem.

She had a feeling, though, that murder was more algebra than geometry. So, how was she supposed to go about collecting the facts she needed to nail Hunsacker? How would she even get enough to impress just one set of police involved? Did she talk to people about Wanda first, or Evelyn, or Crystal? And how did she do it and keep a low profile, so she didn't tip her hand?

Her answer came to her like a gift the next night about ten. She'd just inherited a couple of bikers from a fight in Jefferson County. Both arrived on their stomachs, hands cuffed behind their backs, and leather and chains setting up a racket like a cattle drive.

Evidently there had been a disagreement involving a woman. Billy and Vern had settled it in the time-honored fashion, broken beer bottles and pool cues. They'd also put the bartender in intensive care, which brought out the Jefferson County detectives.

Billy had just expressed a singularly unkind opinion of Casey, which seemed to include a goodly amount of spittle and bad aim. Fully dressed in protective gear to wallow around Billy's blood, Casey took hold of what was left of Billy's hair and held his head very still against her cart.

"Don't fuck with me, boy," she growled, goggle to rheumy eye, knowing from long experience just what it took to get a mean drunk's attention. "You're tied down and I'm not. Besides, nobody likes you here. They're not going to say anything if I sew your lips to the cart."

"That's a fact, Billy," a voice drawled from the doorway.

Startled, Casey looked up. She'd been joined by a gentleman in white shirt and brown polyester slacks that needed either a tighter belt, less stomach, or more butt. He didn't need a badge to be identified.

"Cooperate, you pile of lard," he advised, setting his clipboard down by the sink to give Casey a hand, "or I'll have to ask the lady to step out and we'll discuss your manners in private."

For a blinding moment, her hand still entwined in greasy, bloody hair and her face close enough to be able to enjoy Billy's exotic scent, Casey completely forgot him. Her mind was back in that office downtown, with that smug bastard talking jurisdictions. Well, maybe Jefferson County wasn't part of his jurisdiction, but it was sure part of hers.

"When we're finished here," she offered to the detective with a bright smile, "allow me to buy you a cup of coffee."

"Wild Woman?" Detective Jarvis Franklin echoed, directing a stream of smoke at the ceiling and shaking his head. "Nope. Not a word. You know her?"

Doing her best to appear nonchalant, Casey propped her feet on a table and settled back to take a sip of her coffee. Billy was in the process of entertaining the X-ray staff with his sparkling personality, but the rest of the work lane was in chaos. Casey should have been out helping. But she couldn't pass up a golden opportunity like this.

"I worked up at St. Isidore's before coming here," she acknowledged. "Wild Woman was legend. I had the privilege of doing the town with her once."

Detective Franklin proffered a grin. "Yeah, she's a good ole girl. Too bad for Buddy."

Casey made it a point to shake her head. "I can't believe Wanda didn't even drop him a note. She really seemed to love Buddy."

That provoked a rather indifferent shrug. "That's what Buddy keeps sayin'. Ya ask me? He was probably a little free with his hand, and she decided to do somethin' about it."

"Buddy's still bothering you, huh?"

Another shrug, another long pull from his cigarette. "Down to the station at least twice a week. Won't do any good. All Buddy's gonna get back from this is that car."

Casey straightened a little. "You found her car?" It was a black Firebird, souped up and mean, Wanda's pride and joy. Casey couldn't imagine her leaving it behind, even if it had been Elvis who'd walked in that door to the Ramblin' Rose.

Franklin nodded. "Right where we expected it, the parking lot of the Ramblin' Rose. They remember her bein' in there that night, but can't say as to who she left with. They do remember she was going through her paycheck pretty fast with some lounge lizard, and that she told him she was leavin' the trailer life behind—quite a few times."

"A lounge lizard?"

"One of the regulars. Guy named Bobby Lee who swears up and down he left Wanda at the door singing' 'Love Me Tender.' "

For a moment Casey satisfied herself with listening to the chatter of the paging system, the trundling of the portable X-ray machine down toward room one where they had a new chest pain. She took a deliberate sip of her coffee, trying to time her question with an eye toward offhand consideration, afraid of the step she was taking. She was at work, after all. Anyone could find out what she was doing. Anyone could innocently carry her odd questions back to Hunsacker.

She must have been thinking too loudly. Casey had no sooner looked up to check the door yet again, willing it to stay shut, when it swung open. She jumped, sloshing coffee onto her lap. Her heart skidded. She was sure that she was obvious, that Wanda's name would trigger some kind of instinctive understanding in whoever came in that door. That it would be Hunsacker himself.

It was Barb.

"Having fun?" she asked, an eyebrow arched as she took in the elevated feet and the steaming cup of coffee.

"I'm having a cigarette," Casey said with a smile, turning Barb's frequent excuse against her. She was going to hyperventilate, she just knew it. Barb had been listening in. She had to have been. She'd tell Hunsacker how Casey had asked about Wanda, and he'd figure a way to get Casey fired. Casey just wasn't cut out for this stuff.

Barb scowled. "Have you seen Miller?"

Intent on finishing her coffee, Casey shook her head. "Nope."

Go away. Leave me alone to finish finding out about Wanda. Let me get this over, and I promise I'll never conduct clandestine affairs at work again.

"By the way," Barb announced as an afterthought. "Dr. Hunsacker's coming down for room ten."

Casey nodded. Her cup almost slid out of suddenly sweaty palms. Her chest ached from the effort to stay calm. She felt like a woman entertaining her lover and hearing her husband's key in the front door. Who said this kind of stuff was exciting, anyway?

Barb was out the door by seconds before Casey turned back to Franklin where he was busy aiming smoke rings for the smoke alarm.

"Tell me something," she said, trying her best to sound dispassionate, his answers already beginning to set up a dance of new questions in her. "What if Buddy's right? What if Wanda didn't run off?"

Franklin shrugged again, evidently his expression for all occasions. "Then I'd have to let Buddy call me an idiot." He shot Casey a wry smile that allowed for understanding between two professionals who saw much more of the world than civilians. "But I don't see that happenin'."

"What do you mean I'm overdressed?"

Her attention on the road ahead, Casey offered a

scowl. "We're going to the Ramblin' Rose, Poppi. Not high tea at the Savoy."

Poppi took a second to consider the tea-length, flowered dress and fringed scarf she wore. "You said we were going for a drink," she protested. "You didn't say anything about needing a tattoo and a muscle shirt. And why do I have to come along anyway?"

Casey hit the blinker and slowed into the right-hand lane. "You think I want to go in this place alone?"

Poppi looked around her as even the road deteriorated into potholes and dust and the scenery toward river scrub. The houses were clapboard or mobile lifted on pilings, the preponderance of stores dealing in liquor and guns.

"Heavy," she breathed, the same way she did on a bad trip. "You also didn't tell my why we're doing this."

"Because the police won't."

"And they have guns," Poppi countered evenly.

The Ramblin' Rose was popular even in the afternoon, the gravel lot in front of the shingled ex-VFW post sprinkled with pickup trucks and dented American-made cars. Casey saw more than one HUNGRY? EAT YOUR IMPORT bumper sticker, and was glad she'd thought to drive the old Ford her mother kept in the garage. Swinging in behind a couple of four-bys, she cut the ignition and considered her next step.

"It seemed a good idea at the time," Poppi offered laconically.

Casey had to grin. "Something like that. Ready?"

"For what? Love on a pool table? I'm not sure."

"Finding Wanda's murderer."

Before Poppi could object, Casey opened her door and climbed out of the car. She'd made it a point to dress for the occasion. Jeans, boots, and T-shirt. Simple and unassuming. She hoped she could get what she'd come for and no more. She'd never been to the Ramblin' Rose without Wanda before, and that had been quite a while ago. And now she was here with Annie Hall.

The inside of the Rose was decorated in early Formica, with about six tables, a pool table, and a big-screen TV that was tuned to wrestling. The bar was left over from the VFW, drab and functional in pressboard, the walls gray and hung in bar mirrors, and the shelves lined in beer cans of the world. Casey remembered the menu as being whiskey or beer, with a hamburger or hot dog chaser, and peanuts for hors d'oeuvres. She remembered the clientele as rough. Nothing, it seemed, had changed.

When the bartender caught sight of the two women walking in, he looked behind them for an explanation. When they took up seats at his bar, he cleared his throat.

"Hi," Casey greeted him, remembering him from the time she'd been here with Wanda. The owner, she thought, a pasty, underweight chronic lunger who had been especially enamored of Wanda. "Could we get a couple o' drafts?"

Poppi settled herself on the stool alongside, and wisely kept her silence.

Casey took a look in the mirror to see that several of the players behind her were nudging and leering. She saw two women, neither of whom boasted a full set of teeth or a bra, but she didn't feel any assistance there. She was definitely an outsider. A glaring outsider amid people who didn't care much for the breed.

She did her best to ignore the hollow uneasiness in her stomach. "I've met you before," she said to the bartender as he handed over her drinks. "Charlie, right?"

"Clyde."

She grinned. "Yeah, well, my memory for names is shit. I'm Casey. I came in with Wanda Trigel a couple of times. I used to work with her—well, kind of. In the same hospital."

The bartender immediately unearthed a kind of smile that involved one eyebrow and the middle of his upper lip. "You know Wanda?"

Casey nodded. "She taught me how to tie a cherry stem into a knot with my tongue."

Poppi's eyes widened noticeably, and her first taste of beer was a large one. Still, she kept quiet.

The bartender was grinning with what was left of his own teeth. "That's Wanda all right. You heard from her lately?"

Casey's smile was wistful, even though her heart was galloping again. She felt as if she'd just gone over the top on a Ferris wheel. Maybe this stuff wasn't so bad after all. She took a pull from her own drink before answering, and wiped the side of her mouth with her hand.

"I was kinda hopin' I'd catch up with her here. I heard she left Buddy."

Elbows on the bar, the bartender leaned much too close. It was his way of expressing sincerity. "We haven't heard from her, either. You know Buddy?"

Casey shrugged a little, wishing she could escape the man's breath. "Met him. He seemed nice enough."

She got a nod for an answer. "He is. He's real broke up over this."

"Cop told me that he thought Buddy hit her. What do you think?"

Clyde considered that pretty funny. "Sure he hit her. But after growing up a Millard, she knew how to take a punch."

Casey just nodded. Not much to say about that.

"I don't know," she mused, sipping at her beer and shaking her head. "It just doesn't figure for me, somehow. That's kinda why I came looking to talk to Wanda."

"What don't figure?"

Casey leaned a little herself. "Do you really think Wanda'd just take off like that?"

Clyde straightened a little, looked at Casey as if she were a couple bricks shy. "Sure."

Bad tack to take. Casey waved him off and redirected her question. "No, that's not what I meant. Do you think she'd do it and not at least let Buddy know why?"

"Well, she is impulsive. High-strung, ya know. And she was sayin' something about leaving the trailer. You know how much she wanted a real big house and a garage for her car."

Another arguable point. But Casey had the trump card that nobody seemed to have thought to play. She played it. "Yeah, but would she leave her Firebird behind?"

That brought Clyde straight upright. He looked up to the ceiling, obviously stretching for some thought processes. Maybe it was the gender, Casey thought, stifling her excitement as she remembered Scanlon watching the station ceiling much the same way. They had to look for their ideas. Or maybe they just had to lift their brains a little ways to get them to work.

Without a word, Clyde turned and drew himself a beer. Then he finished it in one long gulp and turned back to Casey, astonished.

"Not," he assured her, "if Elvis himself offered her a ride in his limousine."

"Clyde," Casey said, forcing herself to lean close again. "I've heard Buddy's been hassling the police to find her. I hear he thinks something's happened to her. What if he's right?"

"If he's right," he echoed, his expression suddenly dark, "the Millard boys'll be happy to take care of the slime who might o' done it."

Even Casey had too weak a stomach to consider that.

"The police won't look for her," she nudged with a tinge of outrage. "Maybe her friends should."

"It'd sure show them pussies, now wouldn't it?"

Casey couldn't think of any more appropriate answer than a nod. Now was the time she needed to take the newspaper out of her purse, but she held back, afraid. Wanting too much for Clyde to answer all her questions right here and now by recognizing the picture. Knowing he wouldn't and putting off the inevitable.

But she had no other reason to stay except another beer, and Casey wasn't encouraged by the looks she was intercepting in the mirror from a couple of the pool players. It was put up or shut up in more ways than one. Besides, she couldn't think of any way to bring the alleged lounge lizard into the conversation without sounding like a pussy cop herself.

"Well hey, Clyde. Thanks for the beer. If you do go looking for Wanda, you'll let me know, won't you?" Pulling her purse around, Casey unzipped it and began digging for cash. Her wallet, checkbook, and hairbrush ended up on the counter before she managed to flip the clipping out almost into Clyde's hands.

"Oh, shit, what's that doing in there?" she demanded, swinging on Poppi. "Did you put that in my purse?"

"Not me," Poppi answered evenly.

Clyde picked it up to hand back to her, curiosity nudging his attention toward the picture of the mayor and Hunsacker.

"See that asshole?" Casey demanded, pointing to Hunsacker's smiling face. "Remember that face. He's one of the biggest stiffs in the business."

"Looks like a pussy," he commented.

"Asshole stiffed me on a date," she complained, pointing again. "He's a doctor who worked with Wanda. Took us out for drinks a couple a times and then had his beeper go off before the check came. He ever done that here?"

"In that outfit?" Clyde demanded with a barking laugh.

Casey scowled. "Hardly."

"Never seen him here. Only men Wanda hangs around with here are regulars."

Casey gave the picture another tap. "He likes country western places. Don't be surprised if you see him. And don't say I didn't warn you."

"I won't," Clyde promised, finally accepting the payment for the beers. He never noticed that the picture went right back into Casey's purse with all her other equipment.

"Hey there, sweet thing, how 'bout a game?"

Casey stiffened. She was being addressed by a skinny man with a cue in his hand. She could only hope from the amount of grease he sported that he was on a lunch break from a local garage.

"I don't play pool." She smiled a little hesitantly as she slid off the stool. Behind her, Poppi did likewise. They were no more than ten feet from the door.

He grinned with teeth the color of moss. "I ain't talkin' 'bout pool."

Casey smiled in return and began backing out the door. "Thanks anyway," she demurred, hearing the door squeak in Poppi's hand and praying for sunlight. "Maybe next time."

"A wonderful example of my new game," Poppi said evenly as she punched her car door lock into place a few minutes later.

Casey's eyes were alternately on the parking lot exit and the Rose's door, which thankfully remained closed in their wake. "What?"

"Nirvana," Poppi answered, snapping home her seat

belt. "Can't you just see it? You land on the CEO square.
You decide to close a plant and put a thousand people
out of work so you can increase your profit margins and
buy more prestige. Oh, no, wrong answer. You die and
come back as a lower life form. The guy with the pool
cue and the axle grease between his teeth would do
nicely, don't you think?"

Casey's laughter was explosive. She had a lot of pent-
up tension to relieve after tap-dancing her way through
that bar. "All right," she conceded. "It is a great idea.
You have my money."

Casey felt like laughing all the way back to Webster.
Poppi settled for a smug grin.

"A cherry stem?" she asked with some incredulity a
moment later.

Casey laughed at that, too. "Catch me at the next party.
It's a real nice icebreaker."

"I was hoping you'd show that guy from the pool
table."

"So was he."

Casey found Highway 55 and turned north for the
Meramec River and St. Louis County. She was still tin-
gling with the excitement, the feeling not unlike having
a surprise trauma code at work, dancing along the edge
of disaster, running solely on practice and instinct and
knowing that it would take less than a funny blink to lose
the whole game.

She hadn't won. Winning would have been getting
Clyde to gasp in recognition when he saw Hunsacker's
picture. But at least she'd made it out of there without
blowing it. She'd gotten Clyde to think a little more
about Wanda's disappearance. She'd gotten reassurance
that her instincts about Wanda weren't so far off.

Evens wasn't so bad.

"Did you think up that trick with the newspaper ahead

of time?" Poppi asked, rolling her window down a little and letting the wind in.

"No," Casey said, her voice still laced with adrenaline.

Poppi grinned, shaking her head. "Good. It stunk."

Casey laughed again. "Yeah," she admitted. "It did, didn't it? Good thing I'm a nurse and not a cop."

When Poppi looked over to answer, her eyes weren't quite as bright or exhilarated. "Try and keep that in mind, okay?"

Casey thought of that the next afternoon when she walked onto the work lane. She was still a little pumped up, still surprised that she'd gotten away with her impulsive gamble. After getting back the day before, she'd tried her best to make a list of things about Hunsacker that unnerved her, and what she could do to connect him to three unconnected murders.

If anybody saw that little list, they'd think she'd lost one of her oars. Casey knew she was dealing in intangibles. She knew she was fighting an uphill battle. But she felt righteous. At least she was trying to figure out why people she knew had died. At least she wasn't sitting on her jurisdiction and doing nothing.

Which was why she had to run right into Hunsacker the minute she got to work.

She was on her way to the time clock, her arms full with purse and bag and lunch. Since the morning had been taken up with chapel cleaning, Casey had delayed her planning session until the drive into work. She was on the problem of how to get information out of the labor and delivery crew at Izzy's when she pulled open the door to the back hall and almost bumped right into Hunsacker.

Casey stopped dead in her tracks. She'd been so smug

the day before, felt as if she were invincible, irrefutable. She was a crusader, and Hunsacker was the infidel.

Suddenly she was the target. She gasped, clutched her paraphernalia to her chest like a life preserver. Yesterday Hunsacker couldn't touch her. Today he knew everything she'd ever suspected. He'd instinctively guessed all her secrets, and was going to punish her for them.

It took Casey a full few seconds to realize that he hadn't even recognized her. He was in scrubs, but not the scrubs he usually wore. Not neat and pressed and somehow pretentious, like old school colors. Today they were crumpled and bloody and sweaty. A mask hung by one tie from his neck, and his cap swung from his hand. His eyes, which had always seemed so cunning and sly, were hollow. Dead.

He stumbled to a stop, a hand out as if he were having trouble seeing, faltering a little before he even looked down to find Casey trembling before him.

"Oh," he muttered, "I'm sorry. I . . ."

Tears? Casey couldn't believe it. His eyes glittered with them.

"Dr. Hunsacker," she said, well-honed instincts forcing a hand out to steady him, "are you okay?"

He refocused his attention on her, and Casey felt more troubled. He looked the picture of a soul in torment, and that was a sight Casey never thought she'd see. Her chest, still tight with the terror of exposure, hurt worse with the shock of sympathy.

Hunsacker still hadn't moved. He couldn't seem to drag his gaze away from Casey, nor could he seem to call up any comprehension.

"I'm . . . uh, sorry," he apologized, his hand out to her arm. Casey was stunned by the feel of perspiration on his palm. "Bad day in surgery. I'm just . . . tired."

He wandered away before she could question him.

Head down, shuffling, the paper booties making scuffing noises on the floor. It wasn't until he'd turned the corner toward the doctor's lounge that Casey finally roused herself and finished her business.

The lounge was crowded by the time she made it in. Cigarette smoke hung like a pall over the small room. The secondhand chairs were filled, and the BOHICA boards being perused. The microwave dinged and one of the day nurses pulled out her late lunch.

". . . just heard from the OR crew. She was only fifteen. He was devastated."

Casey's sonar picked right up on the conversation. She didn't want to hear this, but somehow she already knew who they were talking about. Dropping her bag in the corner, she edged over to the knot of people by the refrigerator.

"Who's devastated?" she asked.

Janice, Barb, and Millie looked up.

"Dale," Barb allowed, her use of his first name almost possessive. "Day shift had a young girl with a ruptured tubal pregnancy. Mother denied the girl was pregnant at all until too late. Dale lost her on the table just a little while ago. He picked up the case when Bellamy wouldn't touch it because the girl didn't have insurance."

"Bellamy should die of impacted hemorrhoids," Millie vowed.

Everyone nodded. Casey wanted to say something about seeing Hunsacker in the hall. With anyone else she might have, testifying to the shattering effect of the girl's death on him, commiserating about what hell it was when a good doc lost a tough patient.

With Hunsacker she couldn't. She couldn't get the words of sympathy out. Her chest still stung with it. She could still vividly see the torment in his eyes, the broken shamble of his gait. It was a picture she'd seen before, on good docs, the ones who cared, the ones who took the losses personally and broke their friends' hearts with their pain.

But she couldn't allow it on Hunsacker. She didn't want to feel sorry for him. She didn't want to think of him as human, as fragile, as feeling. She didn't want to have anything to do with the guilt that was already building right behind that ache of empathy in her.

Damn it, just when she was so sure. He had to come along and make her question.

She didn't feel much different by the time she got home that night. The shift hadn't been a busy one, which just meant she had more time to listen to the details of Tammy Whittaker's death. It was a bad death, avoidable but for a mother and an insensitive doctor, leaving Tammy's uncomfortable young ghost hovering over the building. Like Navajos chanting against ghost sickness, the staff told and retold her story, purging outrage, guilt, and shame for the loss of such a young life. They laid blame and offered praise, and except for the frantic nursing crews who had physically held back her death with their hands, the only praise to be allotted this time belonged to Hunsacker.

He'd fought harder, cursed louder, and prayed more desperately than anybody. Stricken OR nurses, over in the ER to share coffee and grief, shook their heads and recounted the final, desperate moments when Hunsacker had sponged and clamped and sweated and screamed, "Damn you, you're not dying on me!"

He hadn't even allowed them to finish their code in surgical ICU as protocol demanded. Operating-room mortality rates were kept down by stapling a dying person shut and pumping on their chest just as far as the ICU to lay the blame on other doors. Hunsacker had told the anesthesiologist to get fucked when he suggested that it was time to do just that. He hadn't given up until he'd held her heart in his hands and known that even that wouldn't convince it to start again.

Children were lost in hospitals. They were never given up easily. By the time the Mother Mary staff finally laid Tammy to rest, they also etched another chapter into the Hunsacker legend.

Casey had listened to all the talk, thought of the weight on Hunsacker's shoulders when she'd seen him, the blood of that child still staining him, and began to wonder.

How could he be the monster she'd thought? If he was really callous enough to murder women who argued with him, would he be capable of losing so much with the death of a patient? If he played control games, abusing patients without their even knowing it, would he be able to turn around and fight such a selfless fight?

Could she be wrong? Could she be investing him with traits only she saw? She hadn't liked him from the moment she'd met him. Would she have manufactured conspiracy where there was only coincidence?

By the time she pulled into her driveway Casey throbbed with contradictions. She hadn't eaten, but she felt sick, unsure suddenly of her own sense, afraid that after all this time she was projecting old memories onto an innocent man. Could a person have post traumatic stress syndrome when the only disaster had been domestic? she wondered. Were her convictions about Hunsacker nothing more than flashbacks?

She'd come to a complete stop, waiting to turn off the car until the Moody Blues answered the question of balance. She felt tired and listless and unwilling to face the lights that were on inside her house.

That was when she realized another car was in her

driveway. Her headlights highlighted it, dark enough to be black, gleaming and sharp. A vintage '67 Mustang convertible, polished and cared for like a bright child, the white top ghostly in the night.

Casey's attention swung back to the house lights. Helen was entertaining somebody in the living room. Casey could see the lights, couldn't see the shadows. She couldn't imagine who was in there. She hadn't known anybody with a Mustang since she'd been out of high school.

Only one way to find out. Switching off the Moodies midsentence, she gathered together her paraphernalia and climbed out of her car. The night was muggy, creeping into the polyester of her uniform like a stale aftertaste. Casey's head ached and her stomach churned. The last thing she felt like was visitors. The last thing she could imagine was who would be so inclined to put up with Helen at eleven o'clock at night.

There was no way she could have anticipated what she found.

Deciding that the front door was the quickest route to an answer, Casey climbed the front porch, her crepe soles swallowing her footsteps. She saw Helen standing before the picture wall in the living room. She couldn't see who she was addressing as she lifted a hand to one of the exhibits. She heard the rumble of an answer, though, and knew it was male.

Both of them came to a surprised halt when she opened the front door. Catching sight of Helen's guest, Casey followed suit. She didn't exactly drop her bags to the floor, but she forgot she had them in her hands. Her eyes were riveted to the man who stood next to the piano on the old oriental rug, a glass of iced tea in his hand, his greeting made hesitant by his exposure to her mother.

Casey's greeting wasn't in the least hesitant. "What are you doing here?" she demanded, and finally remembered to walk in.

# Chapter 8

*HIS STOMACH WAS* killing him. The last few days had been unrelenting frustration, from the moment these two women had left his office to the last interview he'd conducted at nine-thirty down on the stroll. He'd stood in on the Washington autopsies, even though one look at the scene photos had pretty much told the stories. He'd come up empty on witnesses who might tell him what everybody knew, that Cleona's husband had slashed her and her little boy in a fit of crack-induced rage. He'd lost the trail on the gun in the Gray shooting, and fought without success to get a court order for a search on one of the suspects. When he'd come up empty on Crystal tonight, he decided that the only way to complete a perfect evening was a visit with the McDonough ladies.

Only one of them looked glad to see him.

"And this," the little old one said, plucking at his sleeve and pointing to yet another sepia-toned photo on her long white wall, "is Amelia. She was a teacher, you know."

This had to be her house, all shiny surfaces, chintz, and doilies. Scanlon couldn't imagine the younger one having much patience with the Sacred Heart pictures scattered about, the bisque Madonnas with plump, placid faces, and the pile of Liguorian magazines on the table.

And the incense. Scanlon could swear he smelled it, and that was an odor he'd remember in hell, pungent and ancient and mystical. He'd actually looked around when he'd come in the door, afraid he'd see a red votive light betraying a hidden altar. He'd only seen the pictures. Maybe the old lady swung a thurible at them like a Taoist praising ancestors or something.

"I came to talk to you about Crystal," Jack told the daughter where she stood at wary attention.

She hadn't moved from the doorway, braced like a sailor in a high wind with a look of outrage in her eyes. Somehow in the uniform she didn't look as distracted and ineffectual as she had the other day. There was a wiriness to her, a tough determination that reminded Jack of some of the female cops he knew.

"I think I need a beer first," she said without apology. Casting an eye at the iced tea, she lifted an eyebrow. "Interested?"

Scanlon took a look down himself. "Yeah, thanks."

She dropped her gear right there in the doorway and stalked into the kitchen. Left behind, Scanlon was once again commanded to the family album.

"And the twins," the old lady was saying, her voice bright and chirpy. "They both died in childbirth, bless them. They were such lovely, frail things."

Scanlon did his best to cut the soliloquy short. "This all your family?" he asked with a vague gesture of his glass.

"Oh, yes." She sighed with a smile to the collected faces. "All mine. I remember when I bought each one."

Scanlon had just noticed the black woman on the wall up toward the ceiling when he heard that. He looked down at the top of that scarfed head. "Bought them?"

Mrs. McDonough bestowed a beatific smile on him. "Of course. I've collected my family for years. Garage sales are the best places to find them. And book sales, of course."

Scanlon couldn't come up with any better answer than "Uh huh."

He was vastly relieved to see a can of beer appear before him.

The younger Ms. McDonough also offered the wryest of smiles. "Mother has no family of her own, so she collected one. Didn't you, Mom?"

"God gave them to me," she answered in that vague way of hers. "I was just showing them to the father here."

"I'm not—"

"He's a sergeant," her daughter interrupted impatiently. "Not a priest."

The old lady faced right off with her daughter as if Jack weren't even there. "Then why did you call him a bishop?" she demanded.

Both of them turned to him then. Jack scowled, weighed the beer against the tea, and decided that he was going to have to face this one without fortification.

"Past transgressions," he admitted.

The daughter's eyebrow lifted again. "You were a priest?"

"Not diocesan," the old lady insisted vehemently. "It would be sacrilege. He was reading one of those Dutch heretics."

"Jesuit," he admitted.

Both of them stared.

"Oh, my," the little lady breathed.

"Oh, brother," her daughter echoed.

For a minute the three of them just stood there. Jack

finally set the tea down on a doily and concentrated on
his beer.

"Beautiful piano," he observed, motioning stiffly to
the baby grand in the corner. "Do you play?"

The young woman darted a quick look in that direction. "No. That was my brother Benny's talent. I just
dust the thing."

"Your—"

She actually managed a wry smile. "Genetic, not ac-
quired."

Little Mrs. McDonough stiffened a little. Jack recognized the pose and knew better than to pursue it. All that
was left was business. He took a good enough slug of
beer to ignite new fires and faced the daughter.

"Would you like to sit for a minute, Ms. McDonough?"

She seemed amused. "I should have probably said that
first." Even so, she sat on the couch. The mother fluttered for a bit and then alighted onto the other end. Jack
decided not to stand. He wasn't after intimidation here,
just expediency. He chose the wingback, and perched on
the edge.

"I was down on the stroll tonight," he said without
preamble, the beer resting on a knee, his jacket unbuttoned. It occurred to him that he should have left his tie
in the car. Pulling it off in this atmosphere would be like
stripping for Sunday dinner at Aunt Rosa's. Quelling the
discomfort, he got the bad news over with. "Nobody recognized your doctor."

Jack was surprised by Ms. McDonough's reaction. He
expected frustration, maybe contention. What he got was
relief. He was sure of it. She'd been bracing herself for
something, and he hadn't given it to her. Nobody could
accuse her of having a poker face, and within seconds of
his announcement, no fewer than five reactions passed

over it, any number of them adding up to confusion. "You don't think it could be him?"

Hope? He couldn't figure it at all. "It's still pointing right at her pimp. There's one more possible witness who's skipped, but since it's one of the pimp's ex-stable girls, I expect her to name him. Nobody else down there placed the picture of your man."

She seemed to fold into herself a little. Fingering the can on her lap, she gave her attention to the crowd on the wall, as if culling opinions.

"You came all the way out here to tell me," she said, turning back to him. "You didn't even take down my name the other day."

Jack was tempted to do his own perusal of the adopted McDonoughs. "I called Mother Mary. Commendations for initiative and complaints about initiative. But you were right," he allowed. "No recorded flights of fancy. I try never to overlook the possibility of a legitimate lead."

That appeased her. Still, she seemed to be fighting some internal battle. Jack was smart enough to wait it out in silence. Over on her end of the couch, the mother kept her own counsel, her eyes raised and unfocused. Probably praying for his Jesuit soul. A cat had made its appearance, a fat, gray thing with yellow eyes. Mrs. McDonough didn't seem to notice it rubbing against her bare leg.

"You're not discounting Hunsacker completely," Casey finally stated.

"I never discount anything completely," he said. "I just got the idea the other day that you were gonna head off on some kind of crusade, and I don't think you should lose your job over it. There isn't any evidence that says your doctor killed Crystal."

There wasn't any physical evidence at all, which stuck

hard in Jack's craw. No prints, no hairs or fibers. Somebody had beaten Crystal to death and then vacuumed, showing more presence of mind than Jack had ever credited Moses Willis with. But that was something he'd decided didn't need sharing with the ladies from Webster Groves.

Ms. McDonough eyed him, sharp as a lawyer, almost predatory. "You have a nice car."

Jack arched an eyebrow. "Thanks."

"If you decided to leave town for good, would you leave it in a tavern parking lot?"

He smelled the trap, but followed for the information. "Not unless Kathleen Turner was driving me away in one just like it."

Her mouth quirked and she nodded. "Wanda Trigel has a black Firebird. Hotter than your Mustang." She didn't insult him by repeating the story. "She had it put in her will that she was to be buried in that car. The morning after she disappeared, the Firebird was found in the parking lot of the Ramblin' Rose."

Jack was already shaking his head. "I don't want to hear about it." Folding his hands around the still-cold can, he leaned forward and thought about how bad his stomach was going to get. "My chief is a funny guy," he said. "He wants me to spend my time on murders that happen in the city. Crystal was murdered in the city, so that's the one I'm investigating."

"But it could be related."

"The only thing that relates is that Hunsacker knew two of the women and you heard a story that he might know the third," he retorted carefully, even as his gut churned in protest. "And I haven't gotten anything to prove that. Otherwise, you have a woman who left, which doesn't surprise anybody, and another woman who ended up at the wrong corner and got shot, which

I'm afraid isn't unusual there. There were two other murders that night in East St. Louis alone. And not one of them had any report of a white man in the vicinity."

She stiffened, eyes even more torn. "You checked?"

Jack sighed. "I told you. I try not to overlook a legitimate lead. There weren't any witnesses to your friend's shooting. But believe me, somebody would have remembered a rich white guy strollin' around down there with a twenty-two in his hand."

"A twenty-two?" Casey echoed. "I heard it was an AK47."

Jack tried not to smile. "Sorry, it wasn't that exotic. Saturday Night Special, missing wallet and wedding ring. Nothing surprising." Except that the physical evidence didn't add up there, either. Again, no hair, no fibers, no prints of any kind, and that was even more unsettling in an opportunity snatch like that.

Jack had come hoping to allay Ms. McDonough's fears while allowing himself a little more room to do his own quiet look. He had the feeling he wasn't going to have any luck. After her initial reactions of relief at his announcement, he'd hoped he'd walk out with a concession on her part that she'd just retreat into her nice big house here with Madame DeFarge and leave the problem to him. For some reason, his news had only stiffened her spine.

He was going to have to keep an eye on her. If her doctor was anything like she feared, she had no idea what kind of fire she was playing with.

Reaching into his jacket pocket, he pulled out a card. "Do me a favor," he offered, handing it across. "Hang on to this. Before you think of doing something stupid, call me so I can talk you out of it."

Getting to his feet, he set down the mostly full beer

can on another doily. Ms. McDonough followed suit, the card still in her hand.

"Why?" she asked.

Jack sighed. He didn't even realize his hand had strayed, betraying the strain. "Because if I were shot I wouldn't want a cop working on me. He'd have the best intentions, but he'd probably screw something up."

A wry grin broke through all that frustration and uncertainty. "Nicest insult I've ever suffered," she acknowledged. "All right. I'll call."

Pulling her gaze from the ethereal plain, Mrs. McDonough bent to pick up her cat and stand. Her smile was just as vacuous, but she seemed to be trembling a little. "I bet you'd like to play with my pussy, wouldn't you?" she asked.

Jack was glad he'd left his beer can on the table. Otherwise he would have just dropped it on the floor.

"Not when he's on duty," the daughter assured her mother with a painfully straight face. "I'm not sure he's much of a cat man, Mom."

"Maybe," Jack managed in a strangled voice, thinking that the daughter was enjoying his discomfort much too much, "next time."

Five minutes later Jack was back out sliding into his car. Usually he kept to the ritual, settling into the old vinyl, slipping the Charlie Parker tape into the deck, and turning over the engine to listen to the counterpoint a moment before putting the car into gear and backing out. Tonight, he couldn't get his mind off just what it would take to leave a favorite car behind. Charlie Parker never did see the inside of the tape deck.

Casey closed the door feeling even worse than when she'd opened it. She should have been relieved to hear that Hunsacker wasn't tied into Crystal Johnson's murder. After all, she'd walked up that driveway fully intending on absolving the man of guilt for anything but a creepy personality. Well, she'd almost intended it.

She'd wanted someone to let her off the hook, and Scanlon had tried his best to do just that. Only she hadn't let him. The more he'd tried to convince her that she'd be right to just let the whole thing drop, the more she'd argued. Even as she'd remembered what Hunsacker had looked like after the surgery, she'd heard the whispers of doubt.

In the end, no matter what Hunsacker had done that day, Casey just couldn't shake the feeling that he was involved in those two deaths. And she couldn't back away from them until she knew for sure. Even if Scanlon couldn't help her.

"It's nice to entertain gentlemen in the parlor again," Helen said from where she was collecting the remnants. "I'd forgotten."

"It was hardly entertaining," Casey countered instinctively, flipping off the porch light and locking the door. "When did he show up?"

Her mother dusted at the dustless tables with fluttering hands. "We've just become two old maids in this house, Catherine. Just rattling around."

Casey stopped in the door to the living room, her eyes on where her mother hummed and cleaned, as coquettish as a schoolgirl. Even the drab brown couldn't dim her surprising sparkle.

"You should invite people over more often, Mom." And drop that pussy line on all the men. It could turn into a great party game.

"And a priest, too," Helen said to her pictures, the glass of tea in her hand. "Imagine that."

"He's not a Jesuit anymore," Casey retorted, sighing

in capitulation and reaching to turn off one of the lamps on her way to bed.

"Don't be silly." Helen giggled in delight. "That's like saying you're not Irish anymore."

Casey thought to argue, but it occurred to her that her mother was right. There was still a lot of Jesuit in the policeman. It accounted for that ascetic look, for the impression that there were fires banked deep behind those hooded gray eyes.

Casey flipped off another lamp until she and her mother stood silhouetted by the light from the kitchen.

"He's right, you know," her mother suddenly said.

Casey stopped and looked over, but her mother was all shadow. Her voice was suddenly so certain, so clear. Casey wanted to turn the light back on and try to catch that rationality on her features. She wanted to pin her against the wall of delusions, so that she couldn't escape back into the shadows again. But Casey was suddenly just as sure that it was the shadows that had allowed her mother the clarity.

"About what?" she asked instead.

"Leave that man alone. Stay far away so he won't hurt you."

"He's not going to hurt me, Mom."

For a moment all she could hear was her mother's breathing. Soft, quick, like a frightened bird. "In the end they won't listen," she said. "And he'll make you pay."

Casey fought a shiver. The shadows seemed to shift and collect in the deep room. The pictures over on the wall threw off faint reflections like a crowd of people wearing glasses. Suddenly Casey felt stifled and afraid, and it was a fear that had nothing to do with Hunsacker.

"Mom?"

But Helen had expended too much effort. Rustling as if she were shaking out feathers, she carried the glass and cans into the kitchen with the bearing of a nun offering penance.

"You make sure and warn me the next time you invite him over," she chirped, her shoes clicking against the tile floor. "I don't want your gentlemen to think they're not welcome."

Casey turned after her. "He's not—"

Helen spun on her, eyes distant and content once more. "He really is such a nice man, dear. Although I think he worries too much, even for a Jesuit. You tell him that, all right? He needs some weight on him. Good night."

There was only one thing Casey could say in response. "Good night, Mom."

She had the nightmare again that night. The same setting, same outcome. Only this time she heard arguing outside the door, and it frightened her almost as much as staying inside. Casey ended up reading until Helen got up for morning vespers.

There were days when Casey enjoyed a busy shift more than others. The next day was one of those. After the soul-searching she'd been forced into, the ghosts she'd carried through the night with her, she was looking forward to cleansing her palate with a little bloodshed and mayhem.

She got her wish.

She was still clocking in when the first helicopter landed, and it was nonstop business for the rest of the shift. Abe was on, and Marva and Janice, which made the work easier, even fun. If only work could be like this every day, she might not mind doing it for another twenty years or so.

Then again, Casey thought as she stared at the pile of

paperwork she'd have to stay overtime to clear up, maybe the rock band wasn't such a bad idea after all.

Casey used her ten-minute lunch break to call over to Izzy's. It was the next step on her list of things to do, and sometime in the early morning hours when she'd been left alone with the aftertaste of her accusations and the unsettled ghosts of her friends, she'd reached the decision that she had to follow that list. Sgt. Scanlon wouldn't, past his one phone call and his interest in Crystal. He had a suspect everybody wanted to convict, the makings of an easy case, and from the looks of him the night before, a big enough workload without any extra help from her.

She couldn't really blame Scanlon for taking the easy way out. She'd walked that street before herself. But for some reason, this was one of those times when she walked right to the door marked hassle and threw it open.

Her invitation to Betty Fernandez for lunch was made under the guise of setting up some kind of memorial to Evelyn. Betty accepted with alacrity, and Casey felt the dreadful anticipation build in her once again.

She returned to the hall only to discover Rescue 256 running for room three with the latest contestant to sign in, a very hirsute, overweight, sixty-something-year-old man who'd gone into cardiac arrest in one of the local motels. The team was already waiting in the room, so Casey joined the party.

"Down at least ten minutes before the call went out," one of the paramedics panted from where he was sweating and pumping atop his patient. "History of heart condition."

The team tumbled over the patient, assessing, treating, recording. At the door the chaplain blessed the air and left. X-ray pulled their machine in the door and the lab tech hovered alongside Casey waiting for her to strike blood.

"Wife just called," one of the secretaries announced from the door. "She's on her way in."

"No she's not," Janice countered sharply from where she was sliding the identification bracelet around the patient's wrist proclaiming him Mr. B. until they could get his papers completely filled out. "I just put her in the waiting room."

Everybody looked up. Then they looked at Mr. B.

"I don't think that's the wife," the secretary said. "She was just on the phone."

Abe turned to Janice from where he was pulling a sterile towel from a pacemaker kit. "Is your wife young, blond, and have a lot of makeup?"

Janice nodded. "Yeah."

She was met by a chorus. "Then that's not the wife."

"Oh, shit," she groaned, swinging for the door. "I just gave her his wallet."

"He never had a chance to get his pants off," Abe mourned, bending over the dusky chest and probing for the subclavian vein. "Just think, he hadn't even come and he was gone."

But the surprises weren't over. Janice had just walked back into the room clutching Mr. B's wallet when Marva let out a howl.

"Watch out. We got a fashion alert."

She'd been setting up to insert a catheter. When she'd pulled at his trousers, she'd unearthed Mr. B's real secret.

"Sweet Jesus have mercy," she crooned in wonder.

"Leopard skin," Abe mused with a shake of his head. "It doesn't go with the black lace at all."

"Your beast would look lovely sheathed in all those spots, Abe," the X-ray tech offered.

"You'd need bigger spots," Casey retorted.

"*Much* bigger," Michael agreed from where he was assisting Abe.

"Check that woman out there and see if she's missin' some nylons and a garter belt," Marva demanded.

Uncapping the blood drawer's syringe from her line and hooking up the IV, Casey couldn't stop chuckling. She'd wondered sometimes what Ed would look like in twenty years. She'd been right. It wouldn't have been worth sticking around for.

Janice shook her head, her gaze brushing past Casey's and then away before either could react. "Those aren't hers," she announced with some disdain. "She has better taste."

"Where the hell did he get one that wide?" the paramedic demanded, still pumping, his only reaction a funny gurgling noise in his throat as he tried to keep from laughing on top of his patient.

Casey uncapped the epi with her teeth and began to push. "Check his wife when she comes in."

Marva didn't have the slightest compunction about laughing. "Well, what do I do now?"

"You want help?" Abe countered, still probing around in doughy flesh in an attempt to insert the catheter for the pacer. "I'm real good at getting garters loose."

"I'm sure he'd be thrilled."

Abe went on probing without success. "I got news for you. He's never going to be thrilled again."

"Serves him right," Janice announced from the door with surprising conviction. "If I were his wife, I'd bury him in the damn things. Face down, just like he died. In an open coffin."

"I'd pay to see it," Abe retorted, not really paying attention.

Casey wasn't so blithe. She looked up from pushing

drugs to catch the flare of pain in Janice's eyes. Their gazes locked for just a moment, tight and significant across the jumble of staff and equipment.

Casey had forgotten. In everything else that had gone on in the last few weeks, she'd shoved Janice to the background. This time she didn't feel guilty, though. She felt frustrated. Yet another problem, another friend in need of help. Another burden.

They had no sooner called the code when Janice waylaid her. Marva was finishing notes and Casey was pulling equipment.

"Casey," Janice asked, her hands restless. "Are you doing anything for lunch tomorrow?"

Now Casey did feel guilty. She looked up to see the fresh turmoil in Janice's eyes and realized that she was grateful that she had an excuse.

"Oh, I can't Jan," she hedged, knowing Janice wanted to talk about marriage and divorce and decisions. "I'm having lunch with some of Izzy's nurses tomorrow."

Janice, who had never faltered before any situation, who had always remained as poised as a duchess amid the muck and mire of the halls, hesitated. She shifted on her feet, took a shaky breath. She picked at one of her perfect nails, and Casey knew the trouble was big.

"How 'bout after work tomorrow?" she capitulated. "I'm not scheduled for any all-night novenas or anything."

Janice only allowed a brief nod of relief before turning back to work.

In parting she offered a grin toward the still semiclad body on the cart. "It's impressive in person."

Casey grinned back. "Even more impressive in action."

Marva waited only long enough to see the door swing

shut behind Janice. "What Isidore nurses?" she demanded without looking up from her work.

Casey went back to hers, preparing the body for transport down to the morgue. "Some of the OB crew. We're talking about a memorial of some kind for Evelyn."

She must not have sounded nonchalant enough. Marva anticipated her again. "Evelyn your friend who was murdered? That Evelyn?"

Casey refused to look up. "Uh huh."

"The one who was murdered right before you took to reading all the police reports in the paper."

"That's her."

"And you're gonna talk about her memorial."

"That's right."

"You're talkin' about trouble," Marva countered fiercely. "Aren't you?"

Casey tried her best to be offhand. "Yeah, well, you know me. Never satisfied to be gainfully employed and well thought of by my betters."

Marva gave her head a slow, mournful shake. "You really convinced, aren't you? You think Hunsacker's poppin' people in the streets."

Casey suddenly understood the look in Janice's eyes a minute ago. It had been the need to share, to confess. She had it now herself. She wanted somebody else to know what she suspected. Somebody besides a cop who didn't know her, didn't trust her, and probably wouldn't do anything about what she brought him.

"I know for a fact that there are two women from Izzy's who had big arguments with Hunsacker and then died or disappeared," she said. "And a third, the hooker I was reading about the other day when he came in . . ." Casey drew a breath, looked around. Both doors were closed. Nobody could hear her. Still, she thought her voice was too loud. "Grapevine has it that he was seeing her."

"And you think he killed her."

This time Casey didn't flinch from Marva's hard brown eyes. "I think he killed her."

"The same man who cried for an hour after losing that little girl."

"Hitler liked dogs, Marva. How do I know what makes Hunsacker tick? He's . . . there's something about him I can't explain."

"That only you can see."

Now it was Casey's turn to be hard. "How many pelvics have you done with him?"

"A few, why?"

"Tell me, is he gentle? Does he warm up the speculum and wait if his lady's afraid and go in real gentle so he doesn't hurt her?"

Marva's eyes gave her away. She'd seen it, too. "Lots of OBs are assholes. It doesn't make them killers."

Casey straightened, faced her friend with her suspicions, the dread that only a woman could understand, the intangible that made most sense to her. "He does a pelvic on every woman he sees. No matter what. And not out of concern, Marva. I think it's his way of controlling them. Of violating them without their even knowing it. They come to *him* to be hurt. They ask for it. They cave in to that smile and then let him abuse them, and nobody says a thing. Evelyn heard he'd been doing the three-finger special."

Marva battled Casey's words in silence, the repugnance of her accusations tightening the black woman's features and drawing her mouth into a taut line of contention.

"It's still not murder," she countered, struggling to hold on to her neutrality.

"It's a symptom. So is murder. At first, I thought he was just your garden-variety sociopath. You know, amoral, manipulative, that kind of thing. God knows, we got enough of 'em in medicine, one more wouldn't be noticed. But I'm telling you, Marva, I'm beginning to think he's a grade-A psychopath. Serious stuff. *Real* serious stuff. He really gets off on not just controlling people, but hurting them. If you think I'm completely nuts, tell me so. If not, just don't rat on me. I need to find out."

"Baby." Marva sighed, a hand out in commiseration. "You ain't nuts. Not like that. But you is the stupidest creature alive if you think this man's so bad and you still want to go after him."

Fortified by her friend's understanding, Casey offered a smile in return. "I won't argue with you there. I'd rather be back home knitting altar cloths. But I'll be damned if I can let him get away with it."

Marva reclaimed her hand and bestowed another shake of the head. "Jus' as long as you don't know my name when the administration interrogates you."

Casey grinned. "Whose name?"

"You still have to work with him," Marva said. "How you gonna do that?"

Casey took a deep breath and slowly released it. "Hold my tongue and hope he doesn't smell me sweat."

He did smell her sweat. He must have smelled it all the way down the hall, because the minute Casey opened the door from that room, he turned where he stood at the far end and smiled at her.

Casey was getting tired of the way her chest caved in when he did that. She wanted to get a good breath again, and knew she wouldn't until he left the work lane. She wanted to be able to get through a day where her hands didn't sweat and she didn't feel as if somebody had just stripped her bare in public.

And to think that it was just all beginning.

That ubiquitous little notebook in his hands, he strolled toward her. Casey scuttled over to the supply cart and began filling her arms with equipment to resupply her room. She could feel him approach, heard his footsteps like the lap of a deadly flood at her doorstep. Still she worked, crouched down to pull out catheter kits, fighting to overcome the urge to look around, to look up and discover that he knew she'd gone to the police.

Then the back of her neck signaled his proximity. She climbed back to her feet, unwilling to allow him a superior position.

"Been a busy night, I hear," he greeted her, with a smile that put Casey in mind of Pussy in sight of a mouse.

Casey clutched her equipment and straightened, willing herself to answer his smile with a cool one of her own. "You weren't in the lounge talking about how quiet it had been today, were you?"

It seemed he wasn't in the mood for small talk. His eyes promised meaning beyond his words, teased and tormented like a lover holding a surprise behind his back.

"Have there been any more good murders?"

Casey almost dropped the IVs. Instead she fixed her smile in place and headed back to the room. "I don't know," she answered, her own audacity clogging in her throat. "Have there?"

Hunsacker reached across her to push the door open. Casey balked at his proximity. She didn't want to accidentally brush against him, or let him close enough to sense the adrenaline that throbbed through her. Yet she couldn't afford to falter.

"Thanks," she allowed and glided past him, her breath dead still in her chest.

Still insulated in the now-silent room, Marva looked

up. Casey saw the brief flash of surprise in her eyes, the retreat as she bent back over her notes.

"Good grief." Hunsacker grinned at the sight on the table. "Abe said something about an affair to remember, but you really get the full effect in person, don't you?"

"We ain't chargin' admission here," Marva announced without looking up.

Casey dropped her load on the counter and went to better cover the patient. Hunsacker didn't move from the door.

"I was over at St. Isidore's the other day," he said to her, his voice caressing her like a soft hand. "Understand you were married to Ed Baker."

Casey reacted before she thought of it, spinning around to face him. She saw him glance over to where the garish leopard-skin and lace attire lay hidden beneath the drab green sheet.

"Nice guy," he said. Then Hunsacker lifted his gaze to Casey and let it rest there, his new smile feral and knowing. Before Casey could think to counterattack, he walked out.

Casey couldn't breathe. She couldn't move. Outrage spilled through her like hot lye. Fury, frustration. Impotence. She'd just been violated as surely as if he'd had his hands on her, and nobody had known it. He'd just slid a knife in her and slipped out the door.

Damn him. Goddamn him. How did he find out about Ed? How did he know about their marriage, and why taunt her with it? And if he knew about that, what else did he know?

"Casey?"

Casey didn't even hear Marva's concern. She couldn't drag her eyes away from the closed door.

"Casey, honey, what happened?"

Casey flinched at Marva's touch. Startled, she looked

up to remember that her friend had witnessed Hunsacker's actions. Marva had overheard a threat she didn't understand.

"Sweet Jesus, girl, you look like you daddy just came back from the dead."

Casey shook her head, struggling to voice her distress. Tears blurred her vision. She couldn't make Marva understand the poison in Hunsacker's words unless she explained about Ed. And that was just too much for her right now.

"He knows," she said instead, suddenly certain. "Hunsacker knows I suspect him."

# Chapter 9

*BARB SLAPPED OPEN* the door. "What are you guys doin' in here," she demanded, the cacophony of a full work lane spilling in behind her. "Getting fashion tips?"

"Get out," Marva commanded, her hand on Casey's arm, her eyes never leaving Casey's stony face.

Barb stiffened with outrage. "Don't you give me—"

Now Marva did lift her gaze and it landed square on Barb. "I said get out."

Barb got out. Casey barely heard her. She was still trying to settle down, trying her best to regain control over her temper.

"Now," Marva said quietly, still holding Casey in place, Mr. B a mute witness over her shoulder. "You wanna tell me what that was all about?"

"I wondered before," Casey admitted with a shaky breath. "Whether he knew I suspected him. I'm sure he does now. He just . . . I think he gave me a kind of warning."

Marva looked around her as if she'd missed something and could still find it amid the litter of the code. "Warning? What about?"

Casey's smile was grim. Poor Ed. He wasn't getting any anonymity tonight. "Remember the underpants on our friend there?"

"So?"

"Ed has much worse taste. He buys his lacy things at Frederick's."

Marva took another look at the anonymous mass on the cart, and then back to Casey. "Sweet Jesus."

"Nobody knows. I mean nobody. Hunsacker just told me that that's all changed. I think it was a threat about what kind of adversary he's going to be."

"What are you gonna do?"

Casey took the time to drag in a few more breaths. She focused on the red of the needle disposal box at the back of the counter. "I don't know," she admitted in a small voice.

"Tell Tom," Marva insisted, her grip tightening.

Casey swung on her. "Tell him what?" she demanded. "That Hunsacker knows my ex-husband liked pretty things more than I did? Tell him that I think Hunsacker's offing nurses who piss him off, and that now he knows I know? You tell me, Marva. What is Tom going to say to that?"

"But he threatened you, girl."

"You were standing right there. Did it sound like a threat to you?"

"The look on your face sure sounded like he gave you a threat."

Casey shook her head, knowing she had no choice. Caught tight between her suspicions and Hunsacker's power over her, Casey knew she had no one who could help her.

The door swung open behind her. "I can't field a team with only one player," Tom announced in a clipped voice.

"Listen, Tom—" Marva started.

Casey silenced her. "We'll be right out," she said. "We were just cleaning up."

"You aren't the only two players on the team," he threatened. "Just remember, Keith Hernandez was traded, and you can be, too."

Casey looked up to see the pique in his eyes and knew just how far a complaint to him would go. She already had a reputation as a shit-disturber. All she'd need was to lodge a complaint against the hospital's favorite doctor and she'd land on her butt in the proverbial snow. Especially since it seemed the doctor in question knew just how to play this game.

All Casey could do was learn to play it better.

"Dr. Hunsacker was asking me about somebody I knew over at St. Isidore's," Casey lied with an utter sincerity that threatened to make her nauseous. "A nurse who was murdered. We're thinking of setting up a memorial fund for her, and he wanted to know about it. I'm sorry, Tom."

His posture of vexation crumbled halfway through her little speech. By the time she offered him a wan smile, he was ready to reach into his own pocket.

"Oh, that's fine, Casey. I'm sorry," he conceded. "Barb just didn't know what you were so upset about. It's tough when you have to, you know, bang the drum slowly for a teammate."

Casey was glad he left then. She didn't want to laugh in his face.

"Thank God he's off the work lanes." Marva chortled. "Can you imagine him dishin' that kinda crap to Mrs. B out there? He'd get to the part about bangin' slowly and find himself airborne."

Casey shared the laughter. "God, he's getting bad.

Now he's using clichés from baseball *movies*. Next we'll hear how he's the luckiest guy in the world."

Marva shook her head, amazed. "How did you do that? You switched gears so fast I got left in the dirt."

Casey's smile died into real sincerity, the kind that darkened her features into conviction. "I've decided to study the Handbook of Social Success by Dr. Dale Hunsacker. I won't be able to outdistance him if I'm thrown out of the race."

Marva stared. "You're serious. You're not going to quit?"

Casey turned back to finishing her job. "I've already been screwed. The least I can do is deserve it."

Casey wasn't exactly sure what she wanted to get out of her lunch with Betty Fernandez. She needed to keep some kind of contact with St. Isidore's, since any information she could get about Evelyn or Wanda would have to come through that particular grapevine. She needed to hear another view of Hunsacker. Maybe he didn't sit so high over at Izzy's where they had some real doctors. Maybe somebody else over there saw him for what he was.

Well, if somebody did, it wasn't Betty.

A tall, thin, nervous woman with more sincerity than brains, Betty was one of the myriad ex-wives of Dr. Fernandez the Obstetrician. Casey remembered Betty as coming away from her divorce confused and shaken. She didn't look as if six years had settled her in any. Now the focus of her distress was Evelyn.

A memorial, she thought, would be lovely. Casey mapped out a quick idea that put most of the effort neatly in the hands of Izzy's staff and then settled down to the time-honored lunch dialogue—grapevine update. It didn't take much to get the subject around to the holes in the fourth-floor staff.

"Poor Ev," Betty mourned, her salad almost untouched and her wine almost gone. "She loved nursing so much. It's like having a family member die."

"Did you ever find out what happened that night between her and Hunsacker?" Casey asked, her salad gone and her wineglass full. "It still bothers me, thinking about how upset she was over her patient."

Betty emptied her glass and looked vaguely around for more. Casey thought of trading hers for the empty one, but figured that would be a little too obvious.

"I didn't sleep for three nights after the wake," Betty admitted. "You know, after you'd said that you'd talked to her and all." Betty's long forehead creased with hesitation a moment, and then she leaned in a little to share her confidence. "I even read through Mrs. Baldwin's chart. I didn't want to think that Ev had made a mistake, and I knew Dr. Hunsacker wouldn't."

Casey leaned in a little on her side, clasping her hands at the edge of the table to keep them still. "I'd sure feel better knowing that Ev wasn't wrong. She called him, didn't she?"

Eyes wide and moist, Betty nodded. "Five times. It's all in the chart. I think she and Dr. Hunsacker must have just misunderstood each other. They had a terrible argument. I've never seen him so upset. But he had Mrs. Baldwin in surgery within twenty minutes of showing up. Evelyn was just upset about Mrs. Baldwin, I'm sure. She never would have argued with somebody as nice as Dr. Hunsacker otherwise."

Casey nodded in sympathy. "Did she chart what she told him on the phone?" She paused, the next question too important to lose. "Could she have really not told him how badly Mrs. Baldwin was bleeding?"

This time Betty shook her head. "She just charted that she called him, and that he said he wasn't coming in. Poor thing. She must have been too upset . . ."

*Poor Evelyn, she must have been wrong.* Casey fought down her anger, suddenly sure that the only mistake Evelyn had made that night had been not charting exactly what she'd said to Hunsacker. He must have threatened her in that silky, sneaky way of his to leave the matter alone, and she'd ignored him.

Betty was actively dabbing at her eyes now. Casey didn't blame her. Evelyn's death was more tragic than anybody understood yet.

"And Hunsacker stayed with Mrs. Baldwin the rest of the night?"

Betty nodded. "His last note was at about one-fifteen, when she was in recovery."

One-fifteen. Casey's hopes fell. The perfect alibi, in print, in a legal document. How could he have possibly reached the exact spot where Evelyn would become lost in fifteen minutes, when it took at least twenty just to make the Mississippi River? Casey had thought he must have followed Ev off the parking lot. The notes said that instead he'd returned to the floor.

Casey had been running on instinct until now, sure somehow that Hunsacker had been angry enough to hurt Ev, smart enough to learn where she was going and follow, somehow rerouting her into the very place where if she were shot, no one would ever think to point an accusing finger back at an angry doctor twenty miles away. She knew he was smart enough to do it. Way deep inside her where her most primal instincts resided, she felt he was capable of it.

Casey had just figured that once she got the proof that Hunsacker could have been physically tied to the murder, somebody else could come up with the specifics. She'd been outmaneuvered, though.

It still didn't occur to Casey that he couldn't have done it.

"We'll never know," she admitted out loud.

"No," Betty agreed, still thinking of the question of Evelyn's culpability. "Poor thing. I still think of what she must have faced. She was so distraught she must have taken a wrong turn. And died like that. With a weapon that horrible."

Casey looked up, remembering. "Didn't you know?" she asked. "It wasn't an AK47. It was a twenty-two. Saturday Night Special."

Betty's face puckered. "Well, they're not the same at all, are they?"

Which just proved that she was a postpartum nurse and not a trauma nurse.

"No," Casey allowed evenly. "They're not." She refrained from saying that both could get the job done. That was something you said to other trauma nurses, who would nod and commiserate. Postpartum nurses were spoiled with their easy compassion.

"How could he make a mistake like that, I wonder," Betty asked. "He knows so much about guns."

That got Casey's attention. "Who?"

Betty lifted perplexed eyes. "Dr. Hunsacker. I remember he was the one who told us, because he was talking about how the gun was a favorite gang weapon."

Casey flirted with elation, but it did her no good. Why would Hunsacker make a mistake like that? It served no purpose.

"Reports like that always get confused," she simply said. It seemed to satisfy Betty.

Casey shook off her frustration and returned to her

purpose. "Dr. Hunsacker really likes you guys up at Izzy's. He was telling me the other day."

Betty fidgeted a little more, reminding Casey suddenly of Helen. "I don't know," she admitted. "He hasn't been bringing his patients up to Izzy's as much in the last couple of weeks. I miss him."

Casey admitted her surprise. "He hasn't? How come?"

Betty shrugged and went after her water glass, her eyes still moist and uncertain, her distress over Evelyn permeating the atmosphere around their little table. "We don't know. We were afraid it was, you know, the Evelyn thing." Another shrug, this more uncomfortable. "It might be Peter, though. Sometimes he can be difficult, you know."

Peter. Dr. "Wanna Be My Wife?" Fernandez. A rat on the domestic scene, but the kind of administrator who demanded the best from his crew and usually got it. A well-respected bastard.

And Betty thought Hunsacker was having trouble with him. At last Casey was getting somewhere.

"I can't imagine Dr. Hunsacker having trouble with anyone," Casey said. She finally had to lift her wineglass on that one, just to grease the words past her protesting throat.

"Medical egos, I guess. Although the hall gossip is that Dr. Hunsacker had been seeing Peter's latest mistress." Finally something besides distress. Casey caught a definite glint of self-righteous satisfaction on the woman's features. Betty had been Peter's second wife, an upgrade from the waitress who'd worked him through med school. Betty had lasted until Peter had discovered the younger, more passive model.

"That'd explain it," Casey admitted with a grin.

She was gratified to see Betty allow herself to grin

back. But grins didn't seem to last long on Betty. Suddenly her forehead crumbled into distress again.

"Of course, I'm sure he's not seeing her anymore. I mean, why would he?"

Casey wasn't exactly sure how to answer. Betty seemed so intent on her message. "I don't know, Betty."

Picking up her fork once again, Betty shook her head with some resolve. "I just wouldn't want you to, you know, get the wrong impression."

Casey wasn't sure why she needed to reassure Betty, but she did. "Of course not."

Lunch lasted another half hour, during which time they covered old gossip, new gossip, and the vagaries of hospital politics.

Casey learned that nothing more had been heard from Wanda, and that the hospital had waited a total of forty-eight hours after her disappearance to advertise for a replacement. When cleaned out, her locker had given up a number of Elvis pictures, four cartons of cigarettes, and a Tupperware container full of earrings for the four holes she'd punched in each ear. Buddy had wanted to leave her things where they were, sure she was coming back. The hospital administration had insisted, and he'd walked away with her small cache, head bowed so no one saw his tears.

Betty misted up all over again for poor Buddy, sure Wanda was white trash for walking out on her husband that way. Casey kept her silence. She hoped Clyde and the folks down at the Rose had begun their search.

Casey left Betty with promises to get together again over the memorial project and walked back through the mall alone. She was still thinking about Evelyn, about how there should be some way to sit down and figure a way for a white doctor from West County to travel twenty miles in about ten minutes, murder a lone white woman on a corner in East St. Louis, and escape unseen.

Her head was down, her purse swinging in lazy rhythm with her stride. Mall walkers passed her at a fast clip, and the elderly coagulated in slumped knots along benches and planters, which was the closest anybody could get to watching the world go by anymore. Casey smiled at a couple and received courteous nods. She side-stepped a stroller with twins and stopped at a pet-store window to watch puppies.

And then she saw him.

Her steady pace faltered. The man behind her bumped into her and excused himself. Casey apologized. When she turned back, she couldn't find him again.

It had been Hunsacker, hadn't it? There, at the edge of the lane where the shoe store was having a sidewalk sale. Only he hadn't been looking at shoes, he'd been looking at her.

She thought.

It had looked like him—at least she thought it did. Same height, same coloring. And he'd definitely had his eyes on her. But she wasn't sure. It was like a dream, where you could see something but not know what it was, the parts just a little rearranged or vague, and no matter what you did your vision wouldn't clear.

Or maybe it wasn't him and she'd just collected the sum of her suspicions into a recognizable pattern, when all she'd seen had been a nice-looking Yuppie man in a mall.

Even so, she felt unsettled. She wasn't sure suddenly that she wanted to go on, afraid that she'd turn a corner to find him there, waiting for her. Smiling.

Casey shook her head. Maybe Marva was right. Maybe she was getting a bit obsessive. Hunsackers following her everywhere, listening in on her conversations, playing cat and mouse with her in shopping malls. Wouldn't he get off just knowing that he'd upset her so much she'd fabricated him in crowds.

She wasn't surprised at all when she reached the intersection with the shoe store to find no one waiting around the corner. Even so, she slowed a little before reaching it, her palms just the slightest bit sweaty. He'd found out about Ed. He'd killed people, probably in a fit of anger, and covered his tracks somehow. He wasn't a harmless crank. Still, he had other things to do with his day than torment her.

Casey gave her head one last shake and then set back off in search of the uniform store. She'd be seeing Hunsacker soon enough. She didn't need to be inventing him to fill in the lonely hours apart.

Casey didn't get to talk to Janice that night, nor the night after. Neither one of them walked off the halls before three AM. Casey wished she felt more upset about it, but the fact was she still dreaded wading through Janice's problems. Janice was getting quieter every day, more brittle. Casey could see it. She could certainly sympathize, especially if Janice suspected her husband of fooling around. But she wasn't sure she wanted to dig up her own past.

She ended up having to deal with Ed anyway.

The more she thought about it, the more she realized that she had to tell Ed about Hunsacker's knowledge. It was only fair. Ed had let her keep the car after the divorce, the least she could do was let him keep his privacy. She called his office and made an appointment to see him.

Nestled deep in one of the classier medical buildings along Ballas Road, Ed's office reflected his success. He'd built a nice practice for himself specializing in eating disorders and addictive personalities. They were problems not too closely related to his own so that he didn't really have to face himself. His clients were rich, attractive, and grateful. His decor was sleek southwestern with authentic Indian artifacts under recessed lighting and expressionist weavings hanging from his walls. Ed was as happy as Ed got. Casey did her best to be happy for him.

She was surprised every time she saw him that she'd actually been married to him. He was such a passive person. Pale and thin and bespectacled, the kind of kid you liked to hit in school and the kind of man who only inspired confidence as a confidant. A smooth, cultured man to his clientele, he had a bad knack of whining around Casey. To her own eternal mortification, she remembered when that had endeared him to her. But then, her judgment hadn't exactly been award-winning along about that period in her life.

"I'm surprised," he greeted her, walking around his desk to drop a quick kiss on her cheek. He'd affected new horn-rims. They made him look older, more assertive. Of course the image suffered a little when you considered what he looked like in heels.

"I'm sorry to bother you, Ed," Casey answered, doing her best to contain the remnants of disdain her divorce had left her with. "Your practice looks good."

Both of them settled into the beige sectional chairs, civilized and proper, as if they hadn't screamed and battled at each other. Actually, Casey had done the screaming. Ed had ducked every breakable object in the house.

Crossing his leg, he recreased his pants leg and offered Casey his attention.

"You're troubled," he offered in that professional voice of his.

Casey immediately bristled. It had been another problem. Every time she'd tried to confront him, he'd disappeared behind all the catch phrases. "Expand on that. I'd like to hear it. How do you feel about that?" Until she'd shown him how she felt about that. With the breakables.

Today she just wanted to get through this without too much trauma. Crossing her own legs, she worried at the edge of her skirt with nervous fingers.

"Ed, something came up I thought you might need to know about."

He inclined his head just the proper distance. "Go on."

Casey almost smiled. "There's a new doc on staff down at Mother Mary who knows you," she said, her hand stilling as she faced him. "He knows . . . about you. And he made it a point of telling me."

Ed snapped to attention like a sail in a storm. "He what?" Already his voice was beginning to lift. His legs uncrossed, as if he were preparing to bolt. Probably envisioning those artifacts out front disappearing one by one, like his patients.

Casey did her best to wave off the threat. "His name's Hunsacker. He—"

It was Casey's turn for a surprise. "Dale?" Ed retorted with a delighted smile. "Well, why didn't you say so? God, Casey, you scared me. I thought you'd been bad-mouthing me all over town or something."

Casey closed her mouth just in time to keep from gaping like an idiot.

"*You* told him?" she demanded, rigid within the folds of her chair.

Ed wasn't nearly upset enough. Not after what Casey had gone through the other night.

"We're golf partners," he assured her, settling back into his chair. "He's a new member of the club."

"You haven't told any of your other golf buddies that you prefer Maidenform to Fruit of the Loom."

Ed wrinkled his nose a little, as if it were Casey, not

he, with the unique taste. "Alternative choice doesn't intimidate Dale."

Casey almost burst out laughing. Well, that was certainly one way of putting it. She wondered if Ed had any concept just what kind of alternate choice old Dale was into.

"In fact," Ed said with a new smile, suspiciously smug. "Dale's pretty open about his own tastes. And his idiosyncracies." The smile grew wider, as if he were talking golf stories instead of sexual inclinations.

"He likes teddies, too?" The funny thing was, Ed knew that it hadn't been the attire Casey had finally revolted against. As long as he didn't wear it around her, she didn't really care.

"Schedules." He grinned. "I thought I was compulsive. He's got a notebook with every minute of the day accounted for. He jokes about the fact that he always makes love to a woman the same time every day."

"I guess it's easier to keep all those different girlfriends in order."

"He even had a hooker with a bigger notebook than he does."

"A what?"

Ed waved off his admission. He'd never kept a secret around her, divulging patient stories and problems, bouncing ideas off her. He'd always known she'd keep her silence. He didn't realize this time that she couldn't.

"You won't say anything," he assured himself. "He was experimenting, you know how it is. Decided to try her out for a while. She'd actually yell at him if he didn't keep as tight a schedule as she did."

Casey couldn't believe it. Here was a practicing psychiatrist with a seven-figure income, and he was chortling over Hunsacker like a Peck's bad boy. Ed had absolutely no idea what Hunsacker was about. No wonder Casey had ended up healing herself.

Was Hunsacker Ed's new repository of trust? Did Ed tell him all those embarrassing little stories that could so hurt someone if they fell into the wrong hands? Confidences no psychiatrist should divulge to anyone? If Ed had fallen beneath the Hunsacker spell, it would make sense. And if Hunsacker was privy to Ed's secrets, Casey shuddered to think what he could do to the people involved.

Especially her.

"When did you start playing golf with him?" she asked, suddenly afraid of the answer.

"Oh, I don't know. It's been about six weeks or so, I guess. Good handicapper."

"And you talked about me?"

There wasn't any discomfort in Ed's shrug. "We traded ex-wife stories, sure."

Casey's throat closed a little tighter. She didn't even want to think about what Hunsacker had learned about her.

"Funny," she countered quietly, still instinctively wishing after all these years that Ed would show more insight than he did. "He's been a real regular visitor out to M and M the last couple of months. Until the other night, he hasn't said a word about you."

What did she tell Ed? How did she warn him? Ed was just smug enough to carry her warnings right back to Hunsacker as more ex-wife fodder. But he was just vulnerable enough for Hunsacker to shoot him down in flames as an example to her.

Ed settled it for the moment by checking his watch and getting to his feet. "I wouldn't worry about it," he assured her, reaching out a hand to help her to her feet. "I really appreciate your coming to me, Casey. It means a lot to me that you'd think to warn me about a possible problem."

She almost said it then, her hand caught in his, her hesitant smile pale in comparison with the beaming delight on his face. Carefully proportioned to show sincerity. She'd seen him practice that smile in the mirror in the mornings.

"It was the least I could do," she answered, taking her hand back. "Next time, will you kindly send me an update of people in the know? It'd sure save me some grief."

She let herself be steered back across the dun-colored carpeting.

"You'll be the first to know," he promised. "Are you still living with your mother?"

From anybody but a shrink, that would have sounded like an innocuous statement. Casey caught herself bristling again. "Yeah, well, nursing just doesn't pull in the big fees."

Ed chuckled just in time to open the door and be overheard in the waiting room. Several female faces looked up with maternal smiles. Casey imagined they thought he was being spontaneous and genial.

She got another careful peck on the cheek and a wave. Thankfully, she didn't want more.

"One more time, Reeva."

Jack clicked his pen back into gear and leaned over the table. Huffing in indignation, the skinny black woman across the table took a minute to smooth out her spandex skirt and hike her bra strap from where it was slipping down her arm. Pockmarked and bony, she was about sixteen and looked more like thirty.

"Moses come over 'bout six," she recited in a bored monotone. "I knows 'cause we always does it while we watches the news. Moses says he gets a hard-on watchin' other people have troubles. He stay to my place till next mornin'. Tha's it. I got nothin' more to say."

Jack leaned his chair back against the wall and stretched a kink out of his back. He'd been in the interview room for two hours trying to break Reeva's story. If Moses was with Reeva the night Crystal was killed, then he had an alibi. But Jack couldn't imagine any reason Reeva would have stayed inside on a Friday night. He couldn't imagine Moses letting her stay inside. So he settled the chair back on the floor and pulled out a pack of cigarettes.

"How 'bout it?" he asked quietly.

Reeva snatched one like a starving child going for meat. Jack let her light up and savor the first few drags. Across the table from her, he did his own savoring, inhaling the pungent aroma of tobacco as it curled off the end of her cigarette. Even secondhand was better than nothing.

"Why weren't you out at your corner?" he asked.

She watched the smoke curl from the end of her cigarette. "I had my period."

"Doesn't keep you from givin' head."

"When I gets my cramps, I in no mood to be gentle."

Settled quietly in the corner with the notebook and recorder, Barb Dawson lifted one eyebrow. The woman had a point.

There was a knock on the door. Reeva cursed. Jack reached back to grab the handle.

"You available to take a call, Sarge?"

Jack traded looks with Barb. "Take a message, Nick."

The door closed and Jack righted his chair again. Barb hit the play-record button and Reeva ground the last of her cigarette onto the tabletop.

"One more time, Reeva."
"Shee-it."

Casey was back at her list. She'd learned a lot in the
last few days, and she didn't know any other way to keep
it straight. She didn't know how to sort the important
from the useless.

How did you weight the value of grapevine gossip?
Where on the list did you include a perfect alibi that
needed puncturing, or the contrary conviction that the
alibi was a lie? How about an ambiguous threat? An ex-
husband with a big mouth who had the ability to ruin
her?

Casey didn't want to think about the damage Ed could
do in his little golf outings. She'd been as much of a patient as anyone, settling onto his couch when it had still
been vinyl instead of leather and chrome, offering up her
own insecurities and uncertainties. She'd come to Ed for
help and ended up marrying him. In the end, he'd never
really helped her. But he still held her secrets. Secrets
Hunsacker would consume with the greatest of relish
and then spring back on her when she could least afford
it.

Casey was a different person now. Stronger, just as
Marva had said, because she'd had to be. Clearer, more
focused. Much more pragmatic. She knew what a person
could expect in this world, and what she couldn't. And
she knew that the only way to survive was to just keep
putting one foot in front of the other and focus on the
next step and the one after that.

She was just afraid that when she looked up, she'd find
Hunsacker standing in front of her.

Casey wished Sgt. Scanlon would call her back. She
wanted to ask about Crystal's penchant for promptness.

Was she the hooker with the notebook? Would Hunsacker have been in it?

Everything else on her list was probably useless, nothing more than fuel for her own suspicions. But the notebook might be something. Casey looked down at her notes one more time, trying to pull a game plan from them.

She was walking a more perilous tightrope now, with humiliation on one side and unemployment on the other. Each step she took had to be more careful than the last.

Downstairs the doorbell chimed. Casey looked up and sighed. The next step was going to have to wait. She had Janice to deal with first. Shuffling her scattered papers back into order, she slid them away and turned off her lamp.

Janice stood on her porch like a noblewoman on her way to the guillotine. Casey couldn't help but smile as she pulled open the door.

"Finally." She greeted her coworker with a smile she knew must look like one of Ed's. "We have the house to ourselves for the afternoon. Let's eat."

Janice's lips fluttered toward a smile of thanks. "Your mom?" she asked, eyes tracking the high, echoing rooms.

Casey shrugged and pushed the heavy wood-and-glass door shut. "Off saving souls in purgatory."

Janice actually sighed. "I hope she's saving mine."

"Food first." Her tennis shoes muttering on the hardwood floors, Casey led Janice past the entombed silence of the living room back into the cracked and comfortable kitchen.

Casey hadn't wasted her years living with Ed. She knew enough to ease Janice into her problem. Dessert was soon enough.

"I don't know what to do," Janice admitted, picking her chocolate cake into crumbs with the tines of her fork.

Casey spent a moment watching dust motes drift in the sun over by the sink.

"Wanna tell me about it?"

Janice's eyes were wet and huge, her forehead creased like an old letter. Her hands trembled, just a little. She'd been keeping a lot in.

"Your ex-husband ran around on you."

Casey just nodded.

Janice renewed the attack on her cake. "Aaron has done the same thing . . ." Courage seemed to require extra oxygen. Janice filled her lungs and continued. "And it wasn't with women."

Casey's own breath whooshed out. "Oh."

"Men," Janice spat. "A man, anyway. He knows him from the hospital."

Aaron was a nurse who worked at one of the mid-county hospitals, a postcard-perfect hunk with devastating blue eyes and enough hair on his chest to warrant a virgin fiber tag.

"Do you know who it is?"

Janice shook her head. "He swears it was just a fling, just . . . an experiment. Casey, I don't know what to do."

"Wow," Casey muttered. "I never handled that one before. For all Ed's quirks, he did like to be the only one in the bed with a penis."

Janice's look of surprise made Casey smile.

"He's a transvestite, not a bisexual. There's a difference."

"How did you make your decision?"

Casey sighed. "It was a final straw, not the whole reason. His running around was just a symptom of the problems."

Janice nodded, setting her fork down. It clanked listlessly against her plate as she studied the checkered table-cloth. "We've been having problems," she admitted. "We've been married nine years, and it seems like we're having the same arguments without resolving them. I'm frustrated, he's frustrated."

"Does he want to stay married?"

Her laughter was as brittle as her eyes. "Of course he does. He hates change."

"Do you?"

"Want to stay married?" She looked up, her eyes swimming again. "I don't know. I'm afraid I'd stay in it just because I'm as afraid of change as he is. We're comfortable together. We're a habit. Divorce is such a final thing, such an effort."

Casey waited, instinctively knowing there was more. There was.

"There's something else," Janice admitted, her hands on her table, her fingernails lined up like red bullets. "There's someone else."

"For you?"

Janice hesitated, hedged, finally shoved her chair back to give her more room. "I think I'm in love with him. I . . . I feel sometimes like all I want to do is escape with him, and it would take care of everything."

Casey dropped her own fork. "No," she said. "Don't do that."

Janice looked up at her, startled.

Casey faced her, surprised at her own vehemence. Wouldn't it just figure that she'd get into this conversation right after visiting with Ed the Led?

"Believe me when I tell you that running into a new relationship like that isn't going to solve your problems left over from your old one. It's just going to create new ones."

"You did that after Ed?"

"I did that *with* Ed. He was my escape. My savior who understood me and would make me feel better. All I did was step from the swamp into the morass. Trust me, Jan, it isn't the solution."

"Then what?" she demanded, jumping to her feet. "Life with Aaron is impossible right now. He doesn't understand, and I can't make him. We'd been making love less and less even before I found out about . . . the other thing. I think I want to leave, but I'm not sure I have the courage on my own."

"Thinking you want to leave is a lot different than knowing it," Casey advised. "Until you know, tell the other guy to keep his pants zipped."

She actually got a smile out of Janice on that one. A brief flash of revelation that betrayed just what kind of bedmate this new guy was. No wonder she was confused. Sex confused everything.

"You're a woman," Casey challenged her. "You're too intelligent to let your gonads lead you around."

Janice laughed and settled back into her chair. "But they're such lonely gonads."

It was Casey's turn to laugh. "Honey, when they've been singing solo for three years, you come talk to me. Till then, I got no sympathy." Scraping back her own chair, she got up to refill the tea glasses. "Get thee to a counselor, woman. Make Aaron go, too, so he can work out this experimentation shit. Move out if you need to, to see if you'll feel better. Live all on your own for a few months, because chances are that's what you'll be doing anyway if you leave. Then, and only then, will I permit you to run off with Studley Do-Right if you so choose."

Janice looked up with a fair amount of frustrated humor in her eyes. At least it was better than all that angst. "Gee, Mom, it's all so easy, isn't it?"

Casey topped off Janice's glass and turned to her own. "Of course not. But it is logical."

"Which is why we all respect your advice so much."

Casey snorted and sat back down. "If everybody respected my advice, we'd have three more nurses on the work lanes and Ahmed would be put on waivers."

They'd comfortably moved on to dishing dirt when the phone rang. Casey got to her feet, figuring Helen was calling for a ride home from her Sodality blow-out. She was surprised to hear the fatigued growl of Sgt. Scanlon on the other end.

"Can I call you back in about half an hour?" she asked immediately, turning toward the wall. Even Janice could innocently betray her now.

"You can," he retorted shortly. "But I thought you might want to know this now. Wanda Trigel's been found."

# *Chapter 10*

*CASEY COMPLETELY FORGOT* about Janice. "Where?" she asked, already hearing her answer in the caution in his voice.

"Couple of hunters found her down a ditch about half a mile from the Ramblin' Rose."

She didn't realize she'd lifted a hand to the ache in her chest. "And?"

He didn't answer right away. Casey guessed cops were as hesitant to be forthright to civilians as nurses were. "She'd been there a while. There wasn't a whole lot to go on. They think it was blunt trauma to the head."

Casey instinctively nodded. "How did you hear about her?"

Scanlon grunted. "APB's out on some guy she was buying drinks for that night. He's wanted here, too."

So, she wanted to say. I was right. Wanda didn't run off, she didn't leave her car behind. She was dead all the time and nobody looked for her until some poor schmucks in their camouflage and feed hats tripped over her rotting carcass back in the woods.

"He didn't do it," was all she said.

"Jefferson County seems to think so."

It was Casey's turn for a grunt. "They also thought she'd run off with a trucker."

It was news Casey had expected all along. It served to indict Hunsacker yet again in her mind. But she knew just the same it wouldn't help. Nobody would go looking for him just because he'd been called a shit-filled douche bag by the victim. In the end, the news of Wanda's death would only serve to increase Casey's sense of impotence.

"What did you want to tell me?" Scanlon asked. "I was in interrogation when you called."

Casey pulled fingers through her hair and shot a side-long look to where Janice was listening with more than a little interest. "Let me call you back on that. I have company right now."

"Suit yourself."

She wanted him to understand, but she couldn't say anything. "Thank you," she said instead. "I appreciate your calling me with the news."

"I thought you'd want to know."

Hanging up, Casey focused on the shaft of sun again, where it flowed in from the back bay window. Thick and golden and trembling with dust, it reminded her of the sun of cathedrals, ringing with enlightenment and inspiration, swollen with faith. Carrying prayers and incense up through the windows to God.

Carrying back warmth to earth to feed decay, warming a corpse so the bacteria could balloon, so the maggots could feed and grow and hasten dust back to dust. Melting identity and individuality back into fertilizer, the hopes and prayers decaying along with all the other body parts.

"Bad news, Casey?"

Casey offered Janet an apologetic smile. "A friend from back at St. Isidore's. Everybody thought she'd run away from her husband. They found her dead this morning."

Janice's mouth closed into an O of surprise. "God, how horrible. Do they know who killed her?"

"They think so. Somebody she was out drinking with."

Poor slob. Casey hoped he had an airtight alibi, or else he'd get snared in Hunsacker's web, too.

She was just about to return to the table when the phone rang again. She picked it up.

"Is Benny there?"

Well, it definitely caught Casey's attention. "Mom?"

"Catherine, dear, is Benny there?"

"No, of course not." Even so, she caught herself looking around, as if he could have snuck in behind her back. "Why in heaven's name did you ask?"

"Because I've been thinking of him," her mother answered as if Casey were slow. "I'm sure it's a message from Our Lady. She wants me to prepare."

"Good, Mom. Fine. Are you ready to come home?"

"Of course," came the answer. "I have to start dusting."

To dust to dust. Maybe it was a message. Maybe Benny was as dead as Wanda. They hadn't heard in two years And maybe Casey needed an afternoon at the movies to clear her head.

"On my way," she said and hung up.

She didn't get back to Scanlon till later that afternoon.

"Sgt. Scanlon," he answered as if finishing a sentence.

"I'm sorry it took so long to get back to you," Casey apologized. She was sitting back up in her room, her notes condensed to a small list of things Scanlon might like to know. They lay next to her *Taber's Medical Dictionary* and three historical romances on her old walnut desk.

The rest of the room was much the way she'd kept it

when she'd left for school. A canopied bed, window seat, rocker in the corner. The bulletin board with pictures of Paul Newman and Robert Redford had been traded for a series of Erte posters, and the stuffed animals had given way to books and stethoscopes, but it would always be Casey's haven. The top of the house, closest to the sky, the first room the moon found at night and the sun found in the morning. A bubble of quiet in a house that echoed.

"Is it all clear now?" Scanlon asked, just a hint of weary humor in his voice.

Casey couldn't say she was amused. "I've become a little more cautious in the last few days. I seem to have attracted Dr. Hunsacker's attention."

She expected Scanlon to blow her off, so it was a surprise to hear a funny little silence on his end.

"What do you mean?" he asked, suddenly not quite so tired.

"He's playing little games with me. Letting me know that he knows some of my secrets. I'm not sure I want him to have all of them just yet. The company I had over when you called before thinks he walks on water."

"He really has you spooked, doesn't he?"

Casey heard the distant tap-tap of a pen across the line and fought a smile. The sergeant was at work. "I'm looking forward to hearing your opinion of him after you meet."

Another silence punctuated by tapping. "What did you want to tell me earlier?"

"Oh, yeah." She pulled her notes up, glad he'd changed the subject. She knew she'd been cryptic about Hunsacker, but not everyone in St. Louis needed to know about Ed quite yet. "I wanted to ask if Crystal was obsessed with punctuality."

"What?"

"Did she yell at her, uh, customers if they were late for appointments?"

"Well, I'm not sure. I never made a date with her."

"Did she keep a rigid schedule?" Casey persisted.

There was that silence again. It was all the answer she needed.

Did she allow herself to hope now? "I think you'll find Hunsacker's name in her schedule book. Evidently she carried one with her everywhere. He would have seen her the same time every time he visited. Maybe she used some kind of code."

"No," he answered. "She didn't. She wrote everything out. Quite literate for a South Side Hooker. Her book disappeared when she was killed."

Now Casey was silent. She knew Scanlon would be able to hear the throb of bass from her stereo, Joe Cocker singing about help from friends.

She was getting tired of the turnarounds, the chances, the spark of hope only to run headlong into reality. She kept coming close and getting no closer.

"I'd hoped this might be something."

"It does tell me that maybe your doctor did know my dead hooker. Where'd you find out about the book?"

"My ex-husband. He and Hunsacker trade 'women in my life' stories over golf."

This time the tapping stopped. Casey could almost imagine him rubbing at his forehead, elbows on Dawson's desk, his face with that pinched pre-antacid look to it.

"Ms. McDonough—"

Her mother was right. He was still a Jesuit. He issued a complete warning against recklessness with no more said than her name.

"Sergeant," she countered in the same tone. "I have

to know. I have to reach the point where somebody else will listen to me."

"Hearsay evidence isn't admissible in court."

She smiled now. "It's enough to get a search warrant. At least it was on *Miami Vice.* I just want enough so that all you guys will start looking in the right direction."

"You are perseverant, aren't you?"

"My other commendations were for perseverance."

"Can I ask you a question?"

"Sure."

"Why are you so sure? I mean, nobody on earth would tie these three deaths to one person. There's not one damn thing that's the same. Not the weapon, not the site, not the circumstances. There's no pattern here, and what you're trying to tell me is that Hunsacker is a pattern killer."

"I'm telling you he killed three people. I don't know from patterns. I don't care."

"Why?"

Casey shook her head, frustration welling tight in her chest. Certainty, dread, fear, and all overwhelming her sense of logical communication. "It has to do with pelvics, Sergeant."

"Bones?"

"Exams. And unless you're a woman and have ever been through one, I can't tell you why I think Hunsacker's a psychopath just by his fondness for pelvics."

This time the pen seemed to skitter. He must have thrown it.

"Give me a try."

Casey snorted. "What, you're going to give me the church line about not having to be married to counsel couples? Strip, put your feet in stirrups, and make light conversation while somebody's sitting between your legs, and then we'll have something to talk about."

Much to Casey's amazement, Sgt. Scanlon laughed. She should have been furious. She found herself laughing along.

"I've been given a lot of suggestions," Scanlon admitted. "I think that was a first."

"Ask your Detective Dawson about it," Casey countered. "I bet she'd understand."

"Do me a favor," he asked, the levity in his voice dying. "Lay off for a while. I've spent the day interrogating the pimp's girlfriend trying to break his alibi. We also found that possible witness, the one who took off. She's coming in tomorrow morning. We should have something by noon."

"And you still think it's going to be the pimp."

"I still think it's going to be the pimp. If it is, the worst your doctor did was see a hooker with a tight schedule."

Casey didn't know quite what to hope for. It was like all those times Ed had come home late and she hadn't known whether she wanted proof he was seeing other women or not. What did you wish for, innocence or calumny? The anticlimax of relief or the hot flood of self-righteous indignation?

"You'll tell me," she asked. "Won't you?"

He seemed to be thinking about it, tapping something new. Fingers maybe. The sergeant either had great rhythm or was in dire need of magnesium.

"I'll tell you," he finally allowed. "I only hope it satisfies you."

She wanted to say it would. She couldn't. It would be a promise she didn't know she could keep. "Thank you, Sergeant," she did say. "You've been very patient about this."

"Like I said," he answered with the stiff formality of a shy man. "I never pass up a reasonable lead."

Casey hung up the phone wishing she could have told

the sergeant her intangibles. The little things she'd collected about her friends and Hunsacker that began to form a pattern, at least to her. She wanted to see his face when she told him about the way Hunsacker used his information about Ed, how slick and sly he was. She wanted the sergeant to understand about Hunsacker's eyes, because she often felt she was the only one who could see what they really looked like, like the guy in the old *Twilight Zone* who could recognize aliens because he was the only one wearing the right glasses.

Sitting alone in her room at the top of the world with her list, she sometimes felt very foolish, as if she were getting as delusional as Helen. Helen saw saints, and Casey saw sinners. An extension of their lives, a logical end to their beliefs. Casey was afraid she was losing her sense of humor, and if that happened, she'd be as much a ghost as her mother.

It was that dream. The memory of those years when she hadn't known how to break free, when she hadn't had the courage or insight or maturity. She'd come to that apartment a twenty-year old who accepted what she got as inevitable. She'd run four years later and vowed to never look back. Until Hunsacker, she hadn't.

For a long while Casey sat there alone with her suspicions, watching the sun gild the trees and slide toward the horizon. She listened to the croak and chatter of birds and the mutter of traffic over on Elm. For that long she held off the next step, because she didn't want to take it. She didn't want to step out her door into Helen's miasma of fervor, or the real world it held away.

The chapel was the only other room on this floor, a cracked, badly painted, old practice altar Benny had brought home from Kenrick Seminary littered with a forest of holy cards, attended by red and blue vigil lights, guarded by a myriad of Madonnas and one lonely Sacred

Heart. Helen's real family. More real than the faces downstairs she'd made up lives for, more real than her own children who had tiptoed through the house, dreading the sound of their mother's call.

Helen's temple of submission. Her altar of deliverance, built confession by confession over the years until Helen could never escape the finality of her decision, until her children could never run far enough away to quiet the remonstrances.

It was Casey's punishment for taking control that she was caught in her room with the puzzle of Hunsacker to solve. Her penance for not bowing to the power of a greater force. Everyone else submitted, to God or spouses or peer pressure. But not Casey. She had to stand alone. And because she had to stand alone, she was the only one with a clear view of Hunsacker's eyes. She stood on a box of self-pretentious pride that lifted her just high enough to see over that wall of manners he'd erected.

Maybe Helen was right after all. Maybe she should get out there and throw herself at the mercy of the holy cards and be absolved of this insight.

Casey knew better. She was stuck with her pride and her insight and memory of what real impotence felt like to fuel her fight. She wouldn't burn any incense in this house.

Down at city homicide Scanlon bent to retrieve his pen. Crystal's file lay spread out over his desk, where he'd been going over it again when Casey McDonough had called. While he'd been on the phone, somebody had dropped off a note from the captain. It sat on top of the crime-scene photos like a crow looking for leftovers.

The captain was complaining again about Jack's request for overtime. It was the captain's way of telling Jack that he didn't like him. Jack didn't need a note to figure that out. He got the message every time he was called into the office.

Jack wasn't a statistics man. He didn't close files just to clean up the city's numbers. He worried at a case until he was satisfied with it, and that wasn't the way to play the game. City elections were coming up soon, and the captain was the mayor's man. And Jack refused to help the mayor improve his crime stats.

The captain's note made a decent airplane, but it sank fast. Jack turned back to the task at hand.

The ME's shots taunted him. Spread like playing cards, both color and black and white of the crime scene, Crystal's blood dark in both shots, her skin as gray as her floor. Taunting his well-ordered logic.

She'd been a striking woman, tall and commanding, with an athlete's strong features. In the pictures they were misshapen and asymmetrical, like a deflating basketball. Blood matted in her blond hair and spattered the linoleum floor.

It hadn't been a quick death. Whoever had killed her had been in a rare fury. He'd used hands and feet and fingers, battering her until she wasn't recognizable as one of the prettier hookers on the stroll.

And then, after he'd beaten her to death, he'd cleaned everything, including the skin beneath her fingernails.

Scanlon was just turning back to Reeva's interview when the phone rang. His eyes on his work, he palmed the receiver.

"Sgt. Scanlon."

"Jarvis Franklin from Arnold," his caller informed him with a drawl. "Returning your call. What can I do for you now, Sarge?"

Jack started tapping. "Yeah, Franklin, thanks for calling back. I hear you found Wanda this morning."

Franklin snorted. "Coupla boys found what was left. After you and I talked about her car, can't say as I was real surprised. Funny how sometimes you don't pay attention to the nose on your face, ain't it?"

"Well, from the sounds of her, your guess was as good as mine." Scanlon tapped a little faster, not even hearing it anymore. "Tell me something, would you? Did you find anything on the car?"

"Well, I'll tell you, it's funny. Buddy refused to get in that thing after he got it back. Said it'd be bad luck. So we got it in a pretty pristine state. And there was nothin'."

"No latents?"

"No nothing'. It was clean as a soul on Sunday morning. I have a feeling that it was a blind alley. Ole Wanda had that thing over to the car wash every damn week. She musta had it there that day and vacuumed the shit out of it and then just left it at the Rose. And it rained that night. Big storm. Nothin' left of interest on the outside."

The tapping slowed. Scanlon didn't see Barb Dawson look up from her desk and watch. "What about Wanda?" he asked. "Anything?"

That got a real snort, the kind that implied he should have known better. Scanlon could just imagine. Just because he was in the city didn't mean he didn't see his share of decomposed bodies. Jarvis Franklin might have foxes and coyotes, but Scanlon had rats. Rats and heat can do a hell of a job in no time at all.

"Anything that struck you," he amended.

"Why?" Franklin asked. "Got somethin' for me?"

"Nope." Franklin would just love the story of the homicidal obstetrician. Scanlon laid down the pen and took up rubbing. "Just trying to appease that friend of mine that gave me the car idea."

"Only funny thing is her earrings."

"Her earrings."

"Yeah. She wore more earrings than Mr. T. Four on each side. Only one side was missing. All four of 'em. Other than that, she got hit with a big rock and died. We're still lookin' for Bobby Lee Martin, if you see him."

"I got the notice. We'll keep an eye out. Thanks."

He'd barely hung up before Dawson swung his way. "You don't have any friends, Bishop," she prodded, curious.

His fingers closing around his pen again, Scanlon looked over to where the paper airplane stuck ass end out of his trash can. Then he turned to consider the wry light in Dawson's sharp eyes. "Dawson," he said, leaning back and lacing his fingers behind his head, "tell me about pelvics."

There were some benefits to going in to work. It was really difficult to find the energy to weigh the merit of existential existence when you were hip deep in gomers. Control and submission didn't mean squat to a kid with a bean up his nose. When the shift was short three nurses and cursed with Ahmed as one of the docs, the most involved one could realistically get with personal problems was how long your deodorant would last.

Casey didn't get to dinner until almost nine. By then her only coherent thought was how she could get Ahmed deported.

And there, right on top of her bag, was a gift. There was no name attached, but Casey recognized Marva's handwriting. Casey picked up the packet of papers and pulled up a chair.

*Serial, Mass, and Sensational Murders, a Profile.* Casey laughed out loud. Leave it to Marva. Like the detective

fairies, leaving little clues around to help the amateur in-
vestigator solve his case. She should probably run right
home and check her closet to make sure somebody
hadn't left handcuffs in her shoes.

Marva couldn't afford to be involved, and Casey understood. But Marva believed her, and that was all that
counted right now. Especially since there were times
when she didn't believe herself.

Absently picking mushrooms off her pizza and popping them in her mouth, Casey opened the report and
began to scan.

"Serial murders are the murders of separate victims
with time breaks as minimal as two days between victims."

Casey felt a chill of prescience snake down her back.
She had an uncomfortable feeling about this. First line
of the report, and she was already labeling Hunsacker.

A serial killer. Nah. Bundy was a serial killer, Gacy,
Son of Sam. The kind of people who hustled strays and
then chopped them for firewood. Hunsacker wasn't like
that.

The report divided serial murders into two categories,
organized and disorganized. Disorganized killers included the folks who heard voices, saw visions, and
thought their cats were possessed. Psychotics.

After twelve years on the halls, Casey was well acquainted with that particular species. She'd had people
who thought they were everything from Mary Mother
of God to Larry the Cockroach. And, of course, St. Paul.
The only thing keeping St. Paul from ending up on some
DA's list was the fact that he thought Mother Mary's ER
was the Temple of Salvation. If the Temple had had a
Kmart sign over the door, some redheaded checkout
clerk would have been short one head.

Disorganized killers struck when the voices spoke,

which, as any visionary knows, is not a predictable thing. Their urge to kill disappeared with locked doors and regular doses of antipsychotics.

Organized killers, on the other hand, usually fell beyond the range of treatment. Organized killers were usually calm, logical, bright, and charming. They enticed their victims to their deaths just for the sport of doing it.

The human shark, the psychopath. Void of soul, bereft of conscience, hopeless of rehabilitation. Ted Bundy. Handsome, charismatic, manipulative, deadly.

Casey read on, her pizza getting cold on the table, her stomach churning, her trepidation mounting. She didn't even hear the door open.

"What you readin', child?"

Casey jumped and almost knocked over her soda. "Marva, don't do that to me."

Marva's smile was broad and unapologetic. "Good readin', huh? All you ever wanted to know about people who go bump in the night."

Casey shook her head. "They keep talking about Bundy's eyes."

Marva leaned over and grabbed a piece of pizza, then settled herself onto the edge of the table. "Do they?"

Sections of the piece were underlined. Marva knew all about Bundy's eyes. "It's one of the things that first bothered me about Hunsacker," Casey admitted. "His eyes never seemed . . . right."

Marva chewed on her pizza. "Dead," was all she said.

Casey nodded. "I wonder what his feet look like."

Marva almost choked. "You mean about that toe thing?"

"It's a statistic," Casey insisted, needing the levity all of a sudden. "A disproportionate number of serial killers have longer second toes than great toes. Now, the question is, how do we find out?"

Marva grinned. "Tackle him and pull off his shoes."

"Dump a urinal on his Dock-Sides. He doesn't wear socks."

Marva shook her head. "Too obvious."

"And tackling him isn't?"

"All right, we'll have Barb tackle him. She wouldn't mind, and he wouldn't be surprised. Get her to distract him, and we can sneak up while he's not watching."

"I'm not joining a ménage à trois just to play with his toes. That's not my kink."

"Honey, don't tell me what you kink ain't. You' horns gettin' so high, you could just as well start sashayin' up to Abe."

Casey gave a gentle grimace. "Thanks all the same. Some natural wonders are meant to be enjoyed from afar."

Casey didn't think to hide her reading when the door opened again.

"Casey, are you busy?" Steve asked, leaning in. He looked a little bemused, which was an alien expression for him.

"I still have about ten minutes to eat," she said. "Why?"

On the other hand, maybe she should have put the report up. The minute Steve spotted the picture of Ted Bundy on the open page of her report, Casey remembered that he was in the middle of an Abnormal Psych rotation.

"What's that?" he asked, walking on in. "Bundy? Boy, would I have loved to have interviewed him. You don't get a chance to put a serial killer under the microscope every day."

Casey choked back the urge to enlighten him. Why

was it the psych majors didn't see the psychopath under their noses?

"Somebody left this in here," she said, letting him pick it up. "Spooky reading. By the way, how long is your second toe?"

Steve chuckled. "Long enough to pick my nose with. Wanna see my collection of hunting knives?"

Casey actually shivered. "Not funny."

Steve's attention was still on the article he was flipping through. "I'll give you funny. Know what I found out last week? One out of ten serial killers is in the medical profession." Setting down the article, he gave Casey his best psychotic-on-the-loose look. *"Now* you want to see my hunting knives?"

Casey waved him off. "Next incarnation, thanks."

He was already heading back out the door when he remembered why he'd come in in the first place. "Uh, Case. If you're about finished, you got a personal request out there."

Casey closed the article and slipped it back into its envelope. She'd lost her appetite for pizza. "Request for what?" she demanded. "There isn't anybody out there I want to dance with, and I can't do 'Born to Run' without a backup band."

"Dr. Hunsacker."

Steve unwittingly knew just how to get his audience's undivided attention. Casey and Marva both stopped dead and stared.

Steve shrugged. "He's got a lady back in twenty with belly pain. He says he wants you to help him."

Casey exchanged looks with Marva. Then she turned back to Steve. "You're kidding."

"Only about my toes." Now he looked uncomfortable. "He says he'll complain to Jordan if he has to work with anybody but you. It sounded like a joke."

It sounded like it, but Steve wasn't sure. Casey couldn't formulate a decent reaction. She desperately wanted to tell Hunsacker to go to hell. She wanted to crawl under the microwave cart and become invisible. She also very much wanted to know what Hunsacker was up to.

"Tell him I expect a pizza for this," she finally answered.

Relieved, Steve ducked back out. Left behind, Casey and Marva refused to look at each other.

"One out of ten," Casey echoed, her eyes on the door, her head shaking slowly.

Marva didn't move at all. Her gaze was focused in the same direction, as if both of them could divine meaning through the barrier. "Makes sense," she acknowledged.

"Yeah," Casey admitted with dreadful fatalism. "It does, doesn't it?"

Her first thought when she saw him was that he was doing coke. He was high, talking a lot and unable to sit still. When Casey walked onto the hall he was regaling Steve and Janice with tales of a stag party he'd attended the night before. The minute he spotted Casey he grinned with triumph.

"Great." He spun toward her, hands out in welcome. "I was hoping you'd be on tonight. You're always so good to my patients."

Casey slowed on approach, afraid of getting too close, of somehow being sucked into that energy field of his. She was unnerved by the way he looked as if he were enjoying some kind of victory. Both Janice and Steve observed as if they were watching a foreign movie without subtitles.

"You want me to set her up?" Casey asked carefully, not bothering to reach for the chart.

"That would be fine," he said, his smile gluttonous.

Casey quelled a shiver and walked by to get his patient

ready. When it seemed he was going to touch her in passing, she shied like a skittish horse. He laughed.

"Casey here," he announced to Ms. Sydney Frazier a
few minutes later as he gently tapped the inside of her
thigh to get her to relax against his hand, "is my conscience. She doesn't let me forget anything. Do you,
Casey?"

She was close enough now to smell the bourbon. He'd
tried to hide it under mouthwash, but bourbon doesn't
surrender easily. He'd been drinking, was that it? He'd
gotten ripped and then decided it would be great blood-
sport to come in and terrorize Casey?

"And in return, I always try and keep Casey on her
toes," he went on, screwing the speculum into place and
bending for a better look. "I want her to pay close attention to everything, because that's the only way she's
going to learn."

Casey couldn't take her eyes off the back of his head.
Something about his words lodged in her chest, close behind her sternum where she stored her anxiety. And
along her neck. Right down at the base, where those little
flags of instinctive survival resided. They were stirring
again. Something was terribly wrong, and she didn't
know what it was.

Hunsacker dropped the speculum back on the tray
without Ms. Frazier ever once yelping. He'd completed
the pelvic with gentle dispatch. As he flipped the sheet
back down, he turned to make sure Casey had taken note
of it. She felt sick.

"That's all, then," he announced to his patient, his
gaze still fixed on Casey. "Casey'll help you dress."

Casey dismissed his patient without ever saying another word to him. Hunsacker didn't waste much more
time on her. Still leaning against the desk when she

walked back into the hall from cleaning the patient's room, he made it a point to stretch and straighten.

"Well, thanks again. I'll be off." His smile broadened and brightened for her as he slowed to a temporary halt. "It's been another long night, and I have an early day tomorrow."

He was already gone before Casey finally understood.

"Oh, my God," she gasped, scrambling to her feet. "The news. I haven't checked the news today."

Her palms already sweating and her heart rate doubling, she ran for the lounge and the little color portable the doctors had donated for Christmas. Ahmed was there ahead of her watching *Leave It to Beaver* reruns. Casey didn't even apologize. She flipped the channel just in time to see the news return from a commercial.

"And now," the announcer intoned, "to local news."

"What do you mean?" Ahmed demanded, reaching for the knob. "What are you doing?"

Casey slapped his hand away. This was just the news she needed. "Touch that knob and die," she threatened. She never noticed the astonishment on Ahmed's face.

A new contract for teachers, possible fraud charges against a local charity, a fire on the north side.

"And this just in," the announcer said to the accompaniment of dark video that throbbed with flashing lights and the shadows of bystanders. "A Ladue woman was killed tonight in a fiery one-car accident along a deserted stretch of Highway KK in O'Fallon."

Casey stood up. "Give the Beave my best, Ahmed." She felt sick.

She was on her way back toward the work lane when she heard her name being called. She wanted to ignore it. She wanted to walk on out the door and all the way home and hide back in her room where nobody could find her. Then the call came again and she recognized the voice. Casey whipped around on her heel to see Sgt. Scanlon striding her way.

He was still dressed for work, dark shirt, skinny tie, a gray sports jacket that flapped a little as he walked. His face was more animated than she'd ever seen it.

Casey found herself at a dead halt. "What are you doing here?" she demanded, wondering if she'd called him and forgotten already.

Scanlon reached her in two steps and took her by the arm. "Can we go someplace to talk?"

She looked instinctively over her shoulder to where Ahmed still sat and turned instead for room three. It was empty and had a cart in it in case she found herself in need of a place to pass out.

"I've been trying to get ahold of you," Scanlon said as soon as the door had sighed shut behind them. "We're bringing in Hunsacker tomorrow."

Casey couldn't manage anything more than a stupid stare.

Scanlon squinted at her. "You wanted to know. The hooker we were bringing in recognized Hunsacker from the photo. She doesn't remember if she saw him that night, but she knows he was one of Crystal's customers, and that's enough to question him on. It's not a conviction, but at least it's a start. We have a solid link to him."

Still, Casey couldn't formulate an intelligent response. She'd been sucker-punched too many times today already. She just didn't think she could take any more. Scanlon took hold of her, his hands tight around her arms as if contact would help her comprehend. His hair was rumpled and his jacket looked as if he'd crumpled it up and sat on it. Casey found herself wanting to straighten it out. She found herself wanting to fold right into his arms like a tired child.

"Casey," he insisted, giving her a little shake. "You're

the only one who saw this coming. At least enjoy it a little."

She looked up beyond his coat now. Saw the hint of
elation in his eyes and wished she had something better
to tell him. It was too late, though. Hunsacker had gone
to so much trouble to deliver his message.

So she passed it along to Scanlon. "He killed another
woman tonight."

# Chapter 11

*SCANLON HAD HER* by the arms again. "What are you talking about?"

Casey couldn't seem to get past head shaking. "Some lady from Ladue. She went toast off Highway KK out in O'Fallon tonight."

"How do you know?"

She laughed at the insanity of it, even though her stomach tipped again. "He told me. The son of a bitch came in here and demanded I help him with his patient just because he wanted me to know that he'd killed somebody else."

Scanlon took his hands back and shoved them into his pants pockets. Distance, Casey thought distractedly. He's afraid of getting contaminated by my delusions. She could hardly blame him. She was sounding like Helen with her messages from God.

"What exactly did he say?"

Casey looked up to see that deceptive laziness back in his eyes. He was the picture of passive acceptance, his stance relaxed, his jacket flaring out behind his forearms.

It didn't help make her admission any more logical. Casey decided she needed the cart after all. She leaned against it, wrapping her hands around the cool metal frame for balance.

"You remember I told you about the day I figured out he'd killed Crystal. How he carried on this perfectly innocuous conversation about what was in the paper and what a rough night he'd had the night before."

Scanlon nodded quietly. Casey nodded back, badly needing more conviction.

"And how I was convinced he was playing a game with me. Giving me a message nobody else would get."

Another nod, another pause for clarity.

"When he came in tonight, he asked for me to assist him. Said he'd complain to the brass if I didn't. He was . . . hyped, excited. He'd been drinking, too. It's really hard to explain, because he didn't really say anything. It was all in his eyes, in the way he danced around and taunted me. But then, just before he left, so I'd get the message, he said the same thing he said that day. About how he'd really had a rough night." Casey looked Scanlon in the eye and challenged him. "He was telling me he'd done it again. I saw the story on the news."

Scanlon didn't move, didn't offer support or disdain. "Was she a nurse? Somebody you knew?"

Casey shook her head. "They haven't released her name yet. But it's what he was trying to tell me. He was responsible. I knew the minute I saw it."

Scanlon did move then.

Letting his head drop a little, as if he had to consult some inner voice, he turned away from Casey and walked over toward the work-lane door.

Beyond the window Casey could see Steve burrowing in a cart for IV fluids and Janice in conference with Dr. Miller. The light over room six blinked and the phone beeped. Casey wiped her wet palms across the paper sheet and tried to be patient.

"You believed me all along, didn't you?" she asked.

He didn't look back at her. "I told you. I never over-look—"

Casey waved off his excuse. "Yeah, yeah. But you don't think I'm a space ranger."

Still folded into his considerations, Scanlon afforded Casey a ghost of a smile over his shoulder. "You said it. A pain in the ass, but no cookie crumbler."

How could she possibly feel better and worse at the same time? She thought about that Celtic knot she'd stud-ied on Poppi's wall, the endless maze that trapped you before you knew it. She was trapped, drawn in by her instincts and doomed by her persistence. Hunsacker had pissed her off with his manipulations. He'd taunted her with her impotence to stop him, not ever knowing that it was the one taunt she couldn't abide.

Come to think of it, until she'd found herself making lists in her room, she hadn't realized it, either.

She was trapped in a game with a snake. But she'd suf-fered too much turmoil, all those weeks she'd thought herself the only witness. She'd wondered too often whether she was the mad one, whether Hunsacker did no more than remind her of those terrible years in that black-and-white prison. She'd spent too long with only women as her confidants, when women were the last to be heard. And now, finally, she had an ally.

She wanted to thank him, to let him know just how much it meant to her. She wanted again to lean against him, physically just as much as emotionally. It had been so long since she'd been afforded even that much. But that wasn't something Casey allowed anymore.

"So we can go after him for all the murders?" she asked.

Scanlon turned on her, his hands still hidden, his face

still creased with thought. "I'm going to have enough to just get him in for Crystal."

Casey shoved off from the cart, outraged all over again. "But you *know* he did it."

Scanlon refused to flinch from her. "I might when I see him. I might be sure that he's responsible for everything from AIDS to the assassination of JFK. That doesn't matter. I have to take it one step at a time. With luck, and with patience, maybe I can get enough to call in the Major Case Squad, and let them go after him."

"But we don't have that kind of time," she argued, wanting so much for Scanlon to take the whole burden from her, to say, it's okay now. I'll handle it from here. "He's not going to stop."

"He's also on the mayor's Christmas card list."

Casey straightened abruptly, hands on her own hips. "That shouldn't make any difference!"

For the first time, Scanlon lost his temper. "Get ahold of *my* personnel file!" he retorted with enough pique that Janice looked up on the other side of the window.

Casey didn't notice. She didn't take her eyes from Scanlon's, still fighting reality, hoping for a reprieve. Knowing it didn't work that way. Scanlon was just as constrained by the real world as she was. Finally she sighed and shoved her own hands into her lab coat, her posture wilting. So she was going to end up standing alone again. So what else was new?

"Great," she mourned with a sad smile. "Just a couple of pains in a perfect world, huh?"

Scanlon had the good grace to smile back, and Casey couldn't help but like him anyway. Even if he had been a Jesuit.

"New patient to room three. Nurse to room three stat."

Casey started, stared up at the speaker in frustration. "Oh, hell. Wait a minute."

She was turning to head off the invasion when Scanlon spoke up behind her. "Casey, I think you should come back with me tonight."

"I can't—"

Casey had just about reached the door when it slammed in on her. Mike clattered in, pushing a wheelchair with a very pasty, very sick middle-aged man slumped in it.

Casey was on the move the minute she saw him. One whiff and she was running. He had a big GI bleed, the bucket in his hands already sloshing with the blood he'd vomited. It was flecked across his white lips and spattered down his shirt, thick and dark and deadly.

"Mike, get me some saline," Casey snapped, whipping around to get the patient onto the cart before he crumped right on the spot. His eyes were already rolling. "Lots of fluids. Call blood bank and get lab up here. And get me the biggest NG tube you can find.

"Had better days, huh?" she asked the patient with a wry smile. He did his best to stay focused on her as she flipped up the side rails.

"I mean it," Scanlon insisted, sounding kind of funny. "I'm not sure you're safe."

Casey ran for the nurse server and began yanking out equipment. "And see if you can get Ahmed in here!" she yelled to Mike's fleeing back as she swung into a gown.

"Casey."

"No," she answered, pulling on gloves. On the cart, the patient was making funny noises. Casey hopped over and yanked the bed up a little so that he wouldn't aspirate when he puked again. "We're shorthanded."

"You're also my only link to Hunsacker."

Sliding her stethoscope into place one-handed, Casey

looked up from where she bent over to get a blood pressure. "Just a little louder please, so they can all hear it. It will make my life so much easier."

Scanlon was looking white again. Greenish white. Casey couldn't blame him. It wasn't the sight, it was the smell. The worst smells list was a standard around the ER, and hands-down champ was the smell of a gastrointestinal bleed, the kind of pungent, syrupy odor that followed you for days, that wouldn't quite rinse off. The room was awash in it.

"I have to get back and check on that story," Scanlon insisted. "I want you to come with me."

Well, there was a blood pressure anyway. Casey pumped the cuff up again and went for a vein. A big vein. Mike must have impressed somebody out there, because Marva pushed through from the work lane with a couple of bags of Lactated Ringers in her hands and a blood pump.

"You with the patient?" she asked Scanlon on the way by.

"He's with me," Casey answered, slapping at the arm she held to get venous pressure.

Marva stopped a millisecond to smile. "Ain't she a great date?" she demanded. Then she caught the Cathlon Casey flipped to her and got down to business.

"All right now, Jesus, be good to your Marva, help me get this line . . ."

"See?" Scanlon demanded from his corner, his voice sounding even more strained. "There's somebody else here now."

Casey still couldn't find the vein on her side, either. "Are you going to stay in here?" she demanded crossly.

He glared back. "Yes."

Reaching over with one hand, she plucked a pair of

gloves from the box and tossed them to him. "Then get dressed. You get to help."

She should have felt guiltier. Scanlon stuck it out as long as he could. But when the level on the bucket rose again, he opted for retreat. And Casey, in one of her less noble moments, grinned. She finally felt better about having to walk onto Scanlon's turf. He'd walked onto hers and lasted about as long.

"What *was* that?" he asked a while later when she found him sitting in the lounge. He had some of his color back, but his hair was a little wet, so Casey imagined he'd been performing a little fresh-air rejuvenation. Anybody else unaccustomed to that scene would have driven the porcelain bus a block or two. Casey had the feeling that Scanlon hadn't allowed himself to vomit since he was ten.

"That," she informed him with some satisfaction, going back after the cold piece of pizza she'd left behind so long ago, "is what happens to people who do not take care of their ulcers." Munching on congealed dough and cheese, she shot him a meaningful look. "Which of course you have done."

Scanlon's eyes were riveted on her actions. "I thought *my* stomach was strong."

Casey smiled in commiseration. "Like the man says, there's worse things than dyin'. At least for the cleanup crew."

Completely composed once more, Scanlon got to his feet and grabbed his jacket from where it was draped over one of the chairs. "Are you ready to go now?"

Casey considered him. "You mean it. After all this time, *suddenly* I'm in danger? Why wasn't I in danger yesterday?"

Scanlon's smile was grudging and knowing as he shrugged into the jacket. "Because I didn't have any way to prove you weren't a space cadet yesterday. Besides, I didn't know about Elizabeth Peebles yesterday."

Casey couldn't quite get the pizza back up to her mouth. "The lady in the car?"

Scanlon nodded. "Single car, ran into a tree and exploded. Nobody knows why. There aren't any skid marks or signs of another car. She was supposed to be on her way out to her country home. It's going to be a long night, Casey. I need you to tell me everything you can about Hunsacker before I get him in my interrogation room tomorrow."

Casey's answering smile was grim. "If we can stop by my house, I have notes."

Behind her, Marva breezed in with the bag containing her once-clean uniform in hand and scrubs in its place. "Why, hello," she greeted Scanlon with a suspiciously pleasant air. "You stuck it out after all. I was wondering."

Scanlon didn't see fit to react past an enigmatic smile. He busied himself with pulling out car keys.

"Marva," Casey obliged. "This is Sergeant Scanlon. Sergeant Scanlon, Marva Washington."

Marva's eyebrow slid north. "Sergeant?" she demanded, swiveling on Casey.

"Did I tell you I talked to the police?" Casey asked.

"You did not tell me you talked to the police."

Casey's smile was placid. "Well, now the police want to talk to me."

Marva turned to Scanlon. "Make it hurt," she suggested equably, and then walked back out.

Frontenac was a far cry from where Jack Scanlon grew up. The oldest son of an Irish cop, Jack had been raised in Dogtown where Irish cops lived. In the city. He'd been raised on corkball and the fights and fish fries over at church during Lent. The house where his mother still lived was a two-story white frame that looked pretty much like every other house on the block, with a chain-link fence, yard and a porch, and the school playground two blocks away for recreation. He'd bought his first car with the money he'd saved from working at the Steak 'n' Shake, and his father had taken a second job to get Jack through St. Louis University High School.

He hadn't had yard services and pools and preschools. He hadn't been given a car for his sixteenth birthday and another when he wrecked that one. He hadn't had skiing vacations and an allowance that would have supported his sister's family for a month. Jack had had a front porch and two rigid ethnic codes, Italian and Irish. He'd inherited his father's black Irish looks and his mother's Italian determination. He'd also inherited his city neighborhood's disdain for the upscale neighborhoods in the county.

"I want to get a look at that book," he told Dawson as he turned off Conway Road back into one of the newer subdivisions built by all the medical money in the area.

Rubbernecking at the half-million-dollar houses they passed, Dawson just shook her head. "You're gonna be lucky he doesn't file a harassment suit."

"He's a doctor, not a lawyer."

"I'll bet money he calls Murray Abrams before we take our fingers off the front doorbell."

Murray Abrams was the "lawyer who counted" in the upper social circles of St. Louis. Jack refused to take the bet. Checking the address one more time, he turned into a driveway.

Dawson whistled in appreciation. "Screw law and order," she decided. "I want to deliver babies."

The house definitely made a statement, and that was: I have money and can spend it. Two-story stucco with more windows than an airport, it spread out over its acre lot like a modern art museum, white and sleek and classy.

Jack decided it was pretentious. "It's all going to be in that notebook he carries around with him," he said, his gaze on the house. There was a black Porsche in the driveway with BBDOC on the license. "Every nasty little thing he's done, neat and orderly and exact."

"You really think this guy's Dr. Jekyll, don't you?" Dawson squinted over at him. Dawson had sat in on Casey's interview the night before. The neatly wrapped brunette detective had received Casey's allegations without a shred of surprise. A male cop would have hooted for an hour. Which was why she was here.

"I think he's connected with Crystal Johnson's death," Jack corrected her as he reached to open his door. "Until we see how this goes, that's all."

Dawson opened her own door and followed Jack out into the sun. "Thanks for inviting me along, Scanlon. I wouldn't have missed meeting him for the world."

The two of them instinctively matched strides as they walked up the flower-lined walk. Pulling out his identification, Jack leaned on the doorbell. The door opened immediately. They had been watched.

"Yes?"

Jack flashed the badge. "Dr. Dale Hunsucker?"

His suspect leaned an arm against the door frame and smiled. "That's me. Can I help you?"

No surprise. No agitation. He looked as if he were enjoying himself.

"Doctor, I'm Sgt. Scanlon, St. Louis City Homicide. This is Sgt. Dawson." He waited for Dawson to lift her badge. The doctor made a show of looking. "We'd like to ask you to come with us. There are some questions we need to ask."

He was blond and handsome and suntanned. A real

poster boy for the good life. Beyond him Jack could see that the house was decorated in sleek, modern furniture. A lot of white with accents in black and peach. Spare, striking, precise. Jack thought it looked dead.

There was something else. Nothing notable in any other house. In fact one hung on the wall in his mother's house right inside the kitchen where she could use it when the grandkids came over. Here, in this museum, it stuck out like a sore thumb and made Jack itch like hell for a search warrant.

There on the hall table sat a brand-new Dustbuster.

"Questions," the doctor echoed, leaning a little more, smiling a little harder. "Well, sure, come on in."

"We'd rather not. If you don't mind, we'd rather conduct the interview downtown."

All they got was a pleasant shrug. "Sure. Come on in while I get my wallet."

That was when Jack knew that Casey McDonough was right. Dr. Hunsacker hadn't been surprised. He hadn't been upset. And he hadn't asked the first question any sane man would ask when confronted by police. Why?

Casey heard the results of the interview on the news. She'd spent the entire night down in one of those claustrophobic little interview rooms at the back of the city homicide offices answering Scanlon's questions. She'd talked about every incident she could remember involving Hunsacker, every funny look or leading statement. She'd given him Ed's statistics, and information on the other murders that he didn't want to hear about. She'd shared bad coffee, worse hamburgers, and abysmal humor.

Scanlon had driven her home sometime close to dawn, and gone back to start his own shift. He was planning on picking Hunsacker up at eight, hoping to find him still at home on his day off. Casey spent the hours after he left watching the clock, too wired to sleep, too tired to read. She paced in the kitchen while Helen prattled on about miracles and faith, and waited for Scanlon to call.

She wondered if Scanlon had ever found a connection between Hunsacker and Mrs. Peebles. A rich recluse who preferred her own five acres in Ladue to the tony set, Mrs. Peebles had cultivated few tastes that would have caused her to cross Hunsacker's path. She'd been fifty-five, a grandmother, and a patient of Fernandez.

On the surface, Hunsacker had no reason to want her dead. All the same, she was a crispy critter, and he'd been crowing about it. Casey was beginning to believe that if anybody could find out why, it would be Jack Scanlon.

"Aren't you going to help me clean Benny's room?" Helen asked when she saw Casey dressed for work.

Her eye still on the silent phone, Casey just went on stuffing lab coat and stethoscope into her bag. "I'm going to work," she said, wondering why she should have to say anything. She was in a uniform. It was usually a dead giveaway.

"But, Catherine," Helen objected, fingers plucking at Casey's sleeve, her voice high and anxious, "everything's different now, isn't it? I thought we could prepare. I mean, what if we're not ready? What if we lose our chance?"

"What chance?" Casey demanded, too tired and stressed for Helen's catechism games, wanting only to pull away from her mother's grasping fingers.

"Our second chance," Helen insisted. "Don't you see? We have a second chance, and we can't waste it. That's why Benny's coming home. It's why we have to be ready, Catherine. You and I, because it's our responsibility."

"Work," Casey snapped, prying her mother's fingers

loose. "That's what my responsibility is, and if I don't get in on time I don't get a second chance."

Helen's eyes swelled with tears and Casey felt like a heel.

"Don't you understand?" her mother whispered, wringing her hands.

Casey fought to comprehend the frail, trembling woman. She tried to understand her distress. But with Helen, everything was cause for either distress or holy ecstasy. Casey just couldn't keep up anymore.

"Mom," she said, dropping a quick kiss to assuage her guilt. "I'm going to work. Like I do every day. I'll see you in the morning, and we'll do Benny's room then."

Then, because she couldn't stand to look at those frightened, tear-filled eyes any longer, Casey walked out the door.

She hoped for a busy shift. She didn't get it. The hours stretched there, too, with few patients and nothing more than busy work to occupy the staff. Casey went from exhilaration to frustration to fury, somehow knowing that the longer she went without hearing from Scanlon the worse the news would be.

She found out just how bad when she and Marva and Janice were sitting in the lounge eating dinner.

"Who was that guy here last night?" Janice asked as she picked at her prepackaged diet dinner. "Was he your brother?"

Casey almost choked on her tuna salad. "God, no. Benny's as bald as Abe. Except that Benny does it on purpose—at least he did the last time I saw him."

Casey ached she was so tired. She'd tried without luck three times to lie down, and now her eyes felt like misshapen lumps of sandpaper. Her head hurt and she felt as if gravity were sucking her straight through the floor. And she was still jumping every time the phone rang or the door opened. She kept hoping for Scanlon and expecting Hunsacker.

"That was her date," Marva announced from where she was stretched out on the couch, hands folded on her stomach, contemplating the snakebite chart they'd taped to the ceiling. On the wall where the snakebite chart had been was a Peanuts poster with Lucy proclaiming, "I love mankind. It's people I can't stand." "Had a late night of it, too, didn't you, girl?" Marva asked, her gaze never straying from cottonmouths and copperheads.

Cascy obliged them all with a heartfelt yawn. "A late night," she agreed.

"We could have a Japanese dinner where you have to take your shoes off," Marva offered with a straight face.

Casey refused to encourage her.

The news was on. Casey vacillated between wanting to throw everybody out and turn the sound up, and putting her fingers in her ears so she didn't have to find out. She was afraid she'd hear something, and afraid she wouldn't. It had been all day, after all, with no word from Scanlon. Had he learned anything? Had he made any strides, or been caught by bureaucracy? What had he thought of Hunsacker when he'd finally gotten hold of him?

"And in a bizarre twist to a murder case today," the anchor announced only a few minutes later, "a prominent West County physician was questioned by police in the May tenth murder of South Side prostitute Crystal Jean Johnson."

Casey froze. Marva bolted upright just in time to catch the video of Hunsacker down at headquarters.

"Oh, my God," Janice breathed, her fork clattering to the table.

"Officials refused to comment except to say that all leads were being followed in an attempt to solve the mur-

der. Ms. Johnson was found beaten to death in her apartment on Ohio Avenue. No arrests have been made."

Another clip followed, Hunsacker walking back out
into the afternoon sunshine, suitcoat over his arm, lawyer
at his elbow.

"A case of mistaken identity," he assured the smiling
blond female reporter with a look of confused weariness
that evoked harsh lights and rubber hoses. His shirt was
spotless and crisp, his tie deftly knotted, and yet he still
somehow looked rumpled and mussed. He shook his
head and shrugged, like a disaster survivor trying to comprehend his situation. "I can't imagine . . ."

And then Casey was sure he looked right at her.
Pinned her with her culpability, his attitude of the persecuted innocent somehow threatening. She stopped
breathing, the tuna salad caught somewhere around her
second rib, her stomach declining more.

He would be in here tonight, she just knew it. He
would walk straight up to her and gloat, sipping the wine
of her humiliation, and there wouldn't be a damn thing
she could do about it. She felt so suddenly sick.

"My God," Janice repeated, her tone almost reveren-
tial. "Dale. How could they think he'd be involved in
something like that?"

She obviously didn't see Marva and Casey exchange
glances.

But it had to get worse. The news crew had to interview the detective who was good enough to hand them
the juiciest story of the month.

"Date?" Janice suddenly echoed, seeing Scanlon fending off questions with stone-faced determination. "You
just happen to be dating a homicide detective?"

"Imagine that," Marva commented, lying back down.
"An ER nurse dating a cop. You'd only be the—what—
sixth one down here, wouldn't you, Case?"

Casey knew better than to think they were going to get away with it. Janice already had that look of betrayal in her eyes. It wouldn't have mattered if Casey really had been dating Scanlon, if they'd met at the bowling alley and shared a passion for tropical fish and Chinese food; Janice had already branded Casey a traitor. Hunsacker was being persecuted by the police, and Casey had been seen in the company of the same police no more than twenty-four hours before. It was too much of a coincidence.

Which, of course, it was. Casey knew that her secret was out. No matter what turn the whole sordid situation took from here, she would always be found wanting in the eyes of her friends. She'd betrayed a member of her own profession, and that wasn't easily forgiven.

"How could you do that to him?" Janice demanded, chocolate-brown eyes suddenly sore and distant. "He might have seen a prostitute once. He wasn't proud of it. But it's not murder. Do you hate him that much that you'd betray him to the police?"

Casey wished there were some way she could make Janice understand. But the truth was, she'd never understand. She would never hear the real story. Her loyalties, just like everyone else's down here, had long since been cast. Casey's words wouldn't change her perceptions of Hunsacker. Casey's charges wouldn't make any sense.

Janice sat stiff and unyielding and waited for Casey's answer. Casey faced her across the table, her hands clenched into fists on either side of her dinner. She had no answers for her friend.

For the first time in the twelve years she'd walked hospital halls, Casey felt the first chill of alienation. These people had always been her family, her support when she'd bucked the odds and the superiors. They had buffered her and strengthened her and formed the cadre of her universe. They had had her unconditional trust, and she'd had theirs.

Until now. She'd taken a step away, chosen against her little world of medicine. And because she couldn't explain, at least not yet, they couldn't know why. Casey saw it in Janice's eyes, and knew that it wouldn't be long before she saw it in others.

"How?" Janice repeated. "How could you do that to him? How could you betray a confidence like that?"

In the end, Casey didn't answer at all. "I didn't do anything to anybody," she said, and made an effort to return to her tuna.

"You've helped ruin a man's reputation," Janice accused and stalked out.

Marva watched as the door slammed in Janice's wake. "Betray what confidence?"

Casey considered her sandwich without relish and set it back down unfinished. "Knowing that he liked hookers, I guess." Casey pushed her food away. "God, I was really hoping nobody'd know for a while."

Marva just stretched back out again. "You need to talk to that date of yours."

Casey couldn't even manage the energy to throw something at her. And then, of course, the phone finally rang, and it was the right call.

"I'm sorry I couldn't call sooner," Scanlon apologized.

Casey gave in to the temptation to lay her head in her arms. She didn't even want to face Marva anymore. "It didn't do any good," she accused. "Did it?"

"I don't remember promising that it would. We did what we could, and his lawyer did what he could, and now we go on from there."

"What about the witness?"

"Couldn't really positively ID Hunsacker when she saw him. Says he looks different from when he visited

Crystal. She wasn't sure he was there the night of the murder anyway."

"What did he say he was doing?"

There was a pause. "He says he had an emergency at Mother Mary that night, and then went home alone. Believe it or not, we even got the patient record, and he's right there, signed in not more than twenty minutes before Crystal died."

"He's lying," Casey instinctively objected. Suddenly her words sank in and her head came up. "Oh, God, of course."

"What?"

"The time. He always puts the times on his notes—when he gets there, when he leaves. And, of course, once it's in print it's a legal fact. But who says he's telling the truth?" Casey was talking about Crystal, but she was thinking of Evelyn. It would explain the time dilemma, how he could have gotten twenty miles in twelve minutes. He'd just lied on his notes.

"All well and good, but unless you can find somebody who can swear differently, those notes are an airtight alibi."

"Let me look at the chart."

"I didn't mean *you.* I have one of my guys working on it. You'll do a lot better if you aren't seen with us. I have a feeling this is going to turn ugly fast."

"Too late," she assured him, rubbing at her eyes. "I've already been seen with you, and it *is* ugly. Nothing left to do but help. What about Mrs. Peebles?"

She heard the hesitation in his voice and was surprised by the following sincerity. "I'm sorry," he allowed with disconcerting sympathy. "That was my fault. I shouldn't have shown up without warning you."

Casey was surprised by the sting of tears. Leave it to a cop to be the most compassionate person of the day.

"I'll live," she assured him with fraudulent ease. "As you can guess, this isn't the first time I've unsuccessfully bucked the system. Now, what about Mrs. Peebles?"

"Still no connection. No motive."

Now for the big question. Casey shot a look over to see that Marva's eyes were closed, but her antennae were up. Casey needed support on this one, because the answer was so important.

"So," she said, gripping the phone like a handhold on a high tower, her eyes shut against disappointment. "What did you think of him?"

Scanlon shuffled something on his desk. "Well, I'm not sure about AIDS, but I bet he knew Oswald."

Casey's face crumbled into a relieved smile. "What did Dawson think?"

"That he's about the most charming, handsome, intelligent man she's ever met." Scanlon's pause was torture. Casey could hear the ghost of humor return to his next words. "But she wouldn't put her feet in his stirrups unless she had a gun in her hands."

Casey felt herself deflating. She hadn't realized just how much she'd steeled herself against Scanlon's opinion, judging her own suspicions by it, measuring her own sanity against it. His words validated her, absolved her. She wasn't crazy. She wasn't manufacturing leaps of logic that would have put Helen's leaps of faith to shame.

Hunsacker was the villain, not her. He was capable of everything she'd accused him of. She hadn't just manufactured all the funny little things that added up only in her mind. He was bad.

Tears again. Casey wanted to scream. She cried when she was mad and she cried when she was upset and she cried when she was relieved. And right now she was so relieved that she had to squeeze her eyes shut and wipe at her face with her arm, and still her sandwich was getting soggy. For a minute she couldn't even manage to get out the words of thanks that were so important to her.

Scanlon broke the silence first, his end of the line suspiciously still, his voice a little gruff. "You okay?"

Casey nodded three times before she could get the words out. "Yeah . . . uh, yeah, thanks." That made her angrier. She knew damn well he could hear the quaver in her voice. She cleared it and tried again. "I just . . ." That didn't work, either. It seemed instead of dissipating, her tears were building, like a flood that had finally crested.

Scanlon's voice was as gentle as she'd heard it. "A little lonely out there all by yourself on the path of truth and righteousness sometimes."

Casey nodded again, breathing hard to hold herself together. "Yeah."

"If he comes in to work tonight, be someplace else, okay?"

"Okay."

"I'll talk to you again tomorrow. I have some more questions."

Another nod. Another attempt at composure. "Jack?"

"Yeah."

"Thank you."

Casey could definitely hear a smile now. "I never overlook a legitimate lead."

She managed to get the receiver back into the cradle before sobbing.

Marva was already standing next to her, close but not too close, her long face a study in impatience. She thumped a tissue box onto the table in front of Casey and sat down. "What did that boy say to you?" she demanded.

Casey yanked out a couple of tissues and hiccuped with the tears that refused to abate. The smile she gave Marva was a picture of watery exhilaration. "He thinks Hunsacker is pond scum."

Marva straightened, considered, nodded. "A man with some sense," she marveled. " 'Bout time."

"God, I feel so stupid. I feel so *good.*"

"Wages of righteousness, honey. You got a right."

"That's just about what Scanlon said."

Marva nodded. "Good Christian man."

That made Casey laugh. She wanted to explain, but it was hard enough explaining Jesuits to Catholics, much less Baptists.

"So what happens now?" Marva demanded.

"Now," Casey admitted, her flood checked by a backwash of reality, "we just have to prove he's pond scum."

Marva rolled her eyes. "Oh, yeah," she muttered. "That oughtta be easy."

# Chapter 12

*IT WAS ONLY* the first day of June, and already the streets of the city shimmered with heat. The sky was washed out, the air heavy with the smell of hops from the brewery. Sunlight struck sharp shards of lights from car roofs. Pedestrians walked as if through a high tide, battling the humidity and exhaust for breathing space. St. Louis sweltered as it waited for its first big storm of the season, long overdue and badly needed. Natives watched the sky and wiped their foreheads and ached for thunder.

Fewer cops stood out on the headquarters' steps today. They littered the lobby instead, standing in clots of blue beneath the high, echoing ceiling. More visitors crowded onto the stark brown bench in the waiting area, but Casey had the feeling it was more for the air-conditioning than the justice.

Scanlon met her by the elevators behind the control desk.

"Thanks for coming down," he greeted her, hands in pockets, jacket coat splayed back again, attire not appreciably different. Casey wondered if he had a different color dark shirt for every day of the week. The priesthood seemed to have ruined him for pastels. But then, she couldn't imagine him in anything else.

Pulling out one hand, he held the door open until Casey joined him.

"Hey," she said, stepping on board. "Who wants to sleep past eight in the morning anyway? I'd feel more self-righteous if you didn't look like you need the sleep more than I do."

Scanlon almost smiled as he let go of the door and punched a button. "I'm sorry I called you so early. I was tied up yesterday and couldn't get back to you."

"I'm sorry Helen answered the phone."

He resumed his position, eyes up on the progressing numbers. "She wanted my advice on signs from God."

Casey groaned. She hadn't heard that part.

Scanlon shot her a sly look. "Then she said it didn't count since I wasn't Catholic anyway."

Casey offered a weak grin. "She's not sure the pope should have ever reinstated Jesuits back in 1720."

"That's all right," he allowed. "Neither is the pope."

The doors opened to another green and brown hallway. This was Casey's third trip to homicide, and she still got lost in the rabbit warrens that made up the fourth floor. All the crimes investigations units were stationed up here: burglary, juvenile, sex crimes, bomb and arson, homicide. Each section had more people than space and a floor plan that had been laid out about the turn of the century.

Homicide opened up to the left. Scanlon led her through the door into the first office where two detectives looked up and then returned to work. They were members of the service crew, the detectives who responded to a murder call, who worked with the medical examiner and the evidence technicians to secure the scene and get down the details. They conducted initial on-site interviews and collected what data they could before handing the case over to one of the investigating officers next door.

The investigating officers worked the case until it was solved, or until it went back into the file room with only periodic updates to keep it open. There was a flow board in the lieutenant's office delineating each murder, its status, and the team working on it. Casey saw that Scanlon had his name associated with eight different listings.

Two doors down the side hall from the service crews was the sergeant's office, which Hunsacker shared with three other people. It was where Casey had first met him, where she'd sweated and stammered through her story. Walking in today, she smiled easily at the other two men who shared the office with Scanlon and Sgt. Dawson.

The detectives were in the process of shrugging into jackets. One was a tall Viking type, the other compact and Mediterranean. Both dressed much too well for the homicide officers Casey had ever seen. She'd been exposed to the county's lovely brown polyester uniform jacket, and the Jefferson County cowboy look. She'd watched years of *Columbo* and read Waumbaugh, and figured cops dressed like refugees from a bargain basement. Evidently the mandate was different in St. Louis City.

"Where are you going?" Scanlon asked them as he shrugged out off his own jacket.

"We're on the way to make America safe for snitches everywhere," the small one announced, opening his desk drawer and pulling out a gun. He checked it and slid it into a waist holster, his movements quick and broad, as if he could barely contain his anticipation.

Scanlon pulled over two well-used mugs and filled them from the coffee maker. "Got warrants on Ice Man?" he asked.

"Got warrants, got an address, got his girlfriend fixin' us all breakfast if we get there quick enough."

"Casey," Scanlon said almost as an afterthought. "This is Nick Capelli." The skinny one.

He grinned with a set of perfect flashing teeth and slid a black snap brim over his eyes that perfectly matched his tailored black suit, white shirt, and skinny tie. He looked like a hit man. "He never buys *me* coffee."

Scanlon didn't seem to hear him. "And that's Rich Whelan."

The Nordic type nodded from where he was pulling a beeper from a desk drawer. Then he lifted another snap-brim hat from the rack and preceded Capelli out the door.

"Later," they chorused.

Casey lifted an uncertain hand in response.

Waving her to a free chair, Scanlon pulled his out and settled into it. There were more files on his desk, and a stack of return-call messages.

"You know," Casey marveled, still looking after the departing detectives, "it really is different down here."

Scanlon leaned back in his chair and took a first sip of coffee. "How so?"

Casey couldn't help a grin. "My area of the county's a little white bread, if you know what I mean. I guess I expected the cops down here to be the same way. Do you have a hat, too?"

Scanlon inclined his head from behind his coffee cup. He was leaning so far back, Casey wondered how he kept from tipping over. "I have my stingy brim. Sure."

"Stingy brim?"

Scanlon motioned to the black hat that had been left behind atop the coatrack. "Official hat of homicide. Narrow brim, flipped up in the back like a duck's ass."

"So you all look like Mafia dons."

His mouth twitched with humor. "Something like that."

Casey took to her own coffee. The brand down here wasn't much different than what they inflicted over at the hospital, equal parts fuel oil and old socks. "Why do you all wear hats?"

"To protect our heads. Do you know what kind of a mess you can walk into when you show up for a jumper?"

Almost before he got the words out, Scanlon stiffened. Casey could tell he'd spoken before he'd thought about it, revealing more to a civilian than he thought he should have.

But Casey wasn't really a civilian in that sense. "No kidding?" she retorted thoughtfully, and then grinned. "Shows you the difference in our professions. By the time we get 'em, we're worried about keeping our feet clean."

Scanlon didn't move, but Casey had the impression that the distance he maintained between them had just narrowed. Fingering his cup, his expression betraying nothing, he turned his attention to the work on his desk. "How are things doing over at the hospital?"

Casey shifted in her seat, crossing her ankle over her leg and resting her mug atop her jeans. "If I were a person given to clichés, I'd say I'm finding out who my real friends are. Nobody likes a good rumor like a hospital, and the latest is that I accused Hunsacker to pay him back for spurning my advances."

"Did you?"

That brought Casey up short. Even in that straight, uncompromising chair, she stiffened like a queen being accused of treason. "What kind of question is that?" she demanded.

He watched her, passive and quiet, his eyes half-closed again. "It's a question somebody's bound to ask. You leveled a hell of an accusation on him. Why should you be so surprised that somebody'd think you're just being vindictive?''

That brought Casey to her feet, the outrage out of proportion even to his assertion. After all she'd gone through just to get up the nerve to come down here, after the hours of doubt and disbelief, the threat to her career and personal peace of mind, it infuriated her that the first reaction she'd get was that she was just paying Hunsacker back for not returning her sly winks.

It was so damn typical of the way the official world thought. It was so typically male. It was so familiar to her. But Scanlon had become the last person she expected it from.

Frustration propelled her into motion. Turning away from him, Casey stalked to the window and stared out at the pallid, limp day. She clutched that coffee cup in her hands just to keep them still and tapped her toe against the institutional green radiator just to hear the soft clanking.

"It's always back to that, isn't it?" she asked no one in particular. "No matter what I say, nobody will really believe me. After all, everybody knows how emotional women are. Every man on earth knows what happens when a woman has PMS. It's so much easier to blame her bitchiness than have to deal with the possibility that she's really right. It's so much more . . . *understandable.*"

There was no sound behind her, only the echo of voices down the hall, the flat clack of computer keys, the gurgle of the coffee maker. Below her on the street, a police car jockeyed for a parking spot. A spider negotiated the air in front of her, sailing on an invisible lifeline. Tenuous and slippery. Casey wondered if spiders were terrified of the chances they took just to get across a room. Did they remember the wall they left, cold and bitter against their legs, and hesitate before the next one? Or was it all preordained, too deeply imbedded in their instincts for them to refuse? Did they have to sail across, braving the terrifying void to seek substance, no matter what they remembered or wanted?

"And vindictive," she said, her sight internal now, personal. "That's a wonderful word. 'No, of course I didn't molest my child, Judge. My wife's just being vindictive.' 'Don't be silly. I didn't run around on her. She's just being vindictive.' "

Her voice slowed. Her eyes dropped to hands that suddenly trembled. " 'Don't be ridiculous, Officer,' " she finished, her words slowing, trembling as badly as her hands. " 'I never shoved a gun into her mouth and threatened to blow her head off if she left. She's just being . . .' " Casey's breath caught; her words faltered with the poison they hadn't released in so long, the memory that still brought bile up her throat even after seven years. " '. . .vindictive.' "

And she knew exactly how bitter and defeated her voice sounded.

Silence gathered in the little room like dust. The sun was hot through the old glass in the stark, square window. The air smelled like old cigarettes, coffee, and disinfectant. Male smells, power smells, the smells of another station so long ago where she'd had to gather her courage. Where it hadn't helped.

"Do you want to tell me about it?" Scanlon finally asked, his voice straight out of a confessional. If Casey closed her eyes, she could imagine herself back in that tiny, musty box facing the red velvet curtain. Holding her breath, terrified of that smooth, concerned voice that could so easily turn to judgment. The shame already too hot in her to risk more.

Instead, she turned to see that Scanlon hadn't moved,

hadn't changed position or expression. Still watching and waiting and soaking it all in. Surprisingly, she did want to tell him. She wanted to tell him all of it, because deep in those smoke-gray eyes she saw the kind of history that would let him understand. Scanlon was precise, and he was tightly wrapped, but he still couldn't quite hide the rumpled kind of comfort he carried with him.

It didn't matter, though. Casey wasn't shopping for comfort. She'd given that up a long time ago. She smiled, but there was little humor.

"I cannot tell a lie," she admitted. "Hunsacker reminds me of someone. Someone I was powerless against, and it was such a memorable experience that I prefer living with St. Helen of Webster than chance it again."

"The ex-husband?"

Casey could afford humor now as she faced off with Scanlon from across the room. "No," she admitted. "Ed was the change that refreshed. At least for a little while. When you meet him, please don't think less of me. I was a confused little girl then."

Finally allowing himself to move, Scanlon righted his chair and stood for a new cup of coffee. Casey was sure she saw something dark and sad in his eyes. "If all we were judged by were our mistakes, hell would have about as much room as the city workhouse." Turning, he lifted the pot in invitation. "More?"

Casey tilted her head a little, keeping her careful distance from those rumpled gray eyes. "I don't know. Are you about to get all ecclesiastical on me?"

He did smile then, a grudging revelation. "I wasn't ecclesiastical when I could have been."

"Which made you a perfect Jesuit."

"You seem well acquainted with the subject."

She shrugged, relieved to have the conversation turned away from her. "My uncle Martin was a Jesuit.

The only thing he couldn't stand about the church was the fatheads who ran it, most of canon law, and the fact that he wasn't allowed to proselytize in the jungles."

Scanlon held out a hand for her cup. Hesitating only a moment, Casey pushed away from the window and walked back, clenching the mug hard until the telltale trembling in her hands eased.

"Tell him he didn't miss anything," Scanlon offered. "I was in the jungles. It wasn't all it was cracked up to be."

Casey handed him her cup. "With the Jesuits?"

"And the marines."

A hundred new questions popped up. Casey tried to shove them back down. Scanlon returned her cup and she turned for her chair, fascinated anew by the concept of a policeman who had been both a priest and a soldier. What an incredible dichotomy of ideologies to carry into the station with him. What a burden to carry through life, if that sadness in Scanlon's eyes had meant anything.

She wondered what scars the marines had left him with, what guilt the church had left him with.

"So, how *does* a person get from the marines to the priesthood to the precinct?" she asked.

Scanlon smiled then, and Casey thought of martyrs. She thought of the history behind her own smiles and knew better why Scanlon understood so well.

"Logic," he countered dryly. "The marines had none, the Jebbies too much. This is a nice compromise. Most of the mysteries in this job can be solved, but nobody minds much if they don't make sense."

"Do you still believe?"

He sipped at his coffee. "On occasion." But he didn't look very happy about it.

"Then explain Hunsacker to me."

He settled back in his chair and rested a knowing

glance on her. "Well now, that is one nice thing being an ex-priest offers," he allowed. "I'm not troubled at all by the concept of evil."

He did understand. Casey could see it in his expression, heard it in the simple explanation that every textbook of modern medicine and psychiatry would never have allowed. He had seen Hunsackers before, maybe in those jungles, maybe somewhere in a corner of himself, and didn't see the need to cloak the truth in technical jargon or social excuse.

Casey felt the distance she had kept from him lessen just a little, too.

"Do *you* believe?" Scanlon asked.

"In what?" she asked. "Evil? You bet."

"In God."

A much tougher question. An answer no one who knew her had ever heard from her. "No," she allowed with some surprise that it should be a homicide detective she finally admitted it to. "My mother takes care of that for me."

What surprised Casey even more was the fact that she felt so comfortable saying it. Scanlon merely nodded, his eyes considering, his posture easy. Accepting. Somewhere in that grab bag he called a history, he'd lost his distaste for nonbelievers.

It was time to get to the summons that had brought her here. Otherwise she'd get too comfortable, admit too much. Begin to expect answers she had no business hearing. "Can you tell me about Hunsacker's interrogation?" she asked, instinctively straightening in the hard-backed chair.

Scanlon punctuated their move into new territory with a sip of coffee. "Easy," he allowed, tilting his own chair back. "He's innocent, a pillar of the community, and a man targeted by a vindictive woman." Before Casey could say anything, his hand came up. "His words."

"So he denied ever seeing Crystal?"

Scanlon smiled now, and it was dark. "He said he'd been troubled enough when he arrived to seek out a prostitute once. Just divorced and all, new city, new position. He couldn't say which one, he wasn't getting references."

Casey snorted. "He should have at least gotten medical certificates."

"He admitted to having a fight with Evelyn the night she died, but said that it was a misunderstanding he regrets terribly, that there had been a communications problem with a patient. Admits he didn't get along with Wanda, but who did?"

Casey's eyes widened. "You asked him about her?"

"Under the umbrella of establishing an argumentative nature."

Casey sipped at her coffee, thinking of her own pile of disorganized notes, her trouble with coming to grips with three separate—now four separate murders. And she didn't even have to worry about jurisdiction. "What are you going to do?"

Scanlon righted his chair and spent a moment or two tapping at his papers, fingers wrapped in the handle of his mug, eyebrows gathered. He seemed to be coming to some decision.

"Would you be willing to help me?"

Casey was surprised by the question. "What can I do?"

Scanlon tapped a little faster, then stopped. When he lifted his eyes to her, they were dead serious. "Hospitals are as much a closed union as police stations. I need somebody with easy access to information."

"Hearsay evidence?"

He allowed a small grudging grin. "Direction finders.

I also need somebody who knows how to pick apart medical records to find inconsistencies."

"Well, if there's one thing I know, it's paperwork."

"I'll warn you now, we're going to run into some tough obstacles."

"I'm a trauma nurse," she retorted. "I live for trouble."

"In this case," he suggested, "I'd rather you avoid it as much as possible. We have a unique opportunity with Hunsacker, but we also have some unique problems."

"What do you mean?"

*Tap, tap, tap.* "What do you know about serial killers?"

Casey shrugged. "That they keep murdering until they're stopped, and that they have long second toes."

Scanlon chose not to take her bait. "They're usually caught by accident," he instructed her, leaning on his desk like a lecturing professor. "Random killings are the most difficult to solve. Serial killers want to get caught, but at the same time, they take great pleasure in taunting the authorities with their omnipotence. They're not notorious for being sloppy about self-incrimination."

Casey took a deep breath. "Then you'd classify Hunsacker as a serial killer."

"Do you think he's going to stop?" Scanlon asked.

Casey shook her head. "Not after seeing the look in his eyes the other night."

"Then I'd call him a serial killer. The advantage we have here is that usually we have to work back from a number of murders and find the common link. You came to us with the link before we knew about the murders. Of course, the problem is making other people believe that he's actually committing all these murders. If he did kill those four women, he's played it perfectly. Different MO, different jurisdiction, no physical evidence. If you hadn't come along, nobody'd put his name to these."

"How are you going to get him?"

This time it was Scanlon who looked as if he wanted to pace. He shifted in his chair, considered the folders on his desk, picked up his coffee and put it back down again. "The easiest route would be to involve the Major Case Squad. If I could get a concrete link between Hunsacker and more than one murder, I could call them in, and we'd have a better chance of coordinating information on all the murders. Right now, though, nobody has a murder they can't explain by their own turf rules. No surprises, no mysteries. And outside jurisdictions don't like to call out the big boys unless there's a chance of a press nightmare."

He shook his head, obviously well acquainted with the dilemma. Casey wondered whether he'd tried to get his chief to call them out on Crystal already and been slapped down. Picking up his pen again, he fingered it, the sleek silver almost lost in his hand. He had long, spatulate fingers with oversize knuckles. Homely, practical hands. A workman's hands on an ex-priest. On an ex-marine. Casey thought he must have been a logical marine and a passionate Jesuit, which would have doomed him to both. Marines demanded passion and Jesuits logic.

"That book of his," he finally allowed, looking back up, the fire of conviction settled deep in the flat gray of his eyes. He'd been thinking a lot, too. "That notebook where he keeps all his information. That's another common trait among serial killers. A lot of them are obsessive-compulsives. It's not unheard of for them to keep perfect records of what they've done. Keep souvenirs of their kills, maybe pictures. I need to get enough on him to get a search warrant. I've been in touch with the other jurisdictions, suggesting they check his alibis and possibly IDing him on the scene. Of course, you'd think he'd stand out in either East St. Louis or Arnold, but nobody remembers him.''

For some reason Casey thought of the man she'd spotted at the mall, the one who had looked like Hunsacker. The one who had seemed like him, but somehow . . . different. Almost recognizable. The thought disappeared into Scanlon's continued dissertation.

''I'm also going to get some information from Boston on him, background stuff, information on any funny unsolved murders that might have happened back there before he showed up here.''

''Check on his ex-wife,'' Casey suggested. ''After what he said, I wouldn't be surprised if she's in a meat locker somewhere.''

Scanlon made a note. It made Casey think how many obsessive-compulsives there were. They made good nurses, good cops, and good serial killers. There was probably a paper in that somewhere.

''Can you get his medical records?'' she asked.

Scanlon looked up.

Casey smiled. ''If he's a registered psychopath, he's probably got the triad from his childhood. Bedwetting, fire starting, and animal abuse. See if he hurt any other kids when he got to adolescence.''

Now Scanlon was smiling. ''You have been doing your reading.''

Casey toyed with enthusiasm. ''I'm actually beginning to believe we can pull this off.''

Scanlon immediately lost his smile. ''Don't. We haven't begun to feel the backlash yet. In another couple of weeks, this investigation is going to be about as popular as the McCarthy hearings. He's a well-connected man, and he might be able to stop us in our tracks just long enough to get away.''

Casey wanted to argue. She knew it wouldn't do any

good. She'd spent enough time butting her head against the wall over the years to know the size of that headache. From the way Scanlon's hand still strayed to his stomach, she had a feeling he did, too. It was just that for the first time since this had all begun, she felt as if she were going forward.

"Just tell me what to do so we can make the most of the time we have. I want him caught."

That didn't seem to make Scanlon any happier. He caught his hand midway to betraying him and set it back down on the desk. "Be careful," he warned. "I don't want you thinking this is a game. If Hunsacker is the man we think, he's more dangerous than anything you've ever come across. Don't *ever* underestimate him."

Casey shook her head. "I think I'm safe," she admitted with some amazement. "I'm part of the game for him." She set down her cup, thinking, remembering, comprehending. "I've been thinking about it a lot, and I think this all somehow comes down to control for him. Control over women. It's part of his reason for being a GYN. I frustrate him because I haven't bowed yet to seduction or threat, so he's tormenting me with the knowledge that I can't stop him. I think he really gets off on that."

It was so much more complicated, she knew. So intricately woven in Hunsacker's mind that probably no one could ever unravel it successfully. But Casey had seen it in his prancing the other night, the display of power. He didn't consider her a threat. She was his rapt audience, unable to turn away, but unable to bring the play to a close. He performed for her as much as he did for himself.

After all, control wasn't any good if nobody realized you had it. It was a lesson she'd learned a long time ago.

"Sometimes," she admitted softly, "I get the feeling that he's not really after these women. I get the feeling he's after me." She looked up at Scanlon. "You were a Jesuit. You know about the St. Louis exorcism. It's said that Satan wasn't really after his victim, but the priest who exorcised him. Satan didn't want his life. He wanted his soul. Is that something you can say about a serial killer? He doesn't want me dead. He wants me shattered."

Scanlon held her gaze rock steady, and Casey knew that he understood her perfectly. That he respected her fears and intuition. For just a brief moment Casey felt as if he were going to reach out to her, to bridge the distance between them in support.

"I'm not going to let him get away with murdering those women," she vowed, offering a wry smile to lighten her conviction. Then she dropped her gaze, suddenly uncomfortable with the secrets she'd given Scanlon.

"Face it now," he demanded. "We may never convict him for what he did to your friends. He may just be too smart for us."

Casey's reaction was instinctive. "Don't be ridiculous," she objected, stiffening. "He can't just get off scot-free for what he's done."

Scanlon's smile was understanding and weary at the same time. He never expended the energy to move. "You expect justice," he accused gently. "If there's one thing I learned in all those jungles, it's that justice is usually the last thing you get."

If Casey needed any object lessons in the truth of Scanlon's statement, she got them the minute she returned to work. Casey had never felt uncomfortable walking into the lounge before. The hall had always been her arena, her sphere of influence. She had never halted a conversation or provoked silent remonstrances.

The lounge was full when she walked in. Voices faltered. Some dropped dead right on the spot. For a black woman, Marva was unaccountably flushed. Across from her, Barb was so rigid she should have hummed like a tuning fork.

"Hello, fellow babies," Casey greeted them all, although her eyes sought only Marva's stoic support. "It's good to see you all so . . . pink-cheeked."

The conversations stumbled back into gear and a couple of people walked out onto the work lane. Casey dropped her bag into the corner and checked the board.

It went on this way for four days, each day more strained than the one preceding it. Each shift salted with references to back-stabbing and revenge and petty jealousy. Not everyone was against her, but everyone was involved. Everyone watched Hunsacker on the news the second night when he did his portrayal of the wounded innocent, splendid in his lab coat and monogrammed shirt, stethoscope draped around his neck, his office comfortably disordered behind him.

"A desire to discredit me," he said with weary dignity in answer to the anchor's assertion that the police had not dropped him from the investigation. "I don't know what else to charge it to. I'm only afraid that irresponsible accusations like this will injure my patients."

Everyone wondered just why Casey would go all the way into the city just to get back at Hunsacker. And Casey could give them no answer.

The weather still hadn't broken by the fifth day. It hung heavy and sour, the sky a dirty gray and the early summer green dingy. Helen had demanded a morning in the yard, so that by the time Casey made it in to work, she was tired and hot and short-tempered. It galled her that she was beginning to dread the one place on earth she'd always belonged. Work had been wearing badly on her, but not the people. Not her friends. And now Hunsacker had taken those from her, too.

She'd no more than made it in the lounge door when Tom popped his head in the door behind her.

"My office?" was all he said.

Casey heard Barb's self-righteous snort behind her. She ignored it, instead slipping her stethoscope around her neck and sliding her filled pocket protector into her lab coat before heading back out.

When Casey walked into Tom's office, he was balancing his World Series ball in his hands. Casey refrained from groaning. The ball was a bad sign. One of Tom's most cherished themes was teamwork, his favorite speech the one about how the great Cardinal teams of the sixties had been founded on teamwork. How a good ER crew was the same way, able to execute a triple play without dropping the ball (Casey always had a picture of them tossing patients back and forth).

"Casey, there are some things going on I think we need to address," Tom said without looking away from Bob Gibson's signature.

Not really thinking that that needed an answer, Casey just took up her customary position in the facing chair.

Tom rubbed away a little at Julio Javier and Dal Maxville before lifting his gaze back to her.

"I think you know what it's about."

Casey wasn't going to give him any help on this one. She just watched him impassively.

Tom finally managed a sigh. "Casey, correct me if I'm wrong. You had something to do with Dr. Hunsacker's being hauled into the city police station?"

"You make it sound like they threw a net over him and beat him with a rubber truncheon," Casey said equably, even though the anticipation of disaster was already building in her chest. "They asked him some questions."

"They've continued to harass him to the point where he's been frequently mentioned on the news, which has distressed his patients—and this hospital—greatly."

"I didn't call out the minicams, if that's what you're asking."

Tom set the ball back into its holder and steepled his fingers over it again. Absurdly, Casey felt as if she were in *The Babe Ruth Story.*

"Casey," Tom said with a sigh that carried the weight of his disappointment. "I know you have a problem being a team player sometimes. And usually I put up with it, because you have the hands of Ozzie Smith. But I just can't understand what would make you want to turn on a teammate like that."

"He's no teammate of mine," she instinctively retorted, and then regretted it. He was, of course. In the traditional medical parlance. You watch out for the doctors and they watch out for the doctors. You scratch their backs and they'll expect it again.

Casey wanted to get back out of the room. Her vitriol was showing, and that wasn't the way to conduct this conversation.

"What would you like me to do?" she asked. "I was afraid someone was involved in a crime. A bad crime. I've always been taught to go to the police."

Tom shook his head as if he were counseling a kid who'd spray-painted the school gym. "I'm disappointed that you didn't feel you could come to me first. If there were any question about Dr. Hunsacker, don't you think his organization should have the first chance to address it? Didn't Bart Giamatti demand the right to deal with Pete Rose?"

"Pete Rose didn't murder somebody."

"Neither did Dr. Hunsacker." Tom reverted his eyes to the ball, stroking it with his fingers, as if it were crystal instead of horsehide. His voice, when he continued, was patient. A parent dealing with an adolescent. "I know you've had your . . . problems with Dr. Hunsacker. He's told me."

Casey stiffened, willing Tom to face her, her eyes drilling holes into his never-ending forehead as he continued to address his desk.

"And you know"—he shrugged uncomfortably—"that that information is always confidential. I would never betray him or you."

"Exactly what did he say?" she asked, her hands clasped together in her lap, her shoulders aching with the strain of patience. Something had suddenly shifted in the equation, and she couldn't put a finger on it. Something intangible and disconcerting.

Tom dipped his head with discomfort. "That you'd had a . . . well, a little falling out. He begged me to be patient with you." He must have anticipated her reaction, because he finally brought his head and his hand up at the same time. "When I found out that you'd been instrumental in his being investigated, I had to apologize. After all, the manager's responsible for his team. I have to say, he was quite gracious about it."

Casey didn't remember getting to her feet. "You apologized for me without even asking me about it?" she demanded, leaning over his desk, hands flat on either side of the ball, her chest suddenly hot with surprise. "Without so much as asking me if it were true?"

Tom actually backed away a little. "Casey, sit down. You're not helping yourself at all."

Casey straightened, wheeled around on her heel, and paced the other five feet of the office, from Budweiser eagle to framed Musial uniform replica. It was all she could do to force the bile back down. She needed the job, she reminded herself like a mantra to calm her, she needed the job. And unless she somehow saw this through to the end, she wasn't going to have one. Anywhere.

But Hunsacker had just managed to humiliate her again, and she was helpless to do anything about it. And this time, she hadn't even had to be in the same room for him to do it. Maybe it wasn't justice she wanted after all. Maybe it was just retribution for feeling like this.

Casey sat down. Barely.

Tom didn't look any more comfortable. Casey had the fleeting impression he was preparing to ward off blows. It didn't seem like such a bad idea there for a minute.

"You talked to the police on the premises without notifying supervisors," he accused as sternly as he could. "You know that's against policy. Your accusations caused great distress to Dr. Hunsacker *and* his patients *and* this hospital, and if he were a different person, he'd be well within his rights to ask for your dismissal." Now Tom was on a roll, jabbing his desk with his finger to accentuate his points. "Hell, Casey, he could have your license. Is a little spite worth all that?"

"Spite." She breathed carefully, rigid with fury. "You think this is all out of spite?"

"Well, isn't it?"

"Tell me something, Tom," she said, leaning just a little closer, almost satisfied to see him tense in reaction. "What if he did murder that woman? What if *I'm* the one who's right here?"

Tom actually laughed. "Don't be ridiculous. He can't be a murderer. He's been in Millicent Adams' column, for God's sake."

"I mean it," she warned. "Something's really wrong with that man. He's—" Casey stopped, desperate for the right words. Too close to telling the truth, when she knew damn well that one word about multiple homicides would land her own butt right in a padded bungalow over on Fantasy Island with no return ticket. She caught herself just shy of disaster. "Look at his eyes, Tom. Look at the way he acts. He's just too sly. Too . . . slick. It's like he has everybody under a spell."

That brought Tom right to his feet. On an executive, it might have been a threatening move. A man in wire-rims and a white pantsuit didn't quite cut the same figure. "I don't like ultimatums," he advised her, fingers splayed over the desktop. "But I think it's time for one. Mr. Nixon wanted me to suspend you. I managed to avoid it. But, Casey, this is an official verbal warning. You know the play. The next step is a written reprimand, and then dismissal. And much more talk like that's going to usher you right out the door."

Casey reached her own feet and faced him, trembling with fury. Not because Tom was wrong, but because he was telling the truth. She knew it; she'd been expecting it. This was a polite chat, a friendly warning. Next, the gloves came off. And she couldn't stop it.

The staff had always claimed that the CEO of the hospital hadn't been named Nixon for nothing. He wouldn't stand for one of his nurses (he always thought of them as his) to step out of line. He especially couldn't tolerate her threatening his profit margin. And Casey, with her good intentions and unproven suspicions, was doing just that.

"Can I go back to work now?" she asked in a deadly quiet voice. Her chest hurt with the frustration, burned way in behind her sternum. It made her wonder how many of these confrontations Scanlon had had to gestate his ulcer.

Tom faced her, his plain, thin face anxious and earnest. "I don't know," he asked. "Can you?"

It was an effort, but Casey nodded. I need the job, she repeated to herself again and again. I need the job.

"In that case," he said, gaze back on his desk, as if reading a memo, "I know you'll try and be a . . . a good team player. I don't want to hear that you're having any more problems with Dr. Hunsacker. I certainly don't want to hear any more accusations like the ones you've been spreading around."

His eyes came up, pleading. Tom really liked her, Casey knew. The last thing he wanted to do was fire her. She could see, though, that he couldn't comprehend her actions. She bitched and moaned as much as the rest of them, threatening dire consequences, concocting elaborate revenges. But to actually betray a doctor like that. To fabricate such a lie. Because Tom really thought it was a lie.

"One more thing," he managed, tapping his notes again. "You will not talk to police while on the premises unless it is authorized. Is that clear?"

Casey nodded one more time. She wondered yet again whether she should have ever set foot in that police station. She would have known. She would have seen Hunsacker weave his deadly web and been unable to stop it. But she would have been safe. She would have been anonymous and secure.

But she'd done that once. She'd been a coward and crawled away, and she just couldn't do that anymore. She had to at least try. If not for justice, at least for self-respect.

# Chapter 13

*HE MUST HAVE* sensed her humiliation. No more than half an hour after Casey left Tom's office, Hunsacker walked onto the work lane. His reception was enthusiastic and supportive. Millie danced around him and Barb rubbed against him like a cat in heat.

Casey made it a point to stay at the other end of the hall. It wasn't difficult to look busy, and Casey had more than enough reason to stay close to her patients. One was losing a baby and another had already lost her mind. Casey could hear her moaning, the eerie keening haunting and dark.

She tried not even to look down the hall. The excited babble was easy enough to hear, and on occasion laughter broke out. Casey remained bent over her charts, taut with a hundred different resentments.

"Baby, you look like thunder."

Casey acknowledged Marva's arrival with a nod as she scribbled notes.

"Casey, I need a CBC and Type and Crossmatch on room twelve," Dr. Filmont called from where she leaned out the door.

Casey nodded to her, too, and picked up the phone to call the lab. Filmont disappeared back into the room.

"There's something I think you need to know," Marva said in a suspiciously flat tone.

Casey was finally forced to look up. Marva's gaze wasn't on her, but on Hunsacker where he stood with his arm around Barb's shoulder. Casey didn't have anything on the thunder in Marva's eyes.

"Laboratory. Janice."

Casey delivered the message and hung up. Getting to her feet, she reached for requisitions. "I already have a verbal counseling on my record," she warned Marva on the way by. "If this is going to make me mad, maybe you'd better save it."

Marva followed right behind her. "It'll maybe help you understand why the attitude's so bad down here."

Casey knew just by the direction of Marva's gaze what she was referring to.

"Well, since he's obviously Jesus Christ, I must be Judas."

Marva almost cracked a smile. Casey slid Mrs. Trenory's name plate into the stamping machine.

"Wrong analogy," Marva suggested. "Try Samson and Delilah. Or, if the Bible ain't your thing, how 'bout *Fatal Attraction?*"

Casey had a requisition positioned to stamp. All she had to do was slam the machine into place. She stood with her hand on top of it. "What?"

Marva wasn't smiling. " 'Hell hath no fury'?"

Now Casey wasn't even breathing. She could hear Hunsacker's voice, honey slick and seductive, the master instrument of insinuation and innuendo. She thought of how her friends should have known her better.

Her reaction was deathly quiet. "They think I've been sleeping with him?"

Marva turned to her, her eyes uncompromising. Demanding Casey's sensibility. "They think you were."

For a moment movement hung suspended. The babble of the work lane tumbled about them. The air-conditioning clicked on again, fanning their ankles. Outside the picture window at the end of the hall the world stretched away in a sepia wash.

Casey pushed. The stamper slammed hard enough to echo all the way to the picture window. "You couldn't have told me some other time than when Hunsacker's standing twenty feet away?"

Marva refused to flinch from the ferocity of Casey's actions or the frustration in her eyes. "I couldn't tell you before I found out. My theory is that Barb ain't gettin' any, and she's jus' pure jealous. She felt a need to gloat that you had it and lost it."

Casey nodded blindly as she slid in another requisition. At any other time the accusation would have been funny. Casey couldn't care less about what people thought of her, even less what they imagined her sexual escapades to be. Considering what her escapades did amount to, even a rumor would have been more fun than she was having.

But not now. Not with Hunsacker. Not when it would shatter any credibility she had.

Just the thought provoked a new disquiet, a sudden unexplained sense of unbalance. It was as if she'd just been brushed by the gauzy edge of an old dream, unable to recapture it whole. Only emotion remained, the nagging of familiarity.

Slam! What she felt now was uneasiness, and she couldn't remember why. "Where'd she hear it?"

The requisition was not only stamped with a name, but chewed right through. Casey tossed it in the trash and tried again. Marva watched with carefully passive eyes.

"All she said was that everybody knew it. If it's true, it explains some of the . . . undercurrent about this."

That was exactly why Casey believed her. It made such perfect sense after hearing the snide comments about jealousy and the like. It fit in with Tom's stiff comments about a falling out between Casey and Hunsacker. He'd evidently been privy to the gossip as well.

Casey found herself watching Hunsacker as he laughed with Steve. All the time he was jotting something in that ubiquitous little notebook of his. The one Scanlon wanted so badly. The one that would hold all his secrets.

"Do you know that a lot of serial killers are obsessive-compulsive?" she asked, her rote actions once again stilled.

Marva's attention had already been drawn in the same direction. "Is that a fact?"

Not turning away, Casey nodded. "It's a fact. Scanlon says that a lot of them keep records of everything they've done."

Marva's head swung around, her eyes not so passive anymore. "You think he's got an Angel of Death wish list in there?"

It was so visible, so easily accessible. Casey knew that if she could look in that book she'd find out just how careful Hunsacker was, so thorough that he would be able to wipe all trace of himself away from four murders. So thorough he would anticipate anything.

Suddenly an image popped free. Betty, concerned, anxious, trying so hard to communicate something that Casey hadn't understood. Intent that Casey believe that Hunsacker wasn't boffing Dr. Fernandez's mistress anymore.

Because she thought he was boffing Casey.

Betty had heard the same rumor, except mutated just

a little. Just enough to serve some purpose. Casey's breath hissed out. Her hand froze atop the stamper where the requisition waited forgotten. Her gaze leveled on Hunsacker. Hunsacker who would never have left his accuser to chance, who would have used his most potent weapon against her. And suddenly Casey knew where all the rumors had been born.

She should have understood sooner. She should have remembered the minute the innuendos began to circulate. Growing isolation, confusion, misunderstandings, friends who suddenly turned away and never called again. Pain and shame and frustration, because she hadn't understood then what had happened.

The memory was a revelation; a shock. It was like having once had an abscess you thought had long since been cured. Drawn, lanced, squeezed dry, only to realize it wasn't gone at all. She'd just felt a sting, deep inside her, and looked down to see fresh pus, yellow and thick and rancid.

It must have been what Hunsacker smelled on her. Not the fresh humiliation, but the memory, the old decay that jackals like him preyed upon.

"Casey?"

Casey didn't hear Marva. She was listening to old voices, long since locked tightly away in the past when she'd vowed to only look ahead as her cure. She was living a memory suddenly more vivid than even the horror she'd stumbled across.

Even as she watched him, it was as if Hunsacker heard those voices, too. He heard the pain in her head and instinctively turned to sniff it out. Casey didn't move. She didn't look away. She didn't smile. She just met his gaze with the knowledge in her own.

She didn't hear the group around him go still. She didn't see them turn first to him, and then to her, a few settling their righteous anticipation around them like blue-black feathers.

Hunsacker's hand stilled. He held the book between them like a taunt. His eyes shifted, deep inside where the feral fires lived. More than greeting, more even than challenge. He fed on the sight of her, knowing that she'd been isolated and still thinking she didn't know why. He tasted her impotence and smiled.

Casey knew that he would come to her. All around her the work lane stilled like the streets of Dodge City as the sheriff stepped out to face the Clanton boys. Except that this time, only Casey and Marva knew that she was the sheriff.

She could have closed her eyes and known he was approaching. The air prickled around her with his gathering power, his sense of delicious omnipotence. And only Casey felt it. Only she saw the alien in his eyes.

He stopped right in front of her and made it a point to carefully pocket his book. "I'm glad I ran into you tonight," he greeted her. "I wanted to let you know that there are no hard feelings."

*No hard feelings, Casey. I know you were just confused. Come on back to me and everything will be all right. I'll take care of you, just like before. Just like before.*

"Really?" she asked, her own voices echoing his too easily, their poison spilling through her. Even so, she kept her expression neutral, her posture passive. If nothing else, she knew how to play the scene.

Hunsacker smiled and nodded, his eyes terrifyingly compassionate. Public eyes, purposeful eyes so the world could see him as he wanted. "I know you only thought you were doing what was best."

Casey went cold. *I know you,* she thought, daring him. *I know what you are and what you're doing.*

"I appreciate that," she said, her voice as concerned as his, her eyes as sincere. "I hope everything's all right."

*I hope you die. Screaming, begging, stripped naked of all your masquerades so that everyone can see the slug that hides beneath that pretty shell.*

He inclined his head and smiled, the picture of concession. "It might be a while. Once the press gets the bit between their teeth, they don't let go."

*I know you. And I won't turn away anymore.*

They were simple words, an innocuous thought. Casey was stunned by their impact. So shattering it should have rocked her. So revealing Hunsacker should have recognized it. She'd been so afraid of him, scuttling around the shadows to conspire against him and shaking in his presence. She'd had the courage to find out about him, but she hadn't had the courage to confront him. Suddenly that changed.

She recognized him, now, the bogeyman who had lived beneath her bed all these years. The purulence she had to drain once and for all.

*I'm going to win,* she thought. *This time, I refuse to cower or crawl away. I refuse to succumb to innuendo and malice when I know I'm right. I will beat you, and you'll know I'm doing it, because that's the only way to keep the control I've finally managed to wrestle over my life. I will have the courage to fight you face-to-face.*

Her chest caught fire. Her heart thundered in her ears. She stood close enough to this madman to feel the power shimmer from him and knew that he was her second chance. She'd just stopped running and turned to fight. And it wasn't even Hunsacker she was fighting.

Almost as if he'd heard her thoughts, Hunsacker held out his hand and smiled. "Friends?"

Casey smiled back. She knew that everyone else would see relief. Hunsacker would see the challenge. He would see the impotence die in her and know that his adversary had just changed faces.

She grasped his hand. "Friends."

And she knew that he saw. His hand closed tight around hers. She answered. Her eyes never faltered, never strayed before the cold gleam in his. She never flinched before the shock of comprehension that joined them.

Beyond Hunsacker's shoulder, there were murmurs of surprise, some of disdain. Casey ignored them. She gave Hunsacker his message and fought against betraying her triumph. She savored the tart thrill of terror that tasted so different on an aggressive tongue.

His own smile widened. The gauntlet had just been picked up. When Casey finally took her hand back and watched Hunsacker walk on out the door, she hugged her exhilaration to her like a warm afghan. A bright red afghan the color of fresh blood. She was finally going to walk out that door and never look back again.

"Why am I here?" Poppi asked seven hours later.

Casey grinned like a pirate. "Because I needed somebody to talk to. Somebody who'd understand."

Leaning against the triage desk, Poppi lifted an eyebrow. "Saw *Magical Mystery Tour* again, huh?"

Casey swung her bag up over her shoulder and grimaced. "No. More like *Return of the Swamp Creature.* We'll talk about it in the car."

The evening staff was beginning to filter past. Most still cold-shouldered Casey, but she didn't mind as much now. She was righteous, and they would know it. Janice walked out alone, her features drawn and silent, her gate uneven. That hurt. Ever since Janice had confronted Casey, she'd shut down, pulled into herself, accepting support from no one. She'd begun to stretch like a fraying rope, until Casey worried about her. Casey wanted to talk to her, to ask how she was doing. Janice still wouldn't even look at her.

"Well, if it ain't Lucy in the Sky," Marva greeted them, sauntering up with her raincoat on. Rain was nowhere in the forecast, but Marva believed in positive thought. "What are you doin' here?"

Poppi waved an offhand greeting. "Signing up far-sighted investors. Interested?"

Marva slowed to a halt, her face a study in skepticism. "Is this another one of those Toss the Yuppie games?"

"Better." There was no question that Poppi got involved with her projects. Her eyes lit like a cat's on the way to a rabbit dinner. "Nirvana. The game of reincarnation."

Marva set a hand on her hip. "Girl, you been sniffin' that silver polish again, haven't you? Why don't you just stick to jewelry like you're supposed to?"

Poppi wasn't in the least intimidated. "Jewelry is my job. Games are my calling. A hundred dollars, Marva. Think about it. A janitor invested that much in Trivial Pursuit, and now Donald Trump calls him sir."

Marva snorted. "What the heck? You're just nuts enough to do it."

"Come on," Casey nudged Poppi, impatient to get going. "We can hold a partnership meeting later."

Throwing off a shrug, Poppi tipped her head so she looked as though she were peering at Marva over glasses. "She calls me at eleven o'clock to say that she wants to walk to work tomorrow, would I drive her home. And they say I'm flighty."

"Well, she been wired all night."

Poppi looked from Marva to Casey and back again. "Wired."

Marva just nodded. "I think she and Hunsacker had

sex in the work lane with everybody watching. Problem is," she added, resettling her purse to leave, "I'm not sure which one was on top." And without so much as a good-bye, she walked on out.

Poppi turned back from considering the door as it swished shut and pulled her car keys from the depths of her skirt pocket. "Time to go, Casey."

Casey grinned again, anxious to test her newfound determination on the only other person who would understand it. "That's what I figured, Poppi."

The air outside was heavy and metallic-smelling. A sickly orange full moon topped the trees. It was still too hot. The city shouldn't have felt this stale until August. Early summer was a time of upheaval in St. Louis, different weather fronts slamming into each other with the force of football lines right over the Mississippi Valley. The trees should be dancing with wind, and clouds should be boiling over the southwest horizon. Instead it waited, thick and uncertain and distasteful, sapping energy and straining patience.

Tonight Poppi drove her old Volvo. Discreet blue and well broken in, it waited out on the ER parking lot. The two women reached it in silence, both comfortable enough with their ritual of confession that they knew how it would unfurl.

The radio spilled out old Santana. The seats smelled like sandalwood. In the back seat, gardening tools vied for space with a case of jeweler's tools. The Miraculous Medal Helen had given Poppi swung from the rearview mirror and there was probably a lid of grass in the glove compartment.

"Straight home?" Poppi asked, slipping the car into gear.

"I don't care," Casey agreed, settling back into the leather seat like a child into the care of a nanny. She was comfortable. She was protected. This was where she'd made her major decisions in her life, not in front of a priest or within the stiff formality of her living room, but in the succession of front seats Poppi had owned. It was where Casey had smoked her first joint. Where she'd discussed politics and love and the loss of her virginity.

Poppi had rescued her from that apartment in Creve Coeur and helped her ship home her furniture from Ed's house. She'd been there for every major event in Casey's life since Casey had been thirteen.

"I came to a realization about Hunsacker tonight," Casey said without preamble. The car's air-conditioning belched a couple of times and struggled against the heat.

Poppi didn't even bother to look over as she slowed at the end of the emergency drive and waited to turn into traffic. "You finally got his shoes off?"

Casey grinned. "It'd be easier to get his pants off. This is bigger."

Poppi made a funny little choking sound.

Casey waved her off. "You know what I mean. Hunsacker's been spreading rumors around about me. He's told everybody I've been sleeping with him. He evidently told the people at Mother Mary that he'd broken off the relationship, and that that was why I'd ratted on him. He told somebody at Izzy's that we were still sleeping together."

Casey heard the hiss of intaken breath. They pulled up to the stoplight and waited, the light washing Poppi in red.

"Remind you of something?" Casey prodded, already knowing her answer.

Poppi looked over, her eyes hot with remembered fury. They glinted like dark rubies in the light. "Only the last time you were stealing money and seducing young boys."

It still hurt. Deep down, right where all those other old hurts lived, tangled in the mass of threats and deceptions that had been the hallmark of that relationship.

"He came up to me," Casey admitted, that strange headiness returning to battle with the old wounds. "Right there in front of everyone, to forgive me for hurting him."

Silence now. Poppi was waiting. The light changed and they followed the traffic onto the highway.

Casey sat up then, turned in her seat to face her friend. "It was like I was two places at once," she admitted. "Hunsacker would say something and I'd hear another voice echoing what he said, except . . . in a different way."

"What other voice?" Poppi asked, even though she knew better than anyone.

Casey fought down the instinctive panic, knowing of course that just the mention of his name wouldn't bring him back in the door. Gut deep afraid just the same. Which was why she couldn't let Hunsacker win this time. She couldn't live with herself if she failed again.

"Frank," she said, and braced herself. But no wind blew, no hellish chorus wailed in protest. No handsome, charming, vicious man would knock on her door.

"I'm going to purge him once and for all," she promised, turning forward once again. "I realized it when I found I had the guts to shake Hunsacker's hand."

That surprised Poppi more than anything. "You shook his hand?"

Casey couldn't help a new grin, a touch of triumph in her voice. "And I was the one who was on top."

Poppi just shook her head, wondering.

For the next few miles, she kept her attention on her driving. It was after eleven, and more than one of the cars sharing the highway with her didn't seem to find the lane markings that easy to follow. Casey was busy remembering the look in Hunsacker's eyes when he'd realized she'd just called his hand. She smiled with satisfaction that she'd been able to match his grip, his silence, his smile. It was a long way from sobbing and pleading.

Maybe this was the justice she wanted. Nothing more than the chance to stand up to Frank in the only way she could, by using Hunsacker as a surrogate. Maybe all she wanted was evens.

Poppi didn't speak again until the car sat silent in Casey's driveway. "Do you really think this is going to make it all better?" she asked quietly.

Casey looked over to try to discern an opinion in Poppi's eyes. The soft wash of outside light illuminated her white Ralph Lauren blouse and glinted against the gold hoops in her ears, but never reached the upper half of her face.

"What do you mean?"

Poppi shrugged, still faceless in the dark. "I don't know. I'm still not getting good vibes from this. Like you're counting too much on this solving everything you ran away from. The only thing this should solve is who murdered Evelyn."

Casey stiffened, hearing Poppi's opinion for the first time. "Ran away?" she demanded. "I didn't run away. I fled for my life."

Poppi shook her head. "That was different. You haven't dealt with it, Casey. You just pretended it never happened. You've been doing it for seven years, first with Ed and then by sheer force of will."

Casey yanked open her door and stepped back out into the night. "How the hell could I pretend it never happened?" she demanded, slamming the door without car-

ing if Poppi heard the rest of the statement. "I can still
see the scars every time I take off my shirt."

Behind her the other door shut, a softer sound, and
Poppi followed up the driveway. "Tonight was the first
time in seven years you've mentioned the man's name.
You haven't talked about him since you left."

Casey stomped up the steps to the back porch and
threw open the door. "I talked about it with Ed, and all
it got me was another disaster. Thanks, I like it this way
much better. The minute I beat Hunsacker, my ghosts
will all disappear."

Helen was up. Casey stifled a groan. She'd felt so good
no more than fifteen minutes ago, full with her revelation, her sense of achievement. Now, in a period of minutes, Poppi had done her best to burst her fragile
balloon, and Helen waited to drag the rest back to the
ground.

It was worse than she thought. Her mother wasn't just
up, she was on her knees in the living room. Heaving
a sigh of capitulation, Casey dropped her stuff on the
kitchen table and walked on into the living room. Poppi
followed as far as the kitchen.

"Mom?" Casey called, stalling. The lights were off,
only a couple of votive candles flickering on the TV.
They cast an eerie, flickering glow over the watching
faces on the wall. Casey had the most irrational feeling
she'd interrupted a conversation. "What are you doing?"

"I need to confess," her mother whispered, never taking her eyes from the focus of her meditation.

Fighting back another sigh, Casey sat on the couch.
"What for now?"

"Pride. Selfishness. Calumny."

Calumny. Well, that was certainly a new one on the
list. Wherever she was getting her guilt fodder, at least
it was building a better vocabulary. It was a cinch she

wasn't getting her messages from *Wheel of Fortune.* Maybe Ted Koppel.

Casey wondered what the penance was for calumny. "Isn't this a job for the chapel?"

Helen didn't look away from her mission. Hands folded like a first communicant, she lifted her face to the cobwebs at the corner of the ceiling. Casey guessed that was where the angel band massed for things like this.

"Father's coming," her mother informed her. "He called."

"What?" Casey instinctively checked her watch. "You mean the father who was here?"

"Sgt. Loyola."

Casey thought to correct her mother yet again, but decided she liked the analogy. "When did he call?"

"Right after he accused me."

Casey gave in to a little shake of the head. It wouldn't clear Helen's head, but it might help hers a little. "Who accused you? Father Rock?"

"Mick."

Well, at least she was consistent. Mick had been accusing her for over twenty years now. Why should he stop tonight? Casey caught herself looking into the cobwebs as well. Maybe it was her father caught up there with the flies and mosquitoes. But, of course, she wasn't privileged to visions. Not enough guilt, she guessed.

"Did he say when he was coming by?" Casey asked.

"When you were off work. I'm preparing."

"No," Casey countered, getting to her feet. "You're not. He's not doing confessions anymore, remember?"

When Casey slid a hand under Helen's arm to help her up, Helen finally looked over. She really did look as if it had been a hard night at the hairshirt. Her eyes were red-rimmed and wet, her hands shaking when she pulled them apart. Casey's voice instinctively softened.

"It's time for bed, Mom. We'll go see Father Donnelly in the morning, okay?"

Helen searched Casey's face, as if expecting some revelation there, maybe a reprieve. She seemed to sink within herself. "I shouldn't have expected it, should I?"

Casey hated that too-familiar ache her mother's despair set up in her own chest. "What, Mom?"

Tears spilled over. "Another chance. Benny's not coming back, is he?"

The truth? No, Benny wasn't coming back. Benny was as far away as money and circumstance allowed. He was dead or wasted or shuffling along the back halls of Grand Central Station with all the other homeless.

"You'll see him, Mom," she lied, reaching up to tuck a displaced strand of lank brown hair back up under the bandanna. "Once he works out his problems."

Impotence again, the memory of holding on to Benny as he'd run the last time, clutching at his arm, his hand, his memory to call him home. Knowing there was no way to stop him, no way to help him. Marva would have said he wasn't as strong as Casey. Casey wouldn't know. She hadn't seen him in nine years.

The scrape of Helen's feet on the stairs followed Casey into the kitchen where Poppi held out a can of beer for her. She accepted it without a word and drained a third in her first gulp.

"Say one word about ghosts," she threatened blackly, setting her can down to shuck her lab coat and shoes, "and I'll tell Scanlon where you hide your stash."

Poppi's smile was enigmatic. "We're the most frustrated by the traits in others that we recognize in ourselves."

One foot balanced on a chair, her fingers tangled in shoelaces, Casey offered her friend a particularly black scowl. "If you're insinuating that I'm leaning a little too far toward religious fanaticism, I think you need to get a new prescription for those rose-colored glasses of yours."

"If I could use the word *ghosts,*" Poppi offered, sliding into the other chair, "I would remind you that not all ghosts are people. Some are actions we regret. Attitudes. Maybe an incomprehensible passivity." She caught the look of warning in Casey's eyes and leaned back in her chair. "But, of course, I can't use . . . that word."

"My only ghosts," Casey insisted, even though she knew damn well that both of them knew better, "are two cases of incomprehensible bad taste. But I'm past that now. At least I will be once I've made amends for five old broken bones and a plastic surgery bill that almost broke Ed's bank balance."

Poppi was saved from answering by the front door chime. Casey slid off her other shoe and straightened, not sure whether she wanted to answer the door or not. It seemed lately that the good news never lasted as long as the bad news. Unless, of course, Scanlon just wanted to drop by to let her be the first to know that Hunsacker had just been caught red-handed and admitted to the rest.

Casey padded through the hallway. She could see Scanlon silhouetted through the beveled glass in the front door, his head down a little, as if thinking, his shadow a little hunched. When she opened the door, she saw why. And thoughts of miraculous resolutions disappeared like candle smoke.

# Chapter 14

*JACK COULD GUESS* what kind of day Casey had had just by the look on her face. He lifted the six-pack he had in his right hand. "I couldn't face another glass of iced tea."

There were six folders tucked beneath his arm. He was stale and tired. His clothes smelled like cigarette smoke, and his stomach sloshed in coffee. And that was feeling better.

He'd been looking forward to coming over here tonight. After the day he'd had, he needed a little dose of Casey's pugnacious pragmatism. He needed an innocuous surprise or two.

The porch light sapped the color from her face and glinted in the tumble of her dark red hair. She was in her uniform and stocking feet, and she stood as if she were waiting to read a surprise telegram. Jack found himself smiling.

She smiled back as she showed him in. "I never turn down a man bearing a bribe. You're wearing your short brim. It's very cool."

"Stingy brim," he corrected automatically as he stepped past. He hadn't even remembered putting it on.

He'd worn it today on a couple of calls, the first time in quite a few months. Instinct must have taken over when he'd pulled up to the house.

"Since you're in official homicide uniform," Casey said. "I can assume this is business?"

"I have some things I'd like you to look at," Jack admitted, and then stepped farther inside.

It was hard to miss the votive lights on the TV.

"Am I interrupting something?" he asked, attention on the flicker of red along the wall with all the second-hand cousins.

Casey turned to follow his line of vision and her face seemed to wilt in guilty surprise. "Sorry," she apologized with a distracted wave of her hand as she shut the door behind him. "You just missed the reconciliation service."

"Yours?"

She didn't seem to think that was funny. "Don't be silly." All the same, she deserted him to blow out the candles and flip on a few lights. "I refuse to repent for anything. Just ask my mother. Or my administrator."

"Sounds like the pressure's heating up." Even before he had his hat off, Jack was wishing he could take his jacket off with it. It was too hot and sticky tonight to be official. Besides, from the sounds of it, tonight was going to be equal parts business and commiseration.

"It's just hit slow boil," Casey assured him. "I got my first official reprimand today."

He'd been right. By the look on her face, her reaction had been equal parts outrage, frustration, and provocation. Not that he was surprised. If she dealt with her supervisors the way she dealt with everything else he'd seen, he was surprised she still had a job. Which was why he'd been looking forward to seeing her tonight.

"You tell me your story," he offered wryly, "and I'll tell you mine."

Casey came to a stop, struggling for humor. "You, too?"

Jack offered a smile to negate the tenuous position the day had left both of them in. "And that was before the evening news. I can't wait for tomorrow."

"News?" she demanded. "What news?"

"They found out that Franklin down in Jefferson County was interested in Hunsacker, too. In fact, I got him to share some of his stuff with me so I can have you look at it."

She brightened. "He thinks Hunsacker's involved?"

"No. He just can't figure out how anybody else is. His prime suspect went home with one of the other lounge lizards that night, in full sight of her whole flock of kids."

Casey nodded, excitement struggling back through the weariness. "In that case, there's better light in the kitchen." She had pushed open the swinging door into an island of fluorescent and gingham when she added an afterthought. "And Poppi."

Jack assumed that Poppi was the blond. Upscale, upper middle class, in the Webster uniform of designer imprints, she was seated cross-legged on the kitchen counter with a kind of feline watchfulness to her. Jack's instincts told him she was about as run-of-the-mill as her friend.

She cemented her impression with her greeting. "Your vibes could use a little work."

Now he recognized her. Alice in Wonderland after the tea party. Just about what he'd figure to find perched in this house. He was surprised at his own disappointment. He'd deliberately shown up now to exclude audiences. The commiseration, he suddenly realized, wasn't all supposed to be Casey's.

"He's already met Helen," Casey greeted her friend with a scowl as Jack dropped his supplies on the table. "Too much local color can cause permanent brain damage."

"Hey, I'm not the one dressed like Frank Sinatra in *Guys and Dolls,*" she answered equably, then smiled at Jack. "Nice to meet you."

Casey stole two beers from Jack's package and passed one to her friend on the counter. "Sgt. Jack Scanlon, St. Louis City Homicide," she introduced with a flourish of her unopened can. "Poppi Henderson . . ." The can drooped a moment as she evidently searched for an appropriate title.

Poppi jumped right in. "Mother confessor and chronic accomplice," she offered with a pleased little dip of her head. "You have to be the mysterious priest Mrs. McDonough keeps wanting to unburden herself to. Great hat."

Tonight Jack didn't feel so uncomfortable pulling his tie loose. He gave it a tug and unbuttoned the top button of his shirt to give him a little swallowing room. "Thanks."

Funny, he hadn't really thought about that hat for years. It had just been a part of the job, like handcuffs and guns. But he'd thought about it today. He'd thought about that day he'd gone down to Levine's to order it, his official mark of rank. His rite of passage into homicide. Even after all the ritual he'd participated in over the years, it had still meant something to him. He guessed tradition never meant as much unless it was threatened.

He palmed it off and set it down before pulling out a beer for himself. Then he walked the rest over to the refrigerator.

"This looks like the cue to get down to work," Poppi

decided, hopping off the counter. "Unless we're going back to the Rose, I doubt I'll be of much help."

"Just paperwork," Jack assured her, thinking of his jacket again and pulling out a chair without doing anything about it.

Poppi scowled as if he'd said self-immolation. "Thank you, I think I've served my penance for tonight. Besides, all this talk of the Captain Crunch murders depresses me."

Jack settled into his chair, his attention ostensibly on the work he'd brought. He didn't miss the meaningful look that passed between the two women.

"Then you'll be walking tomorrow," Poppi said, standing by the door, beer still in hand.

Casey nodded, her smile too frustrated to be grateful. "Yeah, thanks again, Poppi. I'll talk to you."

"Oh, yeah," Poppi answered, turning to go. "I'm sure you will."

She almost made it all the way out. Casey had already made it over to her chair and pulled it out, rubbing at her temple with the can of beer. She didn't notice that Poppi paused as she opened the screen door. Jack did.

"And, Casey," Poppi suddenly said, her gaze out to the night, her expression curiously amused. "Stop playing footsies with the bad guy. It isn't doing much for your vibes, either."

The chair screeched at the convulsive movement. Casey whirled for a fight. Before she could say anything, her friend was out the door.

Jack forgot his files. His gut had just caught fire again. Casey's friend had delivered that message deliberately, had thought enough of the problem that she'd wanted Jack to know about it. Maybe he'd been wrong about those surprises. There wasn't a damn thing that was innocuous about Casey McDonough.

"Sounds like this is something I need to know about," he offered quietly, suppressing the urge just to shake her and be done with it.

She faced off with him, her eyes much too brittle to be rebellious. Determined, daring, with just a hint of triumph that made Jack really nervous.

"It all began with the affair I've been having with Hunsacker," she said blithely, plopping into her seat and popping the top on her beer. "And how jealous I've been since he dumped me. By the way, you should probably watch your back, too. If there's one thing I should have remembered, it's how much people like Hunsacker enjoy a good reputation bashing."

One of Jack's better traits as a Jesuit had been his ability to see right through a person's most elaborate defenses. It hadn't hurt him any as a cop, either, but it had sure made the job harder to leave at the office.

Casey's defenses weren't in the least complicated. She'd constructed a shell, a tough-kid facade over the little girl who still peeked out on occasion. The problem was, of course, as deftly as she'd crafted her defenses, when they slipped, the view inside was heartbreaking.

Jack wondered what that other man had been like. He didn't have to imagine what the guy had done to her. He saw it every day in his job; he heard it as sharp as shattered glass every time Casey tried to bluster by it. What had made Jack such a lousy Jesuit was that he would have loved the chance to have that son of a bitch on his knees with a gun shoved in his mouth to see just how he liked it.

This was all getting too complicated. He caught himself wanting to reach over to her and do something about the raw disillusionment in her eyes, and he knew damn well just what that would do for him. The job was the job and relationships were something else he'd walked away from. It didn't deaden the fire any.

"I take it everybody believed him," he said instead, pulling a pen from his pocket rather than rub at the new gnawing under his ribs.

She made taking a sip of beer seem a value judgment. "Nothing sells like a hot rumor." She allowed just a little bitter amazement in her expression. "Funny thing is, it's the vindictive bitch story all over again. You'd think that people could at least come up with something unique."

"I'm afraid it still works."

"Oldest rumor in the world, huh?" she countered with a flash of humor. "You're right. Adam probably said Eve fed him the apple because he wasn't paying enough attention to her." And that quickly her expression changed, and the triumph was back, the tentative defiance. It was obvious she didn't figure Jack would be thrilled with her next news. He didn't even notice himself lean back into interrogation position.

"Anyway," she continued, casting for her thoughts in the vicinity of her beer can. "Just about the same time I found out about the rumor business, who should show up on the work lane himself, but Hunsacker. He walked right up to me and forgave me for hurting him."

"Well," Jack said evenly, "you didn't stab him with a scalpel. I would have known by now."

She grinned, the triumph clear.

"I shook his hand," she said. "It was the weirdest thing. Everybody thought he was being great and I was being humble. But the two of us really knew what was going on. He was trying to torture me, and I wouldn't let him." That brought her right back to her feet, rigid and righteous. "I wouldn't let him."

And Jack had thought he couldn't feel worse. She'd taken this whole thing to a different level. They didn't just have cops and robbers anymore, good guys and bad guys. They had failure and success. Sacrifice and redemption. They had penance for two different sets of sins.

"I'm hungry," Casey announced, whipping around for the refrigerator. "Want something?"

Maalox, he thought. "No, thanks."

There was a pile of information to wade through and a new shift to start in less than seven hours. There was an unhappy mayor and a livid captain to deal with, and an avaricious news community to skirt. There was a psychopath out there murdering women just because they annoyed him, and the biggest annoyance was standing across from Jack perusing the contents of her refrigerator. And she'd just dug her nails in deeper. She'd dared Hunsacker to stop her.

This deserved another beer.

Casey was probably deliberately ignoring the scrape of Jack's chair across the floor as he got to his feet. He made sure she wouldn't ignore his message when he reached past her into the refrigerator.

"Let's forget the data we have on the other murders," he suggested.

She refused to turn from her consideration of the refrigerator. "Why?"

Pulling out a beer, Jack afforded Casey a consideration of his own. "If we hurry, we can record all your suspicions so that when you're murdered, we won't have any choice but call out the Major Case Squad. It'll solve all our problems."

Jack didn't wait for an answer. Battling a flush of angry frustration, he popped the can and wandered on over to where the window looked out on the heavy black night.

"I told you," she challenged behind him. "Without me there wouldn't be a game."

He refused to face her. "Without you there wouldn't

be a thorn in my side. Or Jefferson County's or East St. Louis's or O'Fallon's. Even a psychopath knows when the game isn't worth it anymore."

Jack hoped he'd hit the target. The last thing he needed on his battered conscience was the life of a pain-in-the-ass trauma nurse. The last thing his schedule needed was babysitting a feisty redhead with a knack for trouble and, evidently, no sense of caution. The last thing his ulcer needed was the realization that he was becoming too damn fond of those sharp, sad blue eyes to let some psychopath turn them into rat bait.

"I'll be careful," she promised, as if her mother had just told her not to climb a tree. Jack couldn't help but offer a cynical smile out to the darkness where no one would see. Well, that made it all better.

"Stay away from him," he demanded to her vague reflection in the window.

The ghost scowled back at him. "You sound like a jealous husband."

Jack's answering smile was wry. "Jealousy is probably the one thing I was never accused of."

It took her a moment to respond. "You *have* had a busy life. Sorry."

Jack shrugged. "Not everyone finds me charming and understanding."

"Imagine that."

Their gazes met in the glass, hazy and indistinct as if neither were quite real. Jack saw frustration, felt the same. He saw confusion, anger, vulnerability, and hoped he was better at hiding his own. He took another slug of beer and wished fervently he'd just thrown that damn newspaper clipping back into the trash can without thinking about it. Now it was too late. That vague set of blue eyes glaring back at him from the window had managed to steal whatever peace of mind he'd had left. And he knew damn well what kind of chance he had of getting it back.

"Let's get down to details," he suggested, turning around to find her munching on an apple. She tossed the one in her other hand to Jack.

"You could use a little weight," was all she said. "Ya know, I haven't found out about your day at school yet. It must have been a beaut."

Jack couldn't think of anything less appetizing than apples and beer. He juggled the one and drank the other. Better than throwing both, which was what he was tempted to do. "Why do you say that?"

She offered a grin and a vague gesture. "You have that 'God, I want to rub my stomach' look on your face again."

Jack refrained from grinning back, capitulating. For the moment. "Nobody's supposed to see that."

"Every ulcer patient I see has it," she informed him. "Don't forget, I usually don't get them until they've waited too long."

Jack held up the hand with the apple. "Thanks. The visual aids were graphic enough." He tossed the apple again, its flight short and graceless. "Actually, my threat was less personal. The mayor got a call, so my chief got a call, so my captain got a call."

Casey nodded. "Who said, 'Don't be absurd. He can't be a murderer. He was in Millicent Adams' column, for God's sake.' "

Jack shook his head. "No. He's seen murderers there before. But the mayor is up for reelection, and the idea of one of his police persecuting a prominent physician doesn't sit well with him right now."

"Especially when that physician has friends who help contribute to his campaign."

Jack stopped just as he reached his chair. "You ever been a cop?"

She scowled and began mimicking again. " 'You can't accuse her of stealing equipment to use for doing drugs. The hospital's new wing is named after her mother.' The world is not so mysterious after all."

Before he sat down to business, Jack shrugged out of his jacket and hung it over the chair. He never noticed the hand that strayed back to his stomach.

An hour later Casey scraped her chair back. "I still don't see this," she objected, frustrated all over again. "He killed four women, but we're just going to ignore a couple of them."

Jack sighed and leaned back. They'd been over this. "For now. Don't forget, Casey. I'm one person. One fairly unpopular person who has to conduct most of this investigation on his own time. And I'm up against a man who commits the most violent murders, and then tidies up like he was expecting company."

She knew it. She really did. But Casey was a trauma nurse. Her training and experience didn't inure her to waiting or ambiguities. She wanted action now. Any action. She wanted people to know that Mrs. Peebles was as much a victim as Crystal was, even though the O'Fallon police couldn't come up with anything more than unwitnessed suspicious death. Casey wanted someone to ask how Evelyn could have died without witnesses or evidence.

"I'm trying." She rubbed again at the steady ache in her left temple. Her eyes were getting grainy, and all the typewritten words she'd read were beginning to blur. "So we turf Evelyn and Mrs. Peebles for the moment because of lack of evidence."

"Let's call it concentrating on Wanda and Crystal instead," he suggested.

Casey nodded. "Wanda had a fight with Hunsacker. That very night she is seen bragging to Bobby Lee the Lizard that she'll ditch the trailer life right after she has this meeting with some guy outside the Rose at nine-thirty."

"Exactly nine-thirty," Jack emphasized, pointing out an area on the clandestine copy of Bobby's interview he'd brought along. "She emphasized that."

Casey nodded. "Pointing right to Hunsacker. The only other people who are interested in exact time are the White Rabbit and Iranian terrorists. Wanda walks outside into the rain and is never seen again. Her car is left on the parking lot, and her body is found no more than half a mile away. Buddy doesn't know anything about any of this. He's been over the road in his eighteen-wheeler and gets home to find Wanda gone and his brothers-in-law suggesting he find new comfort." What they'd actually said was pussy, but Casey was still too Catholic to say that even to an ex-priest. Thank God Frank Millard hadn't used the *c* word.

"What does it tell you?" Jack asked.

"Tells me she was expecting a windfall from this meeting. I think she was squeezing Hunsacker."

Jack lifted an eyebrow. "Squeezing?"

Casey grinned. "She must have found out something she figured he'd pay to hear."

"She'd do that?"

"In a minute. Wanda was a great tech. Good with women. She hated men, though. Especially authority figures. She was a walking encyclopedia of childhood abuses, and it sometimes spilled over. I can sure see Hunsacker setting her off." She sat a moment, considering the sketchy information, thinking of Wanda. "I wonder what she did with whatever it was she had on him."

"Or if Hunsacker got ahold of it."

Casey looked up to see the homicide officer in Jack demanding pragmatism from her. "Or if Hunsacker got it," she conceded.

He didn't go so far as to nod. But she knew he was judging her in his way. Asking for something from her only he recognized and making his next decisions based on it.

He took another quick look at the paperwork, as if fortifying himself with it. "Is there anybody who might know?"

Casey thought about it a moment. A terrible realization occurred to her. A truth that would have seemed nothing more than expedient no more than a few weeks ago. For a moment she resented Jack for expecting this of her. "Well," she offered as she fingered the grainy photocopies. "He's been dating a good half-dozen people in at least two hospitals. There's bound to be at least one nurse who's mad at him."

It took her some courage to face Jack.

"A vindictive woman?" he asked with a suspiciously crooked eyebrow.

Casey bristled. "Desperate measures," she allowed stiffly. "I'll start nosing around tomorrow and see if I pick up any interesting rumors."

Jack just nodded and scribbled something in his own notebook. Not as nice as Hunsacker's, this one was dog-eared and small, with cryptic messages and even more cryptic drawings crammed into pages that had been curled and creased from fitting into various pockets. Casey wondered briefly what the notations connected with her own name looked like. Probably something along the line of pain in the ass and delusional.

"So," she said, fingering the papers in front of her. "If Hunsacker did pick her up, what did he drive? He has a Porsche. Somebody at the Rose would have said something about it." Or thrown something at it.

"Something rented. Something stolen. Franklin's still checking on it."

Casey allowed herself a smile. "I'd really love to be along when he shows up to interview all the A list who were supposed to be at the fund-raiser with Hunsacker the night Wanda disappeared."

Jack never looked up from his scribbling. "You're looking forward to it more than Franklin is." He stabbed his pen at the other file, the fatter one. "Okay, let's take another look at that chart copy from Mother Mary," he suggested, changing tack as quickly as he checked his watch. "I want to know if there's any chance to break his alibi for Crystal."

There was another question Casey had about Wanda, a curiosity about what Franklin had found among her personal effects when he'd searched. He'd only noted that he hadn't found anything suspicious. Suspicious to a cop might be different from suspicious to a nurse. But Jack had already switched gears. Besides, what Casey was considering wouldn't be something he should know.

Casey pulled the pages back to her again. She didn't need to check her watch to know it was late. She'd been dragging since walking back in this house. And Jack didn't look much better. He'd at least gotten comfortable enough to ditch the formal attire. His sleeves were rolled up and his tie slung over his jacket. He didn't look as if he felt much better, though. There were dark circles beneath his eyes, and the hollows along his cheeks seemed deeper, the creases in his forehead sharper. Captains must hang even more heavily over the head than nursing supervisors.

Casey found herself wanting to pull all the paperwork out of his hands and shove him out the front door. She wanted to lecture him about good food and better schedules and sleep. But he was the same kind of cop that she was a nurse. Only she could leave the emergency room where it was. Murder seemed to follow a person home. She fought a sigh of frustration for both of them and turned to her information.

The chart pages belonged to Mrs. Beverly Williams, late of the postpartum division at M and M. On the night of Crystal's murder, Hunsacker charted having been in to visit the lovely Mrs. Williams along about eight o'clock. The murder had been committed at eight-fifteen.

When contacted, Mrs. Williams couldn't verify when the doctor had been in. The rooms at M and M didn't have clocks in them. She'd been in for five days, after all, each of which had entailed a visit by the doctor. He often visited before dark, she remembered, which would have been anytime before nine.

The nurse on that night had charted once every two hours. She mentioned Dr. Hunsacker in the eight o'clock notes, but failed to mention when he'd come in. "PMD to see pt" is not one of your more eloquent statements.

"PMD," Jack queried.

"Private medical doctor," Casey said. "No information about what he did or how long he stayed. The way these notes read, he could have been there anytime from six to eight." Casey didn't recognize the name of the nurse, but her notes stank. For all you could tell from these, Mrs. Williams did nothing but eat and sleep.

"I don't know how the nurse feels about Hunsacker," she said, wishing she had more of the chart, to see if there was a charting pattern Hunsacker had depended upon to protect himself. All they'd obtained was the one day's worth. "She might cover for him or be willing to hang him out to dry. Want me to find out?"

Jack made it a point to check his watch again.

Casey grinned. "There are still one or two people who'll talk to me. Even at this time of night."

The night supervisor had worked with Casey before her promotion. Getting up, Casey stretched out the kinks and headed for the phone. "I still hate ignoring Evelyn," she admitted. "After all, she's the reason I got into this in the first place."

"We don't have so much as a hint over there," Jack reminded her as he got to his own feet.

Casey shook her head. "But don't you want to know how he did it?"

"I want to know how Paul Newman makes his salad dressing," Jack assured her dryly. "That doesn't mean he's gonna tell me."

The phone was over by the pantry door. Helen had stuck little magnetic holy things on the board alongside, and added the cryptic note, "He won't let you." Casey ignored it.

"By the way," Jack offered, back over by the window. "Just so you know. I found out about the ex-wife."

Casey stopped halfway through the hospital's number. "And?"

His expression was rueful. "Happily remarried with three kids and a cat."

It took a moment for Casey to admit she was disappointed. She'd been hoping for validation at another woman's expense. "Does she talk glowingly of him?"

"Said he was as randy as a barnyard rooster. She put him through school and then he left for the good life."

"Nothing about intimidation, coercion, abuse."

"Not over long distance."

Casey turned back to the phone, pensive. She'd been

sure they would have found something with the ex-wife. "Any medical records yet?"

"Not without a subpoena. I'm looking into his work record, though."

Casey offered a dry grin. "You'll never hear the words *pain in the ass* about Hunsacker from any official."

"I'm looking more for cookie crumbler."

Casey's call took all of seven minutes. In that time she caught up on the night supervisor's bad marriage, good kids, backbreaking schedule, and common passion for romance novels. She also found out that the supervisor knew the postpartum nurse in question. She described her as a pretty, vapid girl with the minimum necessary brain cells for the job and a real need to please. As for whether she got along with Hunsacker, the supervisor implied "got along" was a little mild. "Got along" usually didn't provoke glances that come straight out of the pages of one of her favorite books.

It was all Casey needed to know.

"No chance," she announced, hanging up. "Whether that nurse remembers when Hunsacker walked in the door is irrelevant. She'll swear to whatever he tells her."

She'd been ready to head back to the table when the phone rang again. Casey didn't even think before picking it up. She just figured that the supervisor had remembered something else and called back.

Silence.

"Hello?" she asked again, her voice automatically slowing.

There was someone there. Casey could feel it, skimming the ends of her nerves like static electricity. Recognition, interest. Malice. An invisible entity touching her with no more than thought and intent.

Casey didn't even realize that her hand had come up to her chest, pressing against the sudden stab of fear. The

silence washed over her, tumescent and dark. There
wasn't a word that needed to be said, because the silence
said it all. The heavy, pulsating void carried its own
threat.

*Click.*

Soft, careful, as if the other person didn't want to dis-
turb her, as if the contact were polite and proper. Casey
battled a flush of revulsion.

"Casey?" Jack asked behind her. "What's wrong?"

Casey didn't turn around. She didn't hang up the
phone. For a moment the contact hung suspended, as if
even the phone equipment needed time to assimilate the
message. And then, the flat clacks of disconnection, and
the familiar comfort of a buzz.

It shook Casey out of her reverie.

"Casey?"

She whipped around, his voice too close, as close as
the presence on her line. As suddenly threatening. He
stood right behind her, his features creased with concern,
his cop's instincts too deadly accurate.

Before he got a chance to slip into Casey's brain and
discover the truth, Casey flashed the policeman a smile.

"Wrong number," she said, knowing just what would
happen if she told him. Knowing that he'd interfere before she had the chance to win her victory.

Jack didn't answer right away. He stood across from
her, tense and suspicious, his right hand resting on his
hip, just by his gun. Casey wasn't sure he believed her.
He didn't press it. In the end, they returned to the files
to try to piece together more information, without any
luck. When they finally gave up, he gathered up his
jacket and tie and carried his uneaten apple out with him.

Casey closed the door behind him uncertain what she
should do. She walked upstairs to her room and un-
dressed, still uncertain. Knowing that if she told Jack he

would intervene, and knowing that she didn't want him to. It was too important to let it happen. To prove that she could handle it.

Because Hunsacker had begun to threaten her in a much more personal way. He'd invaded her home.

She really thought that was all. Just that he was upset about whatever had been on the news and thought to step up his reign of terror over her. She went to sleep with the thought that nothing Hunsacker could do would dissuade her. That she was strong now. She could beat him before he hurt her.

The call came at seven in the morning. It startled Casey from her sleep, the buzz a monitor alarm in her somnolent state. A threat in her abrupt jump to sharpness.

There was a phone on her desk, for the conversations she didn't want Helen to monitor. She jumped for it, anxious to intercede before Helen heard that silence. That presence.

"Casey?" It was Millie, and her voice shook with distress.

"Millie, what's wrong?" Casey's stomach sank with awful anticipation. The quaver in the young nurse's voice portended disaster.

It took Millie a minute to pull herself together enough to talk. When she did, it was with outrage, with condemnation. Whatever she was going to say, it was somehow Casey's fault.

"I just thought you should know," she said in a rush. "We just got the call from the police." She sobbed, and Casey wanted to shake her. "Janice is dead. She killed herself."

# Chapter 15

*SHE'D EATEN A .38.* No question, according to the
Brentwood police, who'd been called when her separated husband had stopped by on his way to work to pick
up some things and found her in the bedroom. No question, said the county medical examiner, who inspected
the scene, the remains, and every kind of bodily fluid
they could siphon. Janice Feldman had imbibed enough
alcohol to stupefy a moose and then shoved the gun she'd
purchased the week before into her mouth and blown
out the back of her head.

Yes, her coworkers said. She had been distracted
lately. She'd been having problems at home. She'd even
joked once about committing suicide the "right way" to
prevent common mistakes. Her husband had finally
moved out, and Janice had left behind a note apologizing
for what she was doing to him.

Janice didn't seem like the kind of person who would
commit suicide, they admitted. But then, how many
times had they heard that same song from grieving relatives over the years? No, the investigating detectives
said, women did not as a rule eat guns. But the precedent
had been set during the conversation. That and the note

and the physical evidence pointed to the fact that Janice had been set on proving something to her husband, her friends, and herself.

"What about the guy she was seeing?" Casey asked at work three days later, still stunned, still guilty, still expecting to see Janice stroll down the hall holding a bottle of hydrogen peroxide in her manicured hand to clean some microscopic spot from her uniform. Casey hadn't slept for the last two nights. The phone had been ringing again. And when it hadn't, she'd closed her eyes to see Janice, accusing, distraught, isolated.

"What guy?" Barb demanded with some distaste.

The look in her eyes warned Casey not to make up fairy tales to absolve her own culpability. For some reason, everybody who had sided against Casey in the Hunsacker dispute demanded connection. Their implication was that somehow Casey had caused Janice's desperate act. Casey was too tired to even care.

She looked up from the medication she was mixing. "Janice had begun seeing somebody else. Somebody she said she was in love with." There was another needle cap at the side of her mouth, already misshapen and scarred from chewing.

Barb glared at her from where she stood over the lab FAX waiting for results. "Aaron only moved out last week," she accused.

Casey hadn't even known that. She wondered what kind of decision Janice had made, whether she'd meant to leave for the other man and couldn't in the end, or whether that had fallen through, too. She wanted more than anything to understand why Janice was dead. Why she was dead in such an awful way.

"She told me this a couple of weeks ago," Casey insisted, setting the bottle down and facing Barb.

"The only other man she might have seen was a

shrink," Barb retorted hotly, turning back to her chore. "Dale tried to talk her into seeing somebody."

It was so stupid. Such a little thing that should have blown away all the confusion of the past three days. And it hit Casey like a baseball bat, right between her eyes.

Her knees almost gave out on her. Her chest caught fire. She battled the first tears she'd shed since hearing the news. Not tears of grief. Tears of guilt. Of rage.

Dale.

She should have known. She should have anticipated it the minute Hunsacker had comforted Janice in the lounge. She should have spotted the symptoms in that funny little dance Janice had always done near him. The easiest route to a person's bed is a soft shoulder, and that's just what Hunsacker had provided.

Casey should have understood. After all, she'd been there when Janice had made her promise to Steve about suicide. But so had Hunsacker. And he would have remembered.

"Oh, God," Casey whispered, suddenly blind to the activity around her, hands slippery against the gleaming metal of the medprep, her fingers clawing at nothing more substantial than rage.

He hadn't called to threaten her. He'd called to taunt her. To let her know what he'd done. He would keep calling until she understood and answered him.

"Casey, Mr. Crawley's bed is ready upstairs," Millie announced. "Casey?"

She couldn't even answer. Too many voices already dissented in her ears. Logic told her she was jumping to conclusions. Janice had too much taste to fall for Hunsacker's patter. She would have seen through him in a minute.

But Casey had told herself she was jumping to conclusions before. This time she listened to her instincts, and her instincts told her that Janice had been confused, been in pain. Been desperate. And that was just the kind of chum Hunsacker was attracted to.

Hunsacker had been the other man. He'd slept with her, promised her more than he'd ever intended to give, and then, for some reason, killed her.

And there probably wasn't any way in hell they'd prove this one, either.

"Casey?"

Casey started at the feel of Millie's hand on her arm. "I'll, uh, be right back," was all she said. Then, leaving the syringe full of anticonvulsant medication on the counter, she wheeled around for the lounge.

But Jack wasn't in his office. Casey couldn't leave a message; no one else would understand. She told Detective Capelli to have Sgt. Scanlon call her as soon as he got in, and hung up.

She had to do something. Evelyn was dead, and Wanda, and now Janice. And Hunsacker still hunted with impunity. Her friends. Her coworkers. And as she'd always said, if they didn't take care of each other, nobody else sure as hell would.

Casey sat for five long minutes in the empty lounge, the clatter of the work lane muffled beyond the door, the smoke filter whirring steadily overhead, the distant whine of ambulances prophesying trouble. She still couldn't quite breathe, and her chest hurt, as if something were trying to claw its way out. She had to do something.

There were new notices on the BOHICA board. A flower fund for Janice and a reminder that outpatient psychiatric treatment was only partially covered in the health insurance plan. The official reminder that staff couldn't talk to police on official business in the work lane without the permission of the on-site supervisor.

Casey fought tears again. She pulled at the hard plastic of the needle cap with her fingers, rolling it around between her hands until it left little red grooves on her skin.

Hunsacker was sidling closer. He was raising the stakes, and Casey had to stop him. She had to find some way to silence that boastful laughter. She desperately wanted to talk to Jack about this. To make him understand and get his input. But she didn't really expect him to help. His hands were tied.

Hers weren't.

Concentrate on Wanda and Crystal, he'd said. Well, all right, she would. There were some questions she wanted very much to ask Buddy, some things she wanted to see. After that, she'd get back in touch with her friends over at Izzy's. And maybe she'd just go a little step further and ask her acquaintances in the medical examiner's office for some news about Janice. She'd get enough information for Jack that his request for the Major Case Squad couldn't be turned down.

And tonight, when Hunsacker called, she'd fight back.

Casey didn't call Buddy. Buddy didn't have a phone. She headed back down to the Rose right after work to check in on him.

Nothing much had changed. There was a different song on the jukebox, something about lovers and liars, and fewer people scattered over the vinyl and Formica. Casey walked in alone and hopped up on a bar stool.

Clyde the bartender was pleased as he could be to see her. "I told Buddy what you said," he informed her as he poured her a beer. "We were all set to get up a search party of our own when those old boys found her instead of the rabbits they was huntin'." Setting the foaming glass on the counter, he paused to shake his head, the ashes at the end of his cigarette glowing red right over Casey's beer. "Beer's on the house."

It was his way of saying thank you.

"Thanks," Casey allowed with a smile and took a drink just to get it out of range. Her hands were still shaking. "How's Buddy doing?"

Clyde inclined his head over to one of the tables by the wall. "See for yourself."

Casey couldn't believe her luck. Buddy sat with his back against one of the Budweiser mirrors, a beer in hand and quite a few more on board. Casey remembered him as being a pretty good-looking guy. He looked a lot thinner now, prematurely stooped, his features gray and flat.

She'd never thought much one way or another about Buddy before. Suddenly she hurt for him.

So this was what they looked like later. She'd wondered sometimes when she'd ushered families back out the door from a visit with sudden death, still too numb to know their own grief. She'd been cried on, screamed at, assaulted with that first wave of denial and pain. She'd never seen what they had carried through the next days and weeks. She saw it now, the reality of death weighing Buddy down like an inescapable sentence.

It had to be what Evelyn's husband had felt, what Aaron Feldman felt. It must have been what Helen had faced when her Mick had died so long ago. Casey decided she didn't want any part of it. She was glad she worked the ER, where she could shield herself against the flash of first pain and then shuttle it back out the door before it had the chance to sear her.

"Buddy?" She greeted him, her beer in hand, her voice tentative and more afraid than she realized. She didn't want him turning those lost, lonely eyes on her. She didn't want to be infected with his sorrow.

His eyes were a soft blue. She remembered them laughing. Tonight they looked distant and opaque. Occupant not home, call again later.

"My name's Casey McDonough," she introduced herself, slipping into the other seat without waiting for his invitation. "I worked with Wanda at St. Isidore's."

A dim light flickered. Not interest so much as recognition. "I wanna thank you," he slurred, grabbing on to his beer glass as if it were the only handhold left on a steep slope. A cigarette had burned almost away in the little tin ashtray in front of him, the smoke wreathing him like early fog. "They wouldn't believe me. None of 'em listened. But you did."

Casey shook her head. "I knew Wanda. She loved you, Buddy. She wouldn't have taken off like that without a word." Maybe it was trite. Maybe it wasn't even true. It was all Casey could offer.

Buddy's eyes filled with unshed tears, and Casey battled against her own. God, she hated this. She wanted to get back into her rut, where she was safe and anesthetized against this kind of pain.

"I need a favor, Buddy," she hurried on, trying her best to control her voice. "I don't think the police know what to look for in investigating her murder."

He tried his best to focus on her words. His eyes rolled a little and straightened, settling on a spot on her left cheek. "Pussies," he snarled. He'd obviously been spending a lot of time with Clyde lately.

"Buddy," she said, leaning closer, peering through the haze. "I'm working with another policeman on another murder. A murder I think is related to Wanda's. And, well, if I could find something more solid than they have now . . ."

"But they looked already," he said, his attention inward again. "Rummaged through our place for a coupla hours."

"The cops didn't know Wanda. They don't know hospitals. I do. I might spot something important they wouldn't recognize. Could I look? At her stuff, her hospital stuff." She didn't mention that the police wouldn't have known they were looking for blackmail material. Casey wasn't sure how he'd react to a concept like that. She wasn't even sure he could comprehend it right now. The simple route seemed the best.

It worked. It took him a minute for her words to worm their way past all the alcohol. When they finally did, Buddy came right to his feet with a nod. Then he turned for the door without waiting to see if she'd follow.

"I'm gonna drive Buddy home, Clyde," Casey announced, her beer left forgotten with Buddy's. Clyde just nodded, too.

The Trigel trailer had never been that much to speak of. It was less now. Buddy hadn't spent a lot of time cleaning since Wanda's disappearance. Empty TV dinners spilled out over trash can and sink. Beer cans and cigarette butts littered every available surface. Clothes huddled in rumpled piles over the furniture, and the place reeked of smoke.

Buddy had obviously been sleeping on the couch. The bedroom was dusty and neat, closed off and silent. Casey figured he hadn't gone in since Wanda had disappeared. It made her search easier, but spookier. After pointing out the correct door, Buddy grabbed himself a refill from the fridge and sprawled into a chair in the living room without moving any of the previous occupants, and then just waited.

The contents of Wanda's locker were still stuffed into the cardboard box that sat on the dresser. Just what Casey had heard, five or six pictures of Elvis from puberty to pantsuits, a stash of unfiltered Marlboros, and a cache of cheap, brassy earrings. No diaries, no messages, no surprises. Casey turned away to check the rest of the room.

She found stuffed animals, a shadowbox with tiny turtles, and a lot of jeans. More Elvis and enough makeup to stage a Broadway show. And, tossed in the corner, right behind a chair, a lab coat and white shoes.

Casey hesitated a moment, superstitious and uncertain. Wanda had probably dropped the clothes here after her last night of work, careless with the certainty that they'd still be there the next day to pick up. That she'd be there the next day to do it.

But she hadn't. Casey had the feeling she was the first person to touch them since Wanda had tossed them over the chair and missed, that the police hadn't even seen the little puddle of white back in the corner.

She gingerly reached past a couple of cobwebs and caught the lab coat by the collar. It smelled like cigarettes, too. A name tag was still over the pocket, W. Trigel CNA, Labor and Delivery. Casey went right for the bulging pockets.

Wanda had been a typical hospital pack rat, stuffing her lab coat with things like tape and alcohol swabs just in case she'd need them. Casey stacked those on the dresser along with three pens, scissors, an opened pack of cigarettes, a stash of rubber bands, paper clips, and a tape measure. And one other thing.

Casey almost tossed it right atop the small pile she'd been building on the dresser. It was just a patient label, the kind the computer made up by the hundreds to tag everything from tests to charges on a patient. A white tag with a peelable sticky back with patient name, address, date of birth, and doctor. Casey dropped them in her pockets all the time, grabbing more than enough for what she needed, pulling an extra to remind her to check back on the patient later or update paperwork.

Casey was going to toss it onto the growing pile of debris on the dresser. A familiar object amid more familiar objects. Then she read the information on it, and everything changed. Marilyn Peebles, age 24, address Rolling Rock Lane in Ladue. Doctor, Dale Hunsacker.

Peebles, the same last name as the woman who had been ashed out in O'Fallon. The name they couldn't connect with Hunsacker. But they could now. Casey slipped the label into her own pocket, refilled the lab coat with its cache, and then carefully draped it over the chair where Buddy would find it when he was finally able to open the room on his own. And then she shut the door and tried her best to help Buddy.

The call came at three, just as Casey was trying to fall asleep. She picked up the receiver, torn between wanting it to be Hunsacker and wishing Jack would finally call her back.

Silence.

She almost smiled. You killed her, she thought, straightening in the desk chair. You somehow stuffed a gun in Janice's mouth and blew out her brains, and I know it.

I'm after you, you son of a bitch.

She heard him breathing this time, as if he'd been running. As if he were excited. Well, she was excited, too. She finally had something on him. All she had to do was talk to Marilyn Peebles tomorrow to find out just what it was.

It was all Casey could do to keep her silence, too, to leave her messages implied and secret. It was all she could do to keep from railing at him, demanding an explanation, a reason when she knew darn well the only one she might get was that he enjoyed it.

But she waited. The house creaked and settled around her, listening in, and a breeze fluttered through the curtains at her window. Pussy mewled a floor below and Helen murmured in response. And watching the pearl-gray landscape outside her window, Casey waited.

In the end, she heard the soft click. She didn't wait for the dial tone this time to hang up. Reaching over, she pulled the chain to her desk lamp and consigned her room to moonlight. And when she climbed into bed, she slept better than she had since that first phone call.

Casey made her call the next morning from the same phone so that Helen couldn't overhear. Casey had thought of showing up at the medical examiner's digs up in Maryland Heights, but the fact of the matter was that after twelve years of calling in every emergency-room death she handled, she felt more comfortable dealing with the MEs over the phone. She didn't think she could pick one of them out of a crowd unless he opened his mouth.

It was Pat Martin she ended up talking to, the voice belonging in Casey's mind to a big, brusque Irishman with curly red hair, like hers. She knew he had six kids and a boat he took out on the river, and that he liked a good dirty joke even better than she. She also knew that he asked more questions than a census when he was on, and had a store of unbelievably arcane information on methods of death and destruction. The word was that he also kept a headlight on his desk from his first case, a pileup with four people reduced to road pizza and a car that ended its own life the size of a lunchbox.

"Pat, I hear you got Janice," Casey started in, already rubbing at her temple.

"Yeah," Pat answered, his voice deep and gravelly. "Tough one."

"No question? She really did kill herself?"

"You never think it's going to happen to friends."

Casey scowled. "Don't get all therapeutic on me, Pat. I have a reason for asking."

"She sure as shit wasn't brushing her teeth with that thing," he retorted.

"I thought women didn't eat guns."

"So did I," he admitted. "But she sure made a believer out of me. If she were a thirty-year-old male, I wouldn't have even asked for a note. I'm afraid that fun little conversation you all had about suicide methodology was a little more intense for Janice."

"The note," Casey nudged. "Can you tell me what it said?"

"She didn't mention you, if that's what you mean."

"Pat . . ."

"Okay. All it said was, 'Aaron'—the husband, right?— 'I have no right to do this to you. I'm sorry.' Then she signed it and dotted her I's with Type A."

I have no right to do this to you. Janice hadn't said I can't live anymore, or I have nothing left to live for. She didn't mention lost love or depression. She said she couldn't do something *to* Aaron. What?

"Did you find out anything about the other guy she was seeing?"

"She was a tidy character," Pat said. "No letters, no diaries, no last-minute confessions."

"Just the note."

"Exactly."

"Which doesn't exactly say she killed herself."

"I thought the gray matter on the wall and the powder burns on her upper palate did that."

"Pat, bear with me a minute," Casey begged. "I have a theory for you. A . . . hypothetical situation."

"I live for hypothetical situations."

"Well, here it is. Janice was having lots of trouble in her marriage. She talked to me about it. Evidently Aaron was dabbling with XY chromosome bonding."

"It'd be enough to put *me* in a snit."

"But Janice also said she was seeing somebody else. Somebody she'd considered running away with. It might be someone who would inspire her to write a note like that to Aaron. She *would* have been sorry. She didn't want to hurt him, no matter what he'd done."

"And you think this mysterious significant other blew out her lights." Pat also had a great intuition.

"With all my heart."

This silence Casey recognized. This was a "how do I placate her?" silence.

"He'd have to know just how to do it so it would look just like a suicide," Pat finally offered. "Amateurs don't understand physiology enough to do that."

"He's a doctor."

"He's not a coroner. We're talking blood patterns and stippling and finger placement. She was sitting up when she died, on the side of her bed, unbound and mobile. Hard to make somebody eat a gun without restraints."

"He could. If you have questions, talk to Sgt. Scanlon of the city homicide department. He's looking into some other handiwork of this guy's."

The silence that met this statement was the one of stupefaction. Casey heard the sharp hiss of breath, the creak of a chair.

"You talking about that guy Hunsacker? The one on the news?" Pat couldn't have sounded more surprised if she'd accused the pope.

"Just think about it," she begged, not certain suddenly

what she'd wanted from this conversation. Clarity, certainty. Had she meant to go this far? Had she wanted to spill the story onto the grapevine?

"You said Janice was a neat character," she prodded. "I bet the only thing out of place in that room was the back of her skull."

"Her bookshelf was alphabetized."

Casey instinctively nodded, her eyes down on the doodle she'd drawn of a wave and the words in Janice's note. "You never got to see her at work. Pat, I've never seen another human being who could keep a white uniform spotless for up to twelve-hour stretches down here. I mean spotless. She carried a nail file and a bottle of hydrogen peroxide in her uniform just in case she needed them. Now, you're the medical examiner. Do you *really* think that a broken marriage is enough to overcome that kind of compulsion?"

"Weirder things have happened."

And he'd be happy to tell her about them. Casey didn't give him a chance. "Just promise me you'll keep an open mind. And a shut mouth. I'm in trouble enough as it is for helping with this."

"I'll bet."

"Please?"

He sighed, an expansive sound of concession. "You take care of me, I'll take care of you. What have I always told you? That when you bought the big one you'd be first in line for the saw. Okay, Casey. I'll relook my stuff. Don't expect any miraculous revelations, though. I think you're wrong."

"That's okay, Pat," she admitted. "It's happened before. If I hear anything else, I'll call."

\*       \*       \*

Still no Jack. Casey dialed again, and again he was out. She left another message and headed down for her trip to Ladue.

Casey hadn't anticipated Helen. When Casey let herself out of the house her mother was waiting for her, sitting on the front porch swing, her legs demurely folded at the ankle, clutching both missal and rosary in her lap.

"It's eleven, Mom," Casey protested. "Nothing's scheduled for eleven."

"I want to go with you."

Car keys in hand, purse over her shoulder, jeans already too heavy in the stale morning air, Casey came to a dead stop.

"Go with me?" she demanded, squinting over as if it would help pull her mother into better focus. "Why?"

Helen smiled and fluttered a little. "Because I'm worried about you."

Casey didn't know what to say. She took a minute to look out over the neighborhood where trees hesitated in the still air and the lawns wilted for want of water. The sky was a faded blue, the color of Buddy Trigel's eyes, and it didn't seem alive, either. It made Casey suddenly irritated and impatient.

"You feel badly about that girl," Helen went on, her attention on the writhing silver Jesus trapped between her fingers and the cross. "But that's up to God. God and his tender mother. We can't judge, and we can't forgive. It's a sad thing that she's consigned herself to the fiery eternity of hell—"

"Don't," Casey abruptly interrupted, much too familiar with this line of thought. "She didn't kill herself."

"She did," Helen argued gently, reaching out a hand she knew wouldn't reach her child. "He told me."

"God told you?" Casey retorted, furious that she'd been dragged back into this kind of conversation.

But Helen shook her head. "No, Mick. He told me that you were only hurting yourself by pursuing this, Casey. And I trust him."

"Just when did Daddy appear to you?" Casey demanded.

Helen's eyes teared up. Casey was getting tired of all the crying lately. She wanted a good laugh or two. "He just doesn't want me to feel badly. He wants me to be forgiven, and I don't know if I can do it. But he worries about you, too."

"That's nice of him," Casey said, patting Helen on the shoulder and fighting the urge to run down the steps. "You tell him I'm fine."

"He thinks . . . he thinks you're obsessed by this thing because that man reminds you so much of . . . of Frank."

Casey stiffened. Her mother hadn't mentioned Frank's name since Casey had walked back in the house. It had been like a pact between them, a twisted little vow of silence, and she'd just broken it.

"He's exactly like Frank," Casey admitted, crouching down at her mother's level. "Only worse. And that's why I'm going to get him."

The tears welled over and slid down parchment cheeks. Helen didn't even seem to notice them anymore. Casey was surprised she didn't have grooves in her cheeks like the fabled statue of St. Peter, whose weeping for his cowardice had etched itself all the way into stone.

"Your father was a good man," Helen whispered, hand now finding Casey's arm and clawing it like a last hope. "Don't do this to him."

But Casey could only shake her head, the frustration splintering into rage. She wanted to tell her mother it wasn't her fault she didn't listen to the advice of dead men. She wanted to tell her just what was involved in this game, and why gods and ghosts didn't matter a damn. But she surrendered to the frightened anguish in her mother's eyes.

Patting Helen's trembling hand, Casey regained her feet. "It has nothing to do with Daddy," she assured her. "It has to do with a brutal, evil man who has to be stopped."

She thought that would take care of it, but when she turned to go, Helen scrambled right to her feet behind her and followed.

Perched on the second porch step, Casey sighed. "You'll stay in the car," she warned.

"Of course, sweetheart."

And the two of them went off to catch a murderer.

Jack found the phone message under a stack of new orders. He'd spent the last two days in court testifying on one of his old cases, and the evenings doing some unofficial liaising with the East St. Louis police department in a bar in Sauget. The message was dated yesterday. Taking a good yank on his tie, he checked his watch and decided to try her at work.

It took a good three or four minutes to get him connected.

"This is Casey McDonough," she answered in a brisk, no-nonsense voice that anticipated both confidence and trouble.

Jack settled into his chair and grabbed for the coffee he'd made. "Scanlon," he greeted her. "You called?"

"Three times," she informed him, her voice easing into familiarity. "I was beginning to think you'd run away from home."

"Participating in the antiquated rituals of the court system," he assured her, taking a sip. "And before you accuse me, yes, I am an expert on antiquated rituals."

"Well, Scanlon," she admitted, "you caught me at

lunch. A good thing, because it'll give me time to weave a story about suicide, redemption, and murder."

"Suicide."

"My mother still insists that suicide victims secure themselves a ticket to the Gehenna Express. Being fairly conversant with suicide in all its myriad forms, I tend to disagree with her. But the point this time is that it wasn't suicide."

Jack heard the news in her voice even before she delivered it. "What wasn't suicide?" he asked, pulling his scratch pad over and uncapping his pen. His stomach had been almost quiet the last two days. It looked like the reprieve was over.

"Janice Feldman. You ran into her when you were here, a tall brunette with great bone structure and a spotless uniform."

"She killed herself?"

"My point exactly. She was found four days ago in her bedroom with a gunshot wound through the mouth. She'd been having husband and boyfriend troubles, and the theory was she was despondent and got drunk enough to wipe out her obsession for neatness."

Jack's pen hovered over the still-blank paper. "She ate a gun?" he demanded.

"Women don't do that," she retorted with the kind of brightness Jack knew wouldn't reach her eyes. "They think Janice was their exception to the rule."

"And you don't think so."

"I knew her. I also finally figured out who the mysterious boyfriend was."

He was tapping the pen against a blank sheet of paper and didn't even hear it. He didn't want to ask. He'd just spent two nights butting his head against a brick wall and been summoned into the captain's office again. He didn't want to know that the stakes had been raised again, because he didn't have the chips to call, and it was going to be Casey in the end who was going to lose.

"Hunsacker," he said anyway.

"In a word." Her voice carried an odd exhilaration. Maybe she wasn't as blithe about suicide as she thought. Maybe she'd already vented her grief. Maybe there was something else going on that followed the news. Jack fought an urge to rub away the fire.

"Where was she found?" he asked.

"Brentwood police handled it, and Pat Martin over at the ME's office. I already talked to him."

Scanlon knew he hadn't wanted to hear more. "You talked to him about this?"

"I couldn't get hold of you," she defended herself. "And I didn't want Janice to fall through the cracks. I don't want people to keep thinking she killed herself when Hunsacker did it."

"How do you know for sure?"

"He told me."

Jack had a feeling he'd been waiting to hear this. He closed his eyes and kept his silence, breathless with fury.

"That night you were over," she continued more quietly. "The wrong number. It was Hunsacker, I'm sure of it. He didn't say anything, but I think he was taunting me. The time of death was an hour before that call."

"Did he call again?"

"Every night."

Now Jack made his first notes. "We'll tap the phone. What else?"

"No, you won't."

Jack rubbed at his eyes. It had already been a long day. He didn't need Casey to pick this moment for a fight. "I said we'll tap the phone," he informed her with more steel. "He's getting too close now, and you're not safe anymore."

Casey's voice was as sharp as his. "Unless I'm under arrest, don't tell me what I will or won't do at my own house."

Jack heard it then, the button he must have pushed. It was just amazing how a woman with so much common sense could shut down straight into blind stupidity just because a man told her what to do. Those old hurts must have run real deep.

If she'd brought him any other news, he might have taken more time coaxing her out of it.

"It's you and I, Casey," he reminded her abruptly. "Two people in the whole damn city who think this guy's poison. I can't afford to let you play power games at the expense of the investigation. This has gone too far already."

He could hear her breathing, slow and deep, reeling in control. He did the same and managed to shove down an impulse to send a cruiser out for her, just to make sure she didn't do something stupid.

"Janice Feldman," he repeated back to nudge her into gear. "Brentwood, 1:00 AM, June 12. I'll do some talking. Now, what else?"

It took her a moment, but when she finally answered, her voice had almost regained its control.

"Elizabeth Peebles," she said. "And Wanda."

Jack's pen slowed all over again. "What about them?"

Casey took a good breath. "Did you know that Wanda knew Mrs. Peebles? She met her when her daughter-in-law Marilyn came in to have a baby. Turns out Marilyn went to Dr. Hunsacker and referred the older Mrs. Peebles to him for menopause problems. Momma only went twice, and then stopped altogether until a friend suggested Dr. Fernandez."

"And you know why."

"From what Marilyn said, her mother-in-law was very

troubled about how Hunsacker conducted his office visits."

"How so?"

"It has to do with those pelvics," she said with deliberate patience, reminding him that as yet he hadn't set his feet in stirrups. "He was either too rough or too familiar. Or both."

"And the daughter kept going to him?"

"Funny thing about pregnant women. They get just about to term, and they get really passive with their doctors. They're really afraid of rocking the boat, and more afraid of establishing a new relationship that close to game time."

"Was she having problems with him?"

"Well, that's evidently how this all started. She mentioned something to Wanda while Wanda was prepping her for her C-section. She was trying to understand why she felt so uncomfortable around Hunsacker when everybody else seemed to dote on him. Evidently Hunsacker had been tough and tender to her, too."

"How tender?"

"Enough that if she raised the question, Hunsacker could be investigated, censured, and indicted. She won't raise the question. I asked. But she won't go to him anymore, either."

"And how did you manage to find all this out?"

"Wanda had Marilyn Peebles's name and address in her lab-coat pocket."

Now Jack had to wait a minute for patience. He'd just punched a hole through the paper with his ballpoint. Damn her! She'd just gone off half-cocked again without letting him know. How the hell was he supposed to keep balancing the hunt for Hunsacker with the need to protect Casey? And he hadn't even been into the captain's office yet. He didn't even know whether he was still on the case. Hell, he didn't even know if he was still on the force.

"I asked you to pick up grapevine material," he grated, clenching his pen instead of his jaw. "Not interview relatives."

Her exuberance seemed to have returned. "Nobody else was doing it."

"Don't be an idiot," he snapped. "You make one wrong move, you screw up any hope of hauling Hunsacker in."

"Have I done anything wrong yet?"

"No, but that doesn't make any difference."

"And nobody else in three counties knew that Hunsacker knew Mrs. Peebles. I rest my case."

Jack took a steadying breath. "I'm gonna rest my hand on your backside if you don't contain yourself. Don't you get it yet? Hunsacker's not going to let you traipse around collecting damaging evidence against him. He finds out you met Mrs. Peebles' daughter-in-law and he might meet *you* in some dark parking lot. And who's going to take care of your mother when you end up in a garbage bag?"

It took her a minute to answer. When she did, her voice was subdued and angry. "Not bad," she whispered. "Must be that clerical training that helps you zero in on the guilt reflex so fast."

"Whatever gets the job done."

Jack hung up the phone a few minutes later and leaned back in his chair. Five women, now. Five and counting. Jack saw that he'd written their names in order on his scratch pad. Wanda Trigel, Evelyn Peters, Crystal Jean Johnson, Elizabeth Peebles, Janice Feldman. Each one different, each one as dead as the first. And there were signs that Hunsacker was increasing the tempo of his kills. His down time was shortening, like a woman in labor, so that the next woman was already in danger.

A woman in labor. What an analogy. Jack wondered whether Hunsacker was objective enough about his own murderous pattern to comprehend the irony of the comparison.

Jack looked at his list. Bare facts, statistics, anonymous features that somehow look alike beneath the medical examiner's camera. Eyes half open, as if bored with the whole thing, mouths slack in surprise, skin waxen and thick. It was his secret, the fire behind the Maalox, that he couldn't leave the names on their standardized forms. He took them home with him, to bed and to breakfast, weighing him down like one heavy rock piled on another until there were times when he thought he couldn't get his shoulders up far enough to breathe.

It was Jack's secret that he'd carried his dead from war and from the missions, all clustered around his table in the dark to accuse him, to remind him of his failures. And the victims from his job joined them, sad-faced ghosts with no one to redeem them but Jack.

Even more than that, he carried the names of the next victim and the one after that. He saw the list in his hand and knew it would be longer before it stopped, and those names bore down on him most of all.

This time, though, it was different. This time he'd made the mistake of letting it get personal. It wasn't just going to be innocent victims he had to atone for, it was going to be Casey. Because he knew as well as he knew the list already in his hand, that hers would be added. And he wasn't sure that there was a damn thing he could do about it.

# Chapter 16

"THEN WHY DID Janice go out and buy herself a gun?" Marva demanded when Casey told her. "She didn't hunt no rabbits, girl."

They had the lounge to themselves, Marva milking one of her rare cigarettes and Casey finishing a pile of charts.

"We might never know," Casey admitted, leaning in close. "Maybe she was scared of Hunsacker. Maybe Hunsacker convinced her that Aaron was going to hurt her. Maybe she had a mouse in the closet."

"And maybe she was hurting enough that she just didn't wanna play anymore," Marva argued relentlessly, the smoke that curled from her nose giving her the appearance of a recumbent dragon.

"And blow the shit out of herself?" Casey argued, intense, needing Marva to believe. "Janice wasn't the kind to do it that way. Not when she didn't have to go any farther than the medprep. Hell, Marva, you know damn well that if any of us really wanted to get scrogged, we'd head straight for insulin or potassium or digitalis. All neat and quick and efficient, accessible and anonymous. You wouldn't need a permit or a hundred bucks or the guts to feel the metal against your teeth. You'd drop a vial in your lab coat with a syringe or two, slip into your favorite nightie, put on your favorite music, and get out the tourniquet."

Marva never moved more than an eyebrow. "Sounds like you did a lot of thinkin' on this."

Casey deflated a little. She hadn't felt her fist clench around her pen or her shoulders tighten up somewhere around her ears. "It crossed my mind," she admitted uneasily, wishing Marva would move or flinch or look away. It seemed those soft brown eyes stripped her naked. "A long time ago."

Marva took a minute to at least assure herself of that. With one last drag from her cigarette, she crushed it into the Styrofoam cup she balanced in her lap and blew smoke at the whirring filter in the ceiling. "You got that sergeant working on this?" she asked.

Casey nodded.

Marva nodded back and aimed a finger at Casey's chest. "Then drop it around here. You ain't real popular right now, and that kind of accusation's not gonna help at all."

Marva was about to get to her feet when Casey laid a restraining hand on her arm. "Do you believe me?"

Marva stopped where she was, and those brown eyes settled back on Casey with more worry than Marva would ever admit. "I think that boy has got you fried in hot oil. He's slick and sweet and popular, and you're gettin' sucked into whatever he's doin'. You're losin' your sense of humor, girl, and that's not good."

"People are dying, Marva. What do you want me to do?"

Marva waved that off, too. "Shoot, girl. What I tell you? It's like the good Lord said about the poor. People always gonna be dyin'. Sometimes they's somethin' we can do about it, sometimes they ain't. All you can do is what you can do."

Casey allowed her friend a grudging smile. "You've been a trauma nurse too long."

Marva rolled her eyes and finally got to her feet. *"Way* too long," she said and walked out into the work lane.

It took Casey another ten minutes to complete just one more set of notes. She couldn't concentrate. She was having trouble sitting still. Finally she just gave up and left them for later and went back out to the lane to do some real work.

Maybe it was instinct. Maybe she was developing a sense of smell like Hunsacker. Whatever it was, it drew her back out onto the work lane just as Hunsacker walked in the door.

Casey froze. She'd just laid her hand on a bottle of potassium for the IV she was going to start. She stood there, dead center in the hall, exposed and vulnerable, her suspicions literally in her hand when he spotted her.

"Are *you* going to be helping me with my lady?" he asked with a broad, bright smile.

Casey kept thinking of apples and worms, meat and maggots. Open the bright shiny exterior and see the rot. She couldn't quite match his smile today. Hers would have looked too hostile.

"I think Millie is," Casey said, turning back to her work. Her hands trembled with the sudden flush of adrenaline. She could smell that woodsy cologne he wore, subtle and fragrant. Enticing to the unwary.

He walked very close, smiling, bending his head toward her. "I'd still rather have you help me," he purred, then dropped his voice so that no one else could hear. "You're so thorough about things, ya know?"

Startled, Casey looked up. It was there, that alien that looked out from his eyes, that flat dark entity that consumed emotion. Casey wanted to flinch away from it. She wanted to drop into a ball and cover her head with her hands to protect herself. Rage exploded in her, frustration that he could threaten her in darkness and court her in daylight. But the rage didn't come alone. The minute she let that loose, other, older emotions bubbled toward the surface. Other memories, as deeply imbedded as instinct. He was loosing them like old teeth, and she couldn't allow them free.

So, again, she fought for challenge, for advantage.

I know you, she chanted in the safety of her own silence. I know you and I'll prove it. You can't scare me again.

"I wouldn't want to disappoint Millie," she said with a slow smile of her own, knowing that she couldn't keep the venom from her face as easily as he.

Hunsacker seemed to grow a little. "I'll make it up to her," he promised. "Believe me."

Casey wondered how they could be just casually standing next to each other in a hospital hallway. She felt as if she were battling to stay upright, fighting a wind or storm that threatened to pluck her away. Too bad Jack couldn't tap into this, she thought dizzily. Too bad enmity wasn't admissible in court.

Her courage was costing her.

"I couldn't allow you to do any favors for her like that," Casey retorted, her smile stiffening with meaning, her chest tight. "I'm not sure she'd recover from it."

For a moment he stopped. His smile remained behind like an afterimage, frozen and unreal as the alien retreated to consider Casey's challenge. Casey held her breath, mesmerized, stricken, thrilled. She wanted to tell him about Wanda, about Mrs. Peebles. She wanted him to know she wasn't impotent before his taunting. She wanted to see the surprise on his face when he fell.

"Oh, Dale, there you are," Millie called from the other lane, and the alien slipped away.

Hunsacker lifted his head like a predator sniffing prey. He smiled, his eyes glittering twice as brightly. "Just talking to Casey. Do you have my lady?"

"She's in room six," Millie almost sang out. "Set up and ready to go."

"Would you mind if Casey helped me this time?" he asked in the same way a man would cut in on a dance.

"I get the next two," Millie demanded with a soft pout. Casey wondered if the girl realized she went right up on point every time she talked to Hunsacker. He ever asked her out, she'd do the whole damn dying swan.

"The next three," he promised, and turned back to Casey.

Casey was all set to tell him to go to hell. Then she spotted Tom hovering in the door of one of the rooms, ostensibly checking a chart. His ears might as well have been glued to the back of his head. Casey was getting her chance not to screw up. She wished Marva were close, so she could at least fortify herself with her friend's support. She needed someone to calm the flush of frustration.

"Do you need any Thayer Martin cultures?" she asked instead, focusing on the CPR chart that was peeling from the side of the medprep. As if anybody in a trauma center would need to run to the medprep in the middle of a cardiac arrest to make sure the ABCs of life support hadn't changed since their last code. But lifesaving charts looked good in ERs. It made the staff look sincere about their calling, as if the things were pledges that needed solemn reavowing from time to time. Casey knew the game.

She knew the game, and much as she resented it, she played it now.

Phoebe Griffin was a well-fed, well-pampered woman with a penchant for diamonds and Lucille Ball #4 hair color. Casey didn't like her the minute she walked into the room.

*"There* you are," she whined at Hunsacker, clutching the green paper sheet around her ample waist with both hands as if any minute somebody would come rip it off. "I *told* my Allen that I couldn't stand this any longer. I said I simply couldn't *wait* until office hours tomorrow, especially since you missed my last two appointments. Besides, who wants to wait *hours* in an office when this is so much closer and insurance pays for it?"

"You've been having cramping again?" Hunsacker asked, checking the chart in his hand as he pulled out his notebook.

"Doubled over," she whispered, her eyes large.

Casey squeezed some lubricant onto the opened pelvic pack, the obnoxious sputtering sound saying enough for her. She leaned around a little, trying to see what Hunsacker was jotting down in his book.

She could see the time, and Mrs. Griffin's name. There were a lot of times on the page, a lot of notations, but Casey couldn't make them out.

Hunsacker asked a couple more questions, scribbling, smiling and hand patting, and then slipped out of his jacket for the pelvic. Casey moved around to position Phoebe into the stirrups.

"Well, you know, Phoebe," he was saying as he snapped his gloves into place over the monogrammed cuff of his shirt. "You haven't been behaving. You have to expect to pay some consequences when you haven't behaved. Now, don't you?"

Casey couldn't imagine a supine woman in stirrups looking even more passive, but Phoebe managed it. She simpered and apologized, saying that she just had too many things to do to stay off her feet, especially when she was only a *little* pregnant.

Hunsacker settled onto the stool and flipped the sheet back to expose a lot of unexercised thigh and a black tangle of hair at target area. Phoebe was already squirming.

"I think Casey agrees with me," Hunsacker went on, rubbing the speculum in lubricant and turning back to work. "Don't you, Casey?"

Casey held very still and remained very quiet. Why couldn't anyone else hear this? Why did she hear the subtext in his voice so well and not be able to explain it to anybody else?

Phoebe jumped and yelped. Casey could have sworn Hunsacker smiled. "You have to expect consequences for your actions," he said, turning the speculum. Phoebe jumped again. Casey flinched. "Everybody goes around not paying attention to good advice, just—" Another move, deeper, slow and deliberate. Another yelp. Casey felt the sweat break out on her upper lip. "—abusing themselves or somebody else, and they think they can get away with it. Well, I don't think they can. And I hear Casey doesn't, either."

He bent closer, shoved the speculum in to its edge. Wedged it farther open. Rolled it a little. Casey almost pulled it from his hand. Phoebe was whimpering now, her hands fluttering above her belly in helpless agony.

"Nope," he murmured, stretching it out until Casey actually moved forward to intercede. "Nothing here to worry about."

With a quick, slick movement, he pulled the speculum out and dropped it on the tray. When he did, he looked up to see if Casey had been watching. What he found seemed to satisfy him.

"Is there, Casey?" he asked, and then smiled again,

the smile Casey knew he saved for those phone calls. All teeth and hunger.

Rigid with fury, Casey nonetheless smiled back. "That's what it seems," she allowed carefully.

She hated him, then. Actively, ferociously, blindly. He was Frank at his worst, abusing a woman and then blaming her for it. Smiling that triumphant smile when he got what he wanted. The only difference was that Frank hadn't known how to be subtle.

Casey waited until he'd washed his hands for the third time, pulled his jacket from the chair, and walked on back out of the room.

"Phoebe." She started gingerly, like the first time a toe goes down in a mine field, her voice soft, her eyes concerned. "Can I ask you something?"

Phoebe wiped at real tears of discomfort. "What?"

Casey took a deep breath, knowing how close she was treading to sedition. She could hear her nursing license flutter straight for the incinerator. "Is Dr. Hunsacker always like this to you?"

Phoebe sniffled a few more times, smearing mascara on her tissue and sneaking a look toward the door as if afraid of getting caught.

"He's just . . . angry with me," she murmured, the whine vacant when she was really upset. "I didn't follow his orders at all."

Casey fought down the bile. "And so you deserved to be hurt?"

Phoebe shook her head before she realized it. She stopped, her melting eyes fixing on Casey with confusion and distress. "This isn't the way he usually is. He helped me get pregnant. I didn't . . . I mean, I wasn't complete. He taught me how. You know?"

Complete. Casey had the feeling she was going to hear another Marilyn Peebles story, skirting the edges of the truth for dread of shame, uncertain and yet unwilling to change or accuse.

Casey set a hand on Phoebe's arm. "I just don't like to see women hurt," she admitted. "If you're distressed at all by your care, you have the right to a second opinion. Okay?"

Was that ambiguous enough? Had she saved herself and gotten a message through to Phoebe? Casey felt like a rank coward for not just coming out and saying, Hey, the guy just played Roto Rooter on you. *Do* something about it. But Casey did live in the real world, and as every other time she'd been sorely tempted to say something along those lines because of abuse, neglect, or incompetence, she didn't. Not quite. Even though this time it cost more.

Still Phoebe smiled. Maybe it helped just believing that somebody was on her side. "Thank you. But he's my doctor. I couldn't just up and leave him now, especially with everything else going on. He'd think I didn't trust him."

Casey wondered if Phoebe would ever believe that Hunsacker had really done the things he did, even after what he'd subjected her to. Probably not. It was one of the real frustrations about dealing with people. You just had to realize sometimes that nothing you did would change them.

Casey gave up with no more than a few platitudes and the announcement that Phoebe could get dressed, and walked on out to find Hunsacker waiting for her.

Business was picking up. There were two paramedics restocking from a trip in and a secretary calling parents on a minor. Millie and Abe were discussing something up by room four. And Hunsacker waited for Casey next to the desk by room six, the notebook back in his hand, a prescription pad atop it.

"Questions?" he asked with a perfectly placid face.

Casey fought the revulsion. "Not one," she retorted, walking by to drop the pelvic instruments in dirty hold. She knew she wasn't controlling her expression as well as she should. Hunsacker could probably read every murderous thought that crossed her mind on her way by. It just made him smile.

When she got back to pick up Phoebe's chart, he was waiting. "You need to remind Phoebe about behaving," he said, handing over the finished chart. He was watching her closely, his voice intimate and offensive. "It's your responsibility to make sure she understands that if she doesn't obey me the consequences are her fault."

It sounded so innocent, a doctor concerned about a patient's unwillingness to follow treatment. A man who cared only for his patient's welfare. Casey shuddered under the impact of his real message. She shook with the effort it took to stay in control.

She couldn't challenge him. She couldn't tell him to go to hell, that she wasn't going to be one of the victims in his game. He wasn't going to make her an accomplice.

"When do you want to see her?" she asked instead, chanting her litany of survival to herself, her eyes fixed on the flat black of his.

"Next week, unless she has more problems," he said.

Casey never saw Marva approach. She almost didn't hear the warning in time. Hunsacker's attention veered at the last moment. His gaze skipped over Casey's right shoulder and his eyes widened. Casey turned.

Marva's mouth was open. Her eyes were white-ringed and astonished. She'd just skirted past the two paramedics and turned toward the dirty hold. Unfortunately, her foot caught the edge of a chair that was out just a little too far from a desk.

"Oh, shit!" she cried, her whole body tipping forward like a felled tree.

She was carrying a bedpan full of urine.

Casey jumped out of the way just in time. Marva stumbled and cursed again. Hunsacker tried to duck left. Marva seemed to follow him. At the last minute she caught her balance, but the momentum was too great for the liquid to be contained. A great yellow wave of it splashed over the lip of the bedpan and cascaded down Hunsacker's pants leg.

Casey gaped. A funny gurgling noise struggled free of her throat. She could hear Tom shrieking behind her and Hunsacker shrieking in front of her. She couldn't take her eyes off his shoes, always so fashionable, now sodden and unpleasant.

"You fucking cunt," he breathed, so low only Casey heard him. His gaze lifted from victim to perpetrator, and for the briefest of moments Marva was treated to a visit from the alien.

"Oh, my God," Tom cried yet again as he ran over. "Marva, what did you *do?*"

Marva raised unperturbed eyes to her head nurse and shrugged, the bedpan once again quiet in her hands. "I tripped."

Casey gurgled again. It was getting harder to keep quiet.

"I'm really sorry, Dr. Hunsacker," Marva announced just as placidly, turning back to him. "You should probably get those shoes right off."

"Uh, yes," Casey managed with a jerky nod of the head. "Do you know what pee can do to leather?" Her voice rose on a suppressed giggle.

"Gomer pee." Marva nodded in agreement. "The worst. God only knows what's crawling around in that stuff."

Hunsacker looked as if he'd been hit with a pie. His five-hundred-dollar suit pants were limp and aromatic, and his feet squinched when he moved.

"Scrubs?" Tom begged, wringing his hands. "I'll have a tech get booties for you. We'll take care of dry cleaning."

"It was . . . an accident," Hunsacker said, looking back down.

He gave his leg an uncomfortable little shake and then balanced a hand on the desk. Marva stepped closer. Casey held her breath. There was a soft sucking sound when he pulled his foot free. As usual, he wasn't wearing socks. He held his foot suspended over the terrazzo floor as if he were a wading bird waiting for the tide. A small droplet of urine collected up by his arch and slid along to his second toe to hover, milky yellow and thick, from the pedicured nail.

Casey turned to Marva and lifted an eyebrow in consternation. Marva threw off a shrug of frustration and headed off with the bedpan.

What did they do now? Casey wondered, finally moving herself, leaving Tom to mop up Hunsacker's drenched ego. His second toe was exactly as long as his first toe. They hadn't proved anything. But they had certainly helped relocate Casey's sense of humor.


"When you said you were taking me to lunch, I kind of expected tables and a menu," Casey observed.

"There is a menu," Jack informed her with a wave of his hand. "Right there. Now, do you want a hot dog or a hamburger?"

On a bright day, the zoo was a cacophony of color. Red brick walks, vivid splashes of flowers, trees, glistening black seals, exotic birds, long fingers of blue water in the basins, the earth red of the man-made mountains.

Crowds of kids in playclothes and mylar balloons bobbing in a slow dance over small heads.

Today it was dark and close, the clouds flat with humidity, the trees dusty, and the animals somnolent. School was out, but there weren't a lot of kids. More denizens from the nearby Central West End on lunch break. Just like Casey and Jack.

Casey accepted her hot dog and preceded Jack over to one of the picnic tables.

"You just tired of institutional green?" she asked, waving away sweat bees. "Or is this some kind of message?"

Jack put his food down across from her and swung a leg over the bench. "The captain had me in again yesterday."

Casey had already taken her hot dog in hand. She stopped and looked up at him. "Another cozy little chat?" she asked, suddenly uncertain.

Jack concentrated on the mustard he was squeezing all over his hamburger. He had his hat on again. Casey kept wanting to push it to the back of his head, so he'd look like a Damon Runyan character. The way it sat now, she couldn't see his eyes. She couldn't know what kind of trouble he was in.

"I just decided," he said, spiraling ketchup on top of the mustard without looking up, "that discretion was the better part of valor. I'm on my lunch hour, and unless I spend it with a hooker, he doesn't have any say about what I do."

Casey nodded instinctively. "What about the time he does have control over?"

Jack finally looked up, his expression enigmatic. "I've been given a deadline to come up with something concrete on Crystal, or it goes to somebody else."

His words stole the air from Casey's chest. She couldn't tell what he was feeling, but his movements were precise and controlled, his jaw as tight as an old virgin. He turned back to his lunch deliberately, and she saw the effort it took for him to remain silent in the face of such an affront.

"That's not the normal procedure, is it?" she asked quietly, his frustration a hard ache in her chest.

"During election year," he assured her, "anything's normal."

"Why do you put up with it?" she demanded instinctively, angry for him.

Jack looked a little surprised. "How long have you been a nurse?" he asked.

"Twelve years," she said, her hot dog still waiting in her hand.

"And this is the first time your boss has ever made life difficult for you."

Casey snorted. He'd read her file. He knew just how well she got along with the brass.

He smiled, a small, contained expression that bonded them as fellow strugglers. "I've had enough jobs to know that hierarchy is pretty much interchangeable. Management survives on politics and relies on employees who'll get the job done. I get the job done."

She leaned closer. "Why?"

He shrugged, and it was as controlled and self-contained as the smile. "Because it's what I do best."

Casey had wanted revelation, explanation. She'd wanted him to give her the reason to work past the current crisis. He'd given her the obvious.

"What *do* you believe in?" she asked.

This time the smile was conciliatory. All the same Casey could have sworn she saw darkness at the edges. "Redemption," was all he said. Then he picked up his hamburger and began eating.

"I did get the phone tap," he announced a minute later when he set his lunch down half-eaten.

Casey looked up from checking her potato-chip bag for orphans. "When?"

"I'll drive back home with you to check it. We'll have a tape and a tracer on the call tonight."

"If he makes it."

Jack looked up, worried. "Did he last night?"

Casey offered her own controlled smile. "He didn't have to. He tortured me face-to-face."

That obviously wasn't the answer he wanted. "I told you to stay away from him."

Casey saw something new pass over Jack's eyes, something she'd never noticed before. A sharp, fleeting fear. It surprised her. Even more, it unsettled her, deep where she couldn't explain it. What was he not telling her?

"Virtually impossible to do when he asks specifically for you and your supervisor is eavesdropping to ensure your cooperation."

"Did he say anything?"

"Hunsacker? Oh, yeah. He took the "Inquisitional Pelvic" to new heights, all the while instructing his patient on how if one misbehaves one must pay the price. It was . . . charming."

She didn't seem to be encouraging Jack in the least. "I mean it, Casey," he insisted, leaning toward her. "Stay as far out of his way as you can."

Casey didn't exactly look away. She kept facing the concern in Jack's eyes, knowing perfectly well that he was right. Knowing that she should walk off the halls right now and never force herself to be in the same room with Hunsacker again. But there was more to it than that. She didn't want to back away. She didn't want to forfeit those confrontations, because for the first time she was holding her ground. She wasn't the victim, and it was important for Hunsacker to know.

And there was something else, something that was harder to face.

Jack must have sensed her rebellion. "I'm not kidding about this," he warned sharply. "Winning isn't going to be any good if you have to be dead to do it."

"You really think he'd do that?"

Jack almost sighed. "We checked on Mrs. Peebles. She never made a move to report Hunsacker for abuse. No calls, no letters, nothing the family heard that might have suggested it. So, either he did her to prevent problems, or just because she walked out on him. What do you think he's going to do to you when he finds out we're closing in on him?"

Casey knew what he wanted her to say. Still, she couldn't. She took a deep breath and set her hot dog down, her gaze turned to where beads of sweat crawled down the side of her red-and-white cup. "I don't think you understand," she managed, knowing she had to dredge up the worst for him to at least understand. Hesitantly setting into his hands something that no one else but Poppi knew. "A big part of his game is humiliation. He doesn't want to kill me. He wants to see me crawl. He wants . . ." A fire lit in her chest, the same fire that had finally given her the courage to escape for good. "He wants the satisfaction of knowing that I'm totally helpless against him." She looked up, hating the new tears that threatened. Afraid, uncertain, her balance suddenly lost.

Jack kept his silence, his eyes shadowed by the hat. But Casey saw the set of his features and rushed on. "That other person I told you about?" she said, her voice beginning to falter. "He's married now, living in California. I never pressed charges. I never warned the woman he ended up marrying after I moved out. I just begged him to leave. I . . ." She'd sworn she'd never live through this again, that she was past it. But the shame swelled like a noxious cloud in her, suffocating and rancid. "I got down on my hands and knees, just like he asked, and I begged. Over and over again, promising anything I could think of, agreeing to . . . anything. But it didn't satisfy him. It just seemed to egg him on. He fed on it . . . like, like blood. He needed it."

It was too much. Casey bolted upright and walked off, hands jammed in pockets, breath struggling past the acid. A peacock strutted past her, its tail spread, its mournful cry echoing over the water. Two little kids escaped their mother's clutches to chase it. Casey watched just as long as it took the tears to recede. Then she straightened her shoulders and prepared for confrontation.

She knew Jack would wait where he was, as careful about interloping as Marva. Even so, his eyes gave him away. Deep beneath the shadow of that hat, dark and hot and knowing.

Casey stiffened her resolve. "I asked for it once. I won't do it again."

Jack looked surprised. "You think you *asked* for that?"

But Casey couldn't go any further. Beyond this point lay dragons. When she thought about Frank she thought about reasons and weaknesses, and the shame overwhelmed her. The idea that she'd somehow invited his abuse, perpetuated it with her docility. She'd made it this far away from him by simply turning away. Looking back would be too horrible.

She stood rigidly before Jack, closed off and defensive, afraid now of even the suspicious softness in his eyes, because it meant he might demand inclusion. He might see more than she wanted. "What else have you found out about Hunsacker?" she asked instead.

For just the briefest of moments, Jack looked as if he

were going to protest. Casey challenged him eye to eye, silent and certain, even through the desperation. Terrified of his concern, aching for the cool wash of his pragmatism.

Finally Jack crumpled up the rest of his lunch. "Let's go see the seals," he said and climbed to his feet.

The seals didn't care much one way or the other. Stretched out on the lagoon rocks, they waved at the heavy air and groaned in sealish turpitude. Casey carried her soda along, sipping through the straw just as she had when she'd walked the zoo paths as a kid, when Helen had still remembered to bring them. Jack had his hands jammed in his pockets, his gait clipped and precise, his gaze scanning the visitors rather than the inhabitants.

His attention skimmed the crowd like sonar did an ocean bed, seeing everything, noting anomalies, filing away and collating. A man always on the job. A job that could easily consume.

Casey regretted sharing her burden with him, a man who looked as though he carried enough burdens already. She wished the words had never escaped, that she could push them back into the past where they belonged and let them rot in peace. But he wouldn't have understood otherwise.

She sought levity. "I bet if you were on a cruise ship, you'd look for hijackers."

He looked over at her without much expression. "Maybe."

She sighed, wondering what Jack was like off duty. Wondering if he ever really was. "What do you do on vacation?" she asked, slurping again at her ice cubes.

His quick smile betrayed his frustration. "Read murder mysteries. How 'bout you?"

Casey allowed a grin. "I chase ambulances. What about when you're at home?"

"I never go home."

"That," she admitted, "I think I believe."

She turned her attention to the park, listening to the chatter of people, the rustle of the animals, the distant thread of traffic. At any other time it would have served to decrease her stress level. Today, it made it worse. It made Casey think again of maggots, of the darkness that writhed beneath all this normality.

"So," she finally said. "The news."

Jack had obviously been waiting for her. "I interviewed your ex. He didn't have much to say, except for invoking doctor-patient confidentiality. Nice office."

Casey couldn't look over at Jack. She didn't want to hear about Ed from him. She didn't want to imagine what Jack had thought, sitting in that sterile office, watching Ed rearrange himself into perfect creases.

Jack must have felt her discomfort, because he went on, his gaze still scanning the crowds. "I also got the chance to meet the East St. Louis team. It's a good crew."

Casey looked over in surprise. They'd reached the fence around the lagoon area. To her left a mother was lifting a toddler up past the chain link to see the seals ignore them. Beyond, a couple was celebrating spring in each other's arms.

"Any luck?" she asked Jack.

He pulled his hands out of his pockets to settle them atop the fence. "I managed to raise their suspicions. They don't have any evidence or witnesses. They would desperately like to tie in those two other murders that night, since they were unusual for them, too. Problem is, of course, money. The cops over there don't have any."

"What do you think?"

He shrugged, his attention down at the water that reflected dimly in the flat light. "It's a jigsaw puzzle. We have your friend Evelyn Peters dead from a twenty-two at a stoplight with no witnesses. We also have two local murders, cousins who might or might not have been circling one of the local gangs. They got it with an AK47 and were dumped down by the river."

AK47. Why did that ring bells? Casey tried to remember, to pull up all the bits and pieces of information she'd culled and decide what an AK47 meant.

"The thing about the cousins is that there wasn't any physical evidence," he went on, gaze still out to the seals. "Which sounds like Hunsacker. Except it was with a different gun. The cousins' car was found a week later in a parking lot by the downtown bus terminal where they think the perp took off for parts unknown."

"St. Louis?"

"Yeah. Also, no turn-up on jewelry from Mrs. Peters. The regular channels have dried up. I talked to Franklin about Wanda, and talked to O'Fallon about Mrs. Peebles. Franklin says for you to stay off his turf, and O'Fallon wasn't impressed except to say that Mrs. Peebles's wedding ring was missing. Your friend Martin called to let me know he's trying his hand at the Brentwood police, but the consensus there is that maybe you should be fitted for a beanie."

"What about the gun she bought? Did she say why?"

"Protection. She was going to be living alone. Salesman said she came in with her husband."

Casey sighed, frustrated. Instinctively knowing there was more. "And Hunsacker's alibi for Mrs. Peebles?"

"Another chart. He sure likes to sit in hospitals at night. The daughter-in-law did say that her mother-in-law had gotten some call about a problem at the country house, but didn't know what or who."

"Which leaves us where?"

"Without enough to get a search warrant on him. And

with lukewarm interest from East St. Louis and Jefferson County."

It was a nice day. Casey was standing at the zoo watching the seals and didn't have to go to work tonight. She should have felt better. She felt dragged down and frustrated. "We're not going to get him, are we?"

Jack looked out to the trees and the solid towers of Barnes Hospital that rose beyond. "He'll get sloppy. They all do."

For a minute he seemed content to consider that fact. Casey waited, squinting into the distance along the paths where parents pushed strollers and dates held hands. She saw a single pair of feet strolling beyond the overhanging tree branches and thought it unique. Old people strolled alone, not Yuppies.

"I did get some interesting news," Jack said, turning a little her way. "Want to hear Hunsacker's life story?"

Casey sharpened a little. "I wouldn't even mind hearing how he managed to stay in the Pan Caribbean School of Medicine."

Jack smiled. "Money. Truckloads of it. His family is old Boston Brahmin from Beacon Hill. His father was a hotshot surgeon. His mother was deb of the year, fundraiser of the year, hunt master of the year. You get the idea."

Casey scowled. "I'll be sure to invite them to my next birthday party."

"Can't," Hunsacker said nonchalantly. "They both died in a fire."

Casey almost stopped breathing. "A fire?"

Jack's smile wasn't pretty. Casey thought it was the most satisfying thing she'd ever seen. "Young Dale managed to get out in time. Older brother and sister were away at boarding school. Tragedy of the year."

"What was the verdict?"

Jack shrugged. "Spontaneous combustion from painting supplies. They'd just redecorated the downstairs."

"Anything else?"

"Just that Dale had trouble staying in schools. Even the ones where marks are directly related to donations. Understandable, of course. Dale had had a trauma, and did some acting out. Nobody's talking about just what play he was doing, though."

Casey felt a new thread of hope tempt her. "Any word on family pets?"

"Nothing anybody's talking about. I'm waiting to hear from the family doctor now."

Casey almost laughed, she was so relieved. What a terrible reason to feel better. "So, it wasn't his wife he offed. It was his mother."

She'd just turned back to consider her little pastoral scene. That pair of shoes was still there, walking along the fence. A pair of Dock-Sides, worn without socks. That was what had caught Casey's attention. She looked up, through the leaves, searching for an owner.

"Casey?"

She hadn't realized she'd stiffened up. She was bending now, leaning one way and then the other to get a better look.

She saw him. Smiling. He turned very briefly toward her and nodded his head. And then he walked away.

"Oh, my God," she breathed. "It's Hunsacker."

# Chapter 17

*FIRST JACK LOOKED.* "Are you sure?"

They could both see him, walking away from them, his face in profile. It was just like the mall. One minute Casey was sure, the next she couldn't decide. Those same all-American features, that same jaunty walk. But something . . . something was different.

"I know it's him," she said all the same. "What are we going to do?"

Jack craned his neck for a better view as Hunsacker turned back toward the zoo-line train station. "Not much we can do. He has a right to be here . . . are you *sure?*"

Casey kept looking, mesmerized, revolted. "This happened once before," she admitted. "At Crestwood Plaza. I saw somebody I could have sworn was him, but he looked different. Just a little . . . like, plainer, more normal. I couldn't decide. But I think I was right. I think he was following me that day."

Jack turned back on her, and there wasn't any indecision left on his features. "He's stepping up the pressure," he said. "I've got to get some protection on you."

Casey shook her head, knowing just as well as Jack how difficult that would be for him to do. "I'll be okay."

"Wait a minute," Jack said, turning back, walking a little ways toward where Hunsacker was disappearing over the gentle rise. "You say you weren't sure before. That he looked different."

Casey stared after him, wondering what had just clicked for Jack. "That's what I said."

Jack whipped around on her, his eyes alight. For the first time Casey saw the hunter in him. He threw his arm out in Hunsacker's direction. "You'd swear that was Hunsacker."

Casey took another look. "You want to go find out for sure?"

Much to her astonishment, Jack nodded. "Come on," he urged, grabbing her hand.

"What the hell's wrong with you?" she demanded, tap dancing around a pile of lost snowcone ice in an effort to catch up.

"The hooker couldn't say for sure," he was saying, almost to himself as he ran, his coat flapping past his hips. "She said he looked different when she saw him in lineup. Bundy had the ability to do the same thing. Witnesses couldn't pick him out, because he changed somehow. Maybe Hunsacker does it."

"Like wolfman?" Casey demanded dryly, still hanging on for dear life.

"It's an attitude," he told her without looking away from the now-empty rise. "Look at Bundy's pictures. Each one's different. *He* was different, depending on what he was after. Who says Hunsacker can't do that?"

Casey sidestepped a stroller and hopped a curb. "Honey, I wouldn't put anything past Hunsacker."

Even disappearing into thin air. When they topped the rise, Hunsacker was gone. Jack searched the crowds that swept onto the train, and chased the stragglers who trudged for the parking lot. He disappeared into the men's room and quizzed vendors. Nobody remembered the man Jack described, for good or bad. Hunsacker had simply become invisible.

Casey stood by the train station, battling the urge to look over her shoulder. Sure somehow that Hunsacker was watching her and laughing, and not sure how. The train hooted. A puff of steam shot up from the stack and the train squealed and chugged out of the station. A little black boy with a striped shirt waved to Casey. She waved back.

"He's gone," Jack admitted, coming to a halt beside her. He pulled his hat off and ran a hand through his hair before resetting it. "Well, it doesn't matter. It finally makes sense. I'll get that hooker back in and we'll start all over again."

"And you'll be tossed right out in the snow with your stingy brim."

Jack's smile was full of anticipation. "Can't have redemption without risk," he told her and turned her around to leave.

Jack didn't make it to Casey's house that afternoon. His beeper went off right in the zoo parking lot, and when he called in, was told it was another command performance. Suddenly he wished he hadn't eaten even half that breakfast treat the zoo called a hamburger.

It wasn't just the captain waiting for him. It was the captain, the chief of detectives, and the union lawyer. They huddled in the captain's office like three hemorrhoid patients waiting for the knife. Jack saw the chief take a long drag from a cigarette and wished with all his heart he could have one, too.

"Yeah, Captain?" he asked, knocking on the door frame.

All three men looked up. The captain was old Irish,

florid features and snowy white hair. The chief was younger, neater, with a hawk's face and sparse black hair. The lawyer straightened, slick and sharp, a local version of Jack Kemp. Good old boys all, born to serve, sniffing around power like dogs in heat. The last bastion of white St. Louis democratic politics before the blacks really made inroads. It was one of the things that made Jack so popular. He'd backed the black candidate for mayor, a hotshot new voice out of nowhere who liked to buck the system.

"Come in, Jack." The captain waved him in. Over by the radiator, the chief contemplated what was left of his cigarette and finished it off. The lawyer stepped forward, hand outstretched.

"Crawford Wilson, Sergeant," he introduced himself, even though Jack needed no introduction. Wilson had been called out on his behalf before, a matter of insubordination and suspension. "Good to see you again."

"Crawford." Jack acknowledged him with a quick nod and a shake of his dry, firm hand.

"Let me give it to you straight, Jack," the captain said, rubbing a finger at the side of his bulbous nose. It always made Jack think of Santa Claus. "We were served today with a harassment suit. The city, the department, you."

Jack was tempted to sit down. He didn't. He just pulled off his hat and ironed the duck's ass with his palm. "Dr. Hunsacker?" he asked.

The captain nodded. "Forty million."

Jack couldn't quite contain the quick bark of laughter at the news. "Well, I'll say one thing for him. The son of a bitch has balls."

All three men came to attention. Obviously Jack wasn't taking this seriously enough.

"He claims his practice has been falling off," the captain informed him, his posture more unyielding. "That the notoriety is causing emotional distress. He says you got a hard-on for him, Jack, that nothing but total ruin's gonna cure.''

"That's about right.''

The captain huffed. He was a great handshaker, the captain. He knew more about the political and business figures of this city than the *Post Dispatch*. He knew nothing about his men.

"I'm going to have to take you off the case.''

Jack shook his head. "I'm not going.''

That brought his captain right to his feet. "You'll do what you're told. Or would you rather be pulling nights up on North Market?''

Jack slipped his hat back on his head and slid his hands into his pants pockets to prevent himself from hitting anybody. He rarely got this angry. Usually he just sublimated it all into that growing hole in the lining of his stomach. Today, though, he'd seen Hunsacker change like a chameleon. He'd answered a question that had kept him awake at night. He'd seen a way to reel Hunsacker in before Hunsacker stopped playing games with Cascy and got down to business. But it wasn't going to happen if the captain handed off the Crystal Johnson case.

Jack wasn't going anywhere with the smell of the chase finally in his nose.

"Let me give it to you in a nutshell," Jack said, looking down at the Marine seal on the captain's desk and thinking about how this was what always got him into trouble. He was more than happy doing the work, if the brass just left him alone. They never did. Not in the service, not in the church, not in the department.

When he looked back up, the three men were watching him as if he were a Buddhist monk shaking a gasoline can over his head. "Hunsacker's harassing the nurse who reported him. He's calling her, he's following her. I saw him today. I suspect he's involved in five murders to date, including Crystal Johnson's. Problem is, every murder takes place in a different jurisdiction, so communication is spotty. I've asked for the Major Case Squad and been turned down. Now, if Hunsacker kills this nurse because she's the only one standing up to him, we're gonna have a lot more to answer to than a harassment suit."

"You're only responsible for Crystal Johnson," the captain reminded him, florid complexion now closer to puce. "And so far you haven't come up with squat."

Jack took a breath. It was always the same, caught between what you knew was right and what everyone else thought was expedient. Well, he'd survived before. He sure as hell wasn't going to cave in now. Not if Casey wasn't. "Look at my record, Cap."

No arguing there. It was the one thing that had saved Jack's ass. He might not close cases the quickest or the most conveniently, but his conviction rate was indisputably the highest.

"I can't afford to leave you on this," the captain said. "Do you know what that would look like in the press?"

Jack almost smiled. "It would look like the police can't be intimidated by money."

Crawford Wilson battled a laugh, because, of course, money and power spoke the same language in any city, and the police department here spoke it fluently. The captain just stood there, hands splayed on his desk, eyes glinting fire, certainly envisioning a bigger target area on Jack's ass.

"Can I go now?" Jack asked. "I need to interview my witness in Crystal Johnson's murder again, and get old medical records on the doc. And then I'm talking to the FBI."

"What did I tell you?" the captain bellowed, rigid with fury.

"Jack . . ." Wilson appeased, hand out.

From his corner, the chief finally came to life. "What was your time limit?" he demanded, stepping forward, hands shoved in his own pockets. Nonchalant as a hunting tiger.

Jack turned to him. "A week. I can have an ID that Hunsacker frequented Crystal Johnson today. That means he knew all five women, and had problems with every one. His alibis are mostly his own notes on hospital charts. If I can break one, I can get him. We got personal items missing from victims, like he's taking souvenirs, and not a goddamn shred of physical evidence from any of the crimes. Nothing, like somebody's been vacuuming. This guy is an obsessive-compulsive who washes his hands all the time, schedules sex, and carries a diary around on him like a rosary. A diary that gives me night sweats just thinking about it. Now, what else do I have to do to get somebody to call out the Major Case Squad and coordinate this? Crystal's the weakest link, and that's all I can legitimately investigate right now."

The chief faced off with him, watery blue eyes as sharp as a hawk's, his expression hard. The chief was a crafty politician, but he'd been a real cop before hitting the big leagues. He'd been captain at fifth precinct when Jack had started, up where the wars of North Market were fought.

"Something solid," he growled, sending the captain into another color change. "One bad alibi, one solid ID. One overheard threat. Now get the fuck outta here."

Jack didn't stick around to hear the rest. He heard it as he was striding down the hall toward his office.

"One week!" the captain yelled after him.

Jack left it to the lawyer. He had witnesses to see.

\*     \*     \*

Casey's phone rang the minute she got home. She figured it was Jack reporting on his meeting. She was in for a different unpleasant surprise altogether.

"Girl, you got problems." It was Marva.

Casey had been wiping at the kitchen counter when she answered the phone. The sound of Marva's voice slowed her hand to a stop.

"What problems, Marva?"

"You've been taken off the schedule."

Suddenly Casey couldn't breathe. "What?"

"I saw it when I came in. I had to ask about next week. Your slot's whited out for the next pay period. What did you do?"

"I didn't do anything," Casey objected, white with fury. "What the hell's going on?"

"Get you a lawyer, girl. This looks bad."

"Did you hear anything else?"

There was a momentary pause. "Did you say something stupid to one of Hunsacker's patients? Somethin' like she should act like a rat and desert?"

"No!" Casey caught her breath. Oh, God, of course. She hadn't been circumspect enough after all. Phoebe had walked right back to Hunsacker. "I'll be right over. Make sure Tom doesn't go anywhere. That bastard's gonna have to face me with this."

"I *warned* you!" Tom cried, clutching the baseball like a pacifier. "I told you what would happen!"

"So you take me off the schedule without consulting me?" Casey demanded, leaning over him, red-faced and outraged. "You fucking suspend me without letting me know *why?*"

Tom shot to his feet. "You gave us no choice," he retorted. "Mr. Nixon and the hospital lawyer felt there was nothing else we could do, especially after Dr. Hunsacker initiated an action against your license."

"Because I told his patient she had the option of second opinion."

"Casey, you told her to leave him! He told us exactly what his patient reported to him. You *know* you can't do that. He has every right to censure you. Even worse, you insulted him in front of his patient. During her exam!"

"And just what," she grated, "did I say?"

"That he didn't know how to do a pelvic. That he should be punished for it."

Casey couldn't hold back an indignant laugh. God, and she thought she'd done so well. She hadn't belted him once. "His patient attested to this?"

"An investigation will be made," Tom hedged. "I'm sure you'll be notified if Dr. Hunsacker decides to go through with his demand for your license."

"He's murdering women, and *I* lose *my* license," Casey marveled with a bitter shake of the head. "Now, that's one for the books."

"Casey!" Tom objected. "Don't make it worse."

"Tell me how it can get worse," she snapped before reeling herself in. He was right. She was making it worse. She needed this job. God, she needed *any* job, and suddenly there was a real possibility that she wasn't going to have one. The time suddenly stretched ahead of her, blank and terrifying, the bills piling up, Hunsacker slipping right out of the net so that no one would ever know she was right. And there was nobody out there who could help her with this one, not even Jack.

Casey turned back to Tom and came very close to begging. The realization pushed bile up her throat.

"I'm sorry," she allowed, taking a deep breath, clenching her hands to keep them still. "What can I do?"

She couldn't even mention the hospital's cowardice in

making her come to them. She didn't even mention getting a lawyer of her own, because like most nurses, she was working without a contract. The hospital could fire her for bad breath if they wanted. They wouldn't, of course. They'd make her quit so they didn't have to pay severance. The suspension was just the first sign.

Tom shook his head, his attention back on the ball. "Leave Dr. Hunsacker alone," he pleaded. "You're officially suspended for two weeks without pay. The situation will be reevaluated at that time."

On her way home, Casey drove by the new billboard announcing the newly expanded obstetrical facilities at Mother Mary Hospital. The Hospital with Heart.

Poppi tapped on the back door right around dinnertime. Clad in matching pink sweatsuit and headband, she looked like a Jane Fonda advocate. The truth of the matter was that the only exercise Poppi got was climbing the stairs to her room each night. She wore sweats to commune with the great cosmic forces.

Bent over a pot of chili, Casey didn't bother to wave Poppi in. It was another sacred tradition in the McDonough house. Poppi could smell chili a mile and a half away, and showed up within ten minutes of serving time.

"Looks like it's going to rain," Poppi observed, cushioning the swing of the screen door with her backside so it wouldn't slam.

"It's looked like that for five days," Casey snapped. "I wish it'd just do it and get it over with."

"Gee, you're in a lovely mood. And there isn't any beer left in the fridge." The last sounded more hurt than accusatory as she closed that door, too. Tradition was a delicate thing, and beer was part of the rite of chili.

"Where's Jason?" Casey asked, shaking in just a little

more cayenne pepper. She was sweating already. She might as well make a day of it.

Poppi approached warily. "At class, like every Wednesday night. What's the matter? Too much Latin around the old McDonough homestead tonight?"

Casey refused to look up. "Helen is delivering food to a neighbor who had surgery. It's her Christian duty, you know."

Poppi waved off the acrimony. "You can't spoil my mood, Case. I just got back from a lovely trip."

"Smoked, licked, or injected?"

Poppi's eyes grew very round. "Oh, you are in a snit tonight. And without beer."

Casey reached over and lifted her glass from the counter. Ice cubes clicked amid amber liquid. "We're playing in the big leagues tonight."

Poppi took a minute to digest that one. Leaning back against the counter, she considered Casey with patient eyes. "Want to tell Aunt Poppi about it?"

"Things are getting just a little tense," Casey snapped, slamming the spoon back into the chili.

"Got the hots for the nice policeman?"

"Don't be crass. I told you. I don't date."

"And he's not even a doctor."

"Which is why I let him in my house at all." Casey wasn't sure whether the tears were because of the alcohol or in spite of it. She just knew they were coagulating in her throat, and she hated it. She'd actually thought she was going to feel better that afternoon, and now it was gone. It was worse.

"So, if it isn't a broken heart, what is it?"

"Well, let's see," she mused, taking another sip of what tasted to her like cough medicine. "We'll do it in no particular order. Jack called. He's being sued and a week away from the street, and he lost his best witness this afternoon. I can't get any sleep because I keep getting these lovely phone calls all night, Helen is having visions of Mick who wants me to quit. Today she said that Mick thinks Hunsacker is stealing my soul. And . . . oh, yes, I was suspended today from work. My license is now in jeopardy."

"And?"

Casey swung on her friend. "That's not enough?"

Poppi tilted her head a little. "I don't think so."

Casey deserted the chili for her drink and a little walking space. She should never have hooked up with Poppi. Her friend saw too damn much. "I had to tell Jack. I had to . . . prove the kind of man Hunsacker was, and I couldn't think of another way to do it." That brought the tears closer. Casey forced them back with another long drink. The cold fire bit sweetly. It tasted so much better than the humiliation that had resurfaced.

Casey couldn't tell Poppi what had happened. She couldn't tell it all, because she couldn't explain it, she couldn't define the sick sinking in her stomach at the memory of it.

It had been Jack. It had even been Tom. And then, worse, it had been her own mind sabotaging her sanity.

When she'd arrived home from the hospital, she'd taken her frustration up to her room, beaten, exhausted, dispirited. The only thing left for it, she decided, was to just sleep through it. Especially since she wasn't going to get any sleep that night, either.

Helen had been in the chapel, talking to Jesus about Mick, droning on and on about what a good man he'd been, good breadwinner, good father, good Knight of Columbus. Casey had fallen asleep with the familiar monotone intruding, and carried it into her dream.

The apartment. White on black. Or black on white, she couldn't remember, but the afghan was there, a slash of red that terrified, and her mother's voice just beyond the door. Rising, falling, rising, pleading, like she always did. And Casey frozen, frightened, the tears running down her face, the afghan warm against her little fingers, the only warmth in the dream, in the big, cold room.

This time, though, she cried out. "No, don't!" "Don't! Just let me out!" But instead of being let out, she had to fight. The shadows came, crawling from under the couch, just like her bed, huge shadows that smelled sickly sweet and frightened her, and she fought them, gouging, kicking, screaming. Sobbing.

She'd awakened with a start to find Helen's hand on her arm and her own face wet, her hands clenched around her blanket.

"Jack didn't understand?"

Casey started, submerged back in the shadow world. "He was a perfect goddamn gentleman," she retorted, turning for the sink. The hanging impatiens needed water. She watered them. Then she looked for something else to do.

"It must have taken some guts to share that with a stranger."

"He's not a stranger. He's just . . ."

"A man."

Casey swung back on her friend to find her still leaning against the white counter. Poppi waited passively, years of shared understanding softening her features. For a minute Casey hated her, too. Hated anybody who could face this so easily because she hadn't been through it.

"That's why I hate Hunsacker so much," she insisted. "Because he's so much like Frank, and he's getting away with it, too."

Poppi smiled. "You hate Hunsacker because he reminds you of Frank at all. You haven't had to do that in years."

"I didn't need to." Another litany, another rite of salvation. She was strong now. She didn't need to look back into that abyss and pull truth from it. What truths could you pull from miasma? There was nothing there but poison, and she wanted no more of it. Once this was over, she'd just pack the dream away like the other souvenirs of her life and shove it up to collect dust in the back of her closet.

"Do you know what's the worst part of this?" Casey demanded, walking back to face her friend. "Hunsacker might get away. I let Frank get away with it. I exchanged my freedom for silence and probably sentenced some other poor slob to the same kind of hell. But this time I scraped up the guts to go after this guy, and it probably won't do me any good." She shrugged. "I should give him Frank's number out in LA. He'll probably move out there when this is finished and start over, too."

Poppi shook her head. "I don't believe it," she argued. "Not with your sergeant friend. I don't think he's going to let go of this until he's good and finished. Eventually he'll come up with something."

Casey shook her head. "And in the meantime we have to wait for Hunsacker to ash some other stupid woman. He's going to, ya know."

"How many has he so far?"

"It started with Wanda, and we're up to five."

Poppi nodded for a few moments, her eyes distant and contemplative. Casey figured her for a goner and returned to her chili. "All I know," she said, picking the spoon back out of the thick sauce and beginning to stir with one hand and sip with the other, "is that I'm living for the moment that maggot-ridden, lice-infested bastard is nailed. Fried. Socketed and switched." She sipped again, tamping down the flames a little, because she could hear the clamor of desperate conviction in her own voice. "I will then be a happy woman," she concluded.

Poppi never took her eyes from the stratosphere. "Your problem is your constraint within linear logic," she announced.

Casey looked around, not certain exactly what had brought that on, or what linear logic had to do with fifty thousand volts and a set of metal bracelets. Poppi smiled benignly and turned her vision on Casey.

"How do you know he's only killed five women?" she asked.

Casey reeled her own emotions back in and refocused. "I've been watching," she said. "I've read the papers, and those are the only ones I could come up with."

Poppi's smile grew, placid and ethereal. Dealing with Poppi was like living one giant flashback. "How do you know Wanda was the first?"

Just then the screen door slammed open and Helen scuttled in, a picnic basket over her arm like Dorothy on the way to Oz. "Oh, Poppi dear," she greeted the blond with a bright, albeit slightly out of focus, smile. "Are we having chili again?"

The smell of onions and beans actually outweighed the incense tonight. Casey kept to the kitchen once Poppi left, too unsettled to return to her room and too impatient to deal with Helen. The alcohol hadn't helped. She knew it wouldn't. Still, she had nothing else to take the edge off the panic that dream had provoked. And Poppi, rather than salving Casey's sore subconscious, seemed bent on irritating it.

The house was so quiet Casey could hear the clustered popping of suds around her forearms as she washed the dishes. She could count cadence by the clock on the living-room mantel and locate her mother within two inches by how the house creaked around her. Even Pussy was quiet tonight, floating on little cat's feet and skirting contact for privacy. Casey wished she could be as quiet as Pussy, as invisible when she wanted. It would certainly ease up on some of the humiliation. Well, she thought, there was a good side to her suspension. At least she didn't have to work with Hunsacker for a while.

Casey slid her wrists in under the hot water and let it run until they were splotchy and red. Hot water, now there was a good sedative. She bent her head and closed her eyes, listening to the rush of water, the tinkling of the bubbles, the brush of wind against the trees outside.

She didn't want to think. She didn't want to be afraid, or outraged, or humiliated anymore. She just wanted to get by. She wanted to talk to Jack about baseball or movies instead of murder. She wanted to do her job and come home and feel safe in her room again.

She wanted the ghosts to go away.

But Jack was still coming by tonight. He'd pull out *his* notebook and go over things just one more time, asking questions Casey had answered five times already in the hopes she'd remember something else, setting up probabilities and shooting them down. Watching her with those somnolent eyes of his when she was so vulnerable and raw, when she didn't want anyone to be able to see inside her, especially him.

*Why?*

Damn the alcohol. Damn her for being so weak she'd felt she'd needed it. It only broke down barriers.

Why had she let Frank do it? Why hadn't she even had the courage to stand up on her feet and walk away? She'd crawled. She'd begged. She'd pleaded. Just like she'd wanted so badly to do again this afternoon.

Casey's stomach lurched. The chili she'd only tasted set small brushfires behind her sternum. Because she was the only one who knew. She was the only one who could never ignore the truth, the truth she'd never told another living soul.

When she'd begged, she'd begged him not to go.

She'd begged for more.

The doorbell rang, but Casey didn't hear it. She was bent over the kitchen sink biting back the sudden, hot nausea. Sweat broke out on her face. She pressed a hot hand against her mouth, willing the sickness away. Forcing the memory back.

She was different now. That couldn't affect her anymore.

But dear God, how she wanted Hunsacker to pay for what he was doing to her. She wanted to see him hurt, to see him begging for once, his hands fluttering, helpless to stem the agony someone else inflicted.

She squeezed her eyes shut and breathed deeply and entertained one of the most violent fantasies she'd ever allowed, even about Frank. Even at its worst. She saw herself hitting Hunsacker, stabbing Hunsacker. Shooting Hunsacker, his body jerking like a puppet before the spray from a vicious weapon. An AK47, his favorite gun, the gun gangs were so fond of. And it made her feel better.

Suddenly Casey stiffened. Her eyes opened, but she didn't see the heavy branches that swayed before the kitchen window. She saw Hunsacker in the work lane talking to Steve. She heard his voice, and the answer came to her. The memory she'd been trying to pry loose. The reason the mention of an AK47 had so bothered her before.

"Oh, my God," she breathed to her astonished reflection in the window, an entire jigsaw puzzle falling into place to form an unbelievable picture. "I know how he did it."

The doorbell rang again, two quick jabs, as if the caller were loosing patience or courage. Casey spun around, not wanting Jack to turn away. Her hands still dripped. Wiping them against the sides of her shorts, she trotted into the living room and hit the foyer light. She could see a silhouette through the door, tall, thin, just a little stooped. He probably had more beer, she thought with a sudden grin. *We can toast my brilliant mind and then talk about anything besides murder.*

But she was disappointed when she opened the door. It wasn't Jack who waited out on her porch, but her next-door neighbor. A retired college professor, Mr. Rawlings provided the McDonough ladies with fresh-cut flowers from his garden and a bright companionship for chess or morning coffee. He never intruded, but knew exactly what was going on in the neighborhood from the vantage point of his flower beds. Offering a tentative smile, he held out a small, paper-wrapped parcel.

"I'm sorry to bother you, Casey," he drawled, bobbing his gaunt, age-spotted head in simultaneous greeting and apology. "But this came this afternoon while you and your mother were out. I've been at a garden meeting, and just got home."

"Oh," Casey responded, sure he'd catch her disappointment. She'd so wanted to scoop Jack with her news. "Thank you, Mr. Rawlings. I appreciate your getting it for us."

She accepted the package, surprised at its lightness. It was about the size of a shoebox, wrapped in inside-out shopping bag and tied with a string. It was addressed with large, scrawling handwriting and bore the return address of a post office box in the city. She wondered who it could have been from. She didn't know anybody in the city except, maybe, Jack. On the other hand, it was probably some statue or another Helen had ordered from

Catholic Supply House. They'd long since learned to mail things—especially bills—directly to Casey.

"I've been admiring your visitors' cars," he admitted with a shy smile. "I am an auto buff, you know."

"That is quite a nice old Mustang, isn't it?" she answered absently, knowing he was dying to find out if she was dating again. "I'm thinking of buying it."

His face brightened and fell all at once. "I see. Well, I'm glad for the company for your mother. Tell her I said hello. Good night."

Casey did offer him a smile as she closed the door, already preoccupied by the contents of her package. It was one way she'd never grown up. She still loved to get mail. Any mail, but especially something that smacked as a gift.

She didn't lock the door. After all, Jack was due soon. Already pulling at the string, Casey carried her gift into the kitchen where she could get a knife to minimize the work.

It was a shoebox. The Reebok logo appeared through the last layer of wrapping paper. Casey sat down on the kitchen chair and lifted off the lid.

The box was filled with tissue paper, a funny, variegated kind in white and red and pink. Casey grabbed a handful, and then realized it was wet. She pulled her hand away. Her fingers came away smudged. Red, dark red. Familiar.

She stopped a moment, her hand suspended over the box, her stomach suddenly cold and her neck hot. It wouldn't do any good to wait. She had to know. Gingerly she reached in and pulled the sodden tissue away.

She didn't hear her own whimpering. She didn't realize she'd thrown the box back on the table. Suddenly it was just sitting there in front of her, the paper spilling out over the side like the petals of an exotic flower, and she was on her feet.

Running. She whirled around, the sobs collecting in her throat, the bile spilling up from her stomach. Wretching and sobbing, she just made it to the bathroom under the stairs before she collapsed.

# Chapter 18

*TONIGHT JACK DROVE* with the top down and Bird on the deck. The batter of wind and the wail of a sax was wonderful counterpoint to the chaos back at the station.

The press had caught wind of the lawsuit right after Jack had, and had spent the rest of the day camped out in the foyer. Jack could have dealt with that if he just hadn't lost his prime witness about the same time. He'd sent one of his team out after her, just to find she'd skipped to Chicago to avoid facing her pimp's displeasure. The APB was out, and the truth was Ruthie had never been known to survive outside St. Louis for long, but Jack wasn't sure they were going to get lucky in a week.

The chat with the FBI had done nothing more than confirm his suspicions. He was forwarding them all the data he had to get a full psychological profile, but the agent he'd talked to over at the Behavioral Science Unit in Quantico echoed Jack's suspicions that if Hunsacker's bloodlust didn't get out of hand, he was going to be the very bastard to catch.

Hunsacker plotted out as an organized offender with

higher than normal intelligence, probably a sexual psychopath. Agent Yablonsky even admitted a certain professional admiration for Hunsacker's talent, knowing that if it hadn't been for the quirk of one suspicious woman, not one of the police units involved would have found a link between murders.

The VI-CAP computer didn't come up with any unsolved serial murders from Boston, but like Yablonsky said, if Hunsacker was running to form, he could have offed a whole dormitory and nobody would have figured it out yet. Hunsacker was beginning to escalate his schedule, another classic symptom of the human shark, but unless the good doctor got sloppy in the next week or someone came out of the blue to finger him, there was going to be a real lag time in solving this that spelled real trouble for Casey.

Even Jack's snitches came up empty. They knew Crystal had a high-class clientele, but nobody could produce as much as a rumor with Hunsacker's name on it.

Jack pulled up behind Casey's compact and killed the engine. The night in this insulated little neighborhood was lush with quiet. Trees whispered and lawn sprinklers whirred. A dog barked down the block. For a minute Jack was tempted to turn Bird back on and just sit here, enjoying the warmth. It was something he couldn't afford at his flat. He got gunning pickups and country western at two AM, sirens, the squall of kids, the smell of the brewery. He couldn't imagine living anyplace but the city, but if he did, it might be here. Here where a policeman couldn't afford to live anyway.

The car keys clinked in his pants' pocket as he opened the car door and stepped out. He was carrying a folder of work, since he'd already decided he was going to stay tonight until that call came in. Whether Casey liked it or not, she'd faced this bastard by herself for the last time.

His feet clattered on the wooden steps. There were lights on in the living room and the foyer. Jack rang the bell and waited, scanning the neighborhood. There was a car with steamed windows around the corner. Young love in the suburbs. In the other direction, the dog continued to bark, and a door opened and slammed. The dog stopped. Routine.

Jack wasn't getting an answer at the door. He rang again and peered through the beveled art glass in the door. The foyer was empty, the kitchen lights on. He listened for sounds of approaching footsteps. There weren't any. In the distance a train wailed and faded. The trees sighed again.

And then Jack heard it. A funny, choking sound. He did another quick scan of the still-silent street. Then he checked the door.

It opened in his hand.

"Casey? Mrs. McDonough?"

No answer, but he could hear that funny sound more clearly. He didn't even bother to close the door. Throwing the folder on a hall table, Jack ran for the half-open door at the base of the staircase.

"Casey?"

She was crumpled over the toilet, her face ashen and wet, her hair limp, her body shaking uncontrollably.

"I'm . . . I'm a . . . nurse," she sobbed and wretched again, a wrenching, empty sound that brought Jack out of his jacket.

"What happened?" he asked, grabbing one of those little guest towels and soaking it in the sink. She was scaring him, Casey who was so pragmatic, so solid and straightforward. She looked like a wreck victim.

She couldn't get her breath past the sobs. Pushing her hair away from her face with a trembling hand, she tried to sit back. She almost fell against the wall.

"I thought . . . I . . . that it was from . . . from you," she finally managed, curling her knees against her chest.

Jack crouched next to her, catching her damp hair in his hand, lifting it off her hot neck. He wiped at her forehead with the cloth. She couldn't seem to get her eyes open.

"What did you think was from me?" he asked, wanting to look around, afraid to leave her. She looked as if she were shaking apart. He wiped again, and then slipped an arm around her shoulders. She didn't even seem to realize that she turned to him. She curled into him like a little girl, a whimper escaping her. Jack instinctively pulled her close, his own hands beginning to shake as he wrapped his arms around her. He hurt hard for her.

"Shhh," he whispered, lifting a hand to brush back her hair again, holding tight. "Hey, Casey, it's okay. Take your time."

She clutched at him, her fingers sharp and desperate. "That . . . that . . ."

Jack stroked again, hating this feeling of impotence. Unsure what to do. Terrified of a woman's tears. "Don't . . . don't talk about it if you don't want to," he tried, and felt her stiffen even more.

"And let . . . let *Helen* walk in?" Her head shot up then, almost knocking Jack's teeth together. Her eyes were suddenly blazing through all those tears, an autumn sky after the rain. Straightening, she let only one more little sob escape. "That . . . that son of a bitch!"

Jack couldn't help but grin. "Now, there's the Casey McDonough I know and love. What did Hunsacker do?"

She shuddered again, her skin still hot and pasty. "The kitchen," she managed, briefly losing her bravado to look down at the tile beneath her knees. "I'll, uh, wait here."

"You sure?" he asked. "You're okay now?"

She grimaced. "I'll be okay when I see Hunsacker rot one limb at a time."

Jack grinned again and got to his feet. The front of his shirt was damp and his knees ached. Been a long time since he'd been on 'em. He'd done if for worse things.

He smelled it from the kitchen door and picked up the phone. After dialing 911, he slipped a pen from his pocket and prodded at the tissue.

Jesus. No wonder she'd been in the bathroom puking up her guts. Hunsacker had just taken the art of harassment to new heights.

"What is your emergency, please?"

"This is Sgt. Jack Scanlon, St. Louis City Homicide. I need the police right now at 432 Newbury Place in Webster. And I want a county homicide detective here pronto."

"Do you have a homicide to report, Sergeant?"

Jack's smile wasn't nearly as nice as it had been for Casey. "Tell them they'll see when they show up. Now, get going."

He didn't think the dispatcher would appreciate the allusion to bullfighting. The trophies of victory, ears and a tail. Only humans didn't have tails. But they did have fingers.

Casey supposed she should get up soon. She couldn't believe Helen hadn't been down to investigate the noise yet. Maybe she just figured that Jack had meant all along to bring three squad cars, an evidence unit, and an ambulance to check the phone. The living room sounded like a basketball game was in progress, and Casey could see the crowd of police ringing the kitchen table. She could just imagine what her neighbors were saying.

"No shit," one of the uniforms was whispering. "A Mrs. Potato Head. All it needs is lips and a pipe."

"Shut up, you asshole," his partner commanded with a punch. "Besides, don't you know nothin'? The potato heads don't smoke anymore."

Casey grinned to herself where she was folded up in the corner of the bathroom floor, arms around knees, head cradled on forearms. Just two nights earlier they'd taunted one of the psych patients in the ER who insisted ghosts were following him down the aisles of Schnucks by getting on the PA system and wailing "Heathcliff! He-e-e-eathcliff!" Sometimes you had to be a little nuts yourself.

"Here."

Casey lifted her head to find Jack in the doorway, a glass of Scotch in his hand.

"Do you really drink this stuff?" he demanded.

"Thanks." She smiled wanly, accepting the outheld glass. "No, not usually. But I'm out of beer, and I can't stand the smell of bourbon. It's the poison of choice for West County, and nothing smells worse coming back up after a good slosh around in the ole stomach juices."

Jack shook his head with a smile. "The connoisseurs in the city prefer a good Mad Dog," he said. "Or beer."

Casey's hand was still shaking. The ice clattered in her glass. "I haven't puked over body parts since I was in training," she mused with a little shake of her head.

Jack stepped in and closed the door behind him. "That's a little different," he said. "Don't you think?"

Casey looked up at him. He'd held her and wiped her face and shielded her from the police when they'd barreled into the house. Casey knew it was time to reemerge now, but Jack was here to tell her it could be done at her own time.

"You've been a good sport, Jack," she admitted with a smile that somehow threatened to resurrect tears again. She'd sworn she would never feel this vulnerable around a man again as long as she lived. She'd never let him close enough. Jack seemed to have snuck in and changed the rules. "Thanks."

Jack shook his head, a curt, impatient action. "It shouldn't have gone this far," he argued. "I should have had him in by now."

Casey suddenly wanted to giggle. "Well, that's a 'you're welcome' if I've ever heard one. Should we go talk to the coppers?"

He watched her, his usual reserve suspiciously absent. "Are you sure?" he asked, and she knew he didn't have anything more in mind than what opening that surprise package had done to her.

Casey took a good slug of the Scotch and climbed to her feet. "I never let the bastards get me down, Scanlon. Especially not that one."

She was surprised when Jack laughed. "Good girl." He nodded with approval as he took her by the arms to steady her way up. And then, just before he turned to open the door, he kissed her.

Not much of a kiss. Kind of a matter of punctuation. But quite a surprise nonetheless. And not just for Casey. For just a second before he let go of her to turn them both back out into the fray, Jack looked as if he'd stumbled over a live wire. Eyes sharp, forehead folded into amazement, mouth just a little tight.

Then he shook himself out of it. "You got *cojones,* girl," was all he said. But he smiled, and Casey blushed like a schoolgirl over the rare compliment.

"Bert!" she cried a minute later when she stepped into her kitchen. "Hey, buddy Bert!"

The tall black ex-halfback turned from where he was talking to the evidence crew to flash Casey a bright smile. "Gettin' in trouble again, are you, girl?"

"Yeah, well, when I sent away for those party favors, I didn't expect 'em to be preowned. Where's Ernie?"

"His kid's graduation or some fool thing."

Heading past the knot of men in her kitchen, Casey ignored the pointed looks she was getting. She opened the refrigerator door and pulled out a couple cans of coffee.

"I have a feeling we're all going to be here for a while," she announced. "You guys want leaded or unleaded?"

"Don't be stupid." Bet grinned. Cops and nurses never drank decaf coffee. As old Clyde from the Rose would have said, that was for pussies.

"Hey, Bert," she announced, motioning with the coffeepot to the Irish tweed cap on his head. "You guys wear hats, too."

"Sure we do," he retorted. "Do you know what kind of a mess you can walk into when you answer a jumper call?"

Which was, of course, when Helen decided to show up. Casey heard the rustle behind her, the sudden hush of male voices, and the shuffle of evidence techs as they jumped in front of the box.

"No, no, no, Casey," Helen chirped, walking into the kitchen with a coy wave of her hand. "You mingle with your party guests. I'll serve refreshments."

"No such post office box in the city," Jack announced, hanging up the phone.

"No bodies in any of the local morgues with missing parts," Bert answered from where he sat amid paperwork and the pizza they'd called out for. "One of the guys called the ME from his car. Nothing else unusual witnessed by the neighbors."

The ambulance had disappeared first, then the evidence crew. One Webster car and one county car had stayed to help canvas the neighborhood for information, and one of the Webster detectives had made an appearance to officially hand off the investigation to Bert.

Because of the unique relationship of county to the cities within its boundaries, both the county police and the local police had jurisdiction. The Webster guy had taken one look at the contents of Casey's gift and smiled his gracious concession to the greater manpower and computer capabilities of the county force.

Mr. Rawlings had been escorted in for the first interview. The schoolteacher sat with Helen now on the couch, shaking worse than Casey, unnerved that he should be an accomplice in such a crime. And that after only getting the most euphemistic details. Helen, on the other hand, was chattering away about how lovely it was to have guests again.

Casey finished off her second piece of pizza, trying to drown out both alcohol and coffee. She'd washed her hands eight times, gargled away half a bottle of mouthwash, and changed her clothes, and she still felt like conducting all business from the kitchen sink.

Jack kept watching her, surreptitiously, as if any show of concern would send her screaming into the night. She thought it was sweet. Even so, she would have vastly preferred the kind of evening she'd been spending before the doorbell had rung.

"So," Bert said, munching on a pepperoni slice. "We got a package with no prints, wrapped in a Schnucks bag from one of forty stores, holding three fresh lab specimens from a Caucasian, probably female, cushioned in standard wrapping tissue in a Reebok box you can get only a hundred fifty places delivered by a Fed Ex deliveryman to an old guy who can't see very well, and no word yet from the delivery company where the package was mailed from. Why do I think some ten-year-old's gonna tell us how a guy gave him ten bucks to mail the package?''

Jack rubbed at his eyes with the heels of his hands. "You're catchin' on. I've been trailing this mope for about six weeks now, and I can't even get him to admit he shits in the morning."

Bert offered a policeman's smile. He'd been filled in on the whole story while the evidence techs were playing with the box. "Well, you can count on my help. I just love this kinda shit."

"I'm glad you do," Jack retorted dryly. "'Cause I'm gettin' real tired of it. It's like tryin' to put a jigsaw puzzle together with your eyes closed."

Puzzle. Casey thought about that a minute, letting her brain chug back into gear. She knew there was something she needed to tell Jack, but she couldn't pull it past her mental image of gold earrings spattered with blood, and the idea that her mother might have opened that box. Of course, as out to lunch as Helen was some days, she might have figured it was from a mail-order holy relic house.

"Casey," Jack offered. "Why don't you try and catch some sleep? We'll be here if the call comes in, and you have work tomorrow."

That fast, all her little messages tumbled clear of the fog. She got up and refilled all three mugs.

"I'm not missing that call for the world," she vowed, sitting back down. "I'm not letting him think he can scare me off. Besides, I don't have to go to work tomorrow. Or the day after that. Or, for that matter, the week after that."

Jack stopped with his mug halfway to his mouth. "Why?" he asked.

She smiled brightly. "Because I've been suspended for

slander against a doctor. It *is* slander, isn't it? I can't keep slander and libel straight. I don't *think* I wrote anything down, unless it was in nurse's notes. But I don't think I would have written 'asshole doctor to see victim.' Even if I'd wanted to."

Surprisingly enough, Jack nodded. "Good."

Casey raised an injured eyebrow. "Good? Thanks for the vote of confidence, Scanlon. Seems to me you're about a week away from singing the same tune yourself, buddy."

Jack actually allowed a grudging grin. "I mean I feel a lot better knowing you won't have to face Hunsacker for a while."

"Oh, yeah," she retorted dryly, motioning to all the activity. "It's certainly made a difference so far."

"We'll get him this time, honey," Bert promised.

Casey just laid a hand on his arm. "Don't make promises you might not be able to keep, Bert. This guy has more lives than Rob Lowe." She took a sip of coffee, strong and black and bitter, before continuing. "I did come up with some things this afternoon that might be helpful. It's too bad you weren't around, Jack. It's been quite a day."

Jack offered a tight scowl and pulled his notebook over. "I'd love to hear about it."

She began picking at Bert's pepperoni slice. "Did I tell you that Hunsacker is a gun buff?"

Jack stiffened. Casey guessed she hadn't.

"I'm sorry. There were so many other things, that must have slipped through. He's especially fascinated by gang weapons and the like. I hadn't thought about it all until you told me about those guys who were killed the same night as Evelyn. You said they couldn't connect them all because they were shot with different guns. The cousins had been shot by an AK47. The gang gun."

She got a brace of nods and answered. "At first I thought Evelyn had been killed by an AK47 because I'd heard it from her coworkers. The thing is, they had heard it from Hunsacker. And Hunsacker can sure tell a twenty-two from an AK47, wouldn't you think?"

She could see Jack's gears already working hard. "Let me," she begged, proud of her deduction, knowing he'd hit it just as fast as she. "There weren't any witnesses to Evelyn's murder, because those two men *were* the witnesses. Maybe Hunsacker hid in the back seat of Evelyn's car, or forced her in at gunpoint. He made her drive to East St. Louis, where he knew nobody'd be surprised, and shot her over there. These guys drive up, and he pulls out a second gun, shoots them, and drives them back to the river to dump them. And then he takes their car over the bridge and dumps it at the bus station where he could get a cab home. Voilà, how a white man makes himself invisible in a black community."

Jack's smile was damn near beatific. "That's it," he agreed. "That's it."

Bert shook his head. "The hell with nursing, girl. Come be a cop."

Casey grinned with her little triumph. "Don't tempt me, big boy."

Jack bent to scribble the information down, grinning and shaking his head. "God, this just makes my day. Wait till the East Side guys hear it. We might even get an ID from a cabby."

"Want to hear what else I have?"

That brought Jack's head right back up. "You have more?"

Casey nodded. "Actually, this one's from Poppi."

"The space cadet with the Tammy and the Bachelor hairdo?"

Casey scowled right back. "Don't count Poppi out," she warned. "She has some interesting insights."

Jack snorted. "I'll bet."

"What if," she asked, "there are other murders I missed?"

Jack looked as if he wanted to groan.

"No, I mean it," Casey insisted, leaning over toward him. "Maybe there's something stronger. Maybe we can catch him up with something else."

"And who gets to do this paperwork?" he demanded. "You want a list of unsolved female murders for the last six months from about a ten-county area."

She nodded. "Let me go through it," she said. "After all, I got no place to go. I also know his type of girl. At least we should look."

"She's right," Bert suggested. "The Johnson woman might not be the only woman he's popped in your jurisdiction. Maybe you can make a stronger case."

Jack snorted again. *"Night Court* has stronger cases. I'm just trying to stay ahead of the paperwork."

"Hey," Casey objected. "It's forward momentum, isn't it? It's something. Hunsacker's gotten the last two rounds. Let's get the next one, okay?"

Jack leveled that half-awake stare on her, just a hint of a grin curling his lips. "Whatever you say, Knute."

She grinned back. "Screw you, Copper."

"Casey?"

Casey turned to find Mr. Rawlings at the kitchen door. He'd stopped shaking, but he looked older suddenly, wan and tired. She hopped to her feet.

"Oh, Mr. Rawlings, why don't you go on home? Do you need to talk to him again, Bert?"

"The officer interviewed you, Mr. Rawlings?" Bert asked in his best community-relations voice.

Mr. Rawlings nodded his head. "I . . . I'd stay with

your mother, Casey," he apologized. "But this has quite taken something out of me."

"Of course," she said, a hand on his thin arm. He had asthma and a heart condition. Casey could hear him wheezing and felt guilty for forgetting him. "Thanks so much for sitting with Mom. I know she appreciates it."

Mr. Rawlings patted Casey's other arm in commiseration. "If you need anything . . ."

Casey nodded. "Thank you. Oh, by the way, did you meet Sergeant Scanlon? He's the one who owns the Mustang. Mr. Rawlings has been coveting your car, Jack."

Mr. Rawlings bobbed his head in anxious agreement. "It's a real beauty, Sergeant."

"Thank you," Jack acknowledged with a smile. "It's a good car—289 cubic inch with a dual line Holley four barrel."

Mr. Rawlings looked like Helen when she heard about heaven. Casey couldn't suppress a grin. She just couldn't imagine him squealing into corners, the wind in his three hairs and Skid Row blasting from the stereo.

"Why don't you give it a run, next time I'm over," Jack offered, and Mr. Rawlings looked like he'd met God.

"Oh, thank you. That would be . . . lovely." The old man smiled and bobbed a couple more times. "Good night, then."

"Good night," Bert murmured a second later as the front door could be heard clicking home. "What a lovely idea. Tell you what, I'm gonna leave the phone tag to you guys, and concentrate on getting that list for Casey. Hopefully by tomorrow we'll have a face to go with those ears, and some more information on the sender."

Casey looked down at the table, guilty that she hadn't thought of it sooner. "Look for missing nurses," she suggested. "It's his favorite target to date."

At least it wasn't Marva. The victim had been white. Had been. As awful as the implications of that statement were, Casey didn't even want to think of the alternatives.

Bless Bert's heart. Shoving his cap back on his head, he reached over and gave Casey a fatherly pat. "Hang in there, little girl," he said. "We'll get him."

"Yeah," she said, lifting her eyes in search of support. "We will."

Both men smiled for her. The only problem was, Casey was far too familiar with that look. They wanted Hunsacker as badly as she, but they were too realistic to think that was enough to get them a conviction. It was kind of like telling the parents of a brain-dead child that at least his heart was beating.

Jack stood and held out a hand. "Good to have some help," he said.

Accepting the handshake, Bert laughed and shook his head. "Man, I believe it. Whatever happens, the collar's yours."

Jack smiled. "Nuns taught me to share, DeClue. We can arm wrestle for him later. Call me first thing in the morning."

They headed into the living room to see Bert out. Casey had forgotten that Helen was still out there. She was dusting the piano.

"Oh," she sang when she caught sight of them, "I thought you boys had all gone. I'm sorry."

"Sergeant DeClue's just leaving, Mom," Casey said, pushing Bert none too gently for the door before Helen intercepted them.

Bert nodded and smiled. "Good night, Mrs. McDonough."

Casey closed the door on Bert just as Helen came to life.

"Excuse me, Father." She smiled brightly at Jack, holding her duster to her chest like a crucifix. "Did I introduce you to my family?"

Casey saw the sun rise. She hadn't meant to. She'd meant to stay up just long enough to throw Hunsacker's latest game back at him by not saying a word when he called. Let him think he hadn't affected her with his present. Let him think her suspension didn't mean anything. She'd fully intended on evening out the score by making *him* sweat out her reaction a little. Maybe think the box hadn't shown up at all, or that she was too tough to let it bother her, to let him bother her.

But Hunsacker had figured out just how to torture her even more. He didn't call.

Casey paced downstairs until almost four, making Jack coffee and sandwiches and offering to make up a bed in the guest room if he didn't make it home. She came within a hairbreadth of dusting Helen's family on the wall. That was when Jack walked up and took her two hands in his and gently demanded she go on to bed. He'd wait up for the call. He had work to do. After the day she'd had, she needed some sleep.

Realizing that she was making him crazier than she was making herself, she acquiesced. And spent the rest of the night watching the sky change outside her window.

By seven she gave up and went downstairs. Helen wasn't up yet. Too much company the night before, Casey guessed. The kitchen was empty, Jack's paperwork scattered over the table like notes from an all-night cram session. He'd made a chart, with all the names and information listed on each murder. He'd left four more slots open. It depressed Casey unspeakably.

She found Jack curled up on the couch in the sun room. He'd obviously finally given up himself. His jacket was still out in the kitchen, his tie strewn over the back of the couch, and his shoes in a pile.

The romance books Casey read always seemed to describe a sleeping man as looking like a little boy. Jack didn't look like a boy. He looked like a man. His hair was ruffled and his chin shadowy and his clothes disheveled. He'd tried to get comfortable on a couch that was about four inches too short, and ended up with his feet hanging over the end. There was a hole in his left sock.

Casey looked at his face, which should have been passive and unlined in sleep, and saw just what toll his work had taken on him. He looked gaunt and tired, the creases between his brows permanent, the hollows in his cheeks too deep. A controlled man who saw everything and admitted nothing. Casey watched him sleep for a moment and wished there were something she could do to lift some of that weight. She thought of that funny little kiss he'd given her the night before, and was surprised again how much she wished there were something he'd let her offer in return. And then, not knowing what else to do, she went to make coffee.

"This isn't good," Yablonsky said later that day when Jack got him on the phone. "This guy's starting to take real trophies. And he's giving them to the nurse. He obviously considers her an important part of his image. What do you have on evidence?"

Refreshed only by a shower down in the locker room, Jack rubbed at his eyes and tried to focus on the chart he'd laid out the night before. He'd woken to the smell of fresh coffee only two hours earlier and been surprised to find Casey buttering English muffins when he'd stumbled out into the kitchen, shoes and tie in hand. It was the first time he'd eaten breakfast in two years.

"Oh, Hunsacker was real good," Jack told the agent,

the surprising comfort of a meal in that bright kitchen firing new determination. "Got a street person downtown to walk the package into the Fed Ex office. We probably won't even get a start on finding that guy until the shelters open tonight, and if Hunsacker's true to form, he picked a soup sandwich right out of State San. No evidence from the box except that forensics is happy to say that it was a very professional job. Still no ID on the victim."

"Mmmm. His cycle is shortening. His practice is in trouble, which tells me he's devoting more and more energy to his hunting. And he's graduated to knives. That's real personal stuff with these guys. I'd say he's escalating big time."

"What about the nurse?" Jack asked, taking a slug of coffee to drown the fire of anxiety in his belly. "She seems to think she's safe because he's performing for her." He couldn't get past the picture of her in her robe and bare feet, her hair tousled and her cooking atrocious.

"You mean like the guys who send notes to radio stations. It's possible."

"What are the chances he's gonna change his mind?"

Jack didn't like the silence that met his question at all. "I don't know," Yablonsky finally admitted. "He's sure playing by some of the rules, but he's making his own, too. He's one of the first serials to kill women he knows. I'm not sure I'd put anything past him."

"Great." Just how many nights did he think Casey was going to let him camp out in her back room on the premise that he was waiting for a phone call? "What do I do?"

Yablonsky laughed. "Get him. We can get a complete profile for you by tomorrow, if it'll help. I'd still find out more about his family. That's usually where these guys get their impetus. Do anything you can to get hold of that notebook of his. Get a righteous search warrant for his house. It's all there, somewhere. He's keeping track."

If all Jack needed was confirmation, he'd have felt better. What Yablonsky was telling him was scaring the hell out of him, and that had all come home to him when Casey had greeted him that morning, coffee cup in hand, butter smudged on her cheek, her eyes wide and guileless. By the time he hung up ten minutes later, he found himself rooting around for the Maalox without even bothering to look for witnesses.

"I guess this isn't so bad for six months," Casey said the next afternoon as she picked through the computer printout of murder statistics Bert had brought her.

She was feeling better only because she was doing something again. Hunsacker hadn't called again the night before, and Casey hadn't been able to get Jack to go home again. Worse, she'd caught herself sneaking downstairs close to dawn to cover him up back on the sun-room couch and showering before fixing him breakfast.

Helen had taken up the dangerous new tack that Casey could get her job back with enough plenary indulgences. The news media had just loved the story of the mystery gift, especially since its rightful owner hadn't been discovered yet, and had taken to camping outside Casey's house waiting for her to appear.

Across from her Jack was filling in the latest round of information into his chart. Bert sat alongside, reading the notes Jack had taken from his talk with the FBI. Half-empty plates of ham-salad sandwiches and potato salad weighted down corners, and steins of iced tea supplanted the usual coffee.

"Never mind," Helen said with that small, helpless whine of hers on her way through, as if in conversation with Casey. "I know you're busy. I'll just walk to church."

"I'll be there in a minute, Mom." Casey had already begun thumbing down the list. Maria T. Speers, 79, retired, rape and strangulation, St. Louis, March 12. Bettina Mae Brown, 51, housewife, gunshot wounds to face, Berkley, May 21. Elise P. Soughay, 17, student, assault with a blunt instrument, Washington, February 5.

She looked up to see new shadows and creases on Jack's face. "This is delightful," she said with a scowl. "No wonder cops get so weird. Do you ever see anything nice?"

Jack offered a weary grin. "Now you're asking if I believe in miracles."

"No miracles here," Helen piped up in a mournful voice as she pulled on her white gloves. "We aren't worthy. Benny won't come, and Mick won't stay."

Jack raised an eyebrow. "Mick?" he asked. "Who's that, another brother?"

Casey got to her feet. "A father. The kind who lives on in memory."

"Benny, too?"

Casey paused, uncertain, wishing Jack didn't want this. "I'll tell you about Benny if you tell me about miracles."

When she waded back through the minicams fifteen minutes later, neither Jack nor Bert had moved.

"Yes," Jack said, rubbing a little at his epigastrum. "There are good things that happen. There have to be or nobody'd hang around at all. Now, how about Benny?"

Casey ran her finger down another notch. Latoya B. Farmer, 9, student, rape and suffocation, East St. Louis, January 22.

"Benny is older than I am," she said evenly, thinking absently that of all the pictures of family they had in the house, they had none of Benny. "He tried to be a priest, too. Then he tried to be invisible. That worked a lot better. We haven't seen him in nine years."

"Not everybody knows what to do with the guilt," was all Jack said.

Casey looked up. He smiled, but the purple shadows under his eyes gave it a dark cast, and Casey had the feeling he wasn't joking.

"What would a Jesuit have to feel guilty for?" she demanded. "I see a lot of merit in keeping the church a little off balance. I can't even say I disagree with liberation theology."

"You can't liberate anybody with your hands tied," he countered. "Not by gun and not by crucifix."

"Then by badge?"

He shrugged. "It quiets the most ghosts. Any positive step is better than none at all."

Casey almost forgot Bert was sitting next to her. She was transfixed by the brief flash of vulnerability in Jack's eyes, the real darkness that lay behind all that reason. Now, oddly enough, she thought of a little boy. She thought what Jack must have been like before the ghosts had found him. She wanted to know where those ghosts lived, and how they spoke to him.

Jack deliberately turned back to his work, so she did the same, trying her best to regain a safe distance.

Mary W. Evans, 54, nursing supervisor, hit and run, Sunset Hills, March 3.

Casey was already four names beyond when it struck her. She looked back at the name again.

Evans. Mary W. W for Wilhelmina.

"Jesus Christ," she whispered, stunned. Shaking. She didn't see both men come to attention.

"Recognize somebody?"

It took her a minute to look up from the stark statistics.

Billie. Poor Billie, who couldn't get along with anybody, who had no friends at the end to claim her. Billie, who was not just hit by a car but ripped apart by it. Billie, who had been visited in the end by Dr. Hunsacker because he'd heard she was dead.

Casey grew cold and silent. Angry. Impotent all over again. She'd been wrong. Wanda hadn't been the first. And Casey hadn't even seen it. He'd been right there, making sure, rewarding himself. And she hadn't even guessed. She felt sick to her stomach all over again.

"Casey?"

She looked up then, first at Jack and then at Bert. "Poppi was right," she said, still not quite believing it. "Wanda wasn't the first. Billie was. Billie Evans, the recovery-room supervisor from M and M who was killed on March third. Hunsacker ran over her with his car."

# Chapter 19

*BERT WAS ALREADY* flipping through his notebook. "Tell me about it," he commanded. Jack filled in Billie's name in one of his blank slots. Casey did her best to look back to that night, the first night she'd met Hunsacker. The night she'd battled St. Paul and mourned a woman she hadn't liked.

She remembered Paul. He was hard to forget. She remembered the code, and the condition Billie had been in. She remembered Hunsacker showing up, and she remembered the pelvic, the first one she'd seen him do. But the shift had been a real bitch. It was hard to pull it all together.

She told Bert what she could, trying to keep to facts and not feelings, knowing that neither man wanted to hear how she'd empathized so much with that battered, empty body because Casey had seen so much of herself there. Knowing that they didn't need to hear that it bothered her that she'd put Billie so quickly behind her.

Bert and Jack both scribbled as Casey talked. When she finished, Bert checked back over his own notes from Billie's case. "A black Porsche," he announced, pointing to one specific scribble. "One of the kids who works the nearby theater noticed it speeding away just about the time Billie might have gone down."

"Plates?" Jack asked. "Hunsacker's are personalized. BBDOC."

Bert shook his head. "Kid remembered K and 2, that's all. But they were standard Missouri plates. I remember, we checked all the foreign car places, but nobody reported fixing front end damage on a black Porsche with plates like that. We found shards of glass from the lights at the scene. I'll check again."

Jack noted it. "We'll need to find out if Hunsacker has more than one set of plates."

"He could have stolen 'em, too," Bert noted, getting up for the phone.

"Want me to find out if he was arguing with Billie, too?" Casey asked.

"Did he not get along with her?" Jack asked.

"*Nobody* got along with her," Bert offered from where he was punching numbers. "More than one of her coworkers said they were surprised it had taken this long to happen. One guy offered to put up bail for whoever did it."

Casey couldn't help remembering what Hunsacker had said about Wanda. "No, I didn't get along with her, but who did?" What better reason to kill a person?

But what set Casey apart? She hadn't called him the names Wanda had, but she'd challenged him. Why hadn't he just targeted her along the side of the road like Billie, or lured her to the East Side? Why was she the audience and not the act? Whatever else they found out, Casey wanted that answer first.

"Ernie," Bert said into the mouthpiece, "go get the Evans file. We need to recanvass the hospital, get a possible license from DMV, and recheck all the repair places.

And then, if we're very good little boys, we get to call in a suspect for questioning.''

It took Bert a good ten minutes to fill in his partner. He'd just hung up when the phone rang again. Bert answered it out of instinct. "Some guy lookin' for you, Casey," he announced, handing over the receiver.

Jack went right on alert, jumping up and sprinting for the living-room phone. Casey's heart stumbled. It couldn't be. He wouldn't be calling during the day.

"Hello?"

"Casey, you're home. Good."

Casey sighed in exasperation. "It's okay, Jack," she said into the phone. "It's only my supervisor."

There was a muffled click and then Jack could be heard walking her way.

"What is it, Tom?" she asked, leaning against the wall.

"Well, uh, I have some good news for you."

What? she wondered. A tar-and-feather party? Public flogging? It had only been three days since her suspension. She didn't think she could hold out for Employee of the Month.

"What is that, Tom?" she asked, reeling in her less-than-diplomatic tongue.

"Can you come right in?" he asked. "I'd rather tell you here."

"No, Tom," she answered. "I'm afraid I can't. I have the police here right now. I'm not sure if you heard, but somebody delivered some rather unpleasant gifts to my house the other night."

Well, maybe she hadn't reeled her tongue in quite all the way. Casey could tell by Tom's uncomfortable silence that she wasn't breaking any news to him. Casey wondered desperately what he thought of it. She wanted to ask if he was missing any personnel.

"All right, then," he offered. "How 'bout this? How would you like to come back to work tomorrow?"

Casey instinctively looked over at Jack, as if he could have heard. Maybe he'd be able to come up with a decent reaction. She was drawing a dead blank.

"Casey? Did you hear me?"

"Why?" was all she could manage, stunned by the sudden reversal. She'd just gotten used to the idea that she was an outcast, just beginning to revel in her sense of self-righteous indignation at the idiocy of her workplace and medicine in general.

"Dr. Hunsacker apologized," Tom said. "He said he'd been so stressed by the continuing press that he reacted too strongly. He evidently misheard you during the pelvic, and came in to ask us to reverse your suspension."

"And my license?"

"The board still has to decide, since it's already gone that far."

"And I suppose I'm still on probation."

"For two months. I've scheduled you to return tomorrow. I'm short a couple of nurses, and Barb has to teach a CPR class."

So that was the rush. Not magnanimity, staff crisis. Casey was sorely tempted to tell him no. But she knew better. She'd just paid her bills and knew how much leeway she and Helen had. Once again she bit back her shame at having to surrender for survival's sake.

"Fine," she said, stifling the frustration. "I'll see you then."

Tom didn't ring off yet. Casey knew damn well he was waiting for her to thank him for his efforts on her behalf. But there was only so much Casey could do for her job. By the time she hung up, her AKQ was damn near invisible.

"You're not going to believe this," Casey announced, staring at the phone she'd just replaced.

Jack had returned to his chair, but hadn't sat yet. "Believe what?"

She turned to him, now really needing his reaction. She couldn't trust her own. "My suspension has been lifted. I'm merely on probation now. Hunsacker intervened again."

Casey was confused. Bert was confused. Jack was livid.

"You're not going back to work," he told her simply, his posture rigid, his eyes hard.

Casey's laugh was bitter. "I can't *not* go," she retorted. "This is my job. My career. I'm one screwup away from history."

"You're one whim away from Hunsacker's list!" he shouted.

"You think he's gonna slice and dice me at work?" she demanded, hands on hips. "He's gonna call me in to help with a pelvic and kidnap me instead? Come on, Jack. All he's interested in is getting me to grovel, and he's just done that without once showing his face."

"If you go back, you're playing his game again."

She shook her head, ashamed and furious and tired. "I just told you. I'm already playing it."

"You can't go back to work!" Helen protested the next afternoon as Casey slipped into her lab coat. "I'm used to the company. It's been so lovely having people here."

Having police here, Casey thought dryly as she strapped on her Mickey Mouse watch. "Mom, I don't have a choice. Votive candles aren't free, ya know. Not to mention all those meals for the police." Dinner again, and breakfast. Casey was starting to get used to expecting to see Jack scowling at her in the morning. She was beginning to anticipate it, which unnerved her more than just a little.

She'd walked in last night from dropping Helen off at vespers to hear music. Piano. The notes had cascaded from the walls like sparkling water, jazz improvisation that was both dark and sensuous. Benny had only played classics, and it had a different texture, like old paper. This was asphalt and glass. When she'd walked into the living room, Jack stopped, the look on his face guilty, almost shy. Casey shook her head.

"Is that one of the requirements for the seminary?" she demanded with a wry grin.

He smiled back, and she could see the residue of passion in his eyes, the kind she'd never known from music. She envied him that kind of torment.

"Some temptations shouldn't be avoided," he said, moving to close the keys away again.

Casey stepped forward, a hand preventing him. "You can't imagine how good it sounds," she admitted stiffly. "Don't stop."

He'd been even more uncomfortable than she, as if music were something a man shouldn't admit to. But he'd played, and filled the echoing rooms with a color and whimsy and vitality they'd never known.

Standing here with her mother, Casey missed the life in that music.

Helen took hold of her arm, desperate and unhappy. "Casey, please," she begged. "Since you've been home, it's . . . Mick has . . . I can't let you. Please."

Casey couldn't bear it. Her mother's eyes were huge and wet, her hand trembling. There was dirt under her fingernails from the garden and a cobweb trailing from her bandanna from rooting around in the basement for old letters from Mick.

"Mom, I'm not about to let that man intimidate me into staying home."

Helen's hand tightened. "He's your father," she protested. "You can't talk about him like that."

"I'm not talking about Daddy," Casey insisted, wishing she could pry those fingers loose. "I'm talking about the man I'm trying to put away. The one Sgt. Scanlon is always over here talking to me about. Dr. Hunsacker."

But it didn't seem Helen had heard. "He did his best," she insisted, her grip tighter, her face a study in agony.

He didn't, Casey thought. But it didn't matter now. "Yes, Mom. Now remember, the number's on the board. Call if you need anything." She wasn't going to be able to handle it much longer. There were just too many people pulling her in too many different directions. Jack wanted her to stay home. Helen wanted her in church, and Hunsacker wanted her in his sight. And Casey? Casey just wanted to stop feeling angry and tired and confused.

Helen lifted those startled, frightened eyes to Casey. "Don't go," she begged.

Casey's ghosts stalked her dreams. Helen's were bolder. They seemed to slip out of hiding the minute Casey walked out the door.

"Mr. Rawlings will come over if you want," she soothed, patting the trembling hand as she pulled it loose. "I'll be home as soon as I can."

Casey let herself out the kitchen door and headed around for the driveway. She was all set to swing her bag into the car when she realized she was blocked. There was a Mustang in the driveway behind her, the top down and jazz drifting from the radio.

"You just happened to be in the neighborhood," she taunted.

Jack didn't even bother to smile. "I think you'll find

that your car's broken," he said, his hand draped over the steering wheel. "You'll need a ride to and from work."

She damn near swung her bag at his head. Damn him for looking so tired and worried. She felt guilty for even being pissed that he was trying to control her life.

"I can fix plugs and distributor caps," she warned blackly.

He was unphased. "I heard it was an alternator problem."

Casey didn't move for a minute, fuming. Frozen with indecision. She was unspeakably touched by his concern, furious at his patronization.

"And just how do you get anything else done?" she demanded, finally giving up and stalking his way.

He leaned over and opened her door. "I'm a very organized man."

"Anal," she snarled, plopping into the white vinyl seat and slamming the door shut after her. She saw the crook at the corner of his mouth and ignored it. "Are you going to do this every day for the rest of my life?"

"Only until we get Hunsacker," he assured her and turned the engine over. "I needed to talk to you anyway," he admitted, his attention behind him as he backed out. Two kids swept toward him on skateboards and he waited until they passed.

Suddenly Casey was nervous. "You found the woman?"

"No," Jack admitted, sounding surprised. "She hasn't turned up yet. Yablonsky says there's a good chance she's in Hunsacker's basement until he can safely dispose of her."

"Oh, great." Casey laughed blackly, pushing the hair out of her eyes as they headed down the street. "The Frontenac city council is going to love that one. They don't even have rats in Frontenac. They have 'night squirrels.' Wait till they find out Hunsacker's hosting *Name That Body Part* right under their noses. So, what else is it?''

''What I needed to ask you about was your friend Billie.''

Casey's first reaction was to say ''She wasn't my friend.'' But she remembered the emptiness of Billie's death, those half-open, opaque eyes no one had missed, and she couldn't say it.

''What about her?''

''That envelope on the floor,'' he said, motioning. ''Can you look inside without losing the papers all over Webster?''

Casey scowled at him as she bent to pick up the envelope in question.

He didn't bother to look away from the street. ''De-Clue worked pretty fast. He's talking to Hunsacker now. He found out that the Evans woman had, in fact, had a big falling out with Hunsacker over one of his patients. Nobody heard details, except that she threatened to report him and he threatened her license.''

''A favorite theme,'' she acknowledged.

''Problem is, he has another great alibi.''

''What?''

''You.''

Casey almost let go of the envelope. She stared at Jack in astonishment. ''Me? What the hell did he say?''

''That he was with you when she came in. And that he was at Barnes when she was hit. It's in his notes on a patient there. He says you should know, because you reached him there, and he came right over.''

No, Casey wanted to say. That wasn't right. Something didn't fit. She lifted the paperwork out of the envelope and found copies of her chart on the memorable Mrs.

VanCleve and doctor's notes from a patient at Barnes. There it was on her notes, that Hunsacker had arrived to see his patient at 8:20 PM. And his last note at Barnes read 8:00 PM. Just enough time to get between the two hospitals and park.

"What time was Billie hit?" she asked.

"Near as they can guess, just about eight."

Casey checked the chart and then her notes again. She remembered dealing with the lovely Mrs. VanCleve. She also remembered that her chart had gone on a huge pile to be finished at the end of shift. Casey hadn't charted on it until three hours after the woman had left, and now she realized that something was missing. She wasn't sure what. But something wasn't right.

"He did come in just before Billie did," she murmured, peering at the pages that flapped in the wind. She gave her hair another swipe, already knowing it was useless. "But . . ."

He looked over then. "But what?"

Casey could only shake her head. "I don't know. Something." She looked over at Jack. "Give me some time on this, okay?"

Nodding, Jack returned his attention to traffic. They turned into the emergency drive and pulled to a halt outside the ambulance entrance as Casey stuffed the envelope into her work bag.

"I'll be here at eleven," Jack assured her.

Casey tried another scowl. "What if I don't get off then?"

"I'll read a good book."

"Go home and get some sleep instead."

Jack just shook his head. "I won't get any sleep until this is over. Now, go on and get in to work."

Still, she didn't move. She clutched her bag in taut hands and faced the back end of the ambulance in front of them, trying her best to summon courage, or words, or both. She'd been planning on having time alone to screw her proverbial courage to the sticking post.

Jack was ahead of her. "Casey."

She turned to him, knowing damn well he could see the precarious state of her self-confidence.

Jack's smile was at once dark and empathetic. "Fuck 'em if they can't take a joke."

Casey was surprised by a sharp laugh. The good Sgt. Scanlon was better acquainted with uncertainty than he let on. It said something about the situation she'd landed herself in that it was a man she'd only met going to report a crime who was the one person she could rely on right now.

She flashed him a sharp grin and nodded. "I'm okay, you're okay, but they're morons, right?"

"It's one way to look at it."

At least when she opened the car door she was still grinning.

Casey would never have believed she would be hesitant about walking back on the halls. When the doors swished open before her and the triage staff looked up, she wanted to turn back around. She expected hostility and curiosity, and there was no question she at least saw uncertainty and curiosity on their faces.

It seemed that the shift wasn't going to be normal in any way. When Casey opened the door to the lounge, she braced herself for just about anything. She didn't think that included finding her ex-husband the only person there to greet her.

She instinctively looked over her shoulder, just to make sure she'd walked into the right hospital. Then she turned back to Ed, who was getting to his feet and straightening his double-breasted suit.

"I was wondering if I could talk to you, Casey," he said.

Casey almost ran out to catch Jack before he got away. "What's wrong with the phone, Ed?"

"I hear it's tapped."

Casey abruptly sat. "Where did you get that information?"

Ed walked up to her and held out a hand. "Your supervisor said it was okay if you got on the hall a little late. Let's take a walk."

Casey looked around, fully expecting to see Hunsacker step in the door. "Where?"

Ed sighed. "Casey, you've become paranoid over this whole thing. I'm alone, acting on my own behalf. I just want to talk. And it was your mother who told me about the phone. I think she wanted to scare me off."

Casey didn't know quite what to do, but one thing she'd long since learned about Ed was that he was harmless. Giving in to curiosity, Casey got up and walked out the door with him and headed for the exercise paths that circled the campus.

"The police talked to me, you know," he said, hands in pants pockets, his jacket bunching up around his forearms, head down a little.

"I know," Casey answered, her attention on the little knots of people wandering over the grounds. She still expected Hunsacker to show up out of nowhere.

"You really must have impressed the police with your fear of Dale. They took your story quite seriously."

"And why shouldn't they?" Casey asked.

Ed took a minute to think about that. "Dale has some problems," he admitted, watching the path ahead of him instead of Casey. "Things we've been working through together, about his sexuality and self-image. I won't deny that, and I doubt he would, either. But you've made rash judgments based on only a slice of information, and I think you should know the rest."

"Does he know you're telling me this?"

"No. He'd never let me if he knew."

"Then I don't want to know."

"But you have to. You of all people . . ."

She stopped and swung on him. "I don't—"

"Dale's father abused him." Ed stopped right across from her, his voice implacable and soft. "He beat him mercilessly and locked him in closets for days and humiliated him in public. He molested Dale's sister repeatedly, and Dale couldn't stop it. He's never gotten over it."

Casey instinctively shook her head. "I don't want to hear about it," she demanded, rigid and unyielding. "He's lying to you just to get your sympathy, Ed. He's lying to you like he's lying to everyone. He told everybody at M and M and Izzy's that he and I were having an affair, did you know that?"

Much to her astonishment, Ed nodded. "Casey, he's so afraid he's gay, he does and says outrageous things to protect his self-image."

"Like slicing a woman's ears off?"

The firs whispered with a soft wind. Down the path two people turned at the sound of Casey's strident words, and then walked on, more uncomfortably.

"Somebody is taking advantage of this," Ed insisted. "I can't explain why. I just know that as a psychiatrist, I've evaluated Dale and know he's confused, frightened, full of shame, but that he'd never do what you're accusing him of. He's incapable of violence."

Casey couldn't catch her breath. She couldn't seem to still her hands, rubbing them together as if she could erase some stain. "Did he ask you to intervene, Ed? So I'd lay off?"

Ed shook his head and tried to lay a commiserating

hand on Casey's arm. She flinched from him. "I came on my own when I found out the police were dragging him back in all over again. They're trying to tie him into yet another killing." He shook his head, frustrated, more defensive than he'd ever been with her. "Don't you understand, Casey? He came to St. Louis to try and escape his past, and now you're dragging it all back out again."

"He's lying," she insisted, not knowing what else to say. Desperate and convinced, furious at the compassion Ed demanded. "You're dazzled by him, just like everybody else. You can't see what he's really like."

Whirling away, she tried to walk back to the building. Ed caught her by the arm and forced her to a halt.

"Casey, listen to you," he said, truly concerned. "You're not being logical at all. It's not going to help you to project your unresolved problems onto Dale just to punish other people in your life."

Casey looked over to see that Ed's forehead was pursed, his eyes truly bemused behind the horn-rims. She pulled away from his hold. "The only reason he reminds me of other people in my life is that he acts just like him, only smoother."

But Ed shook his head. "I'm not talking about Frank," he said. "I'm talking about your father."

That brought Casey to a dead halt. "What?"

"Haven't you noticed the resemblance?" he asked, truly surprised. "He looks just like him."

She felt so frightened suddenly. So small and lost. "My father had an *honest* job," she snapped. "He was an officer at the brewery."

"Your father—"

"Is dead," she hissed. "Has been dead most of my life. Thanks for the little talk, Ed, but I have to get back now. I'm sure I hear an ambulance calling."

Ed didn't stop her this time. He stood in the center

of the path, his hands limp by his side, his expression for-
lorn. "Casey—"

But Casey wouldn't turn around. She just walked
faster, her eyes focused on the red emergency sign over
the doors she sought. Which was why she didn't see Dr.
Hunsacker walk out of the trees to her left and stroll
away.

The phone calls started again that night.

Jack had been waiting for Casey just as he'd promised
when she finally got out of work at midnight, slouched
in his front seat reading a book on Immanuel Kant and
the Categorical Imperatives and listening to some strange
kind of fusion jazz on the radio. He asked how Casey's
evening had been, and she snapped at him. The rest of
the ride had been silent.

When she arrived home, Casey thanked Jack for his
consideration and told him to go home and get some
sleep. She still didn't tell him about what Ed had said,
or the fact that of all the people she worked with at M
and M, only Marva and Abe had spoken to her all evening long. She was exhausted and sore and sick, and she
didn't want to deal with having Jack under the roof again
that night.

So she said good night and walked around to let herself in the back door. She brewed a pot of coffee and was
in the process of pulling her shoes off when she realized
that Jack was still sitting out in her driveway, the headlights off and the map light on. Reading Kant.

"Son of a bitch," she muttered and threw open the
front door. "Get in here!"

He rolled down the window. "I'm fine," he assured
her.

"You're a pain in the ass!" she retorted loudly enough
that if it hadn't been that late, all the neighbors could

have taken notes. "And this time you'll sleep in the god-damn guest room!"

She could have sworn she heard a chuckle.

He didn't sleep in the guest room, of course. He dropped his shoes on the sun-room floor and his tie over the couch. He'd evidently decided, however, that it was time to bring a shaving kit with him. That ended up in the downstairs bathroom.

Casey didn't talk to him. She couldn't. She left him the coffee and headed upstairs.

The phone woke her from the middle of a dream. Not the afghan dream, another one. She was sweating and shaking, the echo of a small voice dying in her. "Daddy, no! Don't go!" The words clotted in her chest like old blood.

It rang again, insistent and shrill. Casey jumped from the bed and ran for the phone.

"Hello?"

She heard Jack pick up just because she knew he would. But Hunsacker kept his peace, as always. Casey curled up into her chair, her bare feet flat on the cool wood of the seat, her face buried in a trembling hand, her hair damp and sticky.

He was a menace tonight, a force, like the wind plucking at the edges of her windows, always trying to get in. Persistent, sneaky, wearing. Close to slithering past her defenses and hearing her dreams. Tonight, she didn't think she could hold out. She desperately tried to shore up her anger, her hatred. She recited her litanies as fervently as Helen chanted the rosary, praying for salvation. For . . . what was it Jack said, redemption? For redemption.

But tonight, Hunsacker was too real, too powerful. Casey bit the heel of her hand to keep from screaming at him.

Then, the click. Quiet, controlled, satisfied. Casey couldn't move, couldn't even reach over to replace the phone. She heard the flat hum of a dial tone, and didn't notice that there hadn't been a corresponding click from downstairs. She knew she should go down and talk to Jack about it, should at least tell him she was all right. She couldn't. Curled up in her hard-back chair, like a child against a wall, she held on to the phone, her eyes squeezed shut, her hand against her mouth, frightened for reasons that had nothing to do with murder.

Jack waited for her to hang up. The phone hummed in his ear. The night creaked and moaned around him. Still no corresponding click from Casey's room. Instinctively he looked up, as if he could see through two floors. The call had unnerved him, and he'd heard some of the most awful things one person could say to another. That silence had been turgid, sinister. Jack had felt it crawling up and down his spine like the instinct that the enemy crept beyond the buffalo grass back in the jungle. A huge emptiness with a feral smell to it.

She was too quiet. Too still. Jack finally hung up the phone and climbed the unfamiliar stairs.

The second story was as quaint as the first, family antiques and worn carpeting and more Sacred Heart pictures. Four doors opened off the corridor. Jack didn't try any of them. He headed up again.

The big room brought him right to a stop. Small blue and red votive candles flickered. The smell of incense permeated the wood, and hundreds of curling holy cards crowded the chipped portable altar like a Taoist family shrine. Jack expected joss sticks and paper petitions instead of a kneeler and dispossessed life-size statue of Mary.

He saw the light seeping around the edge of the door

and hesitated. She was still so quiet. And she'd been try-ing to deal with these calls on her own. He wanted to throttle her.

The door was unlocked. He tapped and opened it at the same time, not giving her the chance to beg off. Again, he was brought to a halt. It was like the kitchen downstairs, a flash of color in this pastel house, blues and purples and greens on wall and blanket and curtain, clothes tossed around and books and magazines stacked haphazardly wherever there was room. This was a place with life.

But then Jack saw Casey. All he could think about was finding her on the bathroom floor. She was curled into herself, her hair tumbled over her arms, her bare toes peeking out from under a modest flowered cotton night-gown, her fingers clenched and trembling around the phone.

"Casey?" He heard it. The ache of frustration in his own voice, the grate of fury. He was shaking, and it hadn't been his call.

Giving a little shudder, Casey lifted her head. Her eyes were dry and wide, her face taut. She looked like a mine-site survivor, steeling herself against the pain. Looking into hell and needing the strength to walk away.

"Don't come in," she said quietly in a voice that was surprisingly calm.

Jack halted. His instincts pulled him to her, to take her back in his arms and cushion the fall. His hands, restless with the inability to act, slid into his pockets. His chest hurt almost as much as his gut. "I'm here if you need me," he offered lamely, furious with himself for not hav-ing more. Suddenly impatient with a distance he was be-ginning to resent.

She shook her head, still tightly folded. Still rigid as

pain. "I can't," she whispered, her eyes liquid with turmoil. "It's too easy to do with you."

Jack couldn't quite breathe. He'd spent too many
sleepless hours down on that cramped little couch to be
listening to this. He was too tired and too frustrated and
too attracted. And, she was much too vulnerable.

"I was an Eagle Scout, too," he offered with a wry
grin. "Always faithful, always trustworthy."

Casey tried to grin back and looked as if she were
going to cry instead. "Well, I wasn't," she retorted
thinly, tears finally filling her eyes.

Jack did the only thing he could. He stalked right up
to her and took the phone away. "Come on," he commanded, hanging up the receiver and pulling her gently
to her feet. "You need some sleep."

She started at his touch, skittish and shy. Even so, she
followed. Jack steered her for the mountain of color on
her bed and pulled it back. When she climbed up into
the bed, he covered her up and smoothed the comforter,
much as she had two mornings ago when she'd thought
he'd been asleep.

"I'm here," he repeated, brushing back her hair. "I'll
be here until this is over."

Casey grinned wearily. "I don't suppose that's negotia-
ble."

Jack smiled back. "After we catch Hunsacker, we can
negotiate anything you want."

Giving in to impulse, he bent over and sealed his offer
with another kiss. Not like the one in the bathroom,
more a promise than punctuation. A kiss that betrayed
the fact that he was beginning to need as much as she.
And then, not giving either of them a chance to react,
he turned and left.

\*          \*          \*

Casey didn't get any sleep that night, either. Jangling like a telephone wire in a high wind, she tossed and turned until she heard Helen shuffling around beneath her, and finally got up for the day. Another day with Jack at the breakfast table. Another day hunting Hunsacker. Another day with Helen and the crew at work and the phone, sitting on her desk like a somnolent adder, striking without warning, relentless and deadly.

Jack had already made breakfast by the time Casey got downstairs.

"The call last night came from Creve Coeur," he offered, handing over a mug of coffee. "We're checking to see if our friend was out and about. Is it always like it was last night?"

Casey accepted the cup with a silent nod of thanks. "Every time. He seems to know that silence is worse for me than words."

Jack nodded, sipping thoughtfully at his own cup. He hadn't shaved yet, and was still barefoot, just as he'd been the night before when he'd walked into Casey's room. She'd wanted him to hold her so badly last night, to banish the ghosts. She wanted it again, so she turned away.

"Do you know what Ed tried to tell me last night?" she asked, still incredulous, especially after sitting through that phone call. "That Hunsacker told him this gruesome abuse story. A real Daddy Dearest fairy tale that fueled all his problems."

She looked to Jack for disdain, to reassure her and reinforce her. She needed her outrage so badly right now. She needed his support.

Instead, he contemplated his coffee. "Actually," he said quietly. "It's true."

Casey stopped halfway to the table where her English muffin waited, the butter dripping and the jam red and sweet. Something slipped inside her, something that threatened her balance.

"Come on," she objected again. "Hunsacker'll say anything he can to look sympathetic."

Jack looked up at her, and she didn't like what she saw. "The family hushed it up because of the money," he said quietly. "The place in society. Evidently the famous surgeon went into uncontrollable rages when he drank. He beat his son and molested his daughter, and his wife refused to do anything about it. I read the report yesterday."

Casey couldn't defend herself against something like this. She needed her anger too badly. She needed her sense of distance.

"Bullshit," she accused baldly.

Jack shook his head. "I contacted a detective in Boston. There was always some question about that fire, and he filled me in on the stuff that never hit the news. It's a classic pattern for serial killers, abuse so bad at home that the kid becomes expert at dissociating. All that rage and guilt boiling beneath the perfect facade."

A tiny child, cowering in the dark, weeping with the terror of a sudden bellow, the sound of footsteps. Screams. Helpless and alone and afraid.

No. Hunsacker was a monster. He hurt people just to see it happen. He'd never been a child. He'd never been trapped with no way out.

"Well, good morning, Father. Look what Mr. Rawlings brought us."

Casey actually flinched at the sound of Helen's too-bright voice. She couldn't quite breathe right, couldn't keep the mug still in her hand. She knew Jack was watching her, but she couldn't face him. Her gaze fell instead on Helen, who was too puffy and tremulous for enthusiasm. Casey had hoped she'd be better after yesterday. Instead she looked worse, more strident, like a tightly wound top ready to overbalance. From anxious to desperate, and Casey couldn't say why. But she felt it, too.

"Good morning, Mrs. McDonough," Jack greeted her. "Mr. Rawlings."

Casey turned then to find that Mr. Rawlings had followed Helen in, a bunch of iris and dahlias and gladiolas in his arm. He was smiling at Jack.

"I promised you a ride in the Mustang, didn't I?" Jack asked as Helen gathered the flowers from Mr. Rawlings and went for a vase. Mr. Rawlings smiled the way a person would who had just made a successful transaction. Any other time Casey would have smiled, too. Today she stood silently and stared at her breakfast, her appetite suddenly lost.

"I would like that," Mr. Rawlings enthused with an efficient nod, and then smiled like a boy in a locker room. "Although I have to admit, what I'd really like to do is have a crack at that Porsche."

Casey didn't hear it. She was too distracted, stretched too thin. Jack heard it.

"Porsche?" he asked, his voice deceptively quiet.

Mr. Rawlings nodded. "The one Casey's other friend drives. The one who comes in the afternoons sometimes to keep Helen company."

Casey heard it then. She heard Jack's sudden, harsh silence and turned to see his expression harden to stone. She turned to Mr. Rawlings.

Suddenly her heart was pounding. She flushed with fear. Casey stood very still. Yet she knew everyone could hear the scream of outrage that was building behind her throat. She knew they could see the revulsion that swelled in her chest.

"What other friend?" she asked, her voice strained, desperate to keep it even. She wanted to close her eyes, as if it would make him change his answer. Her hands were clenched around the hot mug, and her chest was frozen. Waiting. Dreading. Knowing.

And still Mr. Rawlings didn't sense the disaster he was announcing. "Why that blond gentleman," he said, and turned to Helen for confirmation. "Didn't I hear you call him Mick?"

Here. Hunsacker had been here, and her mother had invited him in. Casey never heard the mug shatter against the floor or felt the coffee burn her bare leg.

# Chapter 20

"WHAT WERE YOU THINKING?" Casey shrilled, whirling on her mother. "Just what the *hell* were you thinking letting that man in here?"

Jack stepped in front of her. "Casey—"

"No," she snapped, waving away his intervention, glaring at him with accusation. "He was *here*. In my house. In my *house!* And she let him!"

Helen held the flowers in front of her like a shield, the long stems trembling in her grasp, her face paper white at Casey's venom. "I don't recall any visitors," she objected lamely, her eyes skittering away. Turning, she walked toward the door. "Now, I must give these to our lady . . ."

"No," Casey demanded, grabbing her mother's arm and yanking her back around. "Not this time. You're going to talk to me." She wanted to shake her until she rattled, until every ridiculous aphorism clattered right out of her head onto the floor. The urge was so strong, so overpowering that she let go. Helen swayed like a sail in a gust of wind.

"My visitors are my—"

"How long has he been coming here?" Casey demanded, walking right up to her, her hands clenched to keep from striking her own mother. Incensed, terrified, revolted.

Helen shrugged away from her, lifting the vase between them. "A few weeks. He . . . he stopped, and then . . . then he came back yesterday. I missed him." Her attempt at rebellion faltered and died, and she clutched at her chipped green vase as if seeking foundation. "He said you'd leave me if you found out."

"Then why do it?" Casey demanded, taut and disbelieving. Still unable to quite grasp the idea that Hunsacker had touched her things, sat at her table, chatted with her mother while Casey had been working to put him away. "You saw his picture on the television. You knew who he was. Why in God's name did you let him in the door?"

"You don't understand," Helen objected, her eyes filling. "You never did."

"Understand what?" Casey retorted with a wave of her hand. "You invite a murderer into my house, and I'm supposed to understand?"

Casey felt Jack's hand on her arm and tried to pull away. He wouldn't let her.

"We need to discuss this rationally," he advised evenly.

Casey spun on him. "He sat on my furniture," she spat, her eyes burning and her chest so tight she couldn't breathe. "He got them to lift my suspension so he could come back into my house! Don't you understand? He's raped me without even unzipping his pants!"

She'd forgotten Mr. Rawlings. He rustled at her harsh words, too delicate to object, too distressed to stay.

"I'm sorry," he apologized. "I thought you knew. I thought he was a friend."

"Thank you for telling us, Mr. Rawlings," Jack acknowledged him, hand still restraining Casey. "Could I talk to you in a few minutes?"

"Oh, yes." He scuttled from the tension in the room like a fox from a forest fire.

"We need to sit down, Casey," Jack said.

Casey couldn't take her eyes from her mother. She couldn't understand. Truly couldn't. How could her mother have lived through all this, and then blithely invited a serial murderer to tea?

"Explain it to me," she said, still ignoring Jack. "Tell me why you had to invite him in."

"He understood," Helen whimpered, head down, tears tracing a familiar course down hollow cheeks. "He was sent to absolve me."

"Absolve you from what?"

But Helen shook her head, the tears building. "You don't understand. You never did. You have no charity."

"*Tell* me!" Casey demanded, grabbing Helen's arm, endangering flowers and vase. "Make me understand why you want a murderer to make you feel better."

"Because he knew," Helen retorted, her eyes suddenly hot and afraid. She pulled away, standing alone, her flowers brave and bright before her. "He talked to me in Mick's voice. He told me what you can't even tell me. You want me to talk, but it's you who won't talk. You won't even listen. He offered to take my guilt with his."

"Guilt?" Casey demanded. "What guilt? Which guilt? That man doesn't have *anything* to do with us."

But Helen was beginning to fade, to fold into herself with the weight of her words. She began shaking her head, her shoulders shuddering and the vase drooping in uncertain hands. "You don't remember," she said. "You refuse to remember."

"Remember? Remember what?"

"That I killed him!" she shrieked suddenly, all the years of docility exploding along with the vase as it hit the floor. Helen's hands flew to her mouth as if she could shove back in the words. Flowers tumbled at her feet and water splashed over the hem of her dress.

Casey wanted to scream. How many times had they had this conversation? Every Lent, every anniversary, every time she looked at Mick's picture on her mother's dresser. "Aw, God, Mom," she moaned in disgust. "I can't tell you again that leaving the convent doesn't kill a man."

"No!" Helen insisted, still hiding behind her hands, the flowers at her feet like an offering to the Madonna. She was sobbing, now, a new sound of grief. Of horror. "No, no, no. You don't know. You refuse. You turn away and run, because you don't want to know. You want nothing to do with it, with me because of what I did. What I made you help me do. Don't you understand yet? You were with me. You knelt right next to me in the living room every night and helped, you took my message to church with you. You and Benny and I, day after day. Praying to stop his uncharitable acts."

Sudden tears choked Casey. Bile seared the back of her tongue. Her hands sought her ears. She didn't even realize she put them there, shutting out her mother's words. She didn't hear the harsh rasp of her own breathing or the thunder of her heart, a child's heart.

But it was too late. Helen had finally let reality catch up with delusion.

"Every night," she sobbed, her hands clutched to her breast, a mea culpa that bruised. "Every morning when he woke up. Every day for ten years. 'Please, sweet Jesus,' I prayed. 'Help your poor sinner. Give refuge to your children. Grant this one prayer. Save us.' And then he'd come home, and I'd sit across the table from him, waiting, waiting for that last bourbon, and knowing what would come. And I'd pray, 'Please, my lady, my mother and sweet solace, who comforts the ill and oppressed, I don't know what else to do to stop it . . . please.' Every night, our hands like steeples as we prayed together. 'Please. Jesus, Mary, Joseph. Just . . . let . . . Mick . . . die.' "

"No," Casey rasped, her ears hurting, her cheeks wet, her arms too numb to feel Jack next to her.

The dreams. The echoes of that child's voice. The stark, stale terror of the darkness.

Helen crumpled. Jack rushed forward to gather her in. She kept sobbing. "I couldn't take any more. I couldn't take any more, couldn't watch Benny suffer . . . I went to Father, and he said pray for guidance. I went to the police, and they said I'd made my bed, he was my husband. But I was weak. I was evil. And because I was weak, I murdered him. He understood. He prayed, too. He remembered."

Jack led Helen back to the table and gently sat her down. Casey couldn't move from where she stood, numb and frightened and confused. She tasted salt against the palm of her hand, where it shut in the sounds of anguish that clamored in her chest. She heard Helen's sobbing and Jack's soothing murmurs, and still couldn't escape the echoes that suddenly wouldn't end.

Benny. Sweet, serious Benny, who had slept just below her. Who had always crawled into the big room where Helen did her sewing and hid amid the boxes so his father couldn't find him. Who had prayed the hardest, tow head bent over the tips of his trembling fingers, tears splashing the beads of his rosary.

Helen, tiptoeing in her own house to escape her husband's blind wrath, who had never made it any farther than the big room outside Casey's door before Mick had caught her and beaten her, her terrified shrieking and sobbing echoing in the big house.

Casey, trapped in the blackness of her room beyond the terrible sounds, sinking beneath the guilt and shame and terror, wondering why Benny and her mother were so much worse that they had to be hurt and she didn't. Begging to be included just to take away her own shame.

Helen had taken down the sewing machine the day after Mick died. She'd dismantled her sewing room and begun constructing her chapel of guilt, and all these years Casey hadn't realized that she'd prayed at her mother's altar all along.

Casey's door had never been strong enough to blot out the noise. The clatter of furniture, the roaring threats, the pitiful protests, the wrenching cries of pain and terror. She'd lain in her bed and put her hands over her ears and watched the sky. The black, endless, empty sky where nobody lived, where she could be all alone and not hear everything.

Where she wouldn't have to get up in the morning and kiss her daddy hello and feel shame because she loved him so much. Because even as she prayed right alongside her mother and brother, she begged him not to go.

She felt Jack's hand on her shoulder and turned to his embrace. "Damn him," she cursed with blind sobs, her face against the limp cotton of Jack's shirt, fists clenched against his chest. "Damn him, damn him . . . damn . . ."

Jack bent his head over hers. Casey could feel the warmth of his cheek against her, his hand tentatively stroking her hair. He didn't say anything. Just held her so tightly she couldn't escape, couldn't crumble.

Her stomach heaved with revulsion. Her chest closed off. She kept shaking her head, trying to push away the pictures she hadn't allowed in so long, swimming in their recriminations.

She'd been the only one to run to Mick when he'd collapsed. Benny and Helen had sat frozen, their forks halfway to their mouths, their eyes stark as dead fishes, their dread so mixed up with hope they couldn't tell them apart. But Casey could. She'd tugged at her father and screamed, hating herself for it, hating her mother for making her feel this way.

"Daddy, no! Don't go, Daddy, please!"

Outside the window, the sky muttered. The weather service had finally promised rain today, a storm to sweep out all the stagnant air in the city. The sky was tumescent, a dirty green-gray that swirled above the motionless trees.

A storm was coming.

Jack should have known. He should have spotted it the minute Casey talked about the other man, the one who had made her crawl. It was such a familiar pattern, one he'd learned through years of counseling, years of domestic disturbances. Still he couldn't quite quell the rage that ate new holes in his stomach. Rage against a dead man. Rage against a system that had protected him and reserved room in hell for his family.

Helen was up in bed, whimpering and lost. Casey had walked her up, hollow-eyed and spent, her own hands shaking as badly as her mother's. Left behind, Jack had stood in the living room staring at a wasted piano and the harmless family that populated Helen's walls. Family that had given support and succor and love when her real family, her real faith, hadn't.

No wonder Casey had no patience with God. Jack hardly blamed her. He had a few things to say to Him himself.

"The license is K2F-309," he said, phone propped on his shoulder as he read off the notes he'd taken from the interview with a surprisingly observant Mr. Rawlings. He wanted to say something about how thorough the patrolman who'd interviewed him had been, but didn't. It had been his responsibility to follow up on it, and he hadn't.

"I'll get it right over to DMV," Bert promised. "Sounds like it's going to tie right in to Billie Evans. The evidence crew's on its way over to dust for prints. How's Casey?"

"Pretty tapped out. I think Hunsacker's finally getting to her."

"I can't wait till we have this son of a bitch in our hands," Bert retorted. "I'm looking forward to paying him back for this one. Casey's one of the good guys."

It took Jack a minute to answer that. He couldn't quite get past the hard knot in his throat. Casey's scent still lingered on his hands. His shirt was still a little damp from her tears. He'd come a lot closer than he wanted to admit to walking right out of the house and blowing that asshole's brains all over those clean white walls of his.

"We'll get him," Jack promised in a voice every policeman in the city recognized and respected. "And when we do, I get first crack at him."

Bert actually chuckled. "I'll hold your coat. What else can we do right now?"

"The Evans alibi is our best bet until I can get that hooker back from Chicago," Jack said, glad to be back on familiar territory. "I gave Casey copies of the paperwork, and she's trying to come up with something. You'll be over here when?"

"Two hours. When do you leave for Boston?"

Jack checked his watch. "Plane leaves at four. I'm meeting with the Boston detectives tonight, the family and shrink in the morning. Now, you won't leave her for a minute?"

"I'll even have a guy sitting in her waiting room at work."

"Don't let her know. She'll ream you a new asshole and then pitch him right out the back door."

Bert allowed another chuckle. "I borrowed one of the undercover narcs. He'll fit right in."

Jack nodded instinctively as he flipped his notebook closed. "Thanks, man."

"My pleasure. Let's catch this asshole."

"Call in sick."

Casey looked up at the mirror to see that Jack stood behind her. He was dressed for work, with a new dark shirt and skinny tie, his hands on his hips and his jacket splayed back over his arms. Casey could just see the curve of his gun handle behind his right wrist. "Just when I get back to work?" she asked, knowing how lifeless her voice sounded. "They'd demote me to rehab right on the spot."

She could tell he was frustrated. Those creases between his eyebrows were deep, the line of his jaw taut. He looked even more tired than she felt, and she had a feeling he was wishing he had his Maalox bottle. She was surprised at the sharp ache she felt at the thought that he was hurting for her.

Sighing with resignation, she turned to face him. "I'll be okay," she promised. "Marva's on tonight. She'll shore me up."

Jack just shook his head. "I'd rather you didn't leave this house."

"I'd rather I didn't have to walk back into this house," she countered, the nausea surging briefly. Everything she looked at she saw Hunsacker's fingers on. She smelled his cologne when she knew she couldn't, heard his silky laughter in her kitchen where she used to feel safe.

"Bert will be over in a few minutes," Jack reassured her.

Casey could actually grin at that. "It'll almost be worth seeing the expression on some of my neighbors' faces in the morning."

"You don't go anywhere without him," Jack demanded. "You hear me? I don't want you or your mother alone for a minute."

Casey offered an uncomfortable little shrug, her gaze sliding away from his. "I hate this," she managed, surprised by the tears that were still so close, so unpredictable.

She wasn't as surprised as she would have been a week ago that Jack walked right up and took her back in his arms. She folded into him, glad for his strength, his undemanding silence. He didn't wear cologne, his smell clean soap and shaving cream. She thought it smelled like baptism.

"I'll be back tomorrow night," he promised. "If we can establish a pattern from Boston, we can reinforce the circumstantial evidence we have already."

She nodded, eyes closed, heart stumbling past the pictures that once released wouldn't dim. Chest taut with the battle between compassion and hatred. She needed the hatred, but the compassion wouldn't be squeezed out. "I don't want to feel sorry for him," she admitted in a strident whisper. "I want him to be a monster."

"He is a monster," Jack told her, his workman's hands gentle against her back. "But monsters are usually products of worse monsters."

She shook her head blindly, overwhelmed by what she'd realized. "We have so much in common." Except that Casey hadn't been the one flinching away from that powerful, inescapable hand. She hadn't had to hide the bruises and crawl into corners. She'd just had to watch.

"The sons grow up to be serial killers," she observed wryly. "The daughters grow up to be nurses."

Except that Benny hadn't turned to murder to vent his shame and pain. He'd turned to oblivion. He'd disappeared into the mist like a sad, silent wraith, a child-ghost trapped between earth and eternity, just alive enough to be felt, a tug on the conscience, but not seen. Not ever seen again. Maybe it was only the rage that kept the men really alive.

Casey took a few more selfish minutes fortifying herself with Jack's strength. Then, she straightened, shaking herself like a dog trying to rid itself of water. "Okay," she announced, lifting her face to smile up at him. "It's showtime. Be careful in Boston."

Jack was surprised into laughing. "I'm the one with the gun, remember?"

Casey tilted her head in challenge. She wasn't fooling him. She knew it and he knew it. Even so, she needed to get her facade good and set for work. "I'm a nurse," she said. "I don't need a gun to be threatening. Now, head on off. I'll wait for Bert before I leave."

He took her by the shoulders, and for once his eyes were forthright and honest. "Promise me you won't do anything stupid," he demanded, not smiling now. Not teasing at all.

Casey nodded, just as sincere. "Hurry back."

Neither of them said what they were thinking. Casey didn't even know how to phrase it yet. She just knew that she was doing something she'd vowed on everything that had still been holy to her that she would never allow herself to do again. She was anticipating. And she anticipated seeing Jack again even before he left. God, she hoped she wasn't making another mistake.

She got another kiss. This one neither promise nor punctuation. This one hot and slow and savory, the kind that made you forget your troubles and think of only your hormones. Casey's hormones, so badly neglected all these years, sprang right to attention. By the time Jack pulled away, a little breathless and smiling himself, Casey was forgetting every promise she'd ever made to herself. Except the ones about Hunsacker, because until there was some kind of resolution about him, there could be no future for her.

When she left for work, Casey saw that the sky was still unsettled. The temperature had risen; humidity weighted the air. Clouds boiled over in the southwest horizon, angry and threatening. Casey loved storms. She sat up in her room and watched them rip at the city, shaking the ground with their great feet and tearing apart the trees with their cool, swift breath. She didn't feel excited now. She felt edgy, nervous, charged like the air around her. Waiting and uncertain.

"What do you remember about the night Billie came in?" Casey asked Marva as they sat down to dinner.

Marva looked up from her tuna salad. "Not much," she admitted. "Why?"

Casey waved the chart copies at her. "Because somewhere in there is Hunsacker's mistake. I can feel it in my bones, and I can't figure out how to find it."

Marva squinted at her. "I sure wish you wouldn't broadcast that quite so much," she advised. "Barb didn't look too happy at your four-letter professions of love."

"He was in my house," Casey reminded her with a hiss. It was all she could do to eat thinking about it.

Marva nodded, conceding the point. "I already talked to you about that one," she challenged. "You look like warmed-up day-old shit, and work's not gonna help any right now. You should be home in fetal position gettin' your sanity back, not here. Especially here. You shouldn't be within fifteen miles of that man right now. 'Specially if he knows you found out.''

"He's been waiting for me to find out," Casey retorted. "It's part of the game. I had to call in a priest to hear my mother's confession this morning, and I can't sit on any chair in my house without wanting to throw up. It probably tickles him to death."

Marva shook her head. "I hope he lights up like a Christmas tree when they fry him."

"Which is why I'm trying to remember that night," Casey reminded her with another small lift of the papers. "I find I cope better with something positive to do. Now, help me. Remember how busy it was? I did my charting at the end of the shift, and I have a horrible suspicion that I missed something on the VanCleve chart. That's the one that upholds his alibi."

"What he say he was doin'?"

"He was supposed to be in at Barnes twenty minutes before walking in the door here. He got here right before Billie did. I remember. He had bourbon on his breath and was doing his best Dr. Kildare impression. So if he was at Barnes only twenty minutes earlier, he couldn't have gotten ten minutes south of here, found Billie, run her over, and then made it in here before her."

Marva reached for the chart copy. Casey held on to the Barnes notes, looking at the times. The nurse mentioned him arriving at 7:05. She didn't note when he left. His last note timed him at 8:00. And Casey clocked him in at 8:20. But there was something else about the case she should remember, something nagging at the back of her mind.

"Too bad you can't prosecute for doin' unnecessary pelvics," Marva observed, munching on her sandwich. "This lady sure didn't need one."

"I think they're punitive pelvics," Casey answered, swallowing her own bite of ham and Swiss.

Punitive. Punitive. It struck something.

"Give me that chart a minute," she asked.

Leaning across the table, Marva passed it across. Casey took another look. Mrs. VanCleve. UTI. Red fingernails. Diamonds. Bitch.

Casey remembered considering punitive actions against the woman long before Hunsacker had.

"That's it!" Casey crowed, flipping back to her notes again, then rechecking the face sheet. Something rare fluttered in her chest. Hope. Anticipation of the unholiest kind.

"She was a raving, screeching bitch. I remember now. I should have spotted it when I saw the time clocked in and the time Hunsacker came in. We called him for a solid forty-five minutes before we found him and she bitched every second of every minute . . . damn, it's not here anywhere. I know I meant to chart it, especially after the tantrum she threw. I remember asking somebody to get the times on those calls for me."

"But if it ain't on paper—"

Casey's head came up, the hope now agony. "How long do they keep the phone logs from the desk?" she demanded.

Marva shrugged. "Forever, I'm sure. It's paperwork, ain't it?"

Without bothering with the rest of her sandwich, Casey jumped to her feet and ran for the door. Please, God, she thought in sudden, crystal desperation. Let them be there. Let the secretary that night have made clean notes, since she hadn't. Let her be contradicted.

"What are you doing?" one of the secretaries demanded as Casey yanked one file drawer after another open in search of the right paper. Her name was Venice, and she didn't like nurses screwing with her files.

"Phone logs," Casey said. "From March. Where are they?"

"The incinerator," she answered as if Casey were slow.

Casey came to a sick halt. "Please don't say that."

"They keep 'em for a month."

"No," a younger girl answered. "Tom's got 'em. I saw 'em in his office, ya know? It's fer like this study they're doin' so they can get more help or somethin'."

Casey reached for the phone and dialed security.

"You're not going to go into Tom's office, are you?" Venice demanded.

Casey smiled, suddenly wishing she could throw up again. "You bet," she said.

Bert called while she was waiting for security to show up.

"Be careful, little girl," he warned. "We don't have him yet. The plates definitely belong to a black Porsche, but they're registered to a Walter Reed."

Casey let out a wry bark. "Do you know who Walter Reed is, Bert?"

"No."

"The doctor who cured yellow fever. It's also an army hospital."

"That's cute," he retorted. "Not proof. We're waiting for pictures and signatures now. Maybe we can get a match. Until then, you keep your head down."

"I'm gonna break his alibi, Bert," she crowed. "I can feel it in my bones. It's all in those phone logs. Once we have him for Billie, we can break him on everybody else."

She hadn't even heard the lounge door open, she was so excited. Marva's none-too-gentle nudge brought her to attention. Barb was standing in the door, bristling with hostility.

"We're under a tornado alert," she announced briskly into the artificial brightness of the windowless room. Turning her gaze directly to Casey, she finished her message with deliberate warning. "Big storm coming our way. A bad one."

Casey dismissed both her messages without much thought, tired of Barb's tantrums. She was finally getting somewhere, really getting somewhere. She could go back to Buddy's trailer and tell him it would be okay. She could go home to her mother and tell her that Mick had absolved her.

"Trauma code, emergency room seven. Trauma code, emergency room seven."

Casey barely remembered to say good-bye before hanging up the phone on her way out the door.

By the time she and security were in the same place at the same time, Casey thought she was going to lose her mind. All hell had broken loose for a three-hour stretch, and there'd been blood and drunks flying everywhere. They'd just gotten the last upstairs or outside as night shift started to show up.

Casey greeted the oncoming nurses from where security was letting her into Tom's office on the excuse that she'd left her work bag in there. Luckily, the security guard on wasn't diligent enough to wait for her. Casey found the logs within ten minutes.

It took her another half hour to find it. March third, three-to-eleven shift, phone log, recording every doctor called, who placed the call, where the call was placed, whether to office, home, hospital, or through exchange, and when the call was returned. The list of numbers and notes by Hunsacker's name for that afternoon was as damning as it got.

They had placed a call for Hunsacker about another patient at 7:10 through his exchange. He'd answered from Barnes. When Mrs. VanCleve arrived demanding his immediate attendance fifteen minutes later, the call had been replaced. The note next to the time was that Hunsacker had not been contacted because he'd just left Barnes. A full forty minutes before he'd signed off his chart. Repeated calls to the exchange, Barnes, St. Isidore's, and several other locations hadn't located him.

Casey thought she'd feel triumph. She thought she'd feel rockets exploding in her head, singing exultation. She felt oddly empty. It was over. The dance had ended, and she'd just bowed to Hunsacker. It was time to walk away.

Marva was waiting in the lounge along with Barb and a couple of the night crew. Casey lifted the copy she'd made of the log.

"He lied," she announced to her friend. "I have it in black and white. His alibi is pure bullshit."

That frown of worry creased Marva's face, but Casey didn't care. She'd walked on tiptoe too long around here. It was time for them to listen to her and understand. It was her turn to gloat.

Except it was too late for gloating. She just wanted to go home and hand this all off to Bert and crawl into bed until Jack got home the next day. Except that she knew she wouldn't sleep, either. Not knowing that Hunsacker had been in her house, not plagued by that gnawing feeling that if she turned around he'd still be there. Always uncertain, always waiting, even when he was safe inside a five-by-five cell.

Picking her nursing bag off the floor, Casey slid the copy in with the other papers she'd been studying. And then she turned to go.

The new storm was battering the horizon. Casey saw

it the minute she stepped out of the sharp, fluorescent lighting and air-conditioning. Thunder mumbled and cracked. Lightning shuddered in the clouds like distant artillery fire in a World War II movie. The air ahead of it danced in anticipation, trees curtsying welcome, grass shuddering before its onslaught. Gusts of cool air dipped and soared through the familiar humidity like invisible kites.

They were in for it, now. Casey stood for a minute watching it, the capricious wind plucking at her lab coat and winnowing through her hair, and wondered when she was ever going to feel safe enough in her room again to sit on her window seat and welcome that kind of fury.

She should have felt better. Maybe the storm was affecting her, spinning her molecules just like it did the atmosphere's. She walked to her car knowing that she had the end of Hunsacker's career in her hands, and felt furious because she still felt sorry for him. She drove home without calling Bert simply because she wished it had been Jack she could have handed over the final proof to. And she thought of Benny.

The lights were on in the house, Helen's lights and the chapel lights and the lights in the living room. Helen must think that cops needed extra electricity. Either that or she was warding off the storm for Benny. He'd always hated the thunder, even as an adult, cowering from it, hiding from all the windows that let it in. Maybe it was Helen's way to coax Benny back in out of the storm.

Casey pulled in behind Bert's car and shut off the engine. There was a car parked around the corner, but Casey didn't pay any attention to it. That corner was the Mecca of necking spots. She didn't hear the Greasons' dog bark when she got out of the car, so he must have been in already. Good thing Pussy wasn't in heat again.

She would have hated to consign Bert to that kind of shift.

Casey walked into the kitchen and dropped her bag on the floor. She needed something to drink. Then she needed to check on Helen and hand off her information to Bert.

That made her look around. She wondered where Bert had holed up. The house was so quiet, only the refrigerator and the mantel clock keeping her company against the approaching thunder. Casey immediately looked to the sun room, and then realized that it had been Jack who had favored the discomfort of the couch. She found herself smiling at her disappointment at not seeing his familiar form sprawled across the furniture.

Maybe Bert had actually taken her up on the offer of a guest room. Maybe he'd gotten hooked into sitting with Helen while she prayed. Casey almost groaned aloud.

Taking a good slug of iced tea, she pushed the door open to the front hall and headed for the stairs, instinctively flicking off lights and checking windows as she progressed. Lightning flickered in through the big front bays. The wind was beginning to groan at the corners of the house.

Bert had left a cache of paperwork on the hall table, just like Jack. His hat rested atop it, and his jacket was draped over the wingback by the front window. Casey smiled and sipped, reassured by Bert's steadfast presence. Maybe she'd get some sleep tonight after all.

Helen was awake and alone, sitting on her lounger and saying her bedtime rosary. Mick's picture had been moved to the table next to her, where she could see it. Casey wasn't sure what to do about that. Would Helen recover now, or sink deeper into the morass of guilt and self-recrimination?

"Oh, Catherine dear," Helen greeted her with a wan smile, her thumb positioned over the last bead she'd recited. "You're just getting home? I thought I heard you come in already."

"No, Mom. Have you seen Sgt. DeClue?"

Helen made a show of looking around, as if he might be hiding behind the armoire or nightstand. "No, dear, I haven't. He seemed pretty busy, so I came upstairs. Are you going up?"

Casey nodded, backing out just enough to see that the guest-room door was closed. Maybe he'd turned in already. She'd double-check after closing her windows and getting out of her uniform. "I'm pretty tired. See you in the morning?"

Helen thought about it. "I might just . . . visit."

The chapel. Then it wasn't going to get any better. Casey restrained a sigh and smiled a good night before closing the door and climbing the second flight of stairs.

Topping the stairs, she instinctively wrinkled her nose in protest against the incense. The harsh lights washed out the color from Mary's face where she beamed down on her chubby infant and robbed the candles of their mystery. In the dim dusk, the chapel looked quaint, worn like a church tucked in the hills of England where centuries of faithful had rubbed it away with fingers and knees. In the bright light, it looked shabby. A cheap imitation.

Casey walked through it as quickly as she could, now even more uncomfortable with its message, and opened her door. She took another gulp of tea and flipped on the light.

"Oh, good. We've been waiting to see you."

Casey came to a shuddering halt. The glass slipped from her fingers as her mouth opened. She couldn't cry out. She couldn't even breathe. Bert sat stiff and taut on her rocker, a gag stuffed in his mouth, his hands tied behind his back, and his feet tied to the rocker legs. Alongside him, lounging with one of her beers in his hand, a razor-sharp knife bobbing lazily in the other, sat Hunsacker.

He smiled as if Casey had just invited him to dance. "I was really disappointed to see that your good friend Sgt. Scanlon couldn't be here for this," he said. "I especially wanted to see his face when I sliced your ears off."

# Chapter 21

*WHEN A PSYCHOPATH* finally shows himself in the movies, he looks wild. Manic and jerky, as if the poison that fills his brain has spilled out over his nerve pathways. His eyes light and flicker back and forth, and he laughs like Hyde with a beaker in his hand. That isn't the way it happens.

Hunsacker leaned on his side, one elbow on her bright comforter, his eyes settling on her like crows fluttering to a fresh kill. His smile was controlled and pleased, his movements as restrained as a woman at her first formal dinner. He was wearing scrubs, crisp and creased, and looked composed for having been waiting in the shuddering dark of her bedroom with a bound-and-gagged police sergeant.

Casey remembered something she'd read in the material Marva had given her. It said that serial killers were hunters. They just hunted humans. Casey understood that now. She could imagine Hunsacker crouched in a field before dawn, shotgun shouldered and eyes skyward, looking just like this. Waiting, coiling, setting up. A cat curling in on its haunches as it spotted its prey.

The next time she saw one of those movies, when the

killer finally sprang loose, she'd nudge Poppi next to her
and say, No, this is wrong. What they really do is far
more frightening. It's enough to scare you to death before they ever move.

"Nothing to say?" he asked, smiling that self-satisfied
smile of his, his eyes feral. Casey knew Bert was watching
them, trembling with fury. She couldn't afford to look
at him. She couldn't afford to look away from Hunsacker
at all. He might strike without warning.

Lightning seared the sky outside her window and
jolted Casey from her paralysis. The night, it seemed, was
going to shatter instead of the killer.

"I don't . . ." Her voice stumbled over the sudden,
sweeping terror. Thunder slammed into the house, rattling windows and snaking along nerve ends.

Casey had never expected to find him here. Not even
after he'd taunted her with her mother, not even after
the phone calls. She'd balanced her safety on the assump-
tion that he wouldn't sacrifice his audience. The house
groaned with the wind, and Casey shook her head. "I
don't understand."

Hunsacker shifted himself up to a sitting position and
wrapped his arm around the bedpost, the knife still
pointed toward Bert. Casey wanted to scream. She
wanted desperately to run, to slam the door and grab
Helen and flee over to Mr. Rawlings. Her heart thundered with it. Her limbs strained with the temptation.
Her palms had begun to sweat.

But Hunsacker knew her too well already. He only
had to let that knife rise and fall bare inches from Bert's
eyes, his exposed throat, to hold her still.

She couldn't risk Bert. She might get away. She might
even get Helen to react quickly enough to save her, too,
dragging her across the lawn to pound on a closed door

for help in a raging storm. If she did, it would be to come back to find Bert sliced into bloody ribbons.

The lightning glittered along the edge of the blade as if to remind her. It sliced along the edge of Bert's throat, yellow-white against his mahogany skin, dipping into the hollows of his throat that exposed vein and artery and nerve, outlining the path of the blade. There was only so much guilt a person could live with, even to save her own life.

The problem was, Casey didn't know how she could possibly save either of them by staying, either.

"Come on in, Casey," Hunsacker invited, motioning toward the chair where it had been pulled out from her desk. "Get comfortable."

Casey could hardly find breath to speak. "Does the offer come with rope and gag?"

Hunsacker actually laughed. "That's what I like about you," he admitted with a little nod. "I have you hemmed in so tightly at work you shouldn't be able to breathe, and you still insult your supervisor. You got *cojones.*"

Casey stiffened. "Don't say that."

He lifted an eyebrow. "Why? You don't like the compliment?"

"Why are you here now?" she demanded, not moving, not able to act without jerking to a start and stumbling. Dogs did this sometimes; horses, she heard, in a fire. She was frozen in place, only her mouth mobile. Only her mouth that always seemed to get her into trouble anyway. "Sit down," he invited genially, "and I'll tell you."

Casey gave her head a choppy shake. "I'd rather not." Hunsacker's slow smile was truly terrifying. "I'd be happy to convince you," he offered, and before she had a chance to react, he reached over and sliced Bert's cheek.

Casey cried out. Bert flinched, tightened. Blood

welled up from the cut and slid down over the white surgical tape that bisected his face. The knife had swept
within millimeters of his right eye.

"Now, sit," Hunsacker demanded, his eyes back on
Casey.

Her legs shook and her stomach crowded her lungs,
but she managed to get over to the chair. She was turned
at a ninety-degree angle to the door, equally able to see
the bleeding heart of Jesus on one side and the bleeding
cheek of her friend on the other. And behind him, the
storm, still gathering, still building, higher and higher
against the tremulous old walls of the house. Waiting to
pounce, fingers plucking into weak spots, teeth ripping
at exposed viscera. A battle that one day it knew it would
win.

And yet, because it had always withstood, the house
refused to falter.

Hunsacker lifted himself from her bed and strolled
closer. "Actually, I don't want to kill him," he admitted.
"Not yet. I've never had a real audience see my work,
and since Scanlon can't be it, he's my substitute."

Casey clenched her sweaty hands in her lap. She kept
her eyes fixed on Hunsacker's torso as he approached,
the knife bobbing, the erratic light from the window
sluicing along it like bright water, like yellow blood. She
didn't wear earrings, she thought absurdly. Would they
ever be able to identify her? Would they find her, or
would she be lost like that last victim?

"Why now?" Casey repeated, her voice raspy with
strain. "Why not yesterday or last week?"

He crouched down on his haunches before her. Casey
struggled not to flinch away. She could smell his cologne,
that smoky, woodsy scent that was suddenly so much like
the incense in the other room, sickening and heavy and
secretive. She could see all the way back into his eyes,

and there was nothing there. No rage or remorse. The lightning sparked in them only to reveal the crescive anticipation of the hunt. Only the careful, greedy alien that kept seeking her out.

"Because it's over," he admitted in an amused voice, as if he were talking about a play instead of his own murder spree. "You found it tonight, didn't you? I was waiting for you to. It was such a small thing, an oversight when I'm usually so careful. Like these," he said, motioning to the scrubs that were so much a part of him. "Nobody thinks twice about an OB strolling around in them. And the hospital laundry sees so many bloody sets of scrubs, they don't notice one more set. So simple it's brilliant, don't you think?" Casey couldn't answer, mesmerized by his casual dissertation. "All my work is that precise. And yet, all these weeks while we've been courting, I've known I made that one mistake. I've been waiting for you to finally remember." He was delighted, smiling, the knife tip pointed right at Casey's left eye. "I had a secret, and I was waiting for you to find it."

Casey's brain spun. Her chest clamored for air. She fought the urge to press a hand against her sternum to hold her heart inside. She knew he could hear it, was feeding on its terrified staccato. "But there still isn't any hard evidence against you," she protested, trying for anything. "It's all circumstantial."

His smile broadened a little. He lifted his hand, resting the knife tip against Casey's cheek. She shied a little and felt the sharp sting of penetration, just below her cheekbone. "Doesn't matter," he said, his gaze briefly flickering to where Casey felt her own blood welling from the puncture wound. "They're beginning to take you seriously. They never figured me out in Boston, or in New York. Nobody caught on because I was so careful they didn't have any reason to tie the murders together." His gaze slid north again, impaling Casey as surely as his knife. "Until you. I figured if they couldn't catch me in New York, I could live forever in this two-bit wasteland. I could work and hunt to my heart's content. And then the first time you met me, you spotted me. Which is why you'll be my last. My best."

Casey couldn't control the shudder, and it made him smile again. He nodded, satisfied. "Not as brave as you thought, huh? I just have to know, Casey my sweet. How did you know? How did you guess when nobody else did?"

The alien, she wanted to say. That dead, decaying presence that inhabits the backs of your eyes and lubricates your hypnotic voice. "I don't know," she whispered instead. "A . . . gut feeling. The . . . the way you do pelvics."

That provoked the biggest, heartiest laugh she'd ever heard from Hunsacker. "Is that what you told the police?" he demanded. "God, I would have loved to see that."

The knife edged close again, tickling the skin below her eye, so close she instinctively blinked. Sweat began to trickle down between her breasts. Casey couldn't possibly hold still anymore, and yet she did, terrified of that cold, bloody point that caressed her cheek.

Thunder exploded and the house shuddered in protest. Rain slammed against her window. Beyond, trees writhed and screamed. A loose shutter banged against the wall and the wind squealed in delight. But Casey, suspended in breathless agony on the point of a knife, held perfectly still.

"Oh, Casey, there you are."

Hunsacker jerked back. Casey stiffened, the knife missing her cornea by a hairbreadth. She spun toward the door to find Helen standing there, her rosary clutched in her restless hands, her smile tentative and shy.

"A passion play?" she asked, looking around the room. "Really, Casey, Lent's over."

"Mom—"

Hunsacker had gone on point, quivering with restrained energy, ready to pounce either way. Casey's badly frayed composure unraveled dangerously. She didn't even hear the next shattering clap of thunder or notice that Helen shied from it like a nervous horse.

"Come in, Mrs. McDonough," Hunsacker invited, not moving, the knife just inside the shadow of his head.

"Heavens no." She giggled, waving away the invitation, her attention straying to the windows where the storm pounded for entrance. "I never interfere when Casey's entertaining, Benny. You should know that. I will go down and make you children some coffee, though." She'd actually turned away, pulling the door behind her. Casey's heart stumbled to a stop, started.

*Run,* she begged in silence. Get the hell away before he decides he can't count on your delusions.

Helen turned back to them. "Unless you'd like chocolate."

"Coffee," Casey rasped, tears choking her. She'd had a brief surge of hope when her mother had appeared. Helen would run for help. She'd stumble away and Casey would trip Hunsacker as he leapt up to follow. But Helen was lost in the mists tonight. She was wandering somewhere between the Gospel of St. Mark and Tennessee Williams. She nodded brightly and turned away, pulling the door just shy of closing so her daughter could have privacy but not be compromised, without a clue that her daughter would be dead inside a half hour.

"You know what I love about your mother?" Hunsacker asked with a broad smile. "She'll do just that.

She'll walk downstairs and make coffee for when the passion play's over." He nodded, enjoying his observation, his attention never even flickering to the battering, thunderous assault of the storm against the high roof. "I think I'll probably take mine with cream and sugar."

"If you stay to coffee," Casey said. "How do you plan to get away?"

Hunsacker returned his attention to her. She felt it sweep over her like a cold, deadly wave. "Oh, I won't," he assured her. "That's why this has to be my best job. Because after this, they'll make me stop." The knife lifted, sought her skin as if it had a hunger of its own. "I practiced on that last one," he admitted. "It had been a while since I'd let myself enjoy a knife. It's part of the discipline, you know. Using it in surgery on women and not ever hurting them. Clean and sweet and swift, without pain or scarring. Controlling myself when I lay that scalpel against their skin." He pressed the knife close, the edge testing the elasticity of skin like a scalpel the second before penetration when a surgeon sets up his site, gathers his initiative, hesitates before the moment of mutilation. "I lay them open like fish, and then I sew them back up."

The knife sliced along her cheek. Casey knew it was cutting before she felt it. Her body protested even before it allowed the pain. She opened her mouth, the terror too great for words, her eyes tearing and wide, the night sobbing for her.

"But the others, I don't sew back up," he admitted, watching the trail of his handiwork. His eyes glittered in the deathly light now, flickering life where there was none. "I watch the filth spew out of them. I lean close so I can smell it, the sweet stink of death."

He brought his face right up against hers and Casey flinched away. She heard a thud of the beer can hitting the floor, and then his hand wrapped around the other side of her head, holding her against him.

"Yes," he said with a small, satisfied nod. "It smells right on you, too."

Casey fought against the whimpering that bubbled in her throat. She pushed the paralysis away. "Who was she?" she asked, trying to keep contact with those brutal, deadly eyes. "The last one."

He dipped a finger in her blood and tasted it. "Doesn't matter," he said, sucking on the end of his finger like Casey did when she was licking a bowl of icing. "She served her purpose."

"What did you do with her?"

He smiled with satisfaction. "You'll never find her. Nothing but what I've already given you."

Casey's cheek burned. Blood dripped off her jaw and onto the clean white of her uniform. She was trembling now, his touch cold and purposeful.

"What do you think?" Hunsacker asked, turning her head so Bert could see her cheek. Casey could hardly see him through the tears. He seemed no more than a shadow against the storm. "Is that a great cut? And that cunt from Izzy's said I couldn't use a knife. Want to see another?"

Hunsacker lifted the knife toward her other cheek. Casey instinctively defended herself. Pulling away, she brought her left hand up. She never stood a chance. Hunsacker just sliced her palm, from ring finger to thumb.

Casey cried out, jerked away. Hunsacker grabbed her by the hair and held her back on the chair. "I don't think you understand," he told her in a gentle voice, his eyes purposeful. Reaching down behind the chair, he brought up a heavy black gun and pointed it at the same eye he'd showed the knife. "I also have the officer's gun. And you know I like guns, too, Casey. I can kill you both now,

and then go down and slice up your mother . . . or"—
he smiled, slowly, significantly—"you can play along for
a while and still have a chance at escape. What would you
like?"

She was whimpering now, tears mingling with the
blood on her cheek, her hand clenched to hold in the
pain, her fingers already sticky and warm. Staring down
the black, black barrel of that gun where it waited, steady
and silent before her. She didn't even notice the storm
anymore as it threw its greatest artillery at the house.
Windows rattled. Boards moaned and popped. Thunder
echoed nonstop from one hill to the next and back again.
And Casey never heard. Never saw anything but that
gun, the black gleam of blood on the sleek tip of the
knife.

"Tell me, Casey," he demanded softly.

She couldn't speak. He yanked a little harder on her
hair, pulling her head back. He brought the blade down
against her throat. "Tell me."

"Wait," she gurgled, shaking and sick, her eyes instinctively squeezing shut.

"Please," he reminded her, just like a parent instructing a recalcitrant child.

She gasped, sobbed, struggled to regain her control.
"Please."

"Please, Daddy," he taunted. "Don't go."

Casey's eyes flew open. "No—"

The knife bit, so close to her carotid she could feel her
own driving pulse push at the blade. "You heard me,"
he demanded.

"P-please, Daddy, do-don't . . . go."

She was going to vomit; she was going to faint. Her
head swam with fireflies. The house closed in on her,
fetid and cloying, like the smell of funeral flowers. The

smell of her own blood filled her nostrils, thick and metallic. The sweet stink of death.

The knife lifted. Hunsacker raised his head and sniffed. "Ah, there it is." He smiled brightly. "Coffee. I knew I could count on her."

Casey heard him place the gun on her desk, just out of reach. She knew his attention was wavering just a little. She should jump up. She should at least try to disarm him, give them all a fighting chance. She wasn't even tied to the chair, for God's sake.

She didn't move. Her cheek shrieked in protest. Her hand curled in on itself, her middle two fingers limp from the tendons he'd sliced. Her blood splashed color into the faded roses on her oriental rug. Her ears rang with terror.

He'd restrained her with no more than the memory of that terrible knife against her skin, the knowledge of what it could do to her face, her eyes. She couldn't move for fear that the knife would strike before she could escape.

He'd won after all. No matter whether or not the evidence to convict him waited down in her bag on the kitchen floor. He'd made her crawl, made her beg for more, just like before. He'd swamped her in shame, and was going to make her wallow in it before he finally did just what he came to do. She was helpless, and that was his victory.

Still, instinctively, she fought. "You and I have a lot in common," she offered, willing interest into a voice already dead. Facing him, forcing him to see her as a person instead of a target.

Surprised, he looked back down at her. "We don't have anything in common," he assured her, lifting a hand to run his fingers through her hair. "I'm a doctor and you're just a nurse."

Absurdly, Casey giggled. How many times had she heard that one? Every doctor who had ever been threatened by her assertiveness, every resident who had ever been insulted when she'd questioned an order. She didn't think that insult would ever sound the same again.

If she heard it again. The giggle ended in a strangled little hiccup. "No, I mean our fathers," she offered on a voice that wavered with resurrected fear.

"Oh, I don't think so," Hunsacker answered. "Your father was an asshole who worked in a brewery and beat his wife. My father was a well-respected surgeon from a very good family."

Who molded the monster before her with his own hands, Casey wanted to say. "You got along with your father?"

The fingers tugged hard, pulling some hairs from their shafts. "I respected him. Just like everybody."

Silence. Outside, the storm paused, receded before striking again. Casey fought for something more to say, some way to show that she understood what he'd faced as a child.

"I think it's just about showtime," he murmured, his fingers clenching in Casey's hair. "I want to be gone before the storm's over."

Casey could only see one side of his torso. Some of her blood had stained the dull green. He looked as if he'd just walked out of a delivery.

"Take off your clothes," he commanded.

Casey froze. "What?"

He pulled harder, lifting her just a little way up by her hair. "I said take your clothes off. Now, do it."

She began to shake, closing her eyes and then opening them, her hands lifting helplessly, stopping short of interfering. Choking on the new, flashing fear. "I can't . . . my hand."

Hunsacker yanked her straight to her feet. Casey cried out, her good hand instinctively reaching for the pain. Fresh tears burned her eyes, scalded her cheek. *Please,* she wanted to beg. Please don't do this to me. I'll do anything.

I'll do . . .

No.

No. It was what he wanted. He wanted her to beg, to plead. He wanted her on her hands and knees.

Casey wasn't sure how the revelation wormed its way through the terror. She didn't know why suddenly she saw it so clearly when only seconds before all she wanted was to be away from the knife.

He was going to kill her. But the torture he intended was the very act she most dreaded. Not rape or disfigurement. Humiliation. Pleading for him to do anything, just as long as she stayed alive. *Pleading for him to continue.*

If she begged again, he'd win. He'd ruin her in a far worse way than even rape and murder, because she wouldn't have escaped her past after all. She'd let him act out her worst humiliation.

He would make it worse if she begged him.

Casey struggled for composure. She swallowed her tears and let her hands fall back to her side. The knife danced next to her throat, chilly and lethal. There was a new fire in Hunsacker's eyes.

"Say please," he coached. "Please, Dr. Hunsacker, don't do this to me, and I might not make you strip."

She wasn't sure where she got the courage. Maybe it was only blind rage. Instinctive pride. Her breath still caught on sobs. Her heart beat even harder. Her knees wavered. She was going to die. Helen wasn't going to save her and Bert wasn't going to save her. If she didn't save herself, it wouldn't matter. So, she was going to at least fight for her self-esteem.

"Now you're going to have to beg on your knees," he commanded. "And maybe I won't kill you after all."

Casey pulled away and faced him. Silent. Challenging. Pushed as far as she could go.

It took some effort one-handed, but in the end, her uniform lay in a blood-smudged pile at her feet. She stood before Hunsacker in bra and panties. The storm gave a howl and swung back into action. Casey ignored it. She met Hunsacker's gaze with every ounce of deter mination she could muster.

Keep him off center. Keep an eye on the gun. *Do something.*

Hunsacker shook his head in wonder. "You're not nearly as much fun as the last one," he admitted. "She begged for two hours before I killed her." The knife homed in, circling, searching. "I think this time I'll send Scanlon one of your breasts." Hunsacker looked her in the eye, daring her to say something. He let the knife caress her nipple, rasping against the silk like an adder. "Not very big breasts," he taunted with that slick, horrible smile of his, "but nice."

Casey fought down a shudder, then another. She choked on more tears. But she faced him, silent, straight, her hands clenched and her head up.

Anger. White, fierce, brushing at the edges of the terror, demanding room. Casey was furious that she was a victim, that all the other women had been victims to this man without anyone helping or interfering.

"Nothing to say?" Hunsacker asked, letting the knife press deeper, slicing through the fabric. "I'll do it, Casey. Just ask for it."

Thunder shuddered through the house. Rain swept back over it. The wind howled and whined. Casey remained silent.

"Casey, dear?" There was tapping on the door.

Hunsacker froze. The knife slid along the edge of Casey's skin.

She jumped back. "Mom!" she yelled. "Get out of here! You—"

Hunsacker swung at her, the knife fully extended. Casey lunged away. She blindly reached across him for the gun. She was inches from it when he caught her by the hair and yanked her back. Casey screamed, furious, fighting. Both hands up to ward off the terrible slice of the knife. She never heard the crack of a branch. Never saw the lightning sever it or the wind wrench it free. Suddenly it slammed into her window. Glass exploded over the room. The wind swept in, tumbling books and magazines.

Casey shrieked in surprise. Hunsacker whipped around at the sudden fury, dragging Casey around with him. She couldn't take her eyes from the knife, the terrible knife. She kept both hands on his wrist, writhing in his grasp, kicking.

To her left, the door slammed open. It should have swung shut with that wind. Rain pelted her, even across the room. The cold wind stung her. It plastered Hunsacker's hair in his eyes so that he couldn't see well when he turned back to threaten Casey's mother.

Only it wasn't Casey's mother. It was Scanlon.

"Jack!"

Hunsacker pulled her against him, the knife back to her throat. Taut, trembling, very lethal.

Game time was over. Casey went limp.

It was all right, though. Jack was here. He'd take care of her. He'd pull her away from Hunsacker before he loosed that knife on her. Casey felt the sobs breaking free again, even with the razor-thin blade against her throat.

"What the hell are you doing here?" Hunsacker demanded.

Jack had taken up the shooter's position. His clothes were sodden, his hair plastered back. His legs were planted wide for balance and his arms were outstretched, holding his gun in perfect alignment with Hunsacker's head.

"Casey," he said, never looking away from his target. "I had to cancel my trip. Chicago found my witness and I had to go get her."

She tried to nod, but Hunsacker held her too tightly. "He's got a gun," she managed, just before the blade punctured. Another tiny hole, a warning. A promise. She flinched again, tried not to close her eyes or weep. The blade was pressing against her trachea. One slice and she'd be gurgling through her neck, drowning in her own blood. She tried to concentrate on Jack, on helping him get her free, but it was so hard to do.

Jack nodded. "I know. Are you okay?"

She wanted him to look at her. She needed him to tell her that everything was going to be okay now.

"I'm fine," she whispered, even as her blood slid in watery rivulets down her neck, down her chest to stain her bra.

"You can see how sharp the knife is," Hunsacker said in a conversational tone. "I'd hate for it to slip."

"Me, too," Jack agreed. "Because if it did, I wouldn't kill you. I'd cripple you. You'd spend the rest of your life in prison hobbling around on your knees and pickin' your ass with your toes."

Casey could almost hear Hunsacker's smile. "And I," he said, "can disfigure. I can ruin her without ever being enough in the clear for a good shot. So who wins?"

The lightning was in the room now, the thunder spilling over the shattered window. Rain peppered the floor and the wind whirled through to snuff the vigil lights. Casey was shaking again, caught between hope and despair. The knife too close, too quick for Jack to save her. She sated herself on the sight of him, settling all her prayers on him. All her wasted aspirations. Tears spilled over unheeded now that it was too late to care.

"So," Jack said to Hunsacker, "what do we have to trade?"

Casey felt her knees giving out on her again. She could only stand this so long. She could only hurt and dread and hope so much.

"Nothing," Hunsacker said. "See—"

Another branch slammed into the window. The sound was like a fresh explosion. Hunsacker jerked back and around. Casey's eyes flew open to see Jack coiling to spring. The knife had slipped a little. Hunsacker had let go one arm to reach around him.

Casey twisted away. She heard Hunsacker yell at her. Jack fired. Hunsacker jerked and spun back around. Casey saw it, then. He had the gun in his hand.

"Jack, no!" she screamed, whirling on her knees.

She was too late. Hunsacker fired. The impact of the heavy weapon threw Jack back through the door. His gun clattered to the floor out in the chapel where the votive lights had died.

And Casey was left with Hunsacker, who had just leveled his gun back on her.

# Chapter 22

*"BEG NOW,"* he advised, standing over her, the gun wavering in his left hand, the rain slicing his face like tears, his eyes dark hollows in the storm. "That son of a bitch shattered my right elbow. My operating arm."

Casey didn't take her eyes from him. She knelt before him, her chest heaving, her limbs trembling and spent. She saw the blood soak his forearm and wash over his hand. His wasted hand that could have performed miracles.

The knife he'd wielded lay between them on the carpet. Casey could easily reach it and he knew it. She thought she counted on it. He was waiting for her to try for it, to expend her hope on a futile move. Because the minute she wrapped her hand around that blade, he'd put a bullet through her head.

She held hands out to her sides, face up to Hunsacker. In a classic pose of supposition, Bernadette at Fatima, St. Catherine before her Christ. All those martyrs before their executioners. Only Casey wasn't going to be a martyr. Not after what Hunsacker had just done. She had to pay him back for Jack.

Her chest shrieked with impatience. Her hands trembled to be doing something. Anything. Jack could be lying in there dying, and she needed to help. But she held still, because it was the only way.

"I said beg to me, Casey my sweet," Hunsacker grated, shoving the gun closer.

He didn't realize that a gun, in the end, was no more terrifying than a knife. A gun was too abrupt, too imprecise to insinuate its power. It couldn't nick and slice, inflicting punishment before the pain was felt. It couldn't slide home without a sound, which was the most terrifying thing of all.

Casey sobbed and shuddered, but she held still. She knew better than to try for a knife she'd never use. Besides. She didn't need a knife or a gun. She'd just realized that she had an effective weapon at hand. If she could only get that hand to work.

"He's dying out there," Hunsacker taunted, his smile slick. "This is a .357 Magnum. Your friend likes a lot of firepower. You're a trauma nurse. You know what a slug like that can do, ripping through tissue, severing arteries. He could be bleeding to death out there. Maybe you can still get to him if you beg me."

She edged her hands out just a little more. Folded just a little into herself as if she were settling into a better position for pleading. She was really steeling herself to move. The next lightning flash. The next clap of thunder. Anything to get his attention.

"Hunsacker!" Jack yelled. "Here!"

That would work.

Jack rolled across the doorway. Hunsacker swung the gun after him and fired. Casey lunged for the chair and shoved it straight at Hunsacker.

It threw him off balance. She jumped to her feet and grabbed the chair with both hands. Hunsacker was just pulling the gun around to her when she swung the chair right for his knees. He fired. The bullet exploded inches from Casey's head. She dove for the far side of the desk just as Hunsacker lost his balance and toppled.

"Casey!" Jack yelled. "Stay down!"

She sobbed just at the sound of his voice. God, she'd thought he was dead. She'd thought she'd survived just long enough to lose him. She heard Hunsacker's gun thud to the floor. She heard Jack scuttle into the room. And then she heard what could only be fists.

She wanted to get up and help. She needed to help Jack. She knew he'd been hurt, and even though Hunsacker was hurt, too, she knew what his strength was like. He was crazy. Crazy people had no physical limits. She needed to get over and see to Bert. At least to run out that door and get more help.

Suddenly though, curled in her little corner with her knees in the glass and her arms wrapped around her chest, she couldn't move. She just didn't have any more in her. Her chest was on fire from fear. Her cheek and throat ached and her hand still dripped blood down her other arm. She heard the grunts and scuffling, heard Bert's mutters of desperate frustration, heard the dying whine of the wind and the irritable grumble of thunder, and all she wanted to do was hold herself together, because she knew if she let go she'd shatter into a million pieces and never find her way together again.

A gun spun into view. Casey looked up. She could hear Jack and Hunsacker struggling. She saw the gun, out there by itself on her carpet, and knew that she had to be the one to get it. Bert moaned with rage. Casey didn't hear him. She had to move from her position of safety. She shuddered, the terror still a living thing, twisting through her guts and spilling down her legs.

"Casey . . ." Jack panted. "Throw . . . throw something out . . . the window." His words ended in a grunt of pain.

Casey stiffened behind her desk, afraid to look, sure she was going to lift her head and come face-to-face with Hunsacker. Knowing if she did, it wouldn't matter if she lived or not. It would already be too much. She scuttled instead for the gun, not even feeling the glass against her legs. Not feeling the cold wind that raised goose bumps on her naked, wet skin. Only hearing the desperate sounds on the other side of that solid desk, only swimming in her own desperation.

The gun was heavy. She hadn't really ever held one. It drooped in her fingers, surprisingly warm for the chill of the room. She lifted it, weighed it. Briefly squeezed her eyes shut when she realized that by picking it up, she'd consigned herself to action.

"Casey!"

She started. Looked around. For a minute she actually thought of throwing out the gun. Then she found her *Taber's Medical Dictionary* right at her elbow, the pages fluttering in the breeze. Small, compact, heavy enough to make an impact. Symbolic as hell. She picked it up and heaved it as hard as she could. It bounced with several satisfying thumps over the porch roof and off. She hoped that was what Jack meant.

Then she lifted the gun again and crept around the desk.

Hunsacker had his hand around Jack's throat. Jack fought him off, raining bruising blows to his face and head, pulling at his fingers. It was Jack's shoulder that had been hit. Casey could see the blood, black against his shirt, saw the weakness in that hand. She saw the madness in Hunsacker's eyes, and knew that Jack would never break that hold. He was dying and he didn't even know it.

She couldn't shoot. She'd never done it, and they were too close, rolling back and forth. She held the gun impotently out before her, her hands slippery against the grip, pointing it and knowing that it wouldn't do any good. Still sobbing, still trembling so badly she couldn't hold the gun still. She was doing no good. She heard noises downstairs. Footsteps. Help. But they were going to be too late. Hunsacker was already smiling in triumph. Jack's strength was ebbing.

That was when she saw that Hunsacker had managed to grab the knife in his injured hand. And she knew what to do with her gun. Taking it by the barrel in her good hand, she swung it at him. Hard.

He didn't fall. But he faltered, just enough for Jack to get leverage. Forcing those deadly fingers from around his neck, he landed a roundhouse punch that laid Hunsacker flat out. It sent Jack right over, too. He'd used the injured arm.

Casey scuttled over to him.

"The gun," he grunted, doubled over and gasping as he pushed her away.

Looking down, she realized that Hunsacker was already stirring. She turned the gun around and fitted it back in her hands. And then, kneeling just alongside where Hunsacker lay sprawled on her ruined carpet, she nestled it right against his cheekbone.

His eyes fluttered open. Casey shuddered, deep inside her. He stared right at her, Satan spotting a vulnerable soul, and smiled. And just with that small expression, he almost broke the rest of her reserve.

Fury slammed through her. Hatred, as vivid and scorching as the lightning that had seared the sky. Exploding in her chest, racing through her arms, warming the gun in her hands.

It trembled in her grasp, grating against his cheekbone. It dug deep with Casey's fight for control. She suddenly wanted nothing more than to blow his brains out.

To win this game the way Hunsacker would have played it. She saw that cocky, slick smile that told her he knew just what she was thinking, and she wanted to obliterate all thought from that diseased mind. She wanted something back for all the times she'd begged in her life.

She suddenly, desperately, wanted to live out the fantasies that had seen her through his tormenting.

*Beg me,* she thought, just the way she'd thought over the phone, in the hallway, in the patients' rooms. But her litany had changed. Beg me to live, grovel and sweat and shake because I won't listen.

She didn't even hear the pounding of feet up her stairs. She didn't see the crowd of police in SWAT uniforms jostle for position at the door and spill into the room, rifles and pistols and shotguns bristling. She didn't see Jack helped to his feet or Bert untied. She was communicating with Hunsacker.

"Tell me," she said, her voice high and quavery, tears dripping onto Hunsacker's throat. "Tell me you killed them. Admit to it."

His smile just broadened. "Or what?" he asked. "You'll kill me?"

She smiled back, a terrible smile. "And nobody here would see it."

She knew there were other people in the room. But except for Jack and Hunsacker and Bert, they didn't matter. The four of them were the only people in the world, the only ones with voices right now. Casey never took her eyes from Hunsacker, demanding his answer. Demanding retribution.

"I don't think so," he answered. "I want you to think of me. When you turn off the lights and you think you see a shadow, or when you see an almost-familiar face in the crowd. When you look at scrubs or a hospital incinerator. I want you to wonder how I slipped by everybody. How many times I slipped by. I want you to die wondering."

Casey felt the trigger against her index finger, a smooth crescent of steel, cool, compact, efficient. She heard the breath go out of the room. She knew Jack stepped up behind her. She could feel him, a curious warmth that seeped into the edges of her consciousness. He never said a word. Never spoke caution or intervention. He never reached for the gun.

He didn't have to.

Casey saw it. She wasn't sure how close she was to crossing that line, to actually giving in to the poison Hunsacker had fed her. Her hands began to shake so badly that she was abrading his skin. Her jaw ached and her heart stumbled. She was too spent to differentiate between Hunsacker's cruelty and Frank's and Mick's. She just wanted closure on all of it. She wanted to be the one to walk away whole for a change. She wanted them to understand even for that brief millisecond before she pulled the trigger what she'd gone through.

But then she realized what Jack did. She saw, as brief as the flicker of dying lightning, the truth in Hunsacker's eyes. She saw the anticipation, the sudden yearning.

He wanted to die. He wanted her to kill him.

Casey shook her head. She struggled to breathe. Her purpose died in silence. The game was over and nobody won. But at least Casey had stopped being manipulated. Hunsacker had targeted her, because he'd instinctively known she could be the one to kill him. He'd been taunting her to do it all along, to commit the act he hadn't had the guts to commit himself. To shoulder that terrible responsibility. But she wouldn't. And maybe that would be enough.

Very carefully, she lifted the gun away. She removed

her finger from the trigger guard and handed the weapon back to Jack. He plucked it out of her hands.

"Get this piece of shit off the nice lady's floor," he grated, and three of the other cops jumped at the chance.

Casey felt Jack's hand at her shoulder. He helped her to her feet and slid a robe over her shoulders. She couldn't look away from Hunsacker as they cuffed his hands behind his back. He still looked so calm, so composed. If a stranger walked into this room, and somebody said to pick out the serial killer in the crowd, they would have pointed to Jack before they would have singled out Hunsacker. Jack looked angry and frustrated and disheveled. Even after what had happened, Hunsacker looked like a man without worry, without sin. He walked out of the room without once looking back.

"Sarge, you'd better let the paramedics take a look at you."

Jack waved off the SWAT officer's concern. "Get down and tell one of the county guys to find where he left his car. I want it searched." The guy nodded and followed his friends down, and Jack turned back to Casey. He could hear the troop of feet clatter down the stairs along with Hunsacker. He heard Mrs. McDonough's high, thin voice as she greeted everybody as if they were a high-school football team on their way home from a victory. The bullet-proof vest suddenly felt very heavy. Blood slid down his arm and dripped from his now-useless hand. His shoulder throbbed all the way up his neck. His neck felt as if it were on fire. He could still feel Hunsacker's fingers around it.

But right now, his attention was all Casey's. She stood staring after Hunsacker, a robe draped over her shoulders, her face ravaged and her eyes as flat as death. Jack hoped he would never again feel like he had when he'd

swung that door open. He'd taken in the scene in practiced eye, the clutter of debris, DeClue struggling in the
chair by the window, that damn branch only inches from
his head. Hunsacker, his eyes triumphant and deadly,
with that flensing knife at Casey's throat.

Jack had damn near shot him on the spot. He might
have tried if it hadn't been Casey he'd held, if it hadn't
been her throat streaming in blood from the cuts he'd
inflicted, fresh blood welling from the tip of the knife
as Hunsacker had sunk it in just deep enough to make
a point.

God, she'd scared him. Scared him deep where he
didn't think he could feel it anymore. From the minute
he got the news until he'd seen her turn those haunted
blue eyes on him, he'd lived a hundred lives. He'd lived
ten more trying to get Hunsacker away from her before
he had the chance to lay open her throat.

And then, waiting until she'd made up her mind that
Hunsacker wasn't worth killing back.

Standing beside her, watching her stark, ashen face,
Jack shook his head. He'd seen a lot of victims. He'd seen
a lot of perps. He'd never seen anyone with more
strength.

"Come on, Casey," he coaxed, tugging the robe more
tightly around her bare shoulders where now he saw
faint scars from other confrontations. "Why don't we go
on downstairs. It's getting cold up here."

She started at his touch, looked over. Jack bit back a
curse at the brutal slash on her cheek. He hoped that son
of a bitch died bad.

"Why don't you slip on the robe?" he said with a half
smile, his hand back on her shoulder, suddenly needing
to touch her, just to reassure himself that she was all
right. That she was alive.

She looked up at him, tears still sliding unheeded

down her cheeks. "Your arm . . ." she protested, lifting
a hand toward him.

Jack backed away just a little. "Oh, it's okay. Now,
come on."

She actually managed a wry quirk of the lips. "I
thought when you were shot, you weren't going to let
a policeman take care of you."

He smiled back, relieved and awed. She stood in no
more than underwear and a tattered seersucker robe that
was already flowering with blood. Her hair was tangled,
blood streaked and caked her face and throat, and her
eyes were still huge and dark with the residue of violence. And yet she was so poised that Hunsacker had
been the one humiliated rather than his intended victim.

"All right," he conceded. "We'll both be seen."

She smiled, more wistfully, more uncertainly, and
turned to slip her arm through the robe. Between the
two of them they had two decent hands, and managed
the task with a maximum of fuss. And touching. Casey
seemed to need it as much as Jack.

"How did you get here?" she asked, her voice still raw
as Jack finished a one-handed knot on her belt.

Jack smoothed the hair back from her forehead with
a hand that shook. "Your mother. She called 911 and
told them to tell me that Mick was here."

"Mom?" she countered, incredulous.

Jack nodded. He didn't add the part that Helen had
been waiting by the front door with a complete silver tea
service in order to serve him coffee when he slipped in
the door.

He lifted his hand again, and dropped it, frustrated
and suddenly stupid when there was so much that he
needed to say. Like how he'd never been so terrified as
when she'd turned those eyes on him and expected him
to save her. Like he would have suffered anything rather

than have let her end up in Hunsacker's hands. How he'd died just getting that call, and that he'd never let her face something like that again.

Then Jack lifted her hand to tie his handkerchief around it, and saw the damage Hunsacker had inflicted there. His heart stopped all over again.

"You did a good job, Casey," was all he could manage. Stiff and formal and uncomfortable as he clumsily wrapped the sodden white linen and tucked in the edges.

She set those eyes on him again, suddenly a lost little girl where she'd never allowed vulnerability before. "It was so hard for a minute to separate them all," she admitted. "I couldn't tell Hunsacker from Frank from . . ."

Tears swelled and spilled, and she bent her head. Jack lifted it with a finger. "Did I tell you I was a priest once?" he asked. "I'm very good at absolving guilt."

Casey gave her head a little shake. "He should have paid, shouldn't he?"

"I'm not talking about him," he corrected. "I'm talking about you."

Casey stiffened. "I'm not guilty of anything," she countered with the first spark of life.

Jack smiled down at her. "Not bad for starters. We'll work on getting you to believe it."

Casey's answering smile was at once wanton and unsure. "I'd sure like to try," she agreed. It was enough to break a man's heart.

Jack ignored the other cops who still milled around and pulled her close. "We'll begin sessions as soon as we have a full complement of working limbs," he promised. Then he nuzzled against her hair. "Maybe sooner."

He kept his arm around her as they headed down the stairs. "We got the license matchup," he told her, walking her slowly down toward where the paramedics were waiting in the living room. "Hunsacker owns two black

Porsches. He waited a full six weeks to get the damage fixed on the one he hit Billie with. I got in an hour ago with my witness."

"Cookies?" Helen chirped to the crowd, standing at the bottom of the stairs with a tray in her hands and a white gauze apron over her brown dress. "I have tea or coffee, whichever you'd like."

One of the SWAT guys strolled by munching on a ladyfinger. The paramedics were balancing demitasses of coffee on their knees. Bert was flexing his fingers over by the piano as he talked to Ernie, a short, balding Jewish guy who kept shaking his head and grinning at the fix his partner had gotten himself in to.

"I'll tell you," another SWAT member said to his partner as he watched out the door, slapping the water from his cap. "I damn near got hit by lightning when I was standing on that friggin' porch roof. Scared the shit outta me."

"I notice it took you three tries to get the branch through the window, hotshot," the other guy said, munching and grinning. "You're not pitching for the team this summer."

"Bullshit! You try and lob a branch straight up a story in a thirty-mile-an-hour wind and see how easy it is."

Casey was shaking again beneath the flimsy material. Jack held on tighter. She was definitely due for a round of shock. He saw the paramedics looking for someplace to set the coffee as they got to their feet. He wasn't exactly sure yet how he felt about handing Casey off to them.

"Well, Father, there you are," Helen sang, sailing in. "Coffee? Casey, really. You shouldn't greet the guests in your swimwear."

Jack noticed, though, that there were tears in the little woman's eyes as she turned back for the kitchen.

"Uh, excuse me . . ."

One of the paramedics was pointing to the hardwood floor. Jack looked down to see he was dripping blood on it. Damn. No wonder he was starting to feel so washed out. He was going to have to hand Casey off after all.

She was turning to him, her hand coming up, her mouth open to chastise, when a shout went up outside. They all turned. More cries of alarm.

"Stop or I'll fire!"

"Shit!" Jack was already at the door when the shots rang out. Dozens of them, a chain reaction of adrenaline and fear and firepower. Jack reached the porch just in time to see Hunsacker seize under the impact of all those bullets and fall to the lawn.

"What the hell happened?" he demanded, running for him.

Casey was right on his heels.

Hunsacker lay half on the sidewalk, blood pooling beneath him, the handcuffs dangling from one hand, his feet splayed and his eyes open. Really dead this time. He twitched and sighed. A dark stain spread down his pants leg to match the bouquet on his chest. A ragged cloud lifted from the circle of guns that had brought him down, and the air stank with cordite.

"He got out of the cuff," a SWAT sergeant admitted, stunned. That kind of thing just didn't happen. "He actually ran for us. Straight for us."

Jack stood over him, trying to decide how he felt. Furious, because they would never know now. They would never be able to prove that he'd killed all the women they suspected him of. Relieved that he didn't have to worry about his ever getting away.

"He said he didn't want to hang around," Casey said next to him. Jack took her back in his arm. "But dammit, why should he have the easy way out? Now, we'll never know. We'll never find that last girl.''

They all stood there, dark-suited police ringing the dead killer like a circle of priests at a ritual. Silent, staring, wondering. Trying to cull the essence of violence from minerals and water. And into their midst stepped little Mrs. McDonough in her brown dress and bandanna and apron. She knelt right in that pool of blood and lifted Hunsacker's head into her lap.

"It's all right, now, Benny," she crooned, stroking his hair back with trembling hands. "It was the only way. You see, I knew you weren't Mick all along." Her tears spilled onto his face. They were the only tears spent for Dale Hunsacker.

Separating herself from Jack, Casey walked up and bent to her mother. With gentle patience, she helped her back to her feet and walked her back in the house. And Dale Hunsacker was alone again.

"When does the cast come off?" Marva asked.

Casey didn't look up from where she was using an endotracheal guide to scratch beneath the plaster. "Another three weeks," she said. "Then I'm in splints. This tendon shit's a pain in the ass."

Marva grinned. "Well, at least you have your sense of humor."

Casey scowled. "What I have is three more weeks of call backs and telemetry monitoring. I'm ready to tear my hair out."

"Tom thinks he's being magnanimous keeping you on the job. This wasn't a work-related injury, ya know."

Casey knew. She'd been the one sitting in on insurance claims, personnel conferences, and legal meetings. Everybody had just wanted to make sure that Casey didn't file anything official that blamed them for her injuries.

Her injuries she could live with. She still couldn't imagine how they could sleep knowing they were responsible for Janice's death. Because if they hadn't harassed Casey, they might have uncovered Hunsacker's little truths sooner.

As it was, he left on his own terms. The notebook had never been discovered. Just select pages, left right in the middle of his dining-room table to taunt the searchers with the knowledge that there had been more, but they'd lost it. They had his precise schedule for murdering Billie and murdering Wanda. The rest would always be conjecture, circumstance, and chance.

They had found trophies. Dozens of them, earrings, rings, snapshots, keys. Three teeth and a dog collar. They were going to have to pass the artifacts around to all the unsolved homicides in Boston and New York and see if they came up with a match. Buddy got Wanda's earrings. Aaron retrieved a locket of Janice's. Marilyn had Elizabeth Peebles's wedding ring, and Casey had asked for Billie's nursing pin.

"I'm just glad it's over," Casey said.

It wasn't, of course. She still had nightmares. She found herself seeing Hunsacker in crowds, just like before, watching her. Smiling. And, of course, she was still dealing with Mick. But Jack had proven good to his word, and the emotional scars were fading apace with the physical ones.

"How's Jack doing?" Marva asked.

That made Casey smile. She'd been smiling a lot lately, as a matter of fact, from the first walk she'd taken down to sit in his room when he came out of surgery to the ride they'd taken the night before with Mr. Rawlings in the Mustang. Not quite the same ride as Jack, but impressive for a quiet gardener.

"He's as crabby as I am," she admitted, sliding the purloined stylus back in her bag and picking up her iced tea. "They have him on light duty for another three weeks."

"I thought his arm was okay."

Casey grinned. "Not for his arm. For his ulcer. That's what's really ticking him off. They finally caught up with him."

Marva just grinned. "You two were meant for each other."

It was a quiet evening. Baseball was on television and the humidity kept even the kids off the streets. Casey and Marva sat back by room twelve sharing a bag of pretzels and some isolation from Barb, who had never quite recovered.

"So, what now?" Marva asked.

"What do you mean, what now?" Casey retorted. "Now I do my best to keep my job until I get tenured. Which is at least seven more years."

Marva just nodded.

Just about then, a blond head popped around the corner.

"Hey, space cadet," Marva greeted her. "How you be?"

Poppi stepped into the work lane, beaming and clutching a large, fat manila envelope. "Ladies, I have some good news. How would you like to be rich?"

Casey snorted. "Oh, God, not another game. What's this one, Change Partners, the game of Eastern Europe?"

But Poppi wasn't going to be dissuaded. She settled herself onto the edge of Casey's desk and lifted the envelope into view. "No," she countered. "Same game. Nirvana. In which both of you invested a hundred dollars, thereby becoming one-third partners in its future."

Marva stiffened a little in her chair. "You got somebody to look at it?"

Poppi beamed. "I got somebody to buy it. Milton

Bradley is sending their lawyers out next week. We have been asked if we'd like to split two million dollars and a percentage of the sales, with future deals included.''

Casey's jaw dropped. "Get outta here," she retorted instinctively.

Poppi grinned at her. "You're rich, girl. Get a real pool.''

Casey still couldn't comprehend it. Yesterday she'd been on the hospital hit list—the negative kind, pressured because she couldn't assume her full duties, pressured because she was worth a good salary and they didn't want to spend the money on her. Pressured because she'd slammed into Tom's office to offer proof that Ahmed was an imminent threat to the hospital's medical malpractice coverage. Pressured most of all because she'd been right all along, and no one but Marva was going to forgive her for it.

And suddenly Poppi was telling her that none of that mattered. She was independently wealthy. She could sit at home and paint daisies on dinner plates if she wanted. She could buy one of those big old houses down off Skinker and spend the rest of her life trying to find furniture for it. She could stay where she was and turn the dismantled chapel back into a real sewing room for Helen and let her make all the altar cloths and vestments her heart desired. Because somehow she had the instinctive feeling that Nirvana was going to be everything Poppi predicted. Donald Trump was going to call her Ma'am.

"You can quit now," Poppi crowed.

But Casey smiled over at Marva, finally free to enjoy what she loved most.

"No," she disagreed. "Now I can stay."

Suddenly the quiet of the work lane shattered with a familiar bellow.

"Ho, maid, hold! Save me with thy death!"

This time, Casey laughed. In fact she laughed for the rest of the shift and all the way home.